A RIVER OF SILENCE

BY

Susan Clayton-Goldner

Tirgearr Publishing

Published by Tirgearr Publishing
Ireland
www.tirgearrpublishing.com

ISBN 978-1-910234-49-5

A CIP catalogue record for this book is
available from the British Library.

10 9 8 7 6 5 4 3 2 1

DEDICATION

For Jay Thompson, whose long-ago story planted the seed that grew into A River of Silence.

ACKNOWLEDGEMENTS

It's a rare writer who completes a novel in a vacuum. I owe thanks to so many people. To my husband, Andreas, and my children, David and Bonnie. To my beta readers, Jude Bunner, Susan Domingos, Jane Sutherland, Marjorie Reynolds, Bob Olds, and Theresa Wisner. A special thanks to my early reviewers who read the book for me and posted their reviews to Amazon and Goodreads on launch day. Your support means everything to me.

As always, I want to thank James N. Frey—my mentor and friend for two and half decades. He is always just an e-mail away if I need advice or help with plot.

My sincere gratitude to Tirgearr Publishing for taking a chance on me.

Finally, a special thanks to Nichole Ferrari Hamm for my author photo.

"Justice rolls on like a river,
Righteousness like a never-failing stream."
Amos 5:24

PROLOGUE

1988

In only eleven minutes, Detective Winston Radhauser's world would flip on its axis and a permanent line would be drawn—forever dividing his life into before and after. He drove toward the Pima County Sheriff's office in Catalina, a small town in the Sonoran Desert just twelve miles north of Tucson. Through the speakers, Alabama sang *You've Got the Touch*. He hummed along.

He was working a domestic violence case with Officer Alison Finney, his partner for nearly seven years. They'd made the arrest—their collar was sleeping off a binge in the back of the squad car. It was just after 10 p.m. As always, Finney wore spider earrings—tonight's selection was a pair of black widows he hadn't seen before.

"You know, Finn, you'd have better luck with men if you wore sunflowers in your earlobes."

She laughed. "Any guy intimidated by a couple of 14-carat web spinners isn't man enough for me."

He never missed an opportunity to tease her. "Good thing you like being single."

The radio released some static.

Radhauser turned off the music.

Dispatch announced an automobile accident on Interstate 10 near the Orange Grove Road exit. Radhauser and Finney were too far east to respond.

Her car phone rang. She answered, listened for a few seconds. "Copy that. I'll get him there." Finney hung up, then placed the

1

phone back into the charger mounted beneath the dashboard.

"Copy what?" he said. "Get who where?"

She eyed him. "Pull over. I need to drive now."

His grip on the steering wheel tightened. "What the hell for?"

Finney turned on the flashing lights. "Trust me and do what I ask."

The unusual snap in her voice raised a bubble of anxiety in his chest. He pulled over and parked the patrol car on the shoulder of Sunrise Road.

She slipped out of the passenger seat and stood by the door waiting for him.

He jogged around the back of the cruiser.

Finney pushed him into the passenger seat. As if he was a child, she ordered him to fasten his seatbelt, then closed the car door and headed around the vehicle to get behind the wheel.

"Are you planning to tell me what's going on?" he asked once she'd settled into the driver's seat.

She opened her mouth, then closed it. Her unblinking eyes never wavered from his. "Your wife and son have been taken by ambulance to Tucson Medical Center."

The bubble of anxiety inside him burst. "What happened? Are they all right?"

Finney turned on the siren, flipped a U-turn, then raced toward the hospital on the corner of Craycroft and Grant. "I don't know any details."

TMC was a designated Trauma 1 Center and the most serious accident victims were taken there. That realization both comforted and terrified him. "Didn't they say the accident happened near the Orange Grove exit?"

"I know what you're thinking. It must be bad or they'd be taken to the closest hospital and that would be Northwest." She stared at him with the look of a woman who knew him almost as well as Laura did. "Don't imagine the worst. They may not have been in a car accident. Didn't you tell me Lucas had an equestrian meet?"

Laura had driven their son to a competition in South Tucson. Maybe Lucas got thrown. He imagined the horse rearing, his son's lanky body sliding off the saddle and landing with a thump on the arena floor. Thank God for sawdust. Laura must have ridden in the ambulance with him.

But Orange Grove was the exit Laura would have taken on her drive home. The meet ended at 9:00 p.m., Lucas always stayed to unsaddle the horse, wipe the gelding down, and help Coach Thomas load him into his trailer. About a half hour job. That would put his family near the Orange Grove exit around ten.

The moon slipped behind a cloud and the sudden darkness seemed alive and a little menacing as it pressed against the car windows.

Less than ten minutes later, Finney pulled into the ER entrance and parked in the lot. "I'm coming with you," she said.

He shot her a you-know-better look, then glanced toward the back seat where their collar was snoring against the door, his mouth open and saliva dribbling down his chin. It was against policy to leave an unguarded suspect in the car.

"I don't give a damn about policy," she said.

"What if he wakes up, hitches a ride home and takes out his wife and kids? Put him in the drunk tank. I'll call you as soon as I know anything." He ran across the parking lot. The ER doors opened automatically and he didn't stop running until he reached the desk. "I'm Winston Radhauser. My wife and son were brought in by ambulance."

The young nurse's face paled and her gaze moved from his eyes to somewhere over his head.

With the change in her expression, his hope dropped into his shoes. He looked behind her down a short corridor where a set of swinging doors blocked any further view. "Where are they?"

It was one of those moments he would remember for a lifetime, where everything happened in slow motion.

She told him to wait while she found a doctor to talk to him, and nodded toward one of the vinyl chairs that lined the waiting room walls.

He sat. Tried to give himself an attitude adjustment. Maybe it wasn't as bad as he thought. Laura or Lucas could be in surgery and the nurse, obviously just out of nursing school, didn't know how to tell him.

He stood.

Paced.

Sat again. The hospital might have a policy where only a physician could relate a patient's condition to his family.

His heart worked overtime, pumping and pounding.

When he looked up, a young woman in a lab coat with a stethoscope around her neck stood in front of him. She had pale skin and was thin as a sapling, her light brown hair tied back with a yellow rubber band. Her eyes echoed the color of a Tucson sky with storm clouds brewing. "Are you Mr. Radhauser?"

He nodded.

"Please come with me."

He expected to be taken to his wife and son, but instead she led him into a small room about eight feet square. It had a round table with a clear glass vase of red tulips in the center, and two chairs. Though she didn't look old enough to have graduated from medical school, she introduced herself as Dr. Silvia Waterford, an ER physician.

They sat.

"Tell me what happened to my wife and son."

"I'm so sorry," she said. "It was an automobile accident on Interstate 10."

The thread of hope he held started to unravel. "Are Laura and Lucas all right? I want to see them."

Her throat rippled as she swallowed. "There is no easy way to say this, Mr. Radhauser. I'm so sorry for your loss. But there was nothing we could do for them."

All at once the scene bleached out. The tulips faded to gray as if a giant flashbulb had gone off in his face. The doctor was rimmed in white light. He stared at her in disbelief for a moment, praying for a mistake, a miracle, anything except what he just heard. "What do you mean there was nothing you could do? This is a Level 1 Trauma Center, isn't it? One of the best in the state."

"Yes. But unfortunately, medical science has its limits and we

4

can't save everyone. *Your wife and son were both dead on arrival.*"

His body crumpled in on itself, folding over like paper, all the air forced from his chest. This was his fault. Laura asked him to take the night off and go with them. Radhauser would have avoided the freeway and driven the back way home from the fairgrounds. And everything would have ended differently.

He looked up at Dr. Waterford. What was he demanding of her? Even the best trauma center in the world couldn't bring back the dead.

There was sadness in her eyes. "I'm sure it's not any comfort, but we think they died on impact."

He hung his head. "Comfort," he said. Even the word seemed horrific and out of place here. Your wife and son were both dead on arrival. Nine words that changed his life in the most drastic way he had ever imagined.

"May I call someone for you? We have clergy on staff if you'd like to talk with someone."

A long moment passed before he raised his head and took in a series of deep breaths, trying to collect himself enough to speak. "No clergy, unless they can bring my family back. Just tell me where my wife and son are." His voice sounded different, deeper— not the same man who went to work that evening.

"I'm sorry," she said. "But when deaths occur in the ER, we have to move them down to the morgue."

Radhauser stood. Beneath his anguish, a festering anger simmered. Laura was a good driver. He was willing to bet she wasn't at fault. More than anything now, he needed someone aside from himself to blame.

Outside, a siren wailed, then came to an abrupt stop. The sound panicked Radhauser as he headed for the elevator, waited for the door to open, then got inside. He pushed the button to the basement floor. He'd visited this hospital morgue once before to identify a fellow police officer shot in a robbery arrest gone bad. The door opened and he lumbered down the empty hallway.

As he neared the stainless steel door to the morgue, a tall, dark-haired man in a suit exited. At first Radhauser thought he was a hospital administrator. The man cleared his throat, flipped open a leather case and showed his badge. "I'm Sergeant Dunlop with the Tucson Police Department. Are you Mr. Radhauser?"

"Detective Radhauser. Pima County Sheriff's Department."

Dunlop had a handshake Radhauser felt in every bone in his right hand. "I'm so sorry for your loss, Detective."

"Are you investigating the accident involving my wife and son?" Radhauser looked him over. Dunlop wore a pin-striped brown suit with a yellow shirt and a solid brown tie—the conservative uniform of a newly-promoted sergeant. The air around them smelled like antiseptic and the industrial solvent used to wash floors. "Have you determined who was at fault?"

Dunlop hesitated for an instant. "Yes, I'm the investigating officer. From the eyewitness reports, your wife was not to blame. A Dodge pickup was headed south in the northbound lane of Interstate 10 near the Orange Grove exit. No lights. He hit her head-on."

Radhauser cringed. The image cut deep. "Was he drunk?"

"I need to wait for the blood alcohol test results to come back."

The anger building inside Radhauser got closer to the surface every second. Silence hung between them like glass. He shattered it. "Don't give me that bullshit. You were on the scene. What did you see? What did the breathalyzer read?"

Dunlop's silence told Radhauser everything he needed to know. "Did the bastard die at least?"

"He was miraculously uninjured. But his twin boys weren't so lucky." Dunlop's voice turned flat. "They didn't make it." He winced, and a tide of something bitter and hopeless washed over his face. "The idiot let them ride in the pickup bed. Five fucking years old."

"What's the idiot's name?"

"You don't need to know that right now."

Biting his lip, Radhauser fought against the surge of rage threatening to flood over him. "Who are you to tell me what I need to know? It's not your wife and kid in there. Besides, I can easily access the information."

Dunlop handed him a card. "I know you can. But you have something more important to do right now. We can talk tomorrow." He draped his arm over Radhauser's shoulder the way a brother or a friend might do.

The touch opened a hole in Radhauser's chest.

"Say goodbye to your wife and son," Dunlop said, then turned and walked away.

In the morgue, after Radhauser introduced himself, a male attendant pulled back the sheet covering their faces. There was no mistake.

"Do you mind if I sit here for a while?" Radhauser asked.

"No problem," the attendant said. "Stay as long as you want." He went back to a small alcove where he entered data into a computer. The morgue smelled like the hallway had, disinfectant and cleaning solution, with an added hint of formaldehyde.

Radhauser sat between the stainless steel gurneys that held Laura and Lucas. Of all the possible scenarios Radhauser imagined, none ended like this.

Across the room, two small body bags lay, side by side, on a wider gurney. The twin sons of the man who killed his family.

The clock on the morgue wall kept ticking and when Radhauser finally looked up at it, four hours had passed. He tried, but couldn't understand how Laura and Lucas could be in the world one minute and gone the next. How could he give them up? It was as if a big piece of him had been cut out. And he didn't know how to go on living without his heart.

* * *

For an entire year afterwards, Radhauser operated in a daze. He spent the late evening hours playing *For the Good Times* on Laura's old upright piano. It was the first song they ever slow danced to and over their fourteen years together, it became their own.

He played it again and again. The neighbors complained, but he couldn't stop. It was the only way he could remember the apricot scent of her skin and how it felt to hold her in his arms on the dance floor.

Night after night, he played until he finally collapsed into a fitful sleep, his head resting on the keyboard. The simple acts of waking up, showering, making coffee, and heading to work became a cruel pretense acted out in the cavernous absence of his wife and son.

CHAPTER ONE

Ashland, Oregon – Eleven Years Later
October 1999

When his wife, Gracie, handed him the envelope, Radhauser stopped whistling. He read the return address. The Arizona Board of Executive Clemency. His hands shook and his gaze found Gracie's dark eyes and held on. It could mean only one thing. The man who killed his first wife and their thirteen-year-old son was up for parole. It was as if another heart had appeared in his chest and thumped hard. Some things were never over. Life provided its reminders and the pain stayed inside, whether he liked it or not.

Gracie stepped closer. "I can put it through the shredder. We can pretend we never saw it."

The soft hope in her voice was something he could taste, something so good he could never have enough. But this time it wasn't working.

She reached for the envelope.

He pulled it away. "I think this should be my decision."

Gracie frowned and took a step back. She was a decade younger and wildly beautiful with her long limbs and dark hair, bronzed by the autumn light. Though she was barely showing, she wore maternity jeans and a pearl-buttoned, red gingham western smock with a matching red cowboy hat. When their daughter, Lizzie, turned two, they tried to get pregnant again and had nearly given up when Gracie took yet another home pregnancy test. She had raced down to the barn and leaped into his arms like a hundred and ten pound rocket. It was one of the most joyful moments of his life. Out of thin air, a new baby was coming.

Now, she was five months pregnant with a boy. In truth, he'd secretly hoped for another girl. Lucas had been his golden-haired boy and he wasn't sure how he felt about another son. Wasn't sure he could love him as much as he loved Lucas. Radhauser hadn't shared this concern with Gracie, who was ecstatic about a little brother for Lizzie and a son to continue the Radhauser name.

She took another step forward and touched his arm. "Only your decision?"

Though she never claimed to be an angel, she and Lizzie, who was now four years old, had saved him. No doubt about that.

"I'm sorry," he said. "You know I care what you think. It's just that..." He shifted the envelope in his hands. Maybe she was right. Maybe it would do no good—this brutal reopening of wounds. He could forego his right to appear at the hearing and let the board make its decision unbeknownst to him.

But was that what he really wanted? This might be his chance to lift the burden—make a final payment to the ghosts of his first family and put them to rest at last. Maybe opposing parole would do that, but at what cost to him and Gracie?

Often, when he woke in the night, he looked over and watched the rise and fall of her chest just to make sure she was breathing, put his head against her back to feel the warmth and softness of her skin as she slept. Gracie, alive beside him, was one of the greatest miracles he'd ever experienced.

Now, she took his arm and led him down the barn's center alleyway. The air smelled like cedar shavings, alfalfa, and molasses from the evening sweet feed he gave their horses.

Once inside the closed-in stall they'd converted into an office, Gracie gently pushed him onto the desk chair.

He knew it hurt her, the way the grief sometimes caught up with him. Times when he missed his other family with a wrenching sorrow he tried to hide by never speaking of it. Still, there were nights when demons came calling. Nights when nightmares took him back to that hospital morgue. And he awakened in a cold sweat, shaking and choking back panic.

A River of Silence

His anger toward the man who killed Laura and Lucas was an all-consuming, living thing that had lain dormant for a while, but now threatened to infect his life again. "I registered to receive notifications before I met you," he said. "But I thought it would be another five or ten years before any possibility of parole. What if he gets out and drives drunk again? What if he kills another family?"

He felt the gentle weight of her hand on his shoulder. Something always shifted inside him with her touch and the smell of her apple-scented shampoo.

"I suspect he's learned a pretty hard lesson. Please," she said. "What you do will affect Lizzie, me and our son." She caressed the bulge of her belly. "We should at least discuss your options."

When something bothered Gracie, she needed to talk about it with another person. But it wasn't his way. "He didn't think about me or my family's options when he drove in a drunken stupor."

Forty-four-year-old Lawrence Arthur Flannigan had served less than eleven years of a fifteen-year to life sentence for four counts of third-degree murder. After the trial and sentencing, Radhauser hoped he would never see that man again. The thought of looking into his eyes was worse than touching a bad tooth. But he and Gracie lived in Oregon now. What were the chances he would see Flannigan again, even if he were released? "His old man is a former Arizona congressman. He probably pulled some strings."

As if she could feel the heat of his frustration and indecision through his shirt, Gracie took her hand from his shoulder. "His family suffered, too. It's time to let it go." She flipped the switch on the office shredder. It made a shrill, scream-like sound that sent chills up Radhauser's spine.

He shut it off. "Whose side are you on anyway?" He removed his Stetson and raked his fingers through his hair. "If Lucas had lived a normal life, say to eighty, Flannigan took sixty-seven years away. And another fifty from Laura. How could less than eleven short years in prison be enough?"

Gracie shook her head. "I don't imagine those years seemed short to him or his wife and daughter. But think about it. Of

11

course I'm on your side. But what if you give your victim statement and they let him go anyway? Is that going to put you back in the hospital?"

Her words were a slap in the face. He wished he'd never told her about his breakdown or his confinement to the Paloverde Psychiatric Hospital after losing six-year-old Tyler Mesa, his first kidnapping victim. It was a rookie's bad decision. Tyler's death was on him. And that two-week hospitalization almost cost him his badge.

In truth, the last eleven years had been difficult for Radhauser, harder than he ever imagined life could be, but somehow he managed to stay out of the psych ward. "This isn't about me or you. It's about justice for Laura and Lucas," he said, louder than he intended.

She dropped her gaze as she did whenever her compassion came up against his anger. "Are you sure it isn't about revenge?" Gracie looked at him again, as if searching for a man behind the one he projected—a kinder, more worthy and authentic husband.

Revenge. Could she be right? Was it vengeance he sought? No. Gracie was wrong. He'd spent his entire adult life as a detective—a daily battle on behalf of victims who couldn't fight for themselves. Why wouldn't he fight just as hard for his wife and son?

"This is about justice," he finally answered. "How would you feel if it were Lizzie or the new baby? Wouldn't you want the person who took *your* child to suffer consequences?"

The look in her eyes turned breakable. "First of all, Lizzie and this baby are not only my children. They're our children."

His mind raced, thoughts coming too fast to sort. "You know what I meant."

She swallowed hard and looked away from him. "I learned a long time ago I couldn't change your past, no matter how badly I might want to. But I'm your wife now and I'm tired of sharing you with ghosts. If Lizzie could articulate it, she'd tell you the same thing. She's four years old, Wind. She doesn't understand death or having a big brother she's never seen."

He closed his eyes and saw his daughter's face, her long black lashes, the way her dark curls slid over one eye when she danced around the living room, or when she ran and jumped into his arms. His feelings for her were huge and complicated. But Radhauser's mother once told him, 'the dead are alive when we think of them'. He tried to keep Lucas alive by showing Lizzie pictures and telling her stories. It didn't bring him back, but it felt good to remember him full of life. Radhauser opened his eyes.

Gracie turned to face him, two bright pink circles on her cheeks. "Dredging this up will only cause pain. Laura and Lucas are gone. Nothing can hurt them now. But you allow them to go on hurting us. It's a losing battle. And if I thought this hearing would bring you closure, I might encourage..." She stopped short, as if realizing how he felt about that meaningless word.

Closure. How could he find closure when the two people he once loved most in the world were dead? He tried to stop the funeral images in his mind and respond to Gracie, but they kept coming. Two bronze coffins with flowers on top. Sunflowers in the shape of a horseshoe for Lucas. A heart of red roses for Laura. White ribbons that read *wife* and *son* in ornate gold letters.

Her face shadowed by the early evening light through the window behind her, Gracie pulled a yellow legal pad and ballpoint pen from the drawer. She slapped them onto the desk. Her dark eyes flashed. "Do what you have to," she said, a slight edge to her voice. "But don't expect me to be happy about it."

An awkward silence fell over them.

Her mouth clamped into a tight line, her eyes straight ahead. "I need to pick up Lizzie from her play date and get her ready for bed." Gracie lowered her gaze to the floor as if she couldn't bear to look at him again. She slipped through the door without looking back, leaving him alone with his ghosts.

He got up from the chair, then stood in the doorway and watched as her boots kicked up dust in the aisle of the old barn as she headed toward the driveway. Outside the office window, the sun sank behind the mountains, turning the pastures dark.

A part of him wanted to chase after her and tell her that despite its difficulties, the last decade held some beautiful moments for him, like meeting and marrying her, moving to this small ranch in southern Oregon, and finding out she was pregnant with Lizzie and now their son. His life would be over for sure if Gracie left him. Feeling claustrophobic in the small office, he stepped outside and stood beside the double barn doors. He never imagined owning a thirty-two acre horse ranch in Oregon with its lush pastures and looming mountains behind it. Radhauser never lived anywhere except the Sonoran Desert. This was Gracie's dream. And if he were truthful, guilt sometimes gnawed at him, knowing how much Lucas, who'd prized everything connected to horses, would have loved this life.

Radhauser watched Gracie back her red Honda CRV out of the garage and drive down the long gravel lane to the main road. He was still standing there long after the crunch of her tires was replaced by the chirping of crickets.

When he returned to the barn office, the air felt charged. He took a pack of Marlboros from the back of the drawer, tapped them against the desk, then removed the wrapping. He stuck one in his mouth without lighting it. Six months after burying his family, he'd stopped smoking, but sometimes he needed the comfort of a cigarette dangling between his lips, the slight taste of tobacco on his tongue.

He ripped open the envelope and read the letter. Just as he suspected, the man who killed his family was eligible for parole and would be presenting his case to the clemency board on Monday, December thirteenth—in a little more than two months. The letter invited Radhauser to attend and give a victim impact statement.

For five minutes, he stared at the blank notepad in front of him. Sometimes when he was alone and troubled by his latest case or struggling with a decision, he talked to Laura. They'd fallen in love at fifteen and she was his first girlfriend—the first woman he ever confided in. His mother had died when he was a small boy. Laura had opened his heart and taught him how to love. And though she never answered him, it made him feel better to check in with her. "We were happy and Flannigan took so much away from us. Our boy had his whole life ahead of him. What would you do?"

If anyone heard him, they'd think he'd lost it again, but who knew, maybe on some level she listened and understood he hadn't forgotten her or Lucas.

With shocking clarity, a voice spoke inside his head. *Fight for us, Wind.* It was Laura's voice—a voice he hadn't heard for more than a decade. The hairs on his arms lifted.

Gracie wanted him to ignore the hearing and let the man who murdered his family and nearly destroyed his life go free. How could he do that after Laura told him to fight? He loved them so much he would have walked a thousand miles, crossed all the oceans and deserts on earth just to see his wife and son one more time.

Radhauser made his decision. He would fight for them—they deserved that and so much more. He needed to write his victim statement in a way that was clear, concise and poignant. He picked up the pen and wrote three sentences. *My beautiful wife, Laura, was my high school sweetheart—my first love. Our thirteen-year-old son dreamed of being a rodeo cowboy. When Lawrence Flannigan decided to drive drunk, he took that dream and every other one away from Lucas...* When heat built behind his eyes, he put down the pen and closed them.

If only the past could be more fluid and he could find his way back by a route less painful than memory.

CHAPTER TWO

Caleb Bryce, whom everyone called by his last name, pressed the tiny knob that lit his watch dial. 12:50 p.m.—exactly ten minutes later than the last time he checked. Dana's shift at the Lazy Lasso Bar and Grill ended at midnight. *Where could she be?*

He opened the car door. Careful not to bear too much weight on his right leg, he scanned the nearly empty, moonlit parking lot. Bryce had ruptured his Achilles tendon at a softball game two months ago while sliding into third base. He felt like a fool, even as the pain pierced his right calf. The urge to show off for Dana and the boys hadn't been worth the price. But progress had been made, his cast removed, and physical therapy begun.

After limping across the asphalt lot, he entered the Lasso's lobby, then pushed through the polished oak saloon doors into the restaurant and bar. The air was rich with the smell of steaks, ribs, and hamburgers sizzling over an open fire.

Bear Evans, Dana's boss and the owner, greeted him with a wink. "If it isn't my favorite deaf dude," he said, careful to face Bryce so he could read his lips. Bear was a mountain of a black man, around six feet five inches tall, with salt and pepper hair, a matching mustache and more curls on his arms than any black man Bryce ever met. Bear's easy way served him well in his business. With his composed and ready smile, he could calm a drunk or angry customer so fast it was as if a switch was flicked off inside them.

"If you're looking for Dana, she left about an hour ago with Reggie." Bear glanced around the almost empty restaurant. "It's been a slow night. You wanna wait at your usual table?"

16

Bryce swallowed his jealousy and nodded. He thought Dana was over her ex-husband. Maybe she had a legitimate reason for being with Reggie Sterling, but as far as Bryce was concerned, Reggie was bad news. No matter what Dana might believe, he didn't care about her or the kids.

A handsome young man, barely more than a boy, wearing a white apron over his jeans and long-sleeved T-shirt sauntered by them, pushing a broom. He was the son Bear raised on his own.

"Henry," Bear said. "Say hello to Mr. Bryce and then hustle over and bus his table. The one in the far back by the window." He paused, a look of sweet compassion in his eyes. "And by the way, you've done a great job with the sweeping, son."

"Hi Mr. Bryce," Henry said, looking a bit sheepish from the compliment. "How are Scott and Skyler? Can I give Skyler his bottle later?"

The boy had some mental health issues. Bear once told Bryce his eighteen-year-old son had the mind of a seven-year-old.

"Not tonight, Henry. He's fast asleep. But soon, okay?"

Henry smiled.

Bryce was both impressed and amazed by Bear's dedication and patience with his son. Bear was the kind of father Bryce aspired to be.

Bear led him to the booth and took his usual order for a Diet Coke. He had no more than slid onto the bench seat and looked out the window into the parking lot before tumbling into the memory of the night he first met Dana.

The hostess had already seated Bryce at this booth when he noticed the new waitress. In no hurry to order, he watched her move about the room. She was younger than most of the other waitresses, compact and dark, with curly black hair spilling over her shoulders and down her back. Her laugh was infectious and loud enough for even him to hear. He wanted to join right in.

After a few minutes, she paused beside his table and began to talk about the specials that night, pointing out all the items on the menu she liked best.

He turned sideways in his seat so he could more easily read her lips.

17

Dana remained cheerful while she answered mundane questions she was probably asked a dozen times each night. Her smile was open and bright and she didn't react to his speech impediment or ask if he were drunk.

Bryce would have loved to spend more time talking with her, but her gaze left their conversation and clung to the window looking out on the parking lot.

"My name is Caleb Bryce," he said to call her back. "But everyone calls me Bryce. I'm hearing impaired, but good at reading lips as long as you look at me when you speak."

The smile that spread across her face was so wide and warm it hugged his whole body. She shook his hand. "Pleased to meet you, Bryce."

Her attention shifted to the parking lot again.

"Is there a carnival going on out there?" he asked.

When she looked at him again, he saw a splinter of concern, swimming like a minnow in her eyes.

He didn't look away.

She must have seen something in his expression that enabled her to trust him. "I'd give a week's salary for a carnival clown and a lion tamer instead of those two boys I've got sleeping in the car. Scotty's a handful and if he wakes up, he might use the baby as a punching bag." She paused and shook her head. "Sibling rivalry, my butt. Scotty is just like Reggie. He's my ex. Neither of them can stand to be around that baby."

They locked on each other's eyes. He saw her regret and a fierce anxiety she was eager to hide over the uncertainty of her future.

He hesitated to ask, but somehow needed to know. "Are you homeless?"

She put one hand on either side of his face, framing it. "Don't look so worried, darlin'. It's only for a few more weeks. Thanks to Bear, I'll have first month's rent and my security deposit by the end of the month."

Her hands were warm and it was such a gentle gesture. Perhaps the most tender touch he'd ever received.

Bryce stayed at the Lazy Lasso another hour, until closing,

sipping the same Diet Coke and hoping for another chance to talk to her. "I have two extra bedrooms in my house. No strings attached," he said. And he actually meant it.

Dana and the boys had moved in the following weekend.

Now, Bear brought him a Diet Coke and startled him out of the memory and into the present. "Dana will be back soon," he said, placing one big hand on Bryce's shoulder. "I know Reggie can be a jerk, but he's not all bad. He's taken an interest in Henry and been really good to him." He nodded towards his son who wiped down a table across the aisle from the bar. "Reggie got Henry a part-time job washing cars on his father's lot. It's hard to let him go, but I won't always be around to protect him. Henry needs to grow more independent."

Bryce didn't trust anything Reggie Sterling did. His motives were always self-serving. But why burst Bear's bubble?

"Dana's still young and wild. But she knows you're the best thing that ever happened to her and those boys." He squeezed Bryce's shoulder, then hurried over to another customer.

Fifteen minutes later, Dana appeared in the doorway. She was barefoot and wearing her waitress uniform—a denim skirt, red vest, and a white blouse with pearl buttons. A tooled red cowboy boot dangled from each hand. In the soft and subtle glow inside the Lasso, her tangled hair mirrored the golden light from the wall lanterns. When she spotted Bryce, she waved. Her slow, self-conscious gait told him she was drunk, even before he smelled the beer on her breath.

"Are you okay?" he asked. "I was worried."

She nodded.

"Was that Reggie's car I saw outside?"

She slid onto the red vinyl bench across from him.

"You should have called," he said. "I was here at 11 p.m., just like you said. But when you weren't, I had to phone Tilly to watch the kids. You know I'm not comfortable leaving them alone for more than a few minutes, even if they are asleep. I woke Tilly up. She's an old lady and needs her sleep."

Dana sighed—a bottomless, heartbreaking sigh, then turned her face to the window.

He reached across the narrow table and placed his hand on top of hers. "You can talk to me, sweetheart. What's the real problem here?"

When she looked at him, her eyes filled. "I wish I knew. Sometimes I hate my life and I'm only twenty years old. Stupid me getting knocked up at fifteen. I used to blame Reggie because he's older. But it's my own fault. I feel guilty all the time because of the kids." She stopped and looked at him for a moment. "And you. I don't want to hurt anyone. I just want time to be young before I turn into a wrinkled old prune."

He didn't know whether to laugh or hug her. She had no idea how lucky she was to have those two healthy little boys. For as long as Bryce could remember, he'd yearned for a family. He had one and lost it. But he'd found another with Dana, Scott and Skyler. They brought something recklessly alive back into his life. The last thing he wanted was to lose them. "I know fifteen years is a big age difference, but I do remember what being young felt like." He smiled, caressed her hand.

Dana slipped her hand from beneath his and knitted her fingers together. She met Bryce's gaze. Dark semi-circles stained the skin under her eyes.

"Let's go home," he said. "You're tired and a little bit drunk. You'll feel better after you get some sleep."

"Sleep isn't going to fix me," she snapped. "It's too late. You don't get it, do you?" She ripped open her purse, then groped around in the bottom until she found a wadded-up tissue. "We're not working. And it's not like I haven't tried." She stopped and blew her nose, then tore at a loose cuticle beneath her bright red nail polish.

A ripple of panic washed over Bryce. "I have two more classes before I get my degree. I won't be stacking vegetables at Gilbert's Grocery forever." Bryce worked as the produce manager. It was a good job, with health insurance and paid medical leave, but he didn't plan to retire from Gilbert's. He harbored another, more altruistic dream. "I'll teach at the deaf school. We'll have a future. Maybe you can stay home with the kids. We could have a baby together. Round the family out with a little girl."

She shook her head, a look of sadness in her eyes. "Even if I could, I don't want to stay home or have another baby."

"What do you mean even if you could?" Again, he took her hand.

"Nothing," she said. "I like working at the Lasso. I have a life here."

"Waiting on tables of drunks who like to flirt and gawk at your boobs isn't much of a life. You're smart. And you're better than that."

She jerked her hand from his grasp. "I'm tired of your wisdom, all your philosophy of life shit. I want my own place. The tarot has been telling me this for weeks."

"Listen," he said, trying not to raise his voice. "Those cards are just pieces of cardboard. What about the kids? Skyler is only nineteen months old. He needs his mother. But he needs a man around too."

She looked at him hard, a flash of anger in her dark eyes. "Well, maybe I'll find a man. A real man, not a…"

The words she failed to say echoed in his head. *Not a deaf cripple like you.* His face flushed and his hands grew clammy. Those unsaid words both shrunk and pierced him. "A man like Reggie," he snarled. "A man who once stabbed you with an ice pick. A man who can't stand the sight of your toddler. Those boys are happy with me and you know it."

Her face was bright red and contorted. "As much as you like to pretend they're yours, those kids belong to me." She landed a shot where Bryce was most vulnerable.

"I know whose kids they are." He shifted his gaze to the window and looked out at the night sky with its scattering of indifferent stars, then returned it to Dana.

She lifted one hand to wipe her hair away from her forehead. "Good. Because I'm going to find someone else to take care of them at night. And it won't be Tilly, your fabulous black wonder, either."

Bryce stood. "Go ahead. See if you can find someone to love

21

those kids the way I do." He slapped a five-dollar bill on the table to cover the cost of his Diet Coke and limped out of the restaurant. Dana followed.

When they were both in the car, she flipped on the overhead light and turned to face him. They stared at each other like two prize fighters after a round of punches, trying to decide whether to return to the ring.

She must have realized she knocked the wind out of him with her threat to take the kids away and softened. "I'm sorry. I didn't mean to be cruel. You've been a great friend. Really generous and wonderful to me and the boys." Her face brightened, then went dark again. "But when you offered your house to us, you said no strings attached."

The silence between them buzzed in Bryce's ears, louder than any speech.

"Well," she demanded. "Isn't that what you said to me?" Her eyes flashed. The line between them sunk into a deep groove.

"Yes, that's what I said, and I meant it." She was so young and he should have known better. "But I didn't force you to move into my bedroom. You did that of your own accord." About a month after she and the boys moved in, Dana crawled into his bed and snuggled up to his back. He thought she was falling in love with him. Nothing could have made him happier.

He reached across the seat to touch her arm. "I care about your happiness. I just hoped you'd find it with me."

For a few seconds, she remained quiet and still. "It's not your fault," she finally said. "I made a mistake."

"Call it whatever you want. But it worked well for over a year. Those boys are thriving."

Her eyes widened as if the truth found them. "I know. But I'm not." She swallowed hard and looked away from him.

A cloud moved across the moon and the sky was suddenly bereft of light. Bryce gripped the steering wheel with both hands and stared straight ahead into the empty parking lot. A muscle along the side of his jaw throbbed like a heartbeat.

Bryce rarely lost his temper and didn't want to do so now. He turned back to Dana and touched her shoulder. "Look. I'm not trying to run your life. But you know you can't afford a decent place to live and babysitting, too. I can help with…" Bryce stopped himself short of finishing. He didn't want her to know the sad truth—that he'd do just about anything to keep those kids in his world.

CHAPTER THREE

The following morning, Bryce stood in front of the small window over the kitchen sink. It opened onto a warm autumn day. Sunlight filtered through the trees in broad and glimmering bands. The oaks and maples erupted in color and the earth smelled like garden soil recently turned. Dana was tired and drunk last night. She hadn't meant half of what she said. With a good night's sleep, she was sure to see things differently. The sky was already brilliant with two ivory clouds pinned high in the glossy blue. Perfect for a new start.

Pickles, the orange-striped alley cat he adopted more than a decade ago, circled his ankles, nudging his nose against Bryce's legs. A morning ritual. "You hungry, boy?" He poured dry cat food in Pickles' dish and replaced his water.

Dana got up early, showered and dressed before either of the boys finished the blueberry pancakes, in the shape of Mickey Mouse, Bryce prepared for them. He heard her in the living room, laying out her daily tarot cards on the glass top coffee table. After a few moments, she joined them in the kitchen.

He turned away from the window to face her.

She was wearing a pair of hot pink capris, sandals, and a white, lacy tank top, tucked in at the waist. A matching white sweater was tossed over her shoulders. Her hair was still damp from the shower and several dark tendrils curled around her face.

"You look great," he said. "Just right for a picnic in Lithia Park. We can walk down to the Plaza, pick up some chicken and potato salad at Greenleaf. Maybe some French bread and a bottle of that red wine you like."

24

Dana shook her head. Her gaze fixed on him. "Angela is picking me up in a few minutes." Angela was Dana's best friend and worked as the hostess at the Lazy Lasso.

"We plan to get Reggie and the two of them will help me find an apartment." She looked at him, as if checking for a reaction.

Silence hung between them, still and fragile as glass.

The beginnings of a headache, hopefully not a migraine, pressed into the back of his left eye like a thumbtack. "When you got up so early I thought maybe we could do something together, be a family. Besides, I promised the boys."

Four-year-old Scott scurried, barefoot and still in his pajamas, across the tile floor and wrapped his arms around Dana's thighs. "Please...please...please. Come on, Mom. Skyler and me can fish for minnows in Ashland Creek. Bryce has two nets and a big bucket. He said we could go."

"Your dad is coming over later, after I go to work. Maybe he'll take you for ice cream." She untangled herself from Scott's arms, smoothed the wrinkled fabric of her capris, then shot Bryce a look that was anything but happy. "You had no right to make promises to the kids without asking me first."

Dana knelt in front of Scott. "I'm sorry, Scotty, but I already have plans."

"You always have plans without me." Scott got that look of abandonment little kids get when they're excluded.

A look Bryce knew well.

Scott ambled out of the kitchen, his shoulders drooped, and his feet dragged as if he had bricks on them.

Skyler pounded his spoon on the metal tray of his high chair and screamed. He recently discovered he could let out a high-pitched sound. It irritated the heck out of Reggie. But Bryce could barely hear it, and the sparkle in Skyler's dark eyes was so damn cute.

The toddler smiled, pleased with his performance.

After cutting up another pancake for him, Bryce poured what little bit of maple syrup remained in the bottle over them. The

25

last time he made pancakes, the bottle was nearly full. He was sick to death of Dana's ex-husband stopping by to see Scott and raiding their refrigerator as if he owned the place and paid for the groceries. Reggie brought Scott expensive gifts and took him out for treats while completely ignoring Skyler. The man was a real piece of work. What kind of person could throw a nineteen-year-old girl, a three-year-old, and a brand-new baby out of the house and allow them to live in a decrepit old car? According to Dana, when Reggie first saw the baby with his caramel skin, his shock of dark hair and even darker eyes, he claimed Skyler couldn't possibly be his son.

And this denial of paternity, echoed with shadow music from his own childhood, was all the more reason for Bryce to love that little boy. He followed Dana into the bedroom, closing the door behind him. He reached for her arm. "Can we talk privately a minute?"

She jerked away from his grasp. "I told you last night I'm leaving as soon as I find a place."

Bryce's mouth filled with a sour taste and his breathing quickened. "You can't mean that. Scott is warming up to me more every day. And Skyler has never known any other father."

"Maybe it's time he did."

"What's that supposed to mean?"

"I've been talking to Reggie. He's almost ready to step up to the plate and try again."

"He has a house. If what you're saying is true, why search for an apartment?"

She clamped her hands onto her hips. "I said 'almost'. Reggie needs a little more time."

"Moving in with Reggie won't be good for Skyler," Bryce said. "Reggie indulges Scott and completely ignores Skyler. Can't we try harder? It's important to the kids and to me." Again, he reached out to touch her arm.

Again, she jerked away. "Everything isn't about you and the kids. This is about me and what I want. Can't you understand that?"

"No," Bryce said, then paused for a moment, trying to deflect his anger and maintain a steady voice. "I can't understand that kind of selfishness."

"You can call me whatever you want. I'm not changing my mind." She started to leave, then paused and turned back to face him. "Skyler's doctor said to keep him hydrated. Make sure you give him a bottle of that baby apple juice I left on the counter when you put him to bed tonight. Dilute it with two-parts water," she said, as if those instructions made her a good mother. Made her someone who cared. "And don't worry about picking me up. Reggie will do it."

The sound of a car horn intruded. She picked up the bag with her waitress uniform and boots inside and raced toward the front door.

Bryce followed as quickly as he could, his rage building. "You're nothing but a selfish bitch," he shouted, limping down the concrete steps. He picked up a small landscaping rock and threw it at Angela's car. It missed. There was nothing he could do to stop them.

After they drove away, Bryce sat on the bottom step and cradled his head in his hands. Dana didn't give a damn about him or the way he tried to carve out a life and provide some stability for Skyler and Scott. He was merely her babysitter. Nothing else.

Leaning back against the step, he let out a long burst of air and frustration. When he raised his head, Scott stood in front of him, still wearing his footed pajamas. "I hate her. She always goes. And she never takes me with her. She's a selfish bitch."

Bryce sat, unmoving—like a boxer who'd just taken a swift fist to the temple. "I'm sorry I said that, Scotty. Your mother is having a hard time right now and we have to be patient. Maybe she'll change her mind and we can go tomorrow."

Around 10:30 a.m., as was his daily custom, Bryce loaded Skyler into his stroller and they walked to Lithia Park, where he deposited Skyler into a baby swing while he kicked a soccer ball back and forth to Scott. His heart wasn't in it. His head hurt and he kept thinking about Dana and Reggie.

A man dressed in khakis with sharp creases and a denim jacket stood behind Skyler's swing.

Bryce read his lips.

"Is it okay if I push the little guy?" The man was about thirty and well-groomed. An expensive camera with a big telephoto lens hung from his neck. He looked like a man who was part cat, the way he moved as if he had springs instead of joints. He stepped closer to Bryce, intercepted the soccer ball and kicked it to Scott.

"Sure," Bryce said, never taking his gaze away from Skyler. "But not too high. It scares him."

"What's wrong with your voice?"

Bryce gave his usual, half-true, explanation that he'd suffered an accident in childhood that left him partially deaf and susceptible to ear infections that went untreated by his parents who didn't have money to pay for doctors and antibiotics.

"Your little boy is so cute," the man said as he gently pushed the swing. "What's his name?"

"His name is Skyler," Bryce said. "Skyler Sterling."

"May I take a couple photos of Skyler?"

Something about the request seemed suspicious and Bryce said no.

The man laughed and stuck out his hand. "My name is Montgomery Taylor, but everyone calls me Monty. I'm not a pedophile or anything, just a man who likes to photograph kids. And hopes to make a living doing it someday."

Bryce shook hands and introduced himself. They struck up a conversation and when he put Skyler in his stroller for the walk home, Monty walked with them. He told Bryce he lived nearby and often came to the park to practice shooting photographs in different lightings. Taylor was taking photography classes at Rogue Community College. Bryce told him about his dream to teach at the deaf school. And how he was finishing his college education at Southern Oregon University.

Monty seemed like a nice guy and Bryce was going to need a friend if Dana left with the boys. When Monty said he was thirsty,

Bryce invited him inside for a glass of ice water. After pointing Monty toward the kitchen, Bryce put Skyler down for his nap. Scott followed after him.

When he returned from the bedroom, Monty was headed out the front door. He waved, then turned to face Bryce. "Thanks for the water. It hit the spot. Maybe once you trust me a little, you'll let me photograph the boys in the park."

Bryce said nothing. If Dana had her way, he wouldn't spend many more days at the park with the boys.

Later, while Skyler slept, Bryce spotted his neighbor, Harold Grundy, toting a huge, cardboard refrigerator box to the trash bin. "You mind if I take this?"

"Suit yourself, I got no use for it." The neighbor, an older man Tilly called Mr. Grumpalump, stood watching as Bryce hoisted the box and carried it across his driveway.

Scott trailed behind the huge carton. "What's that for?"

"I'm gonna make a playhouse for Cockroach."

"You always do stuff for him. You like him better than me." Scott stared at the ground, then drew a circle in the thick gravel with the scuffed toe of his cowboy boot.

"No, I don't, Scotty." Bryce kneeled on his good knee, eye level with the boy, and lifted Scott's chin with his fingertips. "It's just that your dad gives you so many new toys and takes you out for ice cream. Cockroach gets jealous."

"Me and Dad don't like Skyler. Dad says he screams all the time like a little brat. But you like him. That's why you call *him* Cockroach and me just plain Scotty."

Bryce chuckled. "I call him that because of the way he skitters around the house and can hide himself in teeny little places like that cabinet under the kitchen sink." He patted Scott on the head. "Why don't you help me with this surprise for Skyler? He'll be up from his nap soon."

They dragged the box onto the back deck, sliced it down one seam, turned the printing toward the inside and taped it back together. Bryce cut out windows and a front door. At Scott's suggestion, they painted blue shutters, like the ones on the house they lived in, and printed the words, *Cockroach's House*, in big block letters over the doorway. The paint dried quickly under the heat of the midday autumn sun and they hauled the colorful playhouse into the living room.

The boys soon forgot about the picnic and spent the day playing with their stuffed animals in the cardboard house without their usual squabbles until early evening when Scott demanded a dish of ice cream.

"Not now," Bryce said. "It's too close to dinner. You can have some for dessert."

"You give *him* everything." Scott nodded toward his little brother who stood in front of the screen door, staring out at the street.

When Bryce ignored Scott, the boy lunged forward and shoved Skyler, hard. The flimsy door latch didn't hold and the toddler tumbled, head first, across the narrow porch and down the concrete steps.

Bryce leaped to his feet, ignoring the stab of pain in his right calf, stumbled over the second stair, and then regained his balance. Skyler lay draped over the corner of the bottom step, screaming. Bryce picked him up and was brushing the dirt off the toddler's face just as Scott sprinted across the yard and disappeared behind a neighbor's house.

Assuring himself that Skyler was not injured beyond a bump on the forehead and a few scrapes, and not knowing what else to do, Bryce comforted him for a moment, then lowered the wailing toddler into his crib and chased after Scott.

He discovered him perched on a low branch of a maple tree behind Mr. Grumpalump's garden shed. "Come on down," he pleaded. "You're tired and it's time to get ready for bed."

"You can't make me," Scott snarled, his blue eyes flashing. "It's not even dark yet. Besides, you're not my real dad."

Afraid to leave Skyler alone any longer, there was nothing for Bryce to do but grab Scott under his arms and haul him home. The frenzied boy flipped his head back and forth, kicked the heels of his cowboy boots into Bryce's thighs and groin, and then bit Bryce's forearm hard enough to leave bloody teeth marks.

He flipped Scott to face him. "You better head straight to bed before I do something I'll regret. Like murder." With that threat, Scott spit in Bryce's face and resumed his kicking.

Trembling and at his wits' end, Bryce clamped the thrashing boy under his armpit and swiped his own wet cheek. As he set Scott on the ground in front of him, Dana's instructions leaped up inside his head, 'You have to be firmer with him, Bryce, show him who's boss. He walks all over you.' Bryce swatted the boy on the backside, harder than he meant to, then lugged Scott, still howling and kicking, back into the house.

He deposited the boy in his bedroom, demanded that he stay there, then wrapped ice cubes in a dish towel and held it on the egg-shaped lump swelling Skyler's forehead. When Skyler finally settled down, Bryce filled the tub and bathed both kids without another word. A surge of shame rose in the pit of his stomach when he saw the big red print of his own hand stamped on Scott's pale skin.

He was about to lift Skyler from the tub when the high-pitched buzzer in the hallway announced the telephone. Thinking it might be Dana, he pulled the plug, stood Skyler up in the tub and told Scott to watch his brother. Bryce hurried into the kitchen to answer. He turned down the credit card solicitor, hung up and was headed back to the bathroom when he heard Skyler scream. And it wasn't one of his playful screams either.

The toddler, his face twisted in pain, stood at the back of the tub, clutching his penis.

"My teeth slipped," Scott said. "I was just gonna blubber him on the tummy. My dad is right. Skyler is nothin' but a screaming brat."

Bryce inspected the damage. A pale bruise was already forming, and there were red teeth marks, but Scott hadn't broken the skin. Wrapping Skyler in a towel, Bryce held a cool washcloth over the teeth marks. He sat on the edge of the closed toilet and rocked the boy until he stopped crying. "Does it feel better now, Sky?"

The toddler nodded.

Bryce tossed the other towel to Scott. "Dry off. And put your pajamas on," he demanded. "Now."

Scott obeyed without a word.

Fed up, Bryce gave them grilled cheese sandwiches and tomato soup. Refusing the customary bedtime story, he put them to bed early, closed their door, then clamped the hearing device into his ear, and turned on the living room television.

Less than fifteen minutes later, the doorbell rang.

Bryce ripped out the device and answered.

Reggie Sterling and Henry Evans stood on the porch. A slice of peach-colored daylight lit the sky behind them.

"What do you want?" Bryce asked.

"To see my boy, what do you think I want? I sure as hell didn't come here to see you."

"Scott's in bed."

Reggie checked his watch, a big gold one with a fancy tooled band. "It's only 7:30. He's got another hour before bedtime. Are you trying to keep me away from my son?"

Bryce opened the door. "Go see for yourself. Read him a bedtime story. I wasn't in the mood. But if Skyler is asleep, don't wake him. Scott beat him up pretty bad today."

Reggie stepped inside as if he owned the place, Henry at his heels like an obedient puppy. "That's my boy," Reggie said, as if Scott's beating on his baby brother was something to be proud of. "Tough as nails, that kid. By the way, Dana said I could have one of her cold beers."

Bryce shot him a disgusted look. "I thought you quit. And thanks a lot for drinking our maple syrup."

"Recovering alcoholics get sugar cravings. I'll buy you a new bottle."

"I won't hold my breath," Bryce said. "And just for your information, *recovering* alcoholics don't drink beer."

After Reggie raided the refrigerator, both he and Henry headed down the hallway to the boys' bedroom.

Henry returned a moment later and waited for Caleb to look up. "Skyler wants his bottle," he said. "Can I give it to him again?"

"Sure you can, Henry." Bryce had forgotten all about Dana's instructions to give Skyler a bottle of apple juice.

Henry followed him into the kitchen.

A four-pack of baby apple juice sat on the counter, one of the jars already removed from the pack—another of Dana's attempts to be helpful—the good mother. He twisted the cap and poured the juice into the baby bottle, then diluted it with two-parts water. He screwed on the nipple, shook the bottle, handed it to Henry, then returned to his spot on the sofa.

After about fifteen minutes in the boys' bedroom, Reggie burst back into the living room and stood in front of Bryce, holding the half-empty beer bottle in one hand, the other hand planted on his hip. "You ever lay a hand on my kid or threaten to murder him again and I'll kill you with my bare hands. Do you understand me?"

Bryce's hatred for this man was hot lava rising to the surface. "Get the hell out of my house. And take your tough as nails, spitting, biting, bully of a son with you if you're so damned concerned with his welfare."

Reggie stared at him as if unable to believe what he heard, then headed back into Scott's bedroom. "I'm going to say goodnight to my son."

He returned with Henry, who looked at Bryce and shrugged. "Skyler likes apple juice. I think he'll be quiet now." Henry followed Reggie as he stormed through the front door. Once outside, Reggie turned and slammed it behind them.

The pain in Bryce's head went from a thumbtack behind his eye to a sledgehammer.

The phone rang. Dana didn't make any small talk with Bryce. She wanted to talk to Scott.

Bryce brought the boy to the kitchen phone.

Scott said "okay" three times, then hung up.

"What did Mommy want?"

"For me to take care of Skyler."

Wow. That was one strong case for mother's intuition. Reggie hadn't had time to call her. Did she somehow know Scott pushed Skyler out the front door and took a bite out of his penis?

"Mom said to make sure Skyler drinks his apple juice."

When Bryce lifted Scott so he could see into the crib, the toddler was happily sucking on his bottle.

Scott went back to bed without a struggle. Bryce tucked him in and kissed him on the forehead. "I'm sorry I got so angry with you, Scotty."

The boy grinned. "Mom says I'm a handful."

Bryce tried to laugh, but his migraine had gotten worse. He took three Tylenol from the master bathroom medicine cabinet, put the ice pack on his head and fell asleep on the living room sofa.

At 11:45 p.m., he awakened and lay still, watching the restless flutter of the living room curtains in the night air. His headache was gone. He took the ice pack from his forehead, then lifted Pickles from his chest. Crap. He'd intended to stay awake and check on the toddler every fifteen minutes. Skyler ate his grilled cheese sandwich and the soup Bryce fed him and seemed fine when Bryce tucked him into his crib. But there was always the off-chance his fall resulted in a concussion.

Bryce hurried into their bedroom. Scott was flung out sideways across his bed, his mouth open and moist. His thumb was cocked next to his cheek. Each night as he checked on them, he marveled at the mysterious way sleep transformed Scott from hellion into cherub. It was a privilege to guard their slumber, to be allowed access to this precious part of their daily lives. And he couldn't help but smile as he brushed strands of red hair from the boy's forehead, releasing the powdery scent of baby shampoo. Rolling Scott into the bed's center, he covered him with a blanket before turning his attention to Skyler's crib.

The toddler lay in his favorite sleeping position, one hand under his cheek, butt thrust to the sky and his knees tucked beneath him. Skyler's bed covers were bunched under his legs and

Bryce reached down to release them.

Something was wrong. He flipped on the light.

Skyler's body was rigid. He didn't wiggle or utter a sound. Bryce quickly turned him over. His lips and eyelids seemed darker than usual. Snatching the toddler from the crib, Bryce dashed into the hallway where the light was brighter. When he lifted the toddler's hand to the lamp, Skyler's tiny fingernails were stained the dusty color of blueberries.

Bryce's gut plummeted. Panic raced through him. He shook the little boy. It was like shaking a brick. "Breathe, dammit," he shrieked, and, ignoring the stab of pain in his right calf, he bolted down the hallway, stumbling over his own limbs.

Just inside the entrance to the living room, Bryce tripped over Scott's fire truck and lurched into the coffee table, shattering an oil lamp, turning over the table and the vase of daffodils he bought for Dana, and launching the carefully placed cards of her daily tarot reading.

Instinctively, he broke the force of the fall with his left arm to protect Skyler. It all happened so fast. He flipped onto his back, praying he hadn't injured the stiff and silent toddler still cradled in the crook of his right arm.

He scrambled to his feet, checked Skyler's respirations again. The toddler wasn't breathing. Bryce laid him on the sofa. As he attempted to clear Skyler's airway, the boy had a seizure. Skyler's mouth clamped shut, trapping Bryce's index finger. He jerked frantically, but Skyler's teeth were firmly planted and Bryce had to carry the toddler with him.

He unlocked the front door for the ambulance crew so he wouldn't have to stop CPR or leave the toddler unattended, and then hurried into the kitchen to call 9-1-1. He laid Skyler on the table, felt for a pulse, and tried to force his mouth open. His hands shook.

The trapped finger, painful as it was, pried open a small gap and Bryce positioned his open mouth over Skyler's and forced air into the child's lungs, waited, then breathed into him again. And again.

35

He pumped the toddler's chest, then stopped to blow more air into his lungs. Bryce was unable to remember the cycle, the number of pumps and breaths, and the interval in between. But his mouth and free hand performed as if without need of him. Then magically, a ragged breath rose from the child. And then another.

At the sight of that tiny thorax rising and falling, tears streamed down Bryce's face. With his right hand still trapped, his index finger throbbing, he picked up the kitchen phone and dialed 9-1-1 with his left.

"It's a...a...an emergency." The nervous stutter, gone since his boyhood, reappeared. His eyes glued to Skyler's again motionless chest, he screamed words into the receiver again and again. "The...the...baby...sh...she...isn't breathing. Sh...she's gonna die. It's all my fault. I should have…We need help." Bryce babbled on, not making any sense and he knew it. He dropped the phone onto the kitchen counter, cupped Skyler's chin in his hand and, even though the toddler sucked in an occasional shallow breath, puffed more air between the thin blue lips.

He retrieved the handset.

"Try not to panic, I'll dispatch an ambulance, don't..."

In spite of the amplifier in the phone's earpiece, Bryce didn't hear everything she said. He tried to spill out the details of what happened all at once, imploring her to understand the urgency. "She's go…go…going to…die, dammit."

CHAPTER FOUR

When the pager in his pajama pocket sounded a soft buzz and then vibrated, Radhauser groaned. His eyes shot open. The clock on his bedside table read 12:15 a.m. A call from dispatch this late could mean only one thing. Something terrible awaited him.

He turned off the pager and slipped out of bed, careful not to awaken Gracie. He'd stayed up late in the barn, working on his victim impact statement. She and Lizzie were asleep when he came to bed. Even though Gracie was adamant he ignore the clemency hearing, he hoped she would eventually come to understand why he couldn't.

In the silver glow from the nearly full moon, with her translucent skin and dark hair spread over her pillow, Gracie looked almost ethereal.

He brushed his lips across her forehead. Something moved deep inside him at the touch of her warm skin against his mouth. "I love you," he whispered, then grabbed his jeans, tiptoed down the hallway and inched open the door to Lizzie's bedroom. He tucked her purple blanket around her shoulders, swept his fingers across her cheek. How could his baby girl be four-and-a-half years old already?

Once in the kitchen, he phoned dispatch.

"Hate to bother you this late, Wind," Maggie said. "But we got a 9-1-1 call about an in-home accident. A little kid. The operator said the caller sounded drunk and claimed the accident was his fault. An ambulance has been dispatched. Murph thinks a detective should check it out."

Captain Felix Murphy knew how much Radhauser dreaded any investigation that involved a child. Add a drunk to the equation and he was ready to become a criminal himself. But he wouldn't assume the caller's claim was a real admission of guilt. He'd lived long enough to understand the tightrope humans walked and how the smallest mistake could lead to a fatal plunge. Radhauser was nowhere near the accident that killed his family, but he made the same claim. It was his fault.

He dressed in the laundry room where he kept a change of clothing for nights like this one. Removing the belt buckle Lucas won, he pulled his belt from his dirty jeans, threaded it through the loops of a pair of clean ones and replaced the buckle.

After locking the back door knob, he stepped out into the night. Stars peppered the sky above their ranch in the foothills of the Siskiyou Mountains. He jogged toward the barn overhang where he parked the Crown Vic. The outside air still smelled of sawdust and cedar chips.

Mercedes, Gracie's mare, heard him and nickered—a friendly sound of expectation. "Settle down, girl," he said. "Way too early for breakfast." He sucked in a grateful breath. Marrying Gracie and moving to Oregon had been a good thing. And despite the recent letter from the clemency board, he'd found a peace he never believed possible after losing Laura and Lucas.

The streets were empty and Radhauser arrived at the scene on Pine Street in less than ten minutes. He straightened his steel-gray Stetson, opened the screen and knocked on the oak door of a beautifully restored and well-kept, older Craftsman in Ashland—a small town near the California border, proud of its mountainous landscape, its diversity and the Shakespeare Festival that kept it alive.

"It's the police," he said. "Open up." He waited a moment, then knocked again. It rained earlier and all around him the air smelled like earth and the slight decay of molted leaves. As if on command, four yellow, big leaf maple leaves fell onto the narrow porch. Autumn—that colorful season of death.

When he got no response, he tried the door. It opened into

darkness. Radhauser groped for the switch and the room flooded with light. He quickly scanned the scene.

An overturned coffee table. The shattered globe of an oil lamp littered the blue, ceramic floor tiles with small pieces of glass that caught the ceiling light and sparkled. Water from a spilled vase had formed a puddle on the floor. Tarot cards and daffodils were strewn about. A trail of blood drops led out of the room. *What the hell is going on here?* Instinctively, Radhauser moved his fingers to unsnap his leather holster. He placed his hand on his Glock.

Wedged into a corner at the back of the living room, a large cardboard box, the kind a refrigerator might be delivered in, had been made into a playhouse. Someone had cut out windows and a door and painted shutters on either side of them. Above the door opening, painted in the same Wedgewood blue as the shutters, were the words, *Cockroach's House.* The air around him hummed. *What kind of parent calls his kid a cockroach?*

Radhauser followed the blood drops to a doorway leading to what he assumed was the kitchen.

A man, his back to Radhauser, was attempting to give CPR to a child lying on the kitchen table. He used only his left hand. The other seemed to rest on the child's cheek, the index finger inside his mouth.

Is he trying to clear an airway? The child, barely more than a baby, was as blue as his footed sleeper. His mouth dripped blood.

Radhauser removed his right hand from his Glock. "You're pushing too hard."

The man, seemingly focused on what he was doing, neither responded nor turned around.

"Police," Radhauser said again.

Still no response.

Radhauser touched the man's shoulder.

He spun around, his dark eyes fixed on Radhauser. "Did you bring an ambulance?" His voice sounded like he had mud in his mouth.

Or maybe the 9-1-1 operator was right. Maybe this man was drunk. Radhauser's gaze darted around the kitchen. No empty beer or liquor bottles on the counters. He had a keen nose and could usually smell alcohol from five feet away.

The man was a little shorter than Radhauser, maybe six feet two inches, and looked as if he knew his way around a Nautilus machine. His black hair curled over the collar of his blue denim shirt. He appeared to be in his mid-thirties and stood with most of his weight on his left leg as if his right leg was injured. With that quick glance into his bottomless brown eyes, Radhauser saw a flash of something unexpected. Hidden deep beneath the compassion, fear, and obvious intelligence was an unreachable sadness.

"What's your name?"

The man had returned his attention to the toddler and didn't respond. "Oh my God," he cried. "Why is blood coming out of his mouth?"

Radhauser flipped him around. "Let me take over," he said, then unsnapped the toddler's pajama top and used three fingers to gently press down in the center of his chest, just below his nipples. As he worked, Radhauser tried to remember the manual—how to do CPR with an infant or small child. Little by little it came back to him.

A series of thirty compressions at the rate of 100-120 a minute. He needed to lift the toddler's chin, place his mouth over his mouth and nose and blow. It wasn't easy with a man's finger inside the child's mouth. Two gentle breaths, each one second in duration.

"The blood is yours," Radhauser finally said. The toddler had clamped down on the man's finger with so much force his teeth exposed the bone.

When he found his rhythm, the right speed and depth for his compressions, Radhauser retrieved his badge with his free hand, opened the leather case to show the man, and introduced himself. "Do you have a name?"

"Everyone calls me Bryce." He stared at Radhauser's mouth as he spoke. "The baby. Skyler. He...he...had a seizure. When I tried to stop him from swallowing his tongue, he latched onto my finger."

The man's speech was garbled, but Radhauser was able to

understand him. "Have you been drinking, Mr. Bryce?"

"No, no sir," he said. "I don't touch alcohol. My mother was an alcoholic. I'm hearing impaired from a..." He paused as if trying to choose the right words. "A childhood illness. But I'm pretty good at reading lips. I also sign. My speech defect might make it sound like I'm drunk."

Radhauser counted the seconds between the compressions as he pushed on the toddler's small chest. There was an egg-sized knot on Skyler's forehead that had turned shades of blue, yellow and purple. There were no other visible injuries. *Where the hell is that ambulance?* He glanced at his watch. Though it seemed like an hour since he arrived at the scene, only a few minutes had passed. As if on command, the sound of a siren wailed in the near distance.

"How old is Skyler, Mr. Bryce?"

"Nineteen months."

As Radhauser continued his compressions, Radhauser spotted the gadget to amplify sound on the wall above the kitchen phone. Bryce spoke more clearly than most deaf people Radhauser encountered, probably because he wasn't born deaf. "How old were you when you lost your hearing?"

"Six," he said.

Two paramedics in dark blue trousers and shirts with circular emblems on their sleeves burst through the open door and rushed into the kitchen.

Bryce tried to move out of their way, but his trapped finger kept him connected to Skyler.

The younger paramedic gripped the toddler's jaw with one hand and his cheekbones with the other, releasing Bryce's bloody finger. He introduced himself. "I'm Robert and this is my partner, Frank. Sorry for the delay. Bad accident blocked traffic on Main."

While Frank focused his attention on getting Skyler hooked up to an IV and oxygen, Robert cleaned and wrapped Bryce's finger.

Not needed anymore, Radhauser stepped back into the living room. Knowing how fast a routine accident could turn into a crime scene, he went outside and removed his briefcase and camera from his car. Radhauser wasn't the kind of detective who trusted things to memory. He snapped pictures of the overturned coffee table from every angle, the broken globe of the oil lamp, the scattering of daffodils and tarot cards, the blood spots on the floor and finally the cardboard playhouse, making sure to get a clear shot of the words painted above the door.

After slipping his small notebook from his inside blazer pocket, he jotted down some notes about the scene, Bryce, and what he discovered when he arrived. They'd be useful in filling out his report.

When he finished, he returned to the kitchen.

"Have a physician take a look at that wound," Robert said to Bryce. "You may need a prescription for antibiotics. Maybe even a stitch or two."

Bryce stood, his arms folded tightly across his chest, hands tucked into his armpits, while the paramedics loaded Skyler, now hooked up to an oxygen mask and IV line, onto the stretcher. It was then Radhauser noticed the thick, red rubber band around the toddler's left wrist. Probably a medical alert bracelet of some sort.

The paramedics pushed the gurney through the living room and down the front steps. Bryce limped after them.

Radhauser followed.

The swirling red light flashed across Skyler's tiny body as he was loaded into the ambulance.

Radhauser pushed Bryce closer. "Go ahead. You can accompany him to the hospital." There was no way he would stand around and watch paramedics load Lizzie into an ambulance. He would be inside that rig with her, kneeling on the floor beside her stretcher, holding her hand. Seizing Bryce by the shoulders, he turned him so they were facing. Bryce's eyes were red and filled with so much pain that Radhauser looked away. "Ride with your son. The hospital may require your consent to treat him."

"Skyler's not my son. He belongs to my girlfriend, Dana Sterling. I take care of him while she's at work."

"Do you have medical power of attorney?"

"No," Bryce said, a new flash of fear in his eyes. "Nothing like that."

Radhauser gripped Bryce's arm. "You need to get in touch with her. Tell her to call Ashland Hospital immediately, then head directly over there."

* * *

Dread seeped from his pores as Bryce picked up the receiver to dial Dana at work. All the what ifs darted through his mind. What if he made Scott go to bed and kept Skyler in the living room with him? What if he set the alarm clock every fifteen minutes to check on the toddler? What if he nestled Skyler on the sofa pillow next to him?

If only he could begin this day over and withdraw the furious words he hurled at Dana and Scott. No matter how angry he was, he hadn't meant for any of this to happen. He loved Skyler as much as a man could love a child. As much as he'd once loved his own daughter.

The heel of his hand had gone numb from clenching the phone. His right index finger continued to sting and throb. He dialed and waited for the hostess to answer.

"I need to speak with Dana." His voice was even thicker than usual. "It's an emergency." He clamped his eyes shut, willed her to be there, and to his relief she answered.

"What is it, Bryce?" A slight irritation lifted her voice. "Why are you calling me here? You know how I—"

"I...I had to," he stammered. "It's Skyler. He stopped breathing. I called 9-1-1. They took him to Ashland Hospital, I—"

"Oh my God," she said, her voice thin with fear.

"I'll be there to pick you up in five minutes."

"No," she said quickly. "Reggie is here. He can drive me to the hospital. You stay there with Scott. I'll call you as soon as I know anything."

Before Bryce could respond, Dana hung up.

CHAPTER FIVE

Radhauser stood on the asphalt driveway until every trace of the emergency disappeared except for the wail of the siren as the ambulance raced toward Ashland Hospital.

Concerned neighbors in nightgowns, T-shirts, hair rollers and hastily thrown-on chenille robes and denim jeans, gathered outside the house. Once the show was over, they chatted among themselves for a few moments, then one-by-one straggled back home.

When Bryce reappeared after calling Dana, an older black woman, wearing a pink flowered housedress and a pair of white bunny slippers with dirty ears hobbled over to him. She hugged him around the waist. She was short and heavyset, and her head of tight gray curls didn't reach his shoulder. When she let him go, Bryce introduced her to Radhauser as his neighbor, Miss Tilly.

She stared at the bloody gauze on his finger. "What happened?"

Bryce told her what happened with Skyler, how he'd clamped his teeth into Bryce's finger during a seizure.

"Why ain't you on your way to the hospital?"

"Dana doesn't want me there."

Tilly planted her hands on her hips. "Who cares what she wants." Tilly's voice raised about an octave. A voice someone from across the street could easily hear. "Who made that sorry-ass excuse for a mother the boss of you?"

"Reggie is driving her to the hospital."

Tilly met his gaze. "That Reggie Sterling's got no business acting like he cares. We all know he don't love that boy the way you do."

44

In her eyes, Radhauser saw her love for Bryce. And a lot left unsaid on the subject of Skyler's mom and Reggie. He jotted a note in his book to talk with Dana, Reggie and Miss Tilly.

"If you decide to go to the hospital, bring Scotty over. I'll go make up his bed on the sofa, just in case you need it."

As gently as if she were his mother, Bryce put one hand on each side of Tilly's face, framing it. "The boys and I'd be up that proverbial creek without a paddle if it weren't for you, Miss Tilly." He escorted her back to her house, holding her elbow as she climbed the porch steps. The bunny ears on her slippers slapped the concrete as she walked.

When he returned, Bryce didn't seem to know what to do with his hands. He put them in his pockets, then he pulled them out and swiped them over his pant legs. The blood was already seeping through the gauze on his finger. He stared straight ahead, silent and still, until he started shivering and his teeth made clattering noises. The veins in his neck stuck out like cables.

Fearful he might go into shock, Radhauser led him back inside to a quiet that seemed to have swallowed the small house. This was a man carrying a load far heavier than he could manage, but somehow, he hoisted it up and staggered forward.

Bryce collapsed onto the sofa.

Radhauser sat on the rocking chair facing him. "Who's Scotty?"

"Skyler's older brother. He's asleep in the bedroom. I should probably check on him. I'm surprised the sirens and all the commotion in the house didn't wake him."

Kids. It was as if sleep shut off their hearing. His Lizzie could slumber through a thunderstorm. "I'm sorry to have to do this now, but I need to ask you a few more questions." He nodded toward the overturned table. "It'll only take a minute and then you can go to the hospital."

"Dana made it very clear she doesn't want me there."

"Hospitals are public places. You should go if you need or want to."

Bryce looked at the floor.

Radhauser waited for him to look up again. "Is Reggie Sterling

45

Skyler's biological father?"

Bryce took a few deep breaths, as if trying to collect himself enough to explain. "Reggie is Dana's ex-husband, but he doesn't deserve to be a father."

Radhauser didn't know what to say. "Unfortunately, no one has to pass a test," he finally commented. "Do he and Dana have an amiable relationship?"

Bryce winced at the word *relationship*. "I guess you could call it that."

"You didn't answer my question."

"I'm sorry," Bryce said. "Would you repeat what you asked? I wasn't concentrating."

Radhauser did.

Bryce raised his eyebrows. "He's not much of a father, but Dana gave him the Sterling name. I've never seen the actual birth certificate." His muddled words gleamed, so double-edged they could cut whatever they touched.

"Is there some doubt about Skyler's paternity?"

Bryce took a slow, even, breath. "Reggie thinks so." His gaze washed over Radhauser as if seeing him for the first time.

"What does Dana say about it?"

"Has anyone ever told you that you look like that actor who used to play the Marlboro man?" Bryce's gaze dropped to the hand-tooled boots Radhauser had custom made in Nogales, then returned to his mouth.

"Not all detectives wear wrinkled raincoats like Columbo. But you didn't answer my question. Is there some doubt about Skyler's paternity?"

"Dana claims it doesn't matter." Bryce shrugged. "And I guess it doesn't to her. But it seems to be a big deal for Reggie."

Radhauser was silent for a moment, thinking about how he would feel if he suspected Lucas was fathered by another man. He liked to think it wouldn't matter. Once the boy arrived and was part of his life, he became his son regardless of his genes. But that was probably naïve thinking and it didn't take into account what that kind of suspicion would have done to his relationship with Laura.

What was the matter with him tonight? Despite the upcoming clemency hearing, this wasn't the time to linger in the past. He had a case to investigate. In order to regain his perspective, Radhauser stood and walked across the room, then turned back to Bryce.

"Tell me what happened here."

Bryce told him about the faulty latch on the screen door and the way a push from Scott had sent Skyler tumbling down the concrete stairs.

That would explain the knot on the toddler's forehead, but not the overturned table.

"Why is the table overturned?"

Bryce's gaze stayed fastened on the coffee table while he explained what happened when he rushed into the room to unlock the door for the paramedics. Even after Bryce stopped talking, his thoughts kept coming. Radhauser saw them in his eyes and knew exactly what was happening.

He often looked back on the night when everything changed for him—thought of each precariously stacked moment, one on top of the other. In especially lonely times, he tried to see if he could remove any one moment, change one thing he said or did. And if the outcome could have been different. It was a sick game he played with himself. A game Bryce now played.

He was careful to face Bryce and speak clearly. "How old is Skyler, Mr. Bryce?"

"He'll be two in March."

"And you and his mother live together?"

There was a splinter of hesitation in Bryce's eyes before he nodded.

"For how long?"

"A little over a year now."

"Where does she work?"

Bryce told him.

Radhauser nodded toward the cardboard playhouse. "What's with that?" he asked. "And who is cockroach?"

Bryce stared at him silently, his dark eyes now dull, features flat, as if someone had beaten him down. He seemed caught somewhere between disbelief and actuality. An orange cat brushed against his ankle. Without a word, Bryce picked him up and carried him into the kitchen as if he were sleepwalking.

Radhauser remembered the way his mind wouldn't work after Luke and Laura's accident—that flatness before reality and grief entered. When he was forced to believe the worst.

Before he could ask the question again, a child scurried across the hallway and stood at the entrance to the living room, his thumb in his mouth. The boy looked about Lizzie's age, maybe four or five years old. His strawberry blond hair stuck out on the right side where he slept. He had a sprinkling of freckles across his nose, like Dennis the Menace. The boy had the brightest blue eyes Radhauser ever saw. He wore a pair of black and red Spiderman pajamas.

"You must be Scott," Radhauser said.

Bryce returned to the living room. "It's time to sleep, Scotty. You need to go back to bed."

Scott pulled his thumb out of his mouth. A thin line of saliva trailed after it. "You're not my real dad and you can't make me." The boy's gaze landed on Radhauser. He looked up at the Stetson, paused at the silver belt buckle, then checked out the boots. "Are you a real cowboy?"

"Well," Radhauser said, moving closer and then kneeling so he was eye level with the boy. "I have a small ranch with a barn and three horses. I like to ride the dirt trails up into the mountains. And I shovel out their stalls, brush them down after a ride and keep them well fed. I guess you could say that makes me a real cowboy."

"I want a horse." The boy turned his attention on Bryce. "But he never gives me anything." He looked around the room, his gaze settling on the cardboard playhouse. "I stood on the rail and looked inside. Skyler's not in his crib. How come he's allowed to be up late?"

Radhauser moved aside.

It was obviously painful for Bryce to squat, but he did. He held the boy by his shoulders and looked directly into his eyes. "Skyler got sick and had to go to the hospital. But he's going to be okay, Scotty. He'll be home before you know it."

The boy jerked away, his blue eyes wide and accusing. "Did you hit him?"

Bryce winced and a wave of something hopeless washed over him.

"You did hit him," Scott said. "Just like you hit me. You said you were gonna murder me."

"Listen, Scotty. That's not true. I didn't hit Skyler. I said something to you that I didn't mean. But right now, I need you to cooperate. I'm going to the hospital to check on Skyler. So go get your robe and slippers. Miss Tilly is making up a bed for you." There was anguish in Bryce's voice—a torn slightly hollow sound, as if this day was about to destroy him.

Scott put his hands on his hips. "I'm not going. I hate her." He turned and ran into his bedroom, his bare feet thumping against the floor. "And I hate you, too." The door slammed.

There was a moment of stunned silence.

Radhauser needed to talk to Scott, preferably without Bryce around. This could change everything.

Still, there was something about Bryce that Radhauser had begun to trust—something in the gentle way he treated Miss Tilly. The way he hadn't tried to hide his grief over what had happened with Skyler. And the way he fought through the obvious pain in his leg in order to be eye-to-eye with Scott. It must be tough to be hearing impaired.

Scott seemed like a defiant and angry kid, but if he was telling the truth, Radhauser had no sympathy for a grown man who'd hit a small child and threaten him with murder. If Bryce could do that, what else might he be capable of doing?

Legally, Radhauser shouldn't question a child without a parent or guardian present, but he could with permission. "I have a daughter about Scott's age. Maybe I can calm him down with a story about cowboys. Is that okay with you?"

Bryce nodded, but said nothing.

* * *

When Radhauser finished talking to Scott, he paused outside the boy's door and took a slow, even breath to center himself. A wall of awards hung in the hallway. Caleb Bryce Employee of the Year at Gilbert's Grocery Store for 1987, 1991 and 1994. Seven years of plaques for coaching area Little League teams. Two of his teams won state championships. Three wood and bronze plaques for poems winning first prize in the Oregon State poetry contest.

Somehow Radhauser hadn't taken Bryce for a poet. But he shouldn't be surprised. He'd been a detective for twenty years and learned a long time ago not to judge a man by anything external.

He brushed his fingertips across the etched bronze surface of the Someone Cares award the hospital had presented Bryce for his volunteer work in the newborn nursery. The lavish plaque depicted an adult hand with all the baby's fingers wrapped around the adult's little finger. If you made a judgment based on this wall, you'd believe Bryce was a good man. A poet. A sensitive man who gave back to his community. A man who cared about and supported kids.

Radhauser shook his head to change his mindset. People were multi-layered. Anyone could have a dark side that verged on the dangerous. In his line of work, he encountered elementary school teachers who were pedophiles. Priests who committed murder. Doctors who were sadists.

But he always believed he could read people. That he could stare right into their heads and see what it was they didn't want seen. When one of the other detectives had a solid suspect they couldn't break, they called Radhauser—the man known as the cop who gets a confession every time. Somehow, he missed this one. Had actually felt sorry for that deaf asshole who smacked a four-year-old and threatened to kill him. He returned to the living room.

Bryce sat on the sofa with his head in his hands.

Radhauser tapped him on the shoulder and waited until he looked at him. His face was streaked and wet.

The phone rang, loud as a school fire drill.

Bryce grabbed a tissue from the box on the end table and blew his nose, then hurried into the kitchen to answer. He returned a moment later.

"That was Dana." There was even more mud in his voice now. "She and Reggie are at the hospital. Skyler's in surgery."

His voice was full of prayer and there was so much misery in his eyes that, once again, Radhauser looked away. "It's good both parents are there," he said. "Hospitals are pretty terrible places. Maybe you dodged a bullet."

For the first time that night, Bryce gave Radhauser a weak, somewhat sad smile. "I'd sure as hell need a bullet if that little guy died."

Radhauser was taken aback by his response. But over the years, he learned there was a lot of denial in humans, even ones who weren't suspects. It wasn't so much what a suspect showed you, but what he chose to hide that mattered most. Why hadn't Bryce told him about the fight with Scott? The way he lost control of both his words and his actions. "You mind answering a few more questions?"

Bryce shrugged. "I don't know what else I can tell you."

You can tell me what you did to hurt that little boy. "How often do you take care of the boys?"

"Dana works most nights until at least midnight and often later, so I'm with the kids a lot. She usually sleeps until noon or so."

"Do you feed them dinner and get them ready for bed at night?"

"Since the accident where I ruptured my Achilles tendon, I've been out of work and do most of the cooking."

"Don't you resent it?" Radhauser tried to sound sympathetic, though after what Scott told him, he felt some contempt for this man. He tried to keep it out of his voice. "What kind of life does that leave you? And they're not even your kids."

Bryce explained his relationship with Dana, the injury he sustained to his Achilles tendon and their decision to take the boys out of daycare in order to save money while he was out of work.

He told Radhauser he took a class at the university and had a day every week all to himself. On Dana's day off, he spent the morning volunteering in the hospital, the afternoon in his class and then the library, writing. "It's enough," he said. "Besides, I love Scott and Skyler and most days I don't mind taking care of them."

"Scott says you got pretty angry. That you hit him." Radhauser leaned back in the chair and studied the man's face. The air was charged and the tiny hairs on Radhauser's arms lifted.

Bryce retreated to that place so many suspects go when a cop struck them in the face with a truth. "It's not what you think," he finally said, his face slick with sweat. "I almost never get angry with the kids. I spanked Scott earlier on his butt with my open hand. But I admit, it was ha...ha... harder than I meant to. I don't know...today...I just lost it." Holding his head in his hands, he pressed his splayed fingers against his temples and told Radhauser what happened with Scott. The way the boy screamed, kicked, bit, and spit in Bryce's face. And then later, when the phone rang and Bryce left the bathroom to answer, the 'accidental' bite Scott took out of Skyler's penis.

Radhauser waited until he finished before asking another question. "Do you ever lose it with Skyler, Mr. Bryce?"

His gaze fixed on Radhauser like two hot beams. Some wall inside Bryce seemed to break. "N...N...Never. What do you think I am, some kind of monster? He's just a baby."

"I'm required by law to notify Child Protective Services when there is a suspicion of child abuse, Mr. Bryce."

For a moment, Bryce didn't respond. His gaze stayed fastened on the coffee table. "C...C...Child abuse?" He had the look of a little bucktoothed fat boy facing a big bully on the school playground.

CHAPTER SIX

Radhauser parked in the emergency room lot at Ashland Hospital and hurried across the asphalt. He dodged an ambulance and two police cruisers and then rushed through the double glass doors into the nearly empty waiting room. Glare from the fluorescent lights struck his face like a slap. The heels of his cowboy boots clicked against the polished linoleum. The room smelled like rubbing alcohol, some kind of pine detergent, and fear. Funny, how certain smells could resurrect memories. He took a deep breath. Swallowed the memories back.

He stood in front of the information desk, introduced himself to the on-duty nurse, and showed her his badge. His cowboy hat dangled from his fingertips against his denim pant leg. "I'm investigating an accident and am here to check on Skyler Sterling. I know he's in surgery. Can you tell me anything about his condition?"

She shook her head. "You'll get more information upstairs in the surgery waiting room."

"I'd like to speak to the doctor who admitted him."

"That will be Dr. Barrows." She nodded toward a cluster of multi-colored plastic chairs lining the side wall. "Take a seat. I'll let him know you're here."

Empty Styrofoam cups, one of them scalloped all the way around the rim with teeth marks, dotted the end tables. A gray-haired man with a long beard, wearing blue jeans and a sweatshirt lay sleeping on a green vinyl couch patched with duct tape.

Before Radhauser took a seat, a young doctor in a white lab coat called out his name. The doctor walked a little bent forward like he was in a hurry to arrive at wherever he was going. He led Radhauser into a patient/doctor meeting room. Taking a chair behind a small table, he motioned for Radhauser to sit in one of the molded yellow plastic chairs in front of the table. "How may I help you, Detective Radhauser?"

"I'm the investigating officer in a case involving nineteen-month-old Skyler Sterling. Can you tell me anything about his condition?"

"He was brought in by paramedics around 12:45 a.m., mostly unresponsive. He was cyanotic and his pupils were fixed and dilated. Paramedics said he had a seizure."

"Did your examination show any signs of neglect or abuse?"

"Skyler is a little small for his age, but he doesn't appear to be malnourished. He has an injury to his forehead, some bruising on his chest and a large bruise just under his ribcage. We did full body X-rays. Found no skull or rib fractures. No evidence of old injuries. There was no cranial bleeding. His abdomen was distended so we did an MRI which showed internal bleeding into his abdominal cavity. There was so much blood it was hard to determine its origin. I suspected a torn spleen or liver and called in a pediatric surgeon."

"Would you say his injuries could be consistent with a fall down three concrete stairs?"

Barrows appeared to think for a few seconds. He was a handsome young man with a deep voice you could listen to for hours. "I suppose it's possible," he finally said. "Especially if he struck the edge of the concrete with force."

"Did you notice a red medical alert band around his wrist?"

"Yes, but it was only a rubber band."

That's odd. Why would a 19-month-old put a rubber band around his wrist? Would he have the coordination and finger dexterity to do it? Of course, Scott could have put it there. He made a mental note to ask Bryce.

"What's Skyler's prognosis?"

Barrows stared at Radhauser a moment. "Miracles often happen with little kids. And Daniel Corrigan is one of our finest pediatric surgeons."

Radhauser was heartsick and tired, his whole body was one pulsing ache. He hated cases where a child was hurt. And being in a nearly empty hospital in the middle of the night plunged him into a sense of despair greater than anything he'd felt since the night Laura and Lucas died.

It was time for him to go home and get some sleep. Time for him to mend some fences with Gracie over the clemency hearing.

Once inside his car, his hands started to shake. It was times like this when the darker emotions washed over him. He needed sleep, a shower, shave, and a cup of coffee, but he couldn't steady his hands enough to get the key into the ignition, so he remained in the parking lot and clamped his eyes closed to shut out the memories. But it was too late.

After he finally left the morgue on the night his wife and son died, he couldn't stand the idea of going home to their empty house—facing all the reminders that were scattered throughout. He sat alone in the parking lot of Tucson Medical Center confronting his future without them.

Sometime, after sunrise, he made his way home.

Because the monsoons had lasted longer than usual, it was an especially beautiful spring in Tucson. The air was that electric blue that seemed only to exist in the desert. Prickly pear, pincushion, and barrel cactus plumped from winter rains were in full bloom. Ocotillos waved their red flags and paloverde trees spilled yellow blossoms across the desert floor. Oblivious to his pain, all that new life and beauty only reminded him of everything he'd lost. Perhaps it was always the beauty in life, not its ugliness, that hurt the most.

What did it take to unravel a life? But it hadn't been just one life. It had been a carefully woven tapestry of eight lives—including the driver who hit them, his five-year-old sons, and the wife and teenaged daughter he left behind. All undone by one drunk who might soon be let free.

* * *

Bryce paced the darkened kitchen, uncertain what to do with himself. The window over the sink was open and night air seemed to move through the room like black water. He stumbled over Pickles.

55

The cat yowled.

Bryce realized he hadn't fed the cat all day. He flipped on the light, then poured food into the cat's bowl and refilled his water dish. Pickles circled around his ankles.

Detective Radhauser probably believed he was a child abuser. And maybe he was. He hit Scott too hard. And his negligence in not repairing the latch on the storm door resulted in a severe injury to Skyler.

What was the matter with him, beating himself up like that? Except for those two things, those two awful things, he did nothing but try to make life better for Dana and her boys.

He shoved his hands into his pants pockets, hating this helpless feeling. No one loved Skyler more than he did. He should be with him now, should know what the doctors were doing. Tilly was right. Dana and that imbecile Reggie couldn't forbid him from going to the hospital. Scott would be safe with Tilly. She already made a bed for him on her sofa. Bryce headed toward the center bedroom. He found Scott huddled against the headboard of his bed, staring at Skyler's empty crib.

Bryce flipped on the light and reached for the boy. "It's all right, Scotty."

Scott's gaze darted around the room. "I'm scared," he said, crawling into Bryce's arms. "Did I kill Skyler? Is he dead?"

Bryce picked him up, hugged him against his chest. "No, Scotty." With the smell of Scott's hair, the hated tears rose again and Bryce swallowed them back. "Remember I told you Skyler went to the hospital and that Tilly will take care of you while I go see about him."

"Will you bring him home?"

"Yes," Bryce answered. "As soon as he feels better." He slipped a pair of socks on Scott's bare feet, wrapped a blanket around him and carried him next door.

"Don't you be worryin' none," Tilly said. "I'll watch over him for as long as you need me. He'll be fine." She pulled the sheet back and Bryce deposited Scott on her sofa, tucked a blanket around him and kissed him on the forehead. "Be a good boy for

Miss Tilly," he said, then turned to the old woman. "I owe you another one."

She walked him to the front door and then stepped out onto the porch. "You don't owe me nothin', Bryce. You always doing stuff for me." She stood with her legs apart, her hands planted on her ample hips and watched as he opened the door to his Camry and slid inside.

Bryce backed out of his driveway and headed south on an empty Main Street toward Ashland Hospital. He ignored the twenty-five miles per hour speed limit and drove at fifty. He prayed for Skyler, prayed there would be another chance to chase him around the room with a rubber shark, playing gotcha, Skyler's favorite game. Bryce pretended to bite the toddler's butt with the shark and each time he nipped, Skyler screamed, then exploded in gales of laughter.

It had been years since Bryce prayed, but he could feel his words begging for all they were worth, pleading on bended knees, their bargaining syllables reaching out toward heaven.

He parked outside the emergency entrance, then stopped at the information desk inside the waiting room. "I'm here about Skyler Sterling." He touched his ear, then went through his spiel about being hearing impaired, asking her to look at him when she talked so he could read her lips. "Are you a relative?" She increased her volume and spoke slowly, enunciating every word.

"No. I'm his friend." Bryce lowered his gaze, embarrassed by his faltering speech, the realization he hadn't shaved, or made time for a badly-needed haircut. He hadn't even bothered to run a comb through his tangled, dark curls. "Skyler and his mother live with me and I'm the only father he knows." Bryce raised his gaze in time to catch her canvassing the stubble on his face.

She checked her computer monitor. "He's still in surgery. There's a waiting room on the third floor. That's your best bet for current information." She pointed toward the elevator.

The third floor waiting room was empty. Bryce paced for a few minutes, wondering where Reggie and Dana were, then sat on the edge of one of the chairs. Maybe they went down to the cafeteria for a cup of coffee. He gripped the chrome arms, imagined them sitting across from each other in the empty cafeteria, then stared vacantly at his dusty tennis shoes for a second before he stood and paced again. He was unable to concentrate on anything for more than a few moments.

Bryce was accustomed to quiet. But the silence in this waiting room was knotted and fragile. He paused at a table cluttered with old magazines, picked one up without looking at the cover, then tossed it back.

A little Hispanic girl he hadn't noticed earlier was stacking blocks on the floor in the room's corner. She stared up at him.

His heart thumped so loud in his own ears, he believed the pounding had raised her round, dark eyes to meet his. Calmed for the moment by her stare, he crouched down in front of her. "Where are your parents, honey?"

She ran out of the room and down the hall toward the nursing station screaming, loud enough for Bryce to hear, "Mommy, Mommy. That man talks funny."

He slumped uncomfortably onto the narrow seat of one of the chairs. His hands, folded in his lap, tightened and loosened their grip on each other. The skin on his cheeks burned. What kind of a monster was he? Within the last twelve hours he'd struck and threatened one child, allowed another to be injured severely enough to require surgery, and terrified yet another.

Bryce sensed more than heard the rhythmic click of Dana's boots on the white tile floor. He glanced toward the waiting room's entrance and swallowed hard. She and Reggie were walking side by side. He had his arm over her shoulders as if they were high school lovers wandering the halls between classes.

He clenched his hands into angry fists. What he wouldn't give to punch that pompous Reggie Sterling in the jaw.

When she walked into the waiting room, Dana pulled away from Reggie's embrace and stepped toward Bryce. She still wore her waitress uniform. She looked young, beautiful and frightened. "I didn't know you were here."

It took him a minute to yank himself up onto his feet. He took a breath, considered embracing her.

The set of her jaw stopped him. "I asked you not to come."

Bryce wanted to grab her by the shoulders and shake her into understanding that his love for Skyler gave him more right to be in this hospital waiting room than Reggie Sterling. But he didn't say a word; just stood, only a few inches away, his longing hands clamped against his own thighs.

Dana's hair hung in damp ringlets against her cheeks. "Where's Scott?" She looked around the waiting room.

"Asleep on Tilly's sofa," Bryce answered. "How is Skyler? Please, tell me what's happening."

"You know how I feel about that old woman." She made a frustrated gesture with her hands, turning them palm-side up. Her fingernails were swirled with scarlet polish, a tiny rhinestone set in the center of each.

"For Ch...Ch...Christ sakes, Dana. Don't start that again. It was an e...e...emergency. Tilly was there and I didn't know what else to do. I had to find out about Skyler. I...I...I had to know he was okay."

She stepped back, probably startled by his stammer. "What happened to your hand?"

"When I went to clear his airway to do CPR, Skyler's teeth clamped down on my finger. Please," he begged. "Tell me what's happening with Skyler."

"He's still in surgery," she said. "Some internal injuries, the nurse said. He's bleeding inside." She paused and took in a ragged breath. "What happened?"

"I'm not sure," he said. "Scott shoved him through the screen door and he fell down the steps earlier. But he seemed fine when I gave him his bath and put him to bed."

Reggie moved closer to Bryce. "What did you do to him?"

Bryce looked at Dana. "I'd never hurt him. Surely you know that. You told me I was way too easy on the boys."

She searched his face for a moment, as if looking for some other person. Someone she could believe.

The waiting room door opened.

59

Bryce stopped breathing.

A physician in scrubs, his mask dangling around his neck, entered the room. "I'm looking for the family of Skyler Sterling." All three of them rushed forward.

The doctor introduced himself as Daniel Corrigan, the on-call pediatric surgeon.

"I'm his mother," Dana said.

Reggie and Bryce remained silent.

"I'm sorry." The expression on the doctor's face echoed his words. "We stopped the bleeding, then sutured the incision, and I thought everything would be fine. On the way out of the OR, he had a seizure and stopped breathing. We couldn't bring him back."

"What do you mean you couldn't bring him back?" Dana asked, her dark eyes round and beginning to tear up.

"During the seizure, his heart stopped beating. We tried to shock it back into normal rhythm, but..." His voice trailed off. "I'm so sorry. We did everything we could."

"No," Bryce insisted. "Not Skyler. He...He...can't. He can't be..." Bryce cringed. He couldn't make himself say that word and a toddler's name in the same sentence. Not ever again. It was as final as the closing of a casket. He sank back against the wall, feeling the blood drain from his face and arms.

Reggie pulled a handkerchief out of his pocket and blew his nose. "Are you saying my son is dead?"

The doctor nodded.

It was the first time Bryce ever heard Reggie Sterling claim Skyler as his son.

For Bryce, the questions kept multiplying and reproducing themselves like giant amoebas run wild. There were so many things he wanted to know. Could this have been prevented? Did Skyler's fall down the steps have anything to do with his death? Or had he been injured when Bryce stumbled over the coffee table? If only he had been more vigilant. If only he fixed the faulty latch. If only he left the toddler in his crib while he unlocked the front door for the paramedics.

He told the doctor about the fall, how Skyler had eaten his dinner and seemed okay when he put him to bed. "Skyler had another seizure earlier, just before I called 9-1-1. Do you have any idea what caused them?"

"The MRI showed no evidence of a cerebral bleed," the doctor said. "But the medical examiner will do an autopsy and order a toxicology screen. Hopefully we'll know more when we get the results." He shook his head. "I'm truly sorry for your loss." He turned slowly and left the room.

Bryce dropped onto one of the chairs. The heaviness of loss pressed against him with new weight. He couldn't lift himself above it. He was sinking.

Reggie lunged toward him, grabbed his shoulders and pulled him to his feet, shaking him hard. "You son of a bitch. You murdered my son." A strange hissing sound came out of him, like a teapot when it boiled.

CHAPTER SEVEN

Unable to sleep, Detective Radhauser sat at his kitchen table, drinking a cup of hot cocoa and thinking about the fight he had with Gracie over the clemency hearing. He stood and paced, like someone in an interrogation room, realizing he would crack if he tried to hold out much longer. It was after 2 a.m., but he needed to smooth things over with his wife. And he had no idea how to do that, short of giving in to her wish that he let the board decide Flannigan's fate. He would, if he could. But that hearing was way too important to him. Somehow, he'd make her understand.

He tiptoed down the hallway and into the master bedroom. The bed was empty. Nearly frantic, he looked around the room. A seam of light slipped through the crack at the bottom of the bathroom door. He tapped lightly on the door. When Gracie didn't respond, he opened it.

She was standing in front of the mirror with her pajama top off, poking her right breast with her index finger. "It's growing," she said, referring to a small lump just below the nipple. She was close to tears. Her hands fluttered around her face, as if ready to wipe them away. "Feel it."

He did.

She was right. It was nearly twice the size it was two weeks ago when she first discovered it.

Their faces in the mirror blurred and he swallowed hard against his fear. "Have you made an appointment with the doctor?" He wanted to tell her he was sorry for the way their discussion in the barn had gone—that he loved her more than anything in the world. The words accumulated in his mouth as if they were going to boil over. But he couldn't say them.

"Not yet," she said. "I thought it would go away."

"You have to."

"It's probably only a cyst. You know how pregnancy messes up the hormones. Besides, I'm way too young to have breast cancer. And there is no history in my family. I called my mother to make sure."

Gracie was so alive and full of energy and enthusiasm it was impossible for him to imagine her sick, especially with something like cancer.

"We have to go to the doctor," he said. "If you don't make an appointment, I'll make one for you." He spoke so fast his words tumbled over each other. Nothing mattered to him as much as Gracie did.

A single tear slid down her face. "I'll call tomorrow," she said, turning away from the mirror. She ran her index finger across his cheek.

It was a feather-soft touch, but with the power of an electrical shock. She moved into his arms.

He cupped her head in his hand and held it against his chest. "I love you, Gracie. More than anything in the world."

She wrapped her arms around his waist. "I'm sorry I was such a bitch about the clemency hearing."

He held her tighter. "It's okay." The warmth of her skin seeped through his shirt. "It's not important now. I know you're afraid it might be cancer. And I am, too. But knowledge is power. It might not be anything. If it is, we'll handle it together. You're a fighter."

After they made love and she drifted off, he tucked the blankets around her and, still unable to sleep, returned to the kitchen. He wanted to do something special for Gracie to show her how much she meant to him. Even though he tried to tell her, his mother always said love was action, never just words. "What would you have wanted me to do for you, Laura?" He waited to hear her voice, the way he did in the barn office. But no words came.

Maybe he would surprise Gracie with breakfast in bed. The chrysanthemums were in full bloom. He could cut some blossoms and put them in a small bud vase on her breakfast tray.

As he checked the refrigerator for bacon and eggs, a call from dispatch came in. Skyler Sterling was dead.

The need to weep welled up inside Radhauser's chest like a balloon. He could feel it inside him, that old wave of sadness, with him for over a decade—that awful awareness that tragedy loomed all around us. He left a note for Gracie, got back into his car and headed to Bryce's house on Pine Street. Radhauser's questioning could wait until later in the morning, but he remembered all too well what it felt like to go back to an empty house where a dead child once lived.

Besides, there was something about Bryce. It wasn't easy to put into words, but in his job Radhauser was forced to deal with so many people whose motives and personal agendas were to deceive, that he was drawn to people who gave him the sense they were simply honest and doing the best they could. Despite the fact he'd lost his temper with Scott, Bryce gave him that sense. But Radhauser was also aware of the possibility he could be wrong.

It was nearly 4 a.m., the sky still dotted with stars, the moon icy white and nearly full when he pulled into Bryce's driveway. Radhauser's stomach felt as if he were digesting gravel instead of a cup of hot chocolate. The porch light was on and both living room windows flooded with light.

He stepped out of his car and climbed the stairs onto the narrow porch.

Bent over at the waist, Bryce adjusted something on the screen door.

Radhauser waited for him to look up. When he did, Radhauser touched the rim of his Stetson in a gesture of respect. "I heard about Skyler. I'm very sorry for your loss. May I come inside?"

Bryce loaded his tools back into the red metal toolbox, then stepped aside for Radhauser to enter the house. "I installed a new latch. I should have..." His eyes were red-rimmed.

Once Radhauser stepped inside, Bryce tested the door again. It held, no matter how hard he pushed. "Are you h...h...here to arrest me?"

"No. At this time, we don't have any reason to think Skyler's death was anything but a tragic accident. I could have waited until tomorrow to ask you these questions, but I thought you might want some company tonight." He gestured toward the sofa.

Bryce sank onto the center cushion.

The living room was clean. The tarot cards were stacked neatly on the coffee table, the glass from the broken oil lamp picked up, and everything back in place. Radhauser was glad he thought to take photos when he first arrived. "Are you here alone?"

Bryce nodded. "Scott is still over at Tilly's. She's keeping him until morning. I don't know how I'm going to tell him about Skyler."

"Where's his mother?"

"I don't know. She must still be with Reggie."

Radhauser sat on the edge of the coffee table, face to face with Bryce. He questioned him slowly and patiently and Bryce repeated everything he could remember about what happened. As he talked, his stutter gradually disappeared. If sadness were a color, it would be a gray-blue band wrapped around Bryce's muddy voice.

He remembered his watch read 11:45 p.m. when he awakened on the living room sofa, but he didn't know exactly what time he put the toddler to bed. He said it was earlier than usual because of the difficult day he had with Scott. That Reggie and Henry came by at 7:30 and the kids were already in bed. He didn't know when he pulled Skyler from his crib or how long before he phoned for help. And he was unsure if he spent minutes or hours trying to resuscitate Skyler.

It didn't matter. Radhauser had the 9-1-1 call at 12:05 a.m. Skyler was at the Ashland hospital by 12:45 a.m.

What Radhauser knew and Bryce didn't, was that his final moments with Skyler would stay with him wherever he went. Whatever he did in the future, Skyler Sterling, forever frozen as a toddler, would be there too.

"Did Skyler like to wear a red rubber band on his wrist?"

"No," Bryce said. "Why?"

"I noticed one when the paramedics loaded him onto the stretcher. I thought it was some kind of medical alert bracelet."

"I guess I was so frantic I didn't see it. But it wasn't there when I gave him his bath and put him to bed."

Radhauser jotted a note in his book. A little kid with a rubber band around his wrist was no big deal. But if this house turned out to be a crime scene, he never knew what little detail would turn out to be important. He stood. "You've been through enough for one night. I may have to ask some more questions later so don't leave town, okay? I'll need to talk with Reggie and Dana, too. After we see what the medical examiner finds."

"The medical examiner? Sk...Skyler will have an autopsy? They'll cut him open and take out his organs?"

"It's routine," Radhauser explained. "The medical examiner investigates all accidental deaths. The physicians at the Ashland Hospital aren't sure why he stopped breathing. An autopsy might help them find out. Maybe even help some other kid live."

Bryce walked Radhauser to his car. They stood in silence for a moment beneath the light of a street lamp.

"I thought it was only a seizure, that Skyler would be fine." Bryce shook his head. "People don't die from seizures, do they?"

Radhauser paused, his hand on the car door. He pivoted a little to make sure Bryce could see his lips. "Not usually. But as you know he sustained some internal injuries either in the fall down the front stairs or when you tripped over the coffee table. Or both."

"Either way," Bryce said. "It's my fault."

"Let's wait for the autopsy report," Radhauser said. "Before assigning blame to anyone."

* * *

The Jackson County Medical Examiner's office and morgue was located in Central Point behind the State Highway Patrol Building. It was late afternoon on Thursday by the time Radhauser arrived. The sun wouldn't set for hours, but dark clouds rolled into the Rogue Valley, keeping the sunlight at bay. He hoped it wasn't an indication of things to come.

Radhauser hadn't been able to stop thinking about Bryce. The poor man was torturing himself and Radhauser wanted, more than anything, for Skyler Sterling's death to have come from a natural cause. From something like an undiagnosed heart defect. Even if the medical examiner ruled the death an accident caused by Scott pushing him down the stairs, or Bryce tripping over the coffee table, he would blame himself.

Though Radhauser had been present for more than his share of autopsies and stopped being squeamish, he purposely came late today, not wanting to witness the post mortem on a child as young and small as Skyler Sterling.

He tapped on the ME's office door. His name was Steven Heron, but everyone called him Blue. With his tall, thin frame and dagger-like nose, he actually looked like one of the Great Blue Herons that roamed the banks of the Rogue River. His neck was so long and sinuous, it delivered his head into the room before the rest of his body arrived. Heron was a good man, smart as a Rhodes scholar and with a poet's sensitivity. Radhauser liked Heron, chose to be more respectful, and referred to him only as Heron.

Paying a visit to Heron always brought Radhauser back to his days with the Pima County Sheriff's Department in Tucson, where the ME, a Dr. Irvin Crenshaw, was nicknamed Melon because of his last name and the yellow tint to his skin. He shook his head and tried the door. It was locked.

Assuming Heron was in the autopsy suite, Radhauser continued down the hallway through a set of swinging steel doors labeled *Morgue*, then twenty steps further to a single door with a metal plate engraved with the words *Autopsy Suite*. He stepped into an alcove, dropped his half-filled coffee cup into the trash can, took off his hat and hung it from a hook. He grabbed a green gown and face mask from a stack neatly folded on a metal cart beside the door.

Before heading into the actual autopsy room, where white tiles stretched from floor to ceiling, he thrust his arms into the gown, tied the mask behind his head, and slipped a pair of shoe protectors over his boots. Then he walked toward the autopsy table, the green edges of the gown flapping at his back.

Heron stood beside the stainless steel table, stitching the Y-shaped incision in Skyler Sterling's small torso. Classical music played in the background—Beethovan's 9th Symphony. As always, Heron's posture was perfectly erect in his blue-gray lab coat and matching apron. On a gleaming steel cart beside the autopsy table, his instruments were laid out, as orderly as any operating room surgeon. Like every morgue, this one smelled of disinfectant, formaldehyde, and some other, darker odors like bowel and stomach contents.

Radhauser closed his eyes, then released his wish into the room. *Let it be an aneurysm or a small blood clot in the heart.*

When he opened them again, Heron was pulling the needle through the child's skin, then tying off a stitch.

Radhauser cringed, grateful neither Laura nor Lucas required an autopsy. There was no question about the cause of death. Everyone knew they died by the drunken hands of Lawrence Arthur Flannigan.

Though Heron must have heard Radhauser enter, he wasn't easily distracted. Heron always closed his incisions in small, neat stitches, as carefully as a plastic surgeon would stitch a dog bite on a child's face. When he finished, he looked up at Radhauser's eyes. "How are things on the ranch, cowboy?"

Radhauser made small talk with the ME for a few minutes about the little horse ranch he shared with Gracie, and Heron's childhood summers on his uncle's thoroughbred ranch in Wyoming.

"Have you determined the cause of death?" Radhauser asked.

"I haven't dictated my report yet. But here are the basics. His external examination showed an egg-shaped bump and some bruising on his forehead consistent with a fall." He paused and shrugged. "Pretty common in kids this age. There was no evidence of intracranial bleeding or skull fracture. His abdomen was slightly discolored, probably from the internal bleeding. The surgeon did a good job removing the ruptured spleen and repairing the torn hepatic vein. Under normal circumstances, this would have been sufficient to save the boy."

"What do you mean, normal circumstances?"

"Don't get ahead of yourself, cowboy. I'm getting there. When I couldn't find any obvious reason for his death, I looked at the EKG they did in the hospital. It showed QT interval prolongation."

"Basic English," Radhauser said. "I skipped anatomy and physiology and majored in cowgirls."

Heron laughed. "It is a measure of the time between the start of a Q wave and the end of a T wave in the heart's electrical cycle. Often prolongation is a risk factor for sudden death."

This could be the break Radhauser was hoping for. "Is it what killed Skyler Sterling?"

"No," Heron said. "But it is an important piece of the puzzle. This EKG abnormality is pretty rare in a child without any heart disease. My investigation found nothing wrong with his heart."

"What do you think caused the abnormality in the EKG? Could it have been a mistake?"

Heron held up his hand. "I'll get to that in a minute. But there was one more peculiar finding on my external examination you'll want to know about." He paused, studied Radhauser's face.

Just like Crenshaw, Heron liked to introduce a few dramatic techniques into his presentation. He lifted his left eyebrow. "This kid had a bruise and what appears to be a bite mark on his penis."

Radhauser dreaded asking the question, didn't really want to hear the answer. "You think he was a victim of sexual abuse?"

Heron shook his head. "I don't know. The teeth marks were small. I found no signs of anal tearing or scarring and no semen in his mouth or anus. But one thing is pretty certain, the kid didn't bite himself."

Radhauser said nothing. Bryce had described the shove Scott gave Skyler that sent him through the screen door, across the porch, and tumbling down the steps. The kicking, spitting and biting Bryce endured before he resorted to the slap on the butt. And later the bathtub bite on the penis Scott had given Skyler. Radhauser decided not to mention this to Heron. If the prosecution pursued the bite, tried to blame Bryce for the injury, it would be a feather in the defense cap to prove them wrong. He made a mental note to photograph the bite mark on Bryce's arm for comparison.

"To make a long story short," Heron said. "I found nothing on gross examination, either internal or external, to account for this boy's death."

Radhauser cocked his head. "Then why is he dead?"

"There were raised levels of protein in his blood. This set off an alarm. With further laboratory examination, we found an enzyme called creatine phosphokinase. Upon microscopic examination, I found high concentrations of Haloperidol and its metabolites in his blood, urine, and tissues. This can cause seizures and heart rhythm abnormalities that would explain the QT interval prolongation."

"What the hell is Haloperidol?"

"It's prescribed under the name of Haldol for some psychiatric disorders and for hallucinations in acute alcohol withdrawal."

"How would a 19-month-old get ahold of something like that?"

"Not without adult help," Heron said. "It comes in childproof packaging most adults have trouble opening. And it doesn't taste like anything a child would deliberately want to swallow. I suspect it was mixed with something he ate or drank."

"What are you trying to say?"

Heron handed Radhauser a plastic bag with a pair of blue footed pajamas and a thick red rubber band, then paused as if waiting for the drum roll. "There is no doubt. Skyler Sterling was murdered."

For a moment, Radhauser was too stunned to speak. A blatant murder was the last thing he expected. "Do me a favor and try to keep this murder out of the press for a few more days. And keep that drug detail under wraps for now." Radhauser suspected a kid murder would cause a media uproar. They would probably get some crank calls, crazies confessing to Skyler's murder. He needed a piece of evidence held back—something only the killer would know.

CHAPTER EIGHT

It wouldn't be long before the press learned the big news that a child was murdered in Ashland. In his seven years here, Radhauser had never investigated a child murder. On Friday morning, he got a search warrant for Bryce's house and assigned his partner, Detective Robert Vernon, and Officer Maxine McBride the search. Their patrol car was parked in Bryce's driveway when Radhauser arrived to question the neighbors. "No one home," Vernon said. "Shall we break in the door?"

"Give me a minute." Radhauser was almost certain Bryce's neighbor had a key.

Miss Tilly answered the door wearing a flowered house dress and the same bunny slippers she wore the night of Skyler's death. A hot pink headband held back her steel-wool colored gray curls. She had a sponge mop in her right hand, and her face and forehead glistened with perspiration.

He tipped his Stetson. "Good afternoon, Miss Tilly," he said. "Looks like you've worked up a sweat with that mop." He paused and smiled. "I'd like to talk with you for a few moments if you have time."

"Oh Lordy, Detective Radhauser. I got nothin' but time these days. And call me Tilly. Everyone else does." She propped the mop against the exterior wall next to the front door. Her face lost its friendliness when she spotted the patrol car in Bryce's driveway. "Why are the police over there?"

"We have a search warrant," Radhauser said.

"For what?"

"A child is dead, Ms. Tilly. The medical examiner has listed

71

murder as the cause. And it's my job to find out how and why it happened."

Behind her glasses, her brown eyes were round as quarters. "Murder? Why would that medical examiner think such a thing?"

"Skyler didn't die from his injuries. He died from a drug overdose."

"Bryce had nothin' to do with it. That man won't take nothin' stronger than an aspirin."

"Skyler died as a result of something that happened in Bryce's house. The search warrant gives us the authority to break down the front door. But I hate to do that when I'm pretty certain you have a key."

"I won't be a party to no ransackin' of my neighbor's house. I've seen what the police do on television. And nobody ever cleans up the mess they leave behind."

"There'll be a lot more mess if we have to break in."

She bit her lip, reached down into the pocket of her house dress, and handed him the key. There was a jittery undercurrent of anxiety around her today.

Radhauser took the key and jogged next door to deliver it to Vernon. "Pay special attention to the medicine cabinets. Go through the trash and all the kitchen drawers and cabinets, too. Check the crib to see if you can find one of those kid cups with the little spout or a baby bottle inside."

When he returned to Tilly's house, her door was closed. He rang the bell.

No answer.

He rang again. Knocked.

She opened the door a crack. "I don't approve of what you're doin' to Bryce. So I ain't got the time or anythin' to say to you."

"Don't you want to help Mr. Bryce? I already talked to your neighbor, Harold Grundy. He claims you know Bryce better than anyone in the neighborhood."

"That old man don't know nothin' about anything except himself," she said. "He wouldn't go out of his way to help Bryce or anyone else."

"But you would," Radhauser said. "And so would I."

She opened the door a little wider. "If you're so anxious to help him, how come you let those cops go through his stuff like he's some kind of criminal?"

"Maybe I'm trying to find something that will prove Skyler's death wasn't his fault."

She opened the door and stepped aside so he could enter. "Is that medical examiner person smart?"

"As smart as they come." Radhauser pushed a blanket aside and took a seat on her sofa. He set his hat, crown-down, on the coffee table.

She plopped into the rocking chair across from him.

The house was neat and clean, designed much like Bryce's Craftsman, but without the careful restoration of the floors and woodwork. Her walls were filled with framed family photographs. A large picture of a black Jesus, painted on velvet, hung over the mantle.

She pushed her glasses up and held the bridge to her nose for a second, but as soon as she let go they fell forward again. "What can I do for you?"

"I'd like you to tell me about Bryce. What kind of man is he?"

She smiled as if there was nothing in the world she would rather talk about. "Bryce is about the best man I ever knew." She nodded repeatedly, reaffirming every word. "He treats me better than my own sons. And he gave Dana and them two boys a place to stay. He's a good dad. Watches them boys like a hawk."

"How long have you known him?"

"Ever since he moved in next door." She paused and appeared to be counting something in her head. "His house was the neighborhood eyesore when he bought it. He fixed it up real nice. I reckon it's been ten years now."

"Have you ever seen him lose his temper with the boys?"

She cocked her head and gave him a look that could have peeled chrome off his bumper. "Don't you go blamin' Bryce for what happened. He adored that little boy."

"I'm not blaming anyone. I'm just doing my job. A child is

73

dead and I need to get at the truth."

Miss Tilly tensed, and she sat up straighter. "You want the truth? Nobody ever loved that little boy like Bryce does. Especially not Reggie Sterling."

"Did you ever see or hear Bryce lose his temper with either of the boys?"

"I know what you're getting at," she replied. "And you're dead wrong." She told him what he already knew—that Bryce had smacked Scott on the backside after he pushed the baby out the door and had kicked, bitten, and spit on Bryce. "If you ask me, that boy could use some good old-fashioned discipline."

"Did you witness this incident?"

"I heard Skyler screaming after he went flying through the front door. I was sitting on my porch and saw the whole thing. Scott ran off. I figured he was the culprit and knew he done something bad. Bryce chased after him. I reckon that's when he swatted him, but I didn't see it."

"Did you see them come back?"

"I did. Bryce was carrying Scott underneath his arm. The boy was having a hissy fit, kicking and screaming his head off. I swear, Detective Radhauser, it woulda taken a saint not to whack that boy on his backside. His sorry excuse for a mother does it all the time."

"You don't care much for Dana Sterling, do you?"

"I might as well be honest. Truth of the matter is, no I don't. That woman is a taker. And Bryce is too good for the likes of Dana. You should investigate her. I don't think she ever wanted either of those babies."

"I intend to," Radhauser said. "Were you at home the entire day on Monday? The day of Skyler's injury."

"I'm just about always home. Bryce totes me to the supermarket whenever he goes. And if I'm not feelin' up to it, he takes my list and shops for me. And sometimes he even takes me to my doctor's appointments. Does that sound like the kind of man who'd hurt a baby?"

"Did you see anything unusual that day?"

"Matter of fact, I did." There was satisfaction in her voice, as if she was finally asked a question she was happy to answer. "Ever since he's been off work, Bryce takes them boys down to Lithia Park. Every day it ain't raining or too cold. They leave at 10:30 and get home at noon or a little after. You could set your watch by them. After he gets home, he fixes lunch for them and sometimes me, too, then puts Skyler down for a nap."

"Did he take the boys to the park on Monday?"

"Yes," she said. "And while he was gone, Reggie Sterling shows up with Dana and that boy who works at the Lasso—the owner's son. They had some boxes and packing tape with them."

"Did they go inside the house?"

"Dana just opened up the door and let them inside like she owned the place. They were there for at least a half hour and when they came out, they were each carrying a big box."

"Was the door unlocked?"

She nodded. "Bryce doesn't usually lock it during the day. Scotty is allowed to come and go—as long as he stays in either the front or back yard. Them boxes were taped shut when they left, so I don't know what they stole. I told Bryce about it, though."

Radhauser smiled. He was quite certain she had. Talk about neighborhood watch.

"He just shrugged it off. Said he didn't think he had anything valuable enough to steal. It's not the first time she snuck in there with that Reggie Sterling, doin' God knows what."

"Are you saying Dana was having an affair with her ex-husband?"

"They didn't even bother to close the curtains," she said. "Right there in Bryce's bedroom. And you wonder why I can't stand that woman."

"Were there any other visitors that day?"

"Some man I never seen before walked with Bryce and the boys when they came home from the park. I think he was a photographer. He had a camera around his neck. One of them big ones with the long lens." She indicated the length by holding her hands about a foot apart. "He followed Bryce and the boys inside."

He made a mental note to ask Bryce about this. "There's one more thing I need to ask you about, Miss Tilly." A part of him didn't want to bring this up, knew it would open an old wound for her, but the coincidence was too big. And Radhauser wasn't a man who believed in coincidence—not when it came to a murder investigation.

Tilly sighed, like a woman who'd lived a hundred years. "I'm listening."

"I understand you were once arrested and accused of a crime in Philadelphia."

Her gaze shot over to him as if he accused her of stealing the silverware. For a moment, she stared at him in silence. "You mean that followed me all the way to Oregon?"

"I don't always like it, Miss Tilly, but it's my job to investigate everyone with access to Skyler Sterling on Monday."

She looked at him like she might spit in his eye. "I didn't hurt that baby, Detective Radhauser. And neither did Bryce. Back in Philly, everyone blamed me. I even got fired, but I swear to you, it wasn't my fault."

"Why don't you tell me what happened?"

She gave him a skeptical look. "You gonna believe an old colored woman like me."

He smiled in an attempt to be reassuring. "Until you give me a reason not to."

"It was the sixties and Miss Amy hired me to work in her daycare center. But them northern white folks didn't take kindly to no colored woman watching their babies." She focused her liquid brown gaze on him. "They musta figured some of my black gonna to rub off on their kids' lily-white asses when I changed their diapers." There was pain and a deep resentment in her voice.

"Those were hard times," Radhauser said. "I was a young boy in the sixties. But as a man I'm sorry and ashamed of what went on." It was hard for him to imagine what life was like for her then. Now, Miss Tilly seemed like such an impenetrable woman. It was hard to imagine her ever questioning her place in the world.

She gave him a half-hearted smile. "On the day it happened,

the white woman I worked for was out sick and I had ten kids aged four and under to take care of by my lonesome. I slipped a disc in my back and the doctor prescribed those pain pills to get me through the day. I was always lifting up kids, bending over to change their diapers and wipe their butts."

"Did they accuse you of being an addict?"

"That and a whole lot more." For a moment, her statement hung suspended in the air between them. "I had them pills in my purse on the highest bookshelf. Same place I always put it. Same place the white woman put hers, too. One of the babies had a bad case of diarrhea that day and it was all I could do to keep her clean so she wouldn't get no diaper rash. While I changed her, Wally Meyers climbed up that bookcase, grabbed my purse and found them. He was four-years-old and I reckon he thought they was candy. I called an ambulance as soon as I found my purse on the floor and that pill bottle empty."

"I understand there was a lawsuit."

Time froze. Tilly drew in a long breath as if trying to gather herself. "His parents took me to court, claimin' I didn't like their boy. That I was neglectful and poisoned him on purpose. It was plum awful. But the judge dismissed the charges. I couldn't get out of Philadelphia fast enough. It was in the newspapers, and there wasn't nobody gonna hire me there. That's when I moved to Ashland."

"Do you remember the date of the incident?"

She nodded. "How could I ever forget? It was Wednesday, April twenty-second, 1964."

Radhauser made a note of the date and then stood to leave. "Thanks for your honesty, Miss Tilly."

He liked to think he could sense when someone told the truth, but it wasn't always easy. Humans have lied since they learned to speak and they've gotten good at it, especially when the truth threated their life and freedom.

"Am I a suspect now?" she asked, as if reading his mind.

He gave her a sad smile. "In my business, everyone is a suspect until I learn the truth."

Radhauser checked his watch. Gracie had an appointment with an oncological surgeon in Medford at 3 p.m.

He needed to ask Vernon to follow up and verify Tilly's story.

CHAPTER NINE

Radhauser drove Gracie to the Oncology Clinic in Medford, near the Rogue Valley Medical Center. They arranged for her mother to pick up Lizzie from nursery school and keep her through Saturday morning cartoons. After about a fifteen-minute wait, a heavyset nurse, with a smile far too wide for her job, ushered them into a small office, its pale green walls lined with diplomas celebrating medical school, residency and fellowship completions. It seemed Dr. David McCarthy was well-trained in oncology and women's health.

In the past few days, Gracie had gone through all the tests her Ashland obstetrician felt were reasonable for a woman in her fifth month of pregnancy. When the ultrasound showed the cyst to be a solid mass, they did a mammogram. According to the American Cancer Society, it was relatively safe to have a mammogram when pregnant as only a small amount of radiation was focused on the breast. Gracie wasn't happy with the word *relatively* but her doctor convinced her she needed the test. Technicians placed a lead shield on her belly to block any possible radiation scatter reaching the baby. When the mammogram came back suspicious, too, they did a biopsy.

They'd been called into the clinic for the results and a plan of action. Gracie kept telling him he should be at work, reminding him he was in the middle of a child murder investigation, but he couldn't let her go through this by herself. He was more scared than ever, but was trying hard to hide it from his wife and daughter. Gracie and Lizzie were his life and there was no way he could imagine a world without either of them in it.

Gracie sat in one of the burgundy leather chairs facing Dr. McCarthy's massive desk. Radhauser took the other one. The air freshener, plugged into the wall beneath the window, filled the room with a scent meant to calm patients into believing they were camping in a forest of pines. Radhauser shook his head. Like that could happen to anyone sitting on this side of an oncologist's desk.

He held Gracie's hand as they waited and tried to push a lot of feeling through his fingers and palm. Radhauser wished he were the kind of man who could express his love in words more easily. He squeezed a little tighter.

"I don't know why they couldn't phone us with the biopsy results," Gracie said. "Why do they make us come all the way over here?"

He didn't want to think about the most obvious answer—the results were positive. Besides, it wasn't a long drive. Medford was less than a half hour from Ashland.

Her face darkened. "What if it's bad news? What if the biopsy shows I have cancer? What about the baby?"

He was saved from having to reply by a soft tap on the closed door. A few seconds later, it opened. The oncologist was about forty-five and wearing a pale blue oxford shirt and khaki pants beneath his white lab coat. There was a pager on his belt. "Mrs. Radhauser, I'm Doctor McCarthy," he said, shaking her hand. "I'm an oncological surgeon here at Rogue Valley Medical Center. Your obstetrician has referred your case to me." He was telling her things she already knew, his tone somber and not a hint of a smile on his face.

"Please call me Gracie," she said. "And this is my husband, Winston."

He nodded to Radhauser, stepped forward and shook his hand, then took the high-backed leather chair behind the desk and opened a manila folder.

Radhauser reached over and clasped Gracie's hand again.

"I have the biopsy results on the mass in your right breast," the doctor said. "And I'm afraid it's not what we'd hoped for. The mass is malignant, Mrs. Radhauser. Gracie. You have an aggressive form of ductal carcinoma. I'm very sorry."

Radhauser heard the breath rush out of her body. His mind went blank for a second, as if an electrical current shocked him. He looked at Gracie. She looked at him, and in that moment— that terrible moment—they were connected to each other by a thick band of fear. Fear not only for themselves and Lizzie, but for their unborn child. For a moment, neither of them could find the words to speak.

He could tell Gracie fought tears and he knew she didn't want to break down in front of Dr. McCarthy.

"Will you give us a few moments alone?" Radhauser asked.

"Of course. Just open the door when you're ready to continue." Dr. McCarthy stood, turned sharply on his heels like a soldier and marched out of the room without another word, closing the door behind him.

Radhauser kneeled on the floor beside her, rested his arms along the armrest on her chair, then leaned in close.

Tears were streaming down Gracie's cheeks.

Not knowing what else to do, he stood, put his hands under her armpits, lifted her up off her feet and held her as tightly as he possibly could.

Her shoulders heaved as she sobbed.

"It's okay," he said. "Cry it out." There was nothing he could say or do to change the shock and the fear of having received a diagnosis like this one. But he needed to be strong. He needed to be there for her and put his own feelings on hold. He tried to think of what he might say when the crying stopped and the reality sunk in.

After a few moments, when her body stopped heaving, he set her feet back on the floor facing him, and took her shoulders in his hands. "We can beat this, Gracie. You're young and you're strong." He reached down and stroked her belly. "And we have two very good reasons to fight." It was all he could do to stop himself from dissolving into a pool of tears, too. "I'll be with you. Every step. I'll be there beside you."

Radhauser didn't know what he said that eventually reached

her, but she stretched across McCarthy's desk and grabbed a handful of tissues from the box he kept near the edge. She wiped her face, blew her nose, tossed the tissues into the trash can and then looked up at him and smiled. A great big Gracie-can-do-anything smile.

He felt tears welling again and fought them back. It was something that was happening a lot during the last few days. Each time he talked to or thought about Gracie, an avalanche of tears threatened to wash over him.

She gave him a brave shrug. "Tell the doctor I'm ready. Let's see what it is we're facing."

"That's my girl," Radhauser said.

* * *

McCarthy explained that because of the pregnancy, their options were somewhat limited. He recommended a mastectomy with axillary lymph node dissection to determine if the cancer had spread.

"And if it has?" Gracie asked.

"I'd recommend termination of the pregnancy and an immediate course of chemo and radiation. You are premenopausal and breast cancer is far more dangerous to someone your age."

"No," Gracie said. "Absolutely not. I won't abort our baby."

Radhauser put his hand on her forearm.

The muscles in her arm tightened if she were physically holding on to her child.

"Let's not make a hasty decision," he said. "We can have other babies, Gracie. Think about Lizzie. She needs her mother. We both need you. And your health has to be our top priority."

"I won't do it," she said. "Not under any circumstances. It goes against everything I believe about being a mother. It took us more than two years to get pregnant with him. What if I can't get pregnant again? This is our son, Wind. We've heard his heartbeat and I've felt him move inside me. Our son's name is Jonathan Lucas Radhauser. That makes him real. That makes him a person. I can't just kill our son because it might be better for me." The tears were pouring down her cheeks again.

McCarthy slid the tissue box forward on his desk.

Radhauser grabbed several and handed them to Gracie. Fear sat like a heavy weight on his chest. "What about a lumpectomy?" he asked.

"We could do that," McCarthy said. "But because we can't start chemo or radiation therapy until after your wife delivers, a mastectomy is the safer bet to prevent spreading."

Gracie spoke up. "If you take out the tumor, surrounding tissue and some nodes, and the tissue and nodes aren't malignant, wouldn't a lumpectomy be sufficient?" She looked at Radhauser and smiled. She believed this might actually work. It was there—a slice of hope in her eyes.

"I wouldn't recommend it," McCarthy said. "You'd be taking a big risk."

There was the feeling of a beat being skipped when he said that. And neither she nor Radhauser acknowledged it. They just wanted to keep going in the direction Gracie was leading them.

But McCarthy wasn't letting them off the hook. "In all cases with this type of cancer, even if the area surrounding the tumor is clean and the lymph glands are, too, we still do chemotherapy and radiation. This is an aggressive form and there is no guarantee it won't spread during the four months we have to wait for you to deliver the baby."

Gracie sat quite still for a moment, then turned to Radhauser. Her eyes filled again and she pushed the heels of her hands into them like a small child. Then she moved them and her gaze met his with an expression that chilled him. She looked defeated and actually bent over her belly, bowed by the kind of grief that wouldn't allow her to sit up straight.

He moved to touch her, but she drew away.

"I'll give you some time to think about it," Dr. McCarthy said. "I'm due in surgery. But my nurse can set things up for you."

"If I have the mastectomy, will I be all right?"

"There's a good chance," he said. "Especially if your nodes are clean."

Before Gracie and Radhauser left the clinic, they scheduled a mastectomy for the following Monday.

He drove Gracie home.

She was silent the entire trip, staring vacantly out the window.

The helplessness he felt at not being able to do anything for her was difficult to manage. He wanted to tell her that life was hard and sometimes it knocked the wind out of you. But he wasn't sure it was a message she wanted to hear so he remained silent.

As soon as they walked into their house, Gracie collapsed on the sofa, holding her face in her hands.

"What can I do for you?" he asked, resolved to do whatever she asked of him.

"Just go to work," she said. "I'll be all right. I'm going to take a long bath."

He changed into a suit for Skyler's memorial, then stepped back into the living room. "I'll be home as soon as I can." He had to return to the police station. Murphy called him in for a meeting on the Skyler Sterling murder at 6 p.m. in order to accommodate Gracie's appointment.

"No, you won't be back soon," she said. "You know Murphy is going to pull an all-nighter."

He cringed and felt his shoulders involuntarily slump. "No, he won't. He'll expect me to attend the memorial service for Skyler. I'll check it out and leave early."

She gave him a knowing smile, then headed toward the master bedroom.

As he started for the door, he heard the water running in the bathtub. He was halfway up the driveway to the barn where he parked his patrol car when he turned around and ran back.

He sat on the bathroom floor and rested his arms along the edge of the tub. A part of him wanted to strip and get in with her. The hell with his case. The hell with everything except Gracie and what she needed right now. She used bubble bath and the sweet smell that rose all around them, Tahitian Coconut, was palpable. The label on the bottle showed half-naked natives dancing around a roaring fire pit. A culture that didn't believe in western medicine. A society where a doctor would never surgically remove a woman's breast.

"If I die," Gracie said, closing her eyes so she didn't have to look at him when she said it, "I want you to get married again." She opened her eyes and shot him a look that said she meant business. "And not to some bimbo who happens to be pretty. I want you to find a good mother for our kids."

Gracie was capable of a frightening kind of honesty that he generally admired. But he wasn't ready to hear or even think about the possibility of her death.

"You're not going to die," he said. "I won't let you." But even as he uttered those words, he remembered the agony of Laura's death, the overwhelming feelings of emptiness and loneliness.

"I know how hard this is on you, Wind. I can see in your eyes how worried you are. And if we add that to the upcoming clemency hearing and what's going on with your case, you're pushing yourself too hard. I know you think you're strong and can take on anything the world hands you, but I'm worried about you. You don't sleep and you aren't eating regular meals."

"I'm fine. As long as I have you and Lizzie, I'm tough as shoe leather and can spit nails."

She smiled then, another genuine Gracie smile that made her dark eyes sparkle, and he fell in love with her all over again. He leaned further into the tub, took her face in his hands and kissed her long and hard on the lips.

"You better get to that meeting, lover boy," she said. "You don't want Murphy having an aneurysm."

* * *

Heron had alerted Radhauser that a typist in the ME's office told her boyfriend, an over-zealous reporter for the tabloid *The Talent Tattler*, that Skyler Sterling was murdered. The boyfriend wrote and released his story. Heron was livid. He fired the typist, reminding her of the confidentiality agreement she'd signed.

So, Radhauser wasn't surprised to find news vans lined up on the plaza in front of the police station—the kind with a satellite receiver on top and the name of the television station painted on the side. There was one for each of the local affiliates for NBC, CBS, and ABC.

He pulled into his parking space. A knot rose in his stomach as a fist of reporters jockeyed to attack him. He stepped out of the Crown Vic.

Captain Murphy stood outside the front doors, trying to pacify the reporters, their cameramen following close behind them. Murphy looked agitated—even from a distance of ten yards, Radhauser spotted the sweat on the captain's forehead. Three reporters rushed toward Radhauser, sticking their microphones in his face.

"What can you tell us about the murder of Skyler Sterling? Is the story in the *Tattler* true?"

Not intending to tell those vampires anything, he kept walking.

"Is it true he was only nineteen months old?"

"Was there evidence of sexual abuse?"

The questions came at him like a hive of bees buzzing. Radhauser fought his way through the crowd and pushed open the police station door, the last question echoing inside his head.

"Do you have any idea what killed him?"

He was certain Murphy would soon be asking him for an answer to that and another question. *Who killed Skyler Sterling and why?* There was a fair amount of circumstantial evidence against Bryce, but no matter how hard Radhauser tried, he couldn't come up with a motive. Rage. Jealousy. Revenge. None of them fit.

Reggie was another story. And Dana may have wanted to reunite with him so badly that she killed her own child. What if Tilly wasn't telling the truth? What if she deliberately poisoned a four-year-old child in Philadelphia?

Radhauser grabbed Murphy by the arm and dragged him back inside, locking the door behind them. "Bunch of fucking leeches."

Murphy wiped his forehead with his handkerchief. "How the hell did the media find out about this so quickly?"

"I asked Heron to hold off on releasing the autopsy report until after the memorial service and burial." He told Murphy about the typist and her reporter boyfriend. "I hate that it happened, but at least the drug wasn't mentioned in the article. It gives us something to sort out the crazies who will no doubt call in their confessions."

"I've had four already," Murphy said. "One of them claimed the angel Gabriel descended in her living room and commanded her to send Skyler to heaven."

"Maybe we need to hire a temp just to man the phones."

"What we need is a suspect in custody, Radhauser. And we need one fast."

"I'm working on it, Captain. Vernon and McBride searched the scene with a warrant. If there was anything to be found in the Bryce house, I'm sure they found it."

Radhauser listed the possible suspects and filled his captain in on everything they had so far.

"Talk to every psychiatrist in Jackson County, and I don't give a damn about patient confidentiality. Find out who prescribes Haloperidol and to whom. Check out pharmacies, too. See if you can find a connection to the dead kid."

"I'm already on it," Radhauser said. "Vernon is working on the warrants."

Radhauser thought about the things he learned at the academy and through his own experiences as a detective. Never take the crime scene for granted—let it speak to you before you project yourself inside it. Each one had a unique story to tell. Even if that story was hidden in something that seemed trivial at first glance, his job was to find that story, read it, and figure out exactly what it meant. And that rubber band on the toddler's wrist bothered him.

Murphy let out a long sigh. "No matter what we do, the press is going to be all over our asses until we make an arrest."

CHAPTER TEN

Bryce dressed in his new navy sport jacket, a pale blue dress shirt and a pair of gray slacks—his cordovan loafers polished to shine. He deliberately came late to the 8 p.m. viewing and memorial service for Skyler. Tucked inside his jacket pocket was Skyler's favorite rubber shark. He was surprised to see two uniformed police officers stationed at the front entrance to the mortuary.

He read the lips of one of the officers. "Give the family some privacy." The young woman reporter paid no attention and thrust a microphone in Bryce's face. "What can you tell me about the murder of Skyler Sterling?"

Bryce swallowed hard and kept walking. *Murder?* The press must be fishing for a story. Just a bunch of vultures looking to prove themselves through other people's tragedies.

He fingered the rubber shark in his pocket. When he had a private moment, he planned to place it in the casket with Skyler. The days of chasing him around the house and playing that "bite the butt" game were over, and it seemed appropriate the shark go with Skyler to wherever he was headed now. Bryce stood at the back of the room, observing. The entire room smelled like roses and grief.

He was surprised to see Detective Radhauser in the back row, wearing a dark blue, western-cut suit and his spit polished cowboy boots. The hat dangled from the tip of his index finger.

Bryce stepped over to the detective.

Radhauser turned to face him. "I know this isn't a great time for questions, but I need the name of the man who came home from the park with you on Monday and entered the house."

"Tilly doesn't miss a trick, does she?"

Radhauser laughed. "She gives new meaning to 'neighborhood watch.'"

"His name is Montgomery Taylor." Bryce told Radhauser what happened at the park, how Monty wanted to photograph Skyler, but Bryce had refused. How they'd struck up a conversation and ended up walking home together. "Monty was thirsty and asked for a glass of water."

"Would he have had an opportunity to tamper with Skyler's bottle?"

"I pointed him toward the kitchen while I put Skyler down for his nap. We keep Skyler's bottle in the same cabinet as the drinking glasses. Why? Did someone mess with the bottle?"

"I'm not sure," Radhauser said. "But I'm checking out everyone who had access to Skyler on Monday."

"That thing that happened in Philadelphia was the worst time in Miss Tilly's life," Bryce said. "Please don't upset her anymore. She would never hurt either of the boys."

Radhauser put a reassuring hand on Bryce's shoulder. "I'm doing my job. And for tonight your job is to say goodbye to Skyler."

Bryce's eyes pooled. And then his gaze shifted to Dana.

Tears, darkened by mascara, ran down both cheeks and into her mouth. Her face was smudged with so much misery that Bryce turned his own to the mortuary window, then stepped in front of it, gazing out at the garden lit by spotlights. Golden and rust-colored chrysanthemums, some yellow rose bushes in their second bloom, and an assortment of pansies dotted the carefully planted mounds. Strands of tiny white lights wrapped around the trunks of Japanese maples as if they were Christmas trees.

The open casket sat on a platform at the front of the room. It was no bigger than the old trunk of Christmas decorations his mother had once kept in the attic. Skyler, propped on a white satin pillow, was dressed in a navy-blue sailor outfit, crowned with a starched white collar he would have despised. Two embroidered stripes wrapped around each sleeve. His tiny hands were folded across an appliqued anchor on his chest.

As Bryce stared out into the autumn night, the pressure of a hand on his shoulder turned him around to face Tilly and a muscular young boy about sixteen at her side. They both smiled and Bryce was relieved to find two friendly faces in the crowd of Dana and Reggie's coworkers, friends and family members.

"You remember my grandbaby, Lonnie, don't you? I hope you don't mind he's here. He gave me a ride."

Bryce glanced at his bandaged finger, shrugged, then extended his left hand. "How's that batting coming along?" Years ago, Bryce had spent months of evenings and weekends at the batting cages with a younger, more awkward Lonnie, eager for Little League tryouts.

"Great, thanks to you, Mr. Bryce. I played third base, the hot corner, for Central Point High School last spring." A wide grin lifted Lonnie's face. "I had twenty-seven RBIs."

Bryce dropped his arm over the boy's shoulder. "I'm proud of you. And thank you both for coming."

Tilly nodded toward their seats near the back of the room, two rows in front of Radhauser. Lonnie took her hint and left them alone. When Tilly was certain the boy couldn't overhear, she raised her chin, adjusted her glasses and declared, "He grew up real good, didn't he, Bryce?"

"He sure did, Tilly."

"You holdin' up all right, boy?"

Bryce glanced toward the coffin again. "It's still pretty hard to believe, even though I see it with my own eyes."

"I hate the way that redheaded Reggie Sterling stands up there actin' like he give a damn about the child, when you were the one who loved him." She touched Bryce's arm. "I know that, even if nobody else does."

The service was short, delivered by a clergyman who never met Skyler. To him, and everyone who didn't know the toddler the way Bryce did, it looked as if the little boy had bypassed everything. He wouldn't enter first grade or hit a home run into left field, he would never write a love poem or cradle his own child. But he lived for nineteen months. He reached out and touched, and maybe he absorbed more about living than many adults. Maybe he already discovered everything that really mattered. Maybe, at this very moment, Skyler was running toward a shimmering light somewhere just outside the reach of time. Or maybe it was merely Bryce's need to insist Skyler's life, though short, had a purpose.

At the end of the service, Dana and Reggie stood beside the tiny white coffin. As each family member, friend or co-worker filed by, Bryce read her lips as Dana recited the story of Skyler's death. She began with the tarot crossing card she drew that morning, then moved on to the phone call from Bryce, how she left a tray of drinks on the bar, rushed from the Lazy Lasso to the hospital, and stood next to Skyler's bed as he breathed in for the last time.

Not much of what she repeated was true. It must be Dana's way of coping with the tragedy—to claim she saw it beforehand, perceived it coming through the cards. Her interpretation removed all possibility of prevention, as if nothing or no one could have changed the course of Skyler's life and death, laid out in ten cards on a black velvet cloth.

Bryce waited for his opportunity to say goodbye to Skyler. While Reggie and Dana were involved in a conversation with Bear and Henry, Bryce stepped up to the casket. He lifted Skyler's hands, strangely shocked by their heavy lifelessness, and tucked the rubber shark beneath the toddler's palms. He stood there for a few moments, saying a prayer for Skyler. For some reason, this death brought back all the others.

He shuddered, struggling to clear the memory of his father's suicide. And when he did, the other death, the one he willed himself never again to recall, surged inside him. Grief rose as pure as a song, a hymn sung a cappella.

Bear and Henry stepped up to the coffin.

Bryce moved aside to give them space.

Henry stood, looking at Skyler for a long time. "I guess he won't be screaming anymore."

Bear hushed him and they moved away.

Bryce returned. Above all other things, he vowed he would cherish his days with Skyler and always love the little boy who'd come late into his life and through whom he tasted the promise of a childhood.

Reggie grabbed him by the elbow. "What the hell do you think you're doing?"

The air around Bryce held him down. He swallowed against the strength of something that told him not to move. "I'm paying my respects to a little boy I loved as much as my own son," he finally said.

"Was he your son?"

"You know damn well, I didn't even meet Dana until Skyler was a few months old."

Reggie's pale skin reddened. "If you loved him so damn much, why didn't you keep him safe? Why is he lying in a coffin instead of running around being a kid?" Reggie grabbed the shark from beneath Skyler's palms. "And he doesn't need this cheap piece of shit either."

Detective Radhauser yanked Reggie away from the coffin, took the shark and tucked it back under Skyler's hands. "I suggest you let this man mourn. The way I understand it, he took care of Skyler when you didn't want anything to do with him."

"And who the hell are you to tell me how I felt about that boy?"

He opened the leather case that held his badge. "I'm Detective Radhauser from the Ashland Police Department."

"Then make yourself useful, Detective. Arrest this son of a bitch. He killed my son."

CHAPTER ELEVEN

At Union Square, Kendra Palmer stepped from the back of a limousine, delivered to her father's office straight from the San Francisco airport like a Federal Express package. When she phoned from Medford to schedule an appointment with him, she insisted on taking the shuttle bus. Best get used to it, given the career path she chose. But she wasn't surprised when she spotted George, her father's chauffeur, at the airport gate. Good old Dad had a reputation for getting what he wanted. Her father, Kendrick Huntington Palmer III, believed in the stock market, Ivy League educations, Armani suits, and traveling first class.

She let him score on the limo. Kendra had a much bigger victory in mind.

When she entered Harvard Law School, she didn't have a single doubt she would follow the map her father laid out for her future. Pass the California bar exam, do a clerkship with a prominent judge, and honor her father's wish that she join the family law firm like three generations of San Francisco Palmers before her. But, strange as it sounded, while pursuing her father's dream, she discovered her own.

It wouldn't be easy to convince him she was doing the right thing. Kendrick Huntington Palmer III was a brilliant and complicated man. His cross-examinations were legendary—the way his steel-gray eyes fell on a witness and remained there until a tiny interest stirred, like a slow smile, when he discovered the one thing they most wanted to hide.

Kendra reminded herself she had nothing to hide, and in three years of law school she learned how to debate a point. And she knew how to win. The class follies aimed an entire skit at her, the graduating lawyer most likely to free the guilty.

Keep telling yourself that, she thought, brushing a piece of lint from the gray, pinstriped jacket she wore to please her father. She pulled her long blonde hair back and clipped it at the nape of her neck with a plain gold barrette. Her high-heeled shoes were stylish and yet sensible.

Kendra spent weeks planning a defense of her decision, a rebuttal that would make him understand both her appreciation for everything he did for her, and her need to serve in another way. She would keep it simple. *I've passed the Oregon State Bar Examination and accepted a job in the Office of Public Defense in Ashland, Dad. I'll be able to help people who haven't had the advantages you've given me.* She would tell him how she fell in love with Ashland, its Siskiyou Mountains and alpine ski lodge, its quaint shops, and all the diverse restaurants. How it looked as if a little bit of England dropped into southern Oregon.

Once he realized how important it was to her, surely he would be happy. But no matter how her father reacted, she wouldn't let him stop her. She thought of her dead mother then, the way she always encouraged Kendra to follow her dreams, told her how important they were and what happened when a person didn't have them.

Fortified by the memory of her mother's support, Kendra maneuvered the wide sidewalks crowded with shoppers. A column of tourists waited to board the next cable car. Kendra hurried past them.

In front of her father's brick and granite office building, a woodwind quartet in black tuxedos played a Vivaldi Concerto. Something in the plaintive sound of the oboe caught her attention. She paused to listen for a moment, then tossed a crisp five-dollar bill into a top hat with *The San Francisco Wind* embroidered inside the rim.

Kendra smiled to acknowledge the saxophonist's grateful nod, then slipped through the revolving doors and across the black and white marble lobby to the elevator. She pushed the button for the twenty-second floor and checked her watch. Right on time.

The elevator doors opened on her father's floor. Even though she wasn't born the son he dreamed of, her father loved her and took pride in her accomplishments. Her law degree meant everything to him. It might take him a while, but he would realize it meant something different to her. Squaring her shoulders, she stepped off the elevator, then stood in the hallway, her hand on the doorknob.

A polished brass plate announced the family firm, *Kendrick Huntington Palmer III and Associates*. She sighed, aware of how very much she wanted his blessing, then opened the door into a room full of people eating catered hors d'oeuvres and sipping champagne.

Great. An office birthday party.

Balloon bouquets and bright yellow and red crepe paper streamers hung from the ceiling. A huge, hand-painted welcome aboard banner with Kendra's name on it covered the entire back wall.

Before she could react, her father stood, beaming in front of her. He was a tall, middle-aged man, slender with perfect teeth, tanned skin, and a thick head of wavy dark hair streaked with silver. He was dressed, as he always was for work, in a three-piece Armani suit. He drew back a starched, monogramed cuff and checked his watch. "Right on time." He grinned and kissed her on the cheek. "I'm sorry I missed the party after your clerkship. Your Aunt Edna said you were the star."

"I understood," she lied.

He took another glass of champagne from the silver tray the white-coated waiter offered and thrust it into Kendra's hand. Wrapping his arm around her shoulders, he led her to the center of the room. "May I have your attention," he said, looking like he won a ten million-dollar lawsuit. "I propose a toast to our newest associate, Harvard Class of 1998." He paused, lifted his glass and smiled. "Who just happens to be my daughter, Kendrick Huntington Palmer IV."

Her gaze moved from her father to his secretary and back

again. She fought the urge to announce her plans, raise a toast to a future representing the disenfranchised, but couldn't bring herself to embarrass her father.

When the applause ended, she avoided her father's eyes and scanned the room, looking for Aunt Edna. A half circle of smiling faces, many of whom knew Kendra since infancy, cheered and raised their glasses. Finally, she caught her aunt's attention and smiled. She'd talked with Aunt Edna at the clerkship party and she understood and supported Kendra's plans.

Aunt Edna, her father's sister, hurried toward her.

Kendra loved to watch her walk, the way she loped across the room, projecting enthusiasm and good intentions that arrived an instant before she did. Though she just passed her fiftieth birthday, she didn't look much older than the young woman Kendra first met in childhood, her eyes wide as an autumn sky and shining beneath her clumps of cinnamon-colored curls. None of the magic vanished. Edna had stepped up to the plate after Kendra's mother died.

She hugged Kendra, lips pressed against her ear. "Welcome to the Twilight Zone," she whispered.

Despite her frustration, Kendra laughed.

"How was the interview?"

"You're talking to the newest Jackson County Public Defender," she said. "I've found an apartment in Ashland. It's an amazing town in the mountains, and looks like a little English village. They have a world-renowned Shakespeare Festival. Wait until you see it. I start on Monday." Kendra glanced at her father.

"Don't worry," Aunt Edna said. "We'll adjust his dials later."

Her father's colleagues, a long line of attorneys with offices in the building, shook her hand and patted her on the back. They all said versions of the same thing. *You've made your father very proud. This is the happiest day of his life.*

Kendra clasped each hand, smiled and kept silent. And when the time came, she cut the bright yellow ribbon across her new office door and waited for the party to end.

A half hour later, her father ushered Edna, the last of the guests to leave, toward the door. "I'll see you at the house later. Kendra has something important to discuss with me."

Aunt Edna smiled at Kendra. "Flip those dials carefully," she said, then stepped into the hallway. "We don't want to blow any circuits." She winked. "I'm cooking tonight. Your favorites. So don't be late."

Drawing her back inside the new office, her father nodded toward a chair.

Kendra sat, crossed her legs, leaned into the rose and green tapestry wingback facing a wall of windows, and waited. Like a postcard, the Bay Bridge stretched across gray-blue water flecked with sailboats.

"Did you enjoy the party?"

"Look," she said. "I know how much you want…" She stopped, thought about the conviction in the three-sentence speech she'd prepared, then tried again. "I know you mean well, Dad, but I found something I can be really good at. Something that matters to me." She waited for the explosion.

Instead, he pulled a chair in front of her, their knees nearly touching. He picked up her hands and studied them, stroked the smooth surface of her nails with his thumbs. "If you're determined to get these dirty, The Office of Public Defense in Ashland is as good a place as any, I guess."

Stunned, Kendra didn't know what to say, wasn't sure if he was mocking her. "How did you know?"

He set her hands, palms down, on her knees. "I have my ways."

"I know you think I'm rebelling against my upbringing, but it's more than that. Mostly it's me feeling like I can make a difference. Maybe save someone who might otherwise not be saved." She stopped, knowing she sounded like a bad advertisement for the Peace Corps. "It's idealistic. But I feel like I have to do it. Like it's who I am." She swallowed and waited for him to laugh.

He licked his bottom lip, then bit off a shred of chapped skin. "So do it. I know how much it costs to give up a piece of yourself for someone else."

Searching his face, she wondered if her father might have

once had a different dream for his own life—if her grandfather demanded more than her father wanted to give. She looked for something he left unsaid, but found only his usual poise and composure. *Time to move on*, she thought, grateful for that glimpse into her father's heart. "If you knew my plans all along, why the party?" She cocked her head. "Why make it so hard for me?"

He smiled sadly. "Decisions this important shouldn't be easy. The party was my closing argument. If it didn't convince you, I'd rest my case."

CHAPTER TWELVE

The day after the funeral, Dana returned to the house she shared with Bryce. Leaving Scott in the car with Reggie, she packed clothing into a large suitcase, then filled a box with Scott's toys.

Bryce stepped into the boys' bedroom. "Where are you going?"

"I have to be alone now," she said, her gaze planted on Skyler's empty crib. "Reggie will keep Scott. He'll come over for the rest of our things later."

Bryce felt a softness toward her and a deep regret for all the pain of losing Skyler. She was barely more than a child herself. "Who will take care of Scotty while Reggie works?"

"His father and stepmother have agreed to help out."

Bryce touched her shoulder. "You said she doesn't like kids."

She shrugged.

"But I don't understand," Bryce said. "Where will you go?"

"I'll stay with Angela for a little while. After that…I don't know." She shook her head. Her long hair swayed from side to side and Bryce grazed it lightly with his fingertips before she jerked away.

"You're welcome to stay here, you know that, don't you?"

"It's no use," she said. "It was wrong from the start, over before it even began. We both know that. I've been reading it in the cards for months and I should have listened." Her gaze darted nervously around the bedroom and once again landed on Skyler's crib.

There was nothing more terrible than to face that crib scattered with stuffed animals and toys, the blue plaid blanket with the frayed satin binding he loved to press against his face.

Bryce closed his eyes. Skyler was there again, awake and standing up in the crib. He wore his funny crooked smile that sank a dimple into his left cheek—just like the one on his mother's face. It was an all-too-brief instant of perfect grace, a time when Bryce understood there would be no day in any future year when he could look at a small child without the warmth and weight of his love for Skyler closing in around his heart.

He opened his eyes and tried one last time. "You're wrong. It was good at first. And it can be good again. We need each other more than ever now. I'll be going back to work soon. We'll save our money and buy a new house." No matter how upset he'd been with her immature behavior, Bryce never wanted to play a part in smashing her world.

"No," she said. "Scott is better off with Reggie. I know Tilly thinks I'm a sorry excuse for a mother. And she's right."

"You're not to blame for Skyler's death," Bryce said. "If anyone is, it's me. I'm the one you should blame."

"Reggie wants Scott out of your house. He's his father and he has rights." She picked up the suitcase and walked away. Bryce followed with the box of Scott's toys. Halfway to the car, she turned and faced him again. "Please. Try to understand. I got to get my life together, for Scotty's sake."

Bryce loaded the box into the trunk of Reggie's car, then turned and walked back inside. He didn't want to give Reggie the satisfaction of seeing him stand in the driveway and watch as they drove away.

Once inside, he felt like an intruder, a burglar roaming around his own house. He landed, without thinking about it, back in Scott and Skyler's bedroom. He kept expecting Skyler to toddle down the hallway. He closed the closet door. Behind it, in the bedroom's corner, a tiny red sneaker with a knotted lace paralyzed him. He clutched the small canvas shoe in the palm of his hand. For a long moment, he couldn't move. The pain was unmerciful.

Bryce was once so sure love was stronger than any obstacle. But for the third time in his life, it seemed flimsy when measured against what was lost. Whatever future possibilities he might have invented with Dana and the boys had been recalled, and the truth of his empty life stood before him.

* * *

On Monday morning, Radhauser paced the surgical waiting room at Rogue Valley Medical Center while Gracie had her mastectomy. He glanced at his watch. 11 a.m. Gracie had been in surgery for four hours.

Before they wheeled her away, their gazes locked for a moment. And everything in their years together seemed precariously balanced. Their happiness a kind of arrogance, an abundance they took for granted before her diagnosis.

He checked in at the desk. "Has there been any word?"

The volunteer, an older woman with gray hair and a kind face, was dressed in a pink and white smock. "Dr. McCarthy will come out and talk to you once your wife is in recovery. It shouldn't be long now."

Radhauser sat in one of the uncomfortable vinyl chairs lined up against the wall and picked up a newspaper, the comic section. He read, but couldn't find anything funny. With his and Gracie's future so uncertain, everything he read seemed ironic and dead serious. He tossed the newspaper back onto the table and stood again. This time he stared out the window at the way the sun filtered through the changing leaves in the hospital courtyard. One word hovered, like a prayer, inside his mind: *please.*

"Mr. Radhauser."

He turned to find Dr. McCarthy standing inside a small doorway behind the volunteer's desk. The doctor was wearing green scrubs. A surgical mask dangled around his throat like a necklace. "Follow me."

The doctor led Radhauser into a small conference room with a round table and four chairs—not unlike the one where he received the news of Laura and Lucas' deaths. They seated themselves.

"Everything went well. I believe we got all the cancer and the surrounding tissue appears healthy. But we'll have to wait on the lymph node biopsies. The preliminaries look good."

"When will you have them?"

101

"By the end of the week if we're lucky. I'll call you. And we'll talk again then. Node biopsies are the best prognosticators for long-term survival."

Long-term survival. There it was again—that awful fear lurking like a monster in the closet. The last few days, loving someone with cancer, had been a roller coaster of emotions.

"And the baby?"

McCarthy smiled. "We had your wife's obstetrician with us in the OR, just in case. She and the anesthesiologist monitored the fetal heartbeat. Your son was a trooper, Mr. Radhauser. He didn't miss a beat."

The roller coaster climbed and Radhauser could barely contain his pride at his son's first compliment. *Way to go, Jonathan Lucas Radhauser.* To his surprise, it had been Gracie who'd wanted to include Lucas as the baby's middle name. She claimed it was a way for their son to honor the brother he never had a chance to know. He thought about the fight they had over the clemency hearing and how Gracie said she was tired of living with ghosts. He smiled to himself at her inconsistency. One more reason to love Gracie.

"Do you think we made the right decision? Do you think my wife will be okay?"

McCarthy appeared to ponder the questions for a moment. "Because of the aggressive nature of this cancer, I'd feel slightly more comfortable if we could start chemotherapy in a couple weeks, followed by radiation. But we'll do a course of both once the baby is delivered. It's hard to come between a mother and her child. And I think her chances are good, especially if the lymph nodes are clean."

"Will she be able to carry the baby to term?"

"We may decide to induce a few weeks early or take the baby by cesarean if the nodes give us any reason for concern."

"Can the fact that she has had breast cancer hurt the baby?"

"There are no studies showing that breast cancer itself harms the unborn fetus."

Radhauser stood and shook McCarthy's hand. "I don't know how to thank you."

"No thanks necessary. I'm just doing my job."

"May I see her now?"

A nurse led him to the recovery room. Gracie's eyes fluttered open when he rubbed the back of his hand across her cheek. She was lying on a gurney behind a thin, flowered curtain in a pale blue room that smelled of something antiseptic. A monitor above her head displayed her blood pressure and heart rate. A plastic tube carried fluid from a bag hooked over a metal tree into a catheter in her vein.

He pulled the chair close to her bed and watched for the rise and fall of the sheet that covered her body. When he was certain she was breathing normally, he stepped outside the room, phoned Gracie's mother to tell her the good news, then stood in front of a small window at the end of the corridor.

It, like the waiting room window, looked down on the hospital courtyard where the trees were brilliant with crimson, orange, and gold. In this heightened state of awareness, he saw every leaf on every tree. Birches bright as lemon peels. The sun was high in the afternoon sky and it was all so beautiful. He felt the air entering and going out of his lungs. Gracie and their son were okay. It was such a relief and such an amazing feeling to be alive, as if someone had loosened a belt from around his chest—a belt cinched way too tight. He made no effort to hold back his tears—simply allowed himself to weep with relief and gratitude. This last week put his angst over the clemency hearing into perspective. Maybe he'd mail his victim impact statement and not appear in person.

An hour later, Gracie was transferred to her room. When the dinner tray came, she opened her eyes, smiled at him, and told him to eat. "Then get out of here. And go to work. Before Murphy has a heart attack. I'll see you tomorrow." Her eyes closed.

As he ate a few bites of meatloaf and mashed potatoes, he wondered if Vernon had found Monty Taylor and brought him in for questioning. He pushed the case out of his mind for a few minutes and sat by her bed, watching her sleep. The light over her head was a focused beam that fell on her dark hair in a way that formed a halo. For a moment, Gracie looked like an angel. A case where illusion was so much larger than truth.

* * *

When Radhauser discovered Montgomery Taylor, a new resident in Ashland, had been charged with the molestation of his two-year-old nephew in Indianapolis, Radhauser's pulse quickened. Maybe he was finally onto something that could lead to an arrest. Encouraged, he found Taylor's address. Baum Street, very close to Lithia Park and the Bryce house on Pine.

It was dusk when Radhauser arrived. The house, one of the many Victorian beauties that graced Ashland, was newly painted a Wedgewood blue with dark burgundy trim. He rang the bell.

A woman answered. She appeared to be in her late seventies, dressed in a flowered skirt, bright pink blouse, and ballet slippers. Through the screen door, he caught the scent of mothballs and roses.

She smiled. "What brings a handsome cowboy to my front door? Are you looking to rent a room?" She was a little hunched over and held a cane in her right hand. Her gray hair was cut short in the back, much longer at the sides where it brushed against her rouged cheeks.

He introduced himself and showed his badge.

"I'm Mrs. Carmichael, though the mister died more than twenty years ago."

"I understand Monty Taylor lives here."

"Yes. He rents rooms from me on the second floor." She squinted and stared hard at Radhauser. "Has he done something wrong?"

"I don't know yet," Radhauser said. "That's why I need to see him. May I come inside?"

She straightened her back as if bracing herself for something she didn't want to hear. "He's not home. But I'm sure he's done nothing wrong. He's studying to be a photographer. And sometimes he reads out loud to me."

"Do you know where he is?"

"A poetry reading at the Medford library."

"Would you mind showing me his room?"

She took a step back. "I don't think I should do that without his permission. I have some problems with my hip and don't climb the stairs anymore. Who would watch you?"

"I have a warrant," he said.

She pulled in a sharp breath. Shock widened her eyes as she moved aside, so he could enter.

"It entitles me to search his room, even if he isn't home. And I don't need watching."

"What has Monty done?"

Radhauser didn't want to frighten her by stating Monty was a possible suspect in a murder case. "I don't know that he's done anything yet. I'm early into my investigation. And his name came up."

He showed her the warrant.

Her wrinkled face whitened and her rouged cheeks appeared ever brighter. She handed it back to him, her hands trembling.

"Is Mr. Taylor your only tenant?"

"At the moment," she said. "But I'm advertising for one more. The extra money helps a lot with maintenance. And I enjoy the company."

She hobbled beside Radhauser to the staircase, propped her cane against the railing, and stood, wringing her hands. "I don't know. This doesn't feel good to me. What if he's upset? Tenants expect some privacy."

"I won't disturb anything," Radhauser said. "And you don't have to tell him I was here if it makes it easier for you."

"But what if he knows? Sometimes people can tell if a stranger has stepped inside their private space. It's a vibrational thing."

Just what Radhauser needed, a new-age senior citizen concerned with vibrational energy. "What you tell him is your business. But I need to see the room. Now."

Her lips disappeared into a tight seam as she glanced at his briefcase. "What if you take something that belongs to Monty and hide it in your satchel?"

Radhauser sighed, then opened his briefcase and took out his camera. "I'm required to leave an inventory of anything I take.

But tell you what, how about I leave my satchel on the steps?" He set his briefcase on the bottom stair.

"What are you looking for?"

He had the sense she could see inside him and didn't approve of what she found there.

"It's not right," she said. "You should know what you're looking for."

Radhauser was losing patience. "I won't know until I find it."

"His room is upstairs, down the corridor, first door on the right. His darkroom was originally a nursery. But he said it was perfect because it didn't have any windows. He's serious about his photography and quite good. His bathroom is at the end of the hallway. You won't find a mess. Monty's a neat freak. A perfect tenant."

Radhauser took the stairs two at a time, hurried down the corridor and opened the bathroom door first. The room was clean and smelled like Pine-Sol. He found nothing in the medicine chest except over-the-counter antacids, cough syrup, and aspirin. Nothing that resembled Haloperidol.

When he flipped on the light in the bedroom, he discovered another tidy room. The floor was hardwood and spotless. A camera with a very long telephoto lens sat on the desk. Hang a wooden cross over the bed and Radhauser would believe he was in a monastery.

There was a double bed neatly made with a brown-corded bedspread, matching pillow shams, and curtains at the room's only window. It faced west and traces of brilliant orange and red sky showed through the spaces between the trees. A maple chest of drawers, a bookshelf filled with photography books, and a small desk and chair completed the furnishings.

He snapped some pictures. His search of the drawers showed only stacks of neatly folded clothes. The closet was the same. All the hangers were plastic and pointed in the same direction. His shirts were arranged by color. All the blue ones hung together, then yellow, green and white. A clothes horse, Radhauser decided. With a touch of obsessive compulsive disorder. Probably the kind of man who never passed a mirror without stopping to look at himself.

Monty's darkroom revealed the usual tripods and shelves housing bottles of developer and fixer. It had a strong, unpleasant smell—like a combination of vinegar and bleach. Two stainless steel sinks were set into a cabinet in the middle of the small room. From the twine strung above them, photographs hung to dry by tiny clothespins. Six 8x10-inch pictures of a toddler in a baby swing like the ones at Lithia Park. And every available space on the walls of the stark room was filled with framed photographs. Many of them were disembodied parts. A toddler's hand. One eye. Several of a toddler's mouth. A close-up of a child's ear.

Interesting. And more than a little bizarre.

Radhauser removed the pictures of the mouth and eye and compared the features with the ones still drying on the line. There was a dark spot on the toddler's right eye, as if the pupil had somehow bled into the iris. And his top lip was much thinner than the bottom.

Feeling a combination of disgust and excitement, he took pictures of the photographs, then rehung them. He needed to confirm with Bryce.

But to Radhauser's eye, this toddler looked a lot like Skyler Sterling.

CHAPTER THIRTEEN

The following evening, Vernon phoned Radhauser to remind him of the meeting he'd set up with Monty Taylor, after his shift at the Ashland Co-op ended at 7 p.m. "I can be there in ten minutes." Radhauser checked his watch. 6:54. "Wait for me before you ask or tell him anything.

Vernon and Monty were already seated at the small table in the interrogation room when Radhauser arrived. The walls were painted puke green. The room doubled as the police break room and smelled like left over pizza, stale coffee and cigarette smoke.

Radhauser introduced himself. "Is there anything I can get you? A cup of coffee or a soft drink?"

Monty had a slight frame, with fine, handsome features and dark, neatly-styled hair. Sitting with his back erect, he seemed to be coiled with a kind of animal energy. "You could get me some fresh air. It stinks in here." There was disdain in his voice as he brushed his hair back from his forehead.

Radhauser opened the window to the sounds of traffic flowing steadily across the plaza and a street musician playing *Lady of Spain* on the accordion. "You sure you don't want something to drink?"

"No, thank you. How long is this going to take? I have a photography class at 8 p.m." He folded his hands on the table top.

Radhauser pulled out a chair and sat. The fluorescent lights above them hummed and flickered the way they'd been doing for weeks. Someone needed to replace the damn bulbs.

Monty leaned forward. "I don't know why I'm being questioned by the police. I've done nothing wrong."

The same old story. No one ever admitted to doing anything

108

wrong. "Because when something happens to a child in Ashland, we look at the list of pedophiles and people like you with an arrest record involving a kid." He looked Monty in the eyes. "That little matter in Indiana."

Monty shifted his gaze to the window. It was dark now, except for the streetlights and the golden glow from the restaurants across the street on the plaza. "That was five years ago. And the charge was all a big misunderstanding."

Radhauser leaned back in his chair. "Yes. They usually are. You looking for an apology?"

"No," Monty said. "I'm looking for reasons you called me in here."

"The child in question was about the same age as that nephew you were so fond of."

Again, Monty raked his hair back with pale, trembling fingers.

"You're here because you were in Lithia Park on Monday morning and made advances toward the little boy—the one you wanted to push on the swing and photograph."

"Of course you want to blame me. Once even accused of being a criminal, I'll always be one, right?"

"Do you know Skyler Sterling?"

"I wouldn't say I know him. But I do remember seeing him."

Radhauser leaned his elbows on the table. Liar. Monty had taken dozens of photographs of Skyler. "That child you remember is dead."

Monty jerked back as if he'd been slapped, an incredulous look on his face. "That's so sad. He was an adorable little boy. How did he die?"

"He was murdered."

Monty shifted in his seat. He clasped his hands together and squeezed so hard his knuckles whitened. "Murdered? That beautiful little boy?"

Good. The man was nervous. Radhauser caught something in Taylor's eyes. A hint of both sadness and panic. Was he sad because he hadn't meant to kill Skyler? "Don't you read the paper?"

Monty's face tensed. "No. No, I don't. And what's his murder got to do with me? I may have been arrested, but it wasn't for killing a kid. I'm studying to be a child photographer. I hope to open my own studio. I love kids."

"Sure," Vernon said. "You love them all right."

"How was he murdered?"

"Why don't you tell us?"

Sometimes suspects grew confused or tired and gave up their denials. The one thing that never broke the guilty was unbearable guilt over what they did. If you looked into their eyes, all Radhauser ever saw was regret for getting caught.

"Because I have no idea how he was murdered. Don't try to pin this on me."

Radhauser pulled an envelope from the inside pocket of his western blazer and spread out the photographs he'd taken in Taylor's darkroom. Bryce had verified the photos were of Skyler.

"You had no business in my private space."

"A search warrant made it my business."

"I admit I take pictures of kids in the park. It's part of my class work."

"Hundreds of kids go to Lithia Park every day. Why did you only photograph Skyler Sterling?"

Taylor's face softened. His eyes welled. "Because he reminds me of someone I loved."

Vernon shoved his chair back and stood. "Could it be your nephew—the two-year-old you molested?"

"I was accused. But those charges were dropped." Monty coiled tighter into himself, like a frightened animal with his leg in a steel trap. "It was all a big misunderstanding."

"From what I understand," Radhauser said. "Your sister dropped the charges with the stipulation you leave Indianapolis and never come back."

"She overreacted. I was babysitting for my nephew. We were taking a bubble bath. Nothing happened. My sister, Angela, is an overprotective single mother. Scared of her own shadow. And what if he does resemble Kayden? That doesn't mean I killed him."

Vernon's face twisted in disgust. "That resemblance got you aroused, didn't it?"

Taylor turned his gaze to the window again—to strollers on the plaza enjoying the autumn evening and the accordion music, now a jazzy rendition of *Fly Me to the Moon*. "You want me to confess. To tell you I hurt that kid. But I didn't. I was at school."

Radhauser glanced at Vernon, then back at Taylor. "When you went inside Bryce's house, asked for a drink of water and reached for a glass, you saw Skyler's bottle and decided to drug him. I suspect you meant to tranquilize him, but used a little too much. Maybe you planned to come back to the house and kidnap Skyler once the drug took effect. Did you go into his bedroom? Unlock a window?"

"That's the most ridiculous thing I've ever heard. I did nothing of the sort. I went to my class at 8 p.m. on Monday. Ask my teacher at Rogue Community College. Riverside campus. I came straight home. Ask Mrs. Carmichael. She's like a mother hen and always waits up for me." Monty checked his watch. "I have fifteen minutes to get to class. Please may I go now?"

Even if his alibi checked out, that didn't mean he hadn't put the drug in Skyler's bottle.

"Go ahead," Radhauser said.

Vernon shot Radhauser a look, then turned back to Monty. "Stay close to home."

Monty stood and hurried from the room. Once he was outside the interrogation room door, he turned back. "If you want to question me again, I'm bringing a lawyer with me."

Radhauser hadn't eliminated Monty as a suspect. But why would he drug Skyler, if the plan wasn't to kidnap him after he fell asleep? It would be easy to do. Bryce was deaf and Monty knew it. He could have entered the house without detection. Scott probably wouldn't have awakened. Radhauser's daughter, Lizzie, could sleep through a hurricane. What if Monty returned to the Bryce home after Mrs. Carmichael had gone to bed, and saw the lights on? Or the ambulance in the driveway? He would have raced back to his room at the boarding house.

"As well you should." Radhauser heard the hint of disappointment in his own voice.

Once Monty had gone, Vernon grabbed his jacket from the hook behind the door. "I'll check with the college and his landlady."

"Good," Radhauser said. "And assign McBride to keep an eye on him. Have her stakeout the park playground. Now that's Skyler isn't around, this pervert might start stalking another kid."

CHAPTER FOURTEEN

When Radhauser phoned the Lazy Lasso to find Dana, he was surprised to learn she had returned to work so soon after her son's death. But who was he to judge? The quiet in the house had been more than he could bear and he'd returned to the Pima County Sheriff's office only a week after Laura and Lucas were buried.

As he walked into the restaurant late Monday night, Radhauser was reminded of the Silver Spur in Catalina, just outside Tucson, where he first met Gracie. He thought about the rich, sugary smell of the pineapple upside down cake the Spur served and how he once used it as a daily excuse to see Gracie. His mouth watered.

The decors of the two restaurants were similar—barn wood siding and planked wood floors. Even the waitress uniforms—western skirts and cowboy boots had the same, slightly provocative, air about them. Without the peanuts on the floor, however, the Lasso seemed a bit more upscale. Instead of the bridles and lariats that covered the walls of the Spur, framed photographs of famous country and western singers covered every wall at the Lasso. He tipped his Stetson to Johnny Cash as he stepped through the swinging doors from the lobby into the bar and restaurant.

A chestnut-brown-haired girl with a freckled nose and inquisitive dark eyes greeted him at the hostess podium, the same way Gracie had once greeted him at the Spur. "Welcome to the Lasso. I'm Angela. Dinner for one?" Her long hair was tied up in a ponytail. She looked no more than eighteen.

He touched the rim of his hat, introduced himself and showed his badge. "I'm looking for Dana Sterling. I understand she works here."

Her face lit up. "Dana is my best friend. She's on break right now." Angela nodded toward a booth beside the window where Dana sat smoking a cigarette and nursing a soda.

He slid into the seat across from her. The whole place smelled like red meat grilling over open flames. His stomach growled. Gracie's hospital meatloaf had left something to be desired. But as much as he wanted to take a break for a real dinner, the case wouldn't let him.

"Detective Radhauser." She put out the cigarette. "What are you doing here?"

"I'm investigating the death of your son. I need to ask you a few questions. Is there some place more private we can talk?"

The color left her face. "You can't think I had anything to do with Skyler's death."

He stared at her for a moment, wondering why she jumped to that immediate conclusion, then asked again about a more private place.

"We have a room for birthday parties in the back," she said. "It's empty."

She led him into a small room with a long table that seated fourteen. The walls were painted with balloons, wrapped gifts, and birthday cakes with blazing candles.

Radhauser closed the door and they took seats directly across from each other. "The autopsy report came back," he said. "The ME determined that Skyler died from a drug overdose—not the injuries he sustained from either fall."

"A drug overdose? How could Skyler have gotten hold of any drugs? Bryce is always so careful with the boys. I can't believe…"

"Tilly claims Bryce doesn't take any drugs stronger than over the counter painkillers for his headaches."

"That's the truth. Bryce is a pure-living person. He doesn't drink or smoke. Did Skyler get into the Tylenol with codeine I take for menstrual cramps? I put it on the top shelf in the medicine cabinet. Neither of the boys could reach it without a ladder."

"The drug wasn't anything we found in your medicine cabinet."

"Then how did Skyler get hold of it?"

Angela knocked, then opened the door. "May I come in?" Without waiting for an answer, she stepped up to the table. "Are you okay?" she asked her friend.

Dana nodded.

Angela turned to Radhauser. "May I get you something to drink or eat?"

"Coffee would be great," he said. "Black."

Dana waited until Angela left, then repeated her question. "Where could Skyler have gotten hold of a drug that could kill him?"

"He couldn't have," Radhauser said. "Without adult help."

"What are you saying?"

"Someone murdered your son."

Her eyes widened. She closed them, as if trying to shut out the image his words must have conjured.

Radhauser wasn't sure she was breathing. A fat silence ballooned into the air—a unique stillness with a ticking heartbeat.

Radhauser let himself settle into it. His intuition was strong from listening to suspects lie to him over and over. Gracie jokingly referred to it as his "lying piece of crap detector". It wasn't something he was born with. Radhauser learned to trust his capability to sift through lies and bullshit and get to the heart of a matter very quickly. Dana was a little too calm for a woman whose toddler had been murdered.

She opened her eyes. "Reggie was sad and angry at the memorial," she finally said. "He has his own guilt about not loving Skyler. I mean not loving him as much as he loves Scott. But he didn't mean it when he accused Bryce of killing Skyler."

Angela delivered Radhauser's coffee, then turned to Dana. "You don't look so good. Are you sure you're okay?"

"How could I be okay?" Her voice was edged in sarcasm. "This detective just told me someone murdered my baby. How can anything ever be okay again?" There were tears in her eyes now—the first ones Radhauser had seen since they started this conversation.

Angela looked at him as if checking to see if Dana was telling the truth. "Who would murder an innocent baby?"

"Thanks for the coffee," he replied. "I don't mean to be rude, but I need you to give us some privacy."

Angela saluted. "Yes, sir." She turned and hurried out, closing the door behind her. When she was out of earshot, he continued his interrogation, his gaze focused on Dana's face. "Your friend asked a very good question. Who would murder an innocent baby? And why?"

"I don't know," she said, a hint of irritation in her voice. "Don't you think I'd tell you if I knew?"

"Not if you were trying to protect yourself or someone you loved."

She sucked in her upper lip, and her gaze flicked toward the ceiling before settling on him. "Wait a minute. I was at work when Skyler died."

"I know. But the thing about an overdose is it can be prepared anytime. The medical examiner thinks the drug was administered in something Skyler ate or drank."

"Bryce fed the boys lunch and dinner that day. Breakfast, too," she responded, a little too quickly in Radhauser's opinion. "He made their favorite pancakes. But he wouldn't hurt either of them, especially not Skyler."

"Why do you say that?"

"Bryce always identified with Skyler. But even more so after I told him about Reggie doubting the baby was his kid. Bryce never talks about it, but I think he may have grown up with a man who didn't love him and maybe wasn't his biological father." She paused and thought for a moment. "At least I never lied about it," she said, as if that were something noble, something she could be proud of.

"Finish your story." Radhauser was interested in knowing something of Bryce's past.

"Bryce said he was deaf because his so-called father beat the crap out of him with a baseball bat. And he wouldn't pay for antibiotics when Bryce got ear infections. Don't you see? Bryce would never hurt Skyler. Never."

"I believe you," Radhauser said. "But everyone who had contact with Skyler is a suspect until we determine otherwise. What about your ex-husband, Reggie Sterling?" He already knew Reggie thought Skyler was fathered by another man, but Radhauser wanted to hear Dana's response.

Her face reddened. "He...he thinks Skyler screams too much. He said he couldn't live with a kid that screamed the way Skyler does." She stopped and a look of horror spread over her face. "I mean the way he did."

"You just told me Reggie doesn't believe Skyler is his biological son."

"He doesn't. But he never...I mean Reggie would never..."

"Is he Skyler's father?" Radhauser asked.

She looked wildly around the room as if trying to find something to focus on beside the question he just asked. When she finally answered, her voice was soft. "I don't know," she said, her cheeks flushed. "There was someone else."

Radhauser made a mental note to take a DNA sample from Reggie and call Heron. He kept the DNA of all his murder victims on file.

"Is this someone else aware he may be Skyler's father?"

"No way," she said.

"I'll need his name."

She gave him an uneasy look, then rubbed her hand over her face, pressing so hard the flesh whitened around her fingers. "He's married."

"I don't care if he's the Prince of Wales. I need his name."

"We were drunk," she finally said. "It was a one-night stand."

The air hummed with waiting.

"We don't have to involve his wife. I just need to eliminate him as a suspect."

"I don't know his last name," she said, her cheeks reddening. "His first name was Paul. He was a customer. We...we got drunk together one night and did it in his car. I guess he was ashamed because he never came back into the restaurant again. So, he can't be a suspect. He doesn't know Skyler exists." She paused and her

117

eyes pooled with tears. "I mean existed."

Radhauser gave her a moment to compose herself. "You didn't work at the Lasso then, did you?"

"No, I waitressed for the Bistro in Talent. It was in that outlet mall, just off I-5. Bistro went out of business about two years ago."

"So, why is Reggie so sure Skyler isn't his son?"

"You saw Skyler. He's dark-skinned with black hair and eyes. Scott looks exactly like Reggie. I think he thought Skyler would, too."

"Is that the only reason?"

"He was suspicious because I'd come home so late that night and he said he could smell sex on me. Reggie was drinking heavily back then and real jealous."

"Jealous enough to kill a child he believed was a product of his wife's infidelity? A child he didn't want?"

"No, he's not like that. Reggie would never hurt anyone. He hasn't had it so easy. His mother died when he was a boy. And his father expects him to be perfect. He isn't. But Reggie's a good person."

"From what I understand, this good person kicked you and your two boys out of the house after Skyler was born. You were living in a car when Bryce met you. That sounds like a world of hurt to me."

"Bryce shouldn't have told you that."

"Is it the truth, or not?"

"It's the truth. But like I said, Reggie was drinking heavily back then. Ever since he got sober, we've been trying to work things out. Last night, he said he thinks we should start over."

Why not, Radhauser thought—*now that the screamer he couldn't live with, the reason for the divorce, was dead?*

"How about you, Ms. Sterling? Did you want to get back together with your ex-husband bad enough to get rid of the toddler who stood in your way?" Radhauser argued with conviction, his voice slightly raised and his words sharpened to cut deep.

But in truth, he was nowhere close to giving Murphy the suspect he wanted. Radhauser was fishing. He needed a motive.

And the only two people who had a clear one so far seemed to be Dana and Reggie Sterling.

Her look could have melted the skin on Radhauser's face. "No, damn you. What kind of mother do you think I am? I loved Skyler and it didn't matter to me who his father was. I carried him inside me for nine months. He was my baby. And Reggie is coming around. He asked me to move in with him."

For a moment, Radhauser didn't speak. He thought about Gracie and how adamant she was about keeping their baby, even if it endangered her life. Softening his tone, he asked, "Some reason why you and Reggie didn't start over before now? You've been seeing him for a while, haven't you?"

Again, her gaze fixed on him. She took a cigarette from her purse and lit it. In the flare of light, her face was so smooth she looked even younger than her twenty years. She stared at Radhauser through the flame.

"I'll phrase it another way," he said, lowering his voice a bit. "Don't you think it's a bit suspicious Reggie asks you to move back into his house after Skyler is dead?"

"It's not like that. We've been talking about it for weeks. Ask Reggie if you don't believe me."

"I intend to." Radhauser sat back and sipped his coffee. It had gone cold. "Did you return to Bryce's house after you left with your friend, Angela, the morning before Skyler died?"

"No," she said. "I was with Angela and Reggie all day and then at work. We were looking for an apartment for me."

"Are you sure?" It didn't escape him that she just lied, told him she and Reggie had been discussing a reconciliation for weeks before Skyler's death. If that were the case, why would she go searching for an apartment?

"Yes. I'm sure."

"That's funny," Radhauser said. "I have a witness that puts you, Reggie, and Henry Evans at Bryce's house at about 11 a.m. on Tuesday."

"That nosey bitch. Always watching every move I make. She hates me for some reason."

"Were you there or not?"

"They helped me pack up some of my things. I knew Bryce would be upset when I moved out and I thought it would be easier on him if I did as much as possible when I knew he wouldn't be home. He's pretty predictable." She paused and let out a small laugh. "That's another word for boring. Bryce takes the kids to the park around 10:30 every morning."

What she said made perfect sense about packing when Bryce wasn't around.

"If you didn't do anything you're ashamed of, why lie about it?"

She hung her head. When she looked up again, her face was streaked with tears. "I didn't want you to think I'd hurt my own baby."

CHAPTER FIFTEEN

On Tuesday morning, Sterling Ford customers were clustered around the service area. The dealership, located just off the Interstate 5 at the outskirts of Ashland, was garnished with red balloons and strips of multicolored streamers as if they were hosting a child's birthday party.

Radhauser parked, then took a minute to call the hospital to check on Gracie—asleep and doing well according to the nurse. Next, he placed a quick call to Lizzie's grandmother. He sighed. Both his girls were fine.

Sterling Ford's showroom floor was so shiny Radhauser could see his reflection. He straightened his cowboy hat and browsed the new cars on display for a moment.

A cherry red Explorer. A bronze Crown Victoria four years newer than his police-issued one. A bright blue Mustang. He studied the lines of the car, wished Ford had kept the original crisp lines of the 60's Mustangs. It was his favorite car in high school and he at one time hoped to restore a classic one with Lucas.

Now, it appeared life was giving him another chance and perhaps he and Jonathan would someday make that dream come true.

Radhauser read the sticker on the Mustang's window. A starting price of a mere $16,470. The little bungalow he and Laura bought in Tucson, just before Lucas was born, had cost only a thousand dollars more. He sucked in a breath. The whole showroom was filled with that wonderful new car smell—leather, clean rubber and Simoniz car wax.

"In the market for a new car, Detective?" Reggie looked like a New York bank executive, dressed in a charcoal gray three-piece suit and a starched yellow dress shirt with a gray and yellow striped tie. His red hair was neatly parted on the side and looked as if it had been blown dry by a stylist. He wore a pair of loafers that competed with the floor for best shine. Reggie was what Radhauser's father would have called a prissy pants.

"No," Radhauser said. "I'm looking for you. I have a few questions I need to ask about Skyler's death."

"Why do you have questions for me? I wasn't anywhere near that house when Bryce killed my son."

His son? Now that Skyler was dead, it seemed Reggie took every opportunity to claim him.

Lie number one.

"Is there somewhere more private we can talk?"

Reggie led Radhauser into his office. With its thick red carpeting and mahogany desk and credenza, it was as posh as a New York law firm. Reggie sat, like a big shot, behind his desk in a leather chair as high as the one in Judge Shapiro's courtroom.

Radhauser took one of the white leather chairs in front of the desk. An amazing collection of antique pewter Ford cars, from the Model T to the classic Mustang, lined the bookshelves above the credenza. He took off his hat and set it on the table between the two chairs, then shifted his attention to Reggie.

He fidgeted with his hands. The tips of his fingers and nails were stained yellow. Nicotine. Reggie was a smoker, and a heavy one from the looks of his hands. There was a no smoking sign on his desk.

"I'm dying for a cigarette," Radhauser said.

"Me, too. My old man won't let anyone smoke inside. Do you want to go outside to the smoking area?"

"No," Radhauser said. "I actually quit more than ten years ago. I just have a few questions. It won't take long."

Reggie Sterling had an open face with a light scattering of freckles the same red color as his hair. There was no way he could doubt that Scott was his son. He looked just like his father. Reggie's smile was eager and slightly forced, like an amateur actor performing the theater role of someone open-hearted and innocent who only wanted to be helpful.

"Would you care for a cup of coffee?" He nodded toward an expensive-looking coffee maker on top of a mahogany file cabinet.

"No, thank you," Radhauser said. "I just had one with Dana."

Reggie squirmed in his leather desk chair, but said nothing.

"Did you kill Skyler?"

"Are you kidding me? What the fuck are you talking about? That asshole Bryce killed my son. At the very least he wasn't paying attention. Kids are unpredictable. They can get in a lot of trouble if you ignore them. Scotty was just being a little boy. He didn't mean to push Skyler down those stairs. And Bryce should have fixed the latch on that storm door. Everybody knows you have to be careful with a toddler."

"The medical examiner has a different theory. He says Skyler was poisoned with a drug overdose. I believe you visited Bryce's house on two separate occasions last Monday, the day before Skyler died. Once around 11 a.m. and again around 7:30 p.m. Am I wrong?"

Reggie's eyes widened and his pale skin turned red. "What is the medical examiner's theory?"

An angry wave washed over Radhauser. He lifted a pen from the holder on Reggie's desk, looked at it absently for a moment, then set it back down. "The medical examiner's report concluded Skyler was murdered."

"Negligent homicide," Reggie said, as if he was an attorney pleading the case. "I told you, Bryce murdered my son."

"I'm not so sure," Radhauser replied.

"Why the fuck not?"

"Because Caleb Bryce loved Skyler. Everyone I've talked to has told me that. I was wondering... How did you feel about him?"

"Am I a suspect? Is that why you're here?"

"As I told your ex-wife and current girlfriend, Dana, everyone is a suspect until I can determine otherwise."

Something flashed, mean and cold, in his pale blue eyes. "So what if I was in the house? I often stop by the Bryce house to see my son." He paused, then corrected himself. "My sons. Why would I kill my own boy?"

Lie number two.

Radhauser could tell his questions were irritating Reggie, so he kept asking them. "Since when did you start claiming Skyler as your son? It's my understanding you kicked Dana and both boys out of your house because you were certain Skyler was fathered by someone else."

Reggie's skin grew even redder.

When he said nothing, Radhauser continued. "I'd like to get a DNA sample from you today to establish Skyler's parentage. Is that okay with you? You might as well say yes. Because if you don't, I'll return with a warrant."

There was a moment of hesitation. "No warrant necessary. I got nothing to hide. Besides, it'll be good to finally prove I'm right." Reggie Sterling's story flipped back and forth like a seesaw.

Radhauser wanted to punch him in the face. Instead, he took the swab from his jacket pocket, removed it from its plastic container, swabbed Reggie's mouth with a little more force than was needed, and returned it to the container. He planned to drop it off at the ME's office on his way home.

"Is the fact that you believed Dana conceived him with someone else the only reason you hated Skyler?"

"I didn't hate him. He was a baby. Nobody hates a baby."

Lie number three.

"Several people, including your acknowledged son, Scott, have stated that you did."

Reggie's disdain for Radhauser was palpable. He could feel it growing like bread dough.

"Skyler screamed all the time. Redheads have sensitive ears and I couldn't stand that high-pitched sound he made when he wanted something. He wouldn't use words. Even as a toddler, Scott never did that." His voice faltered for just a moment, a pause or an intake of breath that didn't seem quite natural. "Of course, it didn't bother that deaf retard, but it drove me crazy."

Radhauser wished he had enough evidence to lock up this

arrogant asshole today. He would like nothing more than to slap some cuffs on his wrists and haul him to jail. "Crazy enough to want to silence him?"

"What are you trying to say here? Do I need a lawyer?"

"You're certainly entitled to one," Radhauser said. "But this is just routine questioning. I'm asking the same things of everyone who saw Skyler on Monday."

Reggie's gaze shifted to the glass wall of his office. "It feels personal."

Several potential customers browsed the showroom, opening car doors and sitting behind the wheels, imagining what it would be like to own the car.

"Can we finish this up?" Reggie asked. "My dad is attending a Ford convention and I need to get back to work. He'll kill me if he finds out I missed a sale."

"Do you and Dana plan to reconcile?"

"I hope so. My mother died when I was ten. It was hard without her. I want Scotty to grow up with both his parents."

"How noble," Radhauser said.

Again, Reggie's eyes flashed. "Look, I know you don't like me much, but that doesn't mean I'd kill a baby, even one I wasn't fond of."

"You have to admit, it's pretty coincidental that that baby you didn't believe was your son, that baby whose screams made you crazy, is out of the way just in time for your reconciliation with his mother."

Reggie stood, nearly knocking his chair over in the process. "This interview is over. If you want to talk to me again, I'll have my lawyer present."

"Thank you for your time, Mr. Sterling. I'll be in touch." Radhauser stood, put his cowboy hat back on, and turned to leave. He felt the heat of Reggie's stare on his back. Halfway through the office door, Radhauser turned around. It was a hunch, based on something Dana had said. And the *Alcoholics Anonymous Big Book* on Reggie's credenza. "One more thing. Have you ever been treated for alcohol addiction?"

Reggie opened his mouth to speak, then closed it. His clenched his eyes shut and seemed to be biting back against something he preferred not to talk about.

Radhauser waited.

"Why is that any of your business?"

"In a murder investigation, I make everything my business."

"I might as well tell you." Reggie opened his eyes. "Because I know you'll find out anyway. My dad did an intervention a few months ago. I was drinking pretty heavy. I hated him at first. But the old man probably saved my life. I went through the Sunrise Drug and Alcohol Treatment Center last summer. I got myself in pretty bad shape after Dana and Scotty left."

Radhauser noted he made no mention of Skyler.

"The withdrawal was hell. They practically had to put me in a coma. But I'm okay now. I go to meetings. I stopped all the hard stuff. And I only drink a beer every once in a while. Only one. And only with Dana."

Lie number four.

It would be a rare alcoholic who could stop at one beer. And Bryce already told him about the beer Reggie took from his refrigerator while Dana worked at the Lasso.

Radhauser tried to keep the sarcasm out of his voice as he thanked Reggie for his honesty, then turned and smiled to himself.

Nothing made him happier than when one of his hunches turned out to be true.

He left the showroom, then phoned Vernon to get a warrant for Reggie's treatment records.

"Consider it done," Vernon said.

Tomorrow, Wednesday morning, after he picked up Lizzie and her grandmother, they would bring Gracie home from the hospital. Once they settled in, he planned to pay a visit to the Sunrise Treatment Center.

* * *

As the receptionist instructed, Radhauser grabbed a cup of pretty-good coffee in the lobby area and took a seat in one of the modern, burgundy leather chairs in the Sterling Library. It appeared to be a newly-completed addition to the Sunrise Treatment Center and first class all the way. You entered the library through double French doors. The walls were richly paneled in cherry with bookcases on three of them to match. The room smelled like fresh paint, new carpet, and leather.

Gracie had cried happy tears when she saw Lizzie—as if they'd been separated for a month instead of just three days. The early morning rain had washed the fields on their ranch and they glittered with moisture. Puffy white clouds moved across the bright blue sky. A perfect Oregon day. Radhauser had wished he could stay home with them.

But Murphy was antsy.

And Radhauser, obsessed with learning who killed Skyler Sterling and why, needed to speed up his investigation, go where the evidence took him.

The French doors of the library opened and the medical director of Sunrise Treatment Center, Dr. Barry Collingswood, joined him. He was a handsome, tall, well-built man with tanned skin. The director gave Radhauser an easy, dimpled smile, with a perceptible gap between his front teeth.

Radhauser stood and the two men introduced themselves.

Collingswood's hair fell over his left eyebrow as he reached out to shake Radhauser's hand. He tossed his head back to keep the shock of hair out of his eyes. He wore brown trousers and a pale green shirt, covered by a lab coat with his name embroidered in navy under the pocket. His black-rimmed glasses made him look a little like Clark Kent. After they shook hands, he took the chair across from Radhauser.

Director Collingswood looked around and nodded, a man well-pleased by what he saw. "Isn't this a lovely space? It's been open about six months now."

"Was it a gift from Reginald Sterling, Sr. at Sterling Ford?"

He stared at Radhauser for a moment. "As you can imagine, Detective, our benefactors like to remain anonymous," he said in a way that told Radhauser he hit the nail on the head.

"The receptionist called it The Sterling Library," Radhauser said. "Nothing very anonymous about that."

"Whatever the source," Collingswood said, "it's a wonderful place for our patients to read and contemplate." He nodded towards a line of small desks that faced windows looking out on the manicured gardens. "Perfect for completing 4th step personal inventories and getting to work on the 5th step as well." He raised his right arm and swept it across the air, pointing to a wall of windows. "What better place to find health, forgiveness and peace."

Radhauser tried to imagine Reggie in the library. Maybe he sat at one of the desks his father paid for and completed his personal inventory—didn't like what he found. Maybe his time here caused him to reevaluate his life and what mattered. Perhaps it was what accounted for his desire to try again with Dana.

As if giving a tour to the family of a prospective resident, Collingswood continued. "We have a large selection of inspirational books. Some of the best fiction ever written. And, of course, all the Hazleton publications on alcoholism and its most effective treatments."

Radhauser said nothing.

"But you're not here to talk about our library, are you? How may I help you, Detective Radhauser?"

"I'd like to talk with you about one of your patients. Reggie Sterling."

"As I'm sure you're more than aware, our patient records are confidential."

"And as I'm sure you're more than aware, Dr. Collingswood, even patient confidentiality can be waived when it's part of a criminal investigation, especially murder." Radhauser handed him the warrant.

Collingswood looked it over, pushing his hair out of his eyes with his right hand. "Excuse me for a moment," he said, then stood and walked out of the room. He came back a moment later with Reggie's file in his hand. "What exactly do you want to know about Mr. Sterling's stay with us?"

Radhauser asked the preliminary questions. Date he was

admitted and released. Did he enter of his own accord or was it a family intervention? Was he a compliant patient? Did he complete the program?

According to Collingswood, Reggie entered the center in July after an intervention arranged by his father and other members of the Sterling family. This confirmed what Reggie had said.

"He arrived with a blood alcohol five times the legal limit and enough to kill someone with a system not adapted to daily consumption of large amounts."

"Did he complete the program?"

"Yes. Reggie spent three weeks longer than the average patient. He was released a little over two months after he entered. According to the center's records, Reggie attended the recommended thirty meetings in thirty days. As far as I'm concerned, Reggie was a compliant patient who contributed to the group sessions and seemed to be committed to his recovery. But the recidivism rate for alcoholics is very high." Dr. Collingswood shrugged. "I can't predict whether or not Reggie will remain sober."

From what Heron told Radhauser, Haloperidol was often prescribed for hallucinations during acute alcohol withdrawal. "Did he suffer hallucinations during withdrawal?"

"Reggie's withdrawal was difficult—one of the worst the center had ever seen."

"Did you or your staff administer any drugs to help him through the withdrawal phase?"

Collingswood opened the file. "I'm sure we did. We don't like our patients to suffer any more than necessary. Alcohol withdrawal is not a pretty sight." He spent a moment reviewing the patient notes. "Reggie hallucinated. He believed spiders and snakes crawled all over his skin. He screamed, tried to scratch them off and actually caused his skin to bleed."

"So, what did you give him to help with the withdrawal?"

"Benzodiazepines are the medications of choice for treating alcohol withdrawal because of their rapid onset sedating qualities. But they have a high risk of liver failure. Antipsychotics may lower the seizure threshold and, consequently, increase the risk of seizures associated with alcohol withdrawal. Even after using benzodiazepines, Mr. Sterling exhibited psychosis and acute agitation, which is not uncommon with acute withdrawal. We administered Haloperidol or more commonly, Haldol. It has the benefit of a rapid tranquilization."

Perfect. Just what Radhauser wanted to hear. "Did he go home with a prescription for Haldol?"

"No," Collingswood said. "We wean our patients off once they complete the acute phase of withdrawal. Usually after a week or two at the most."

"Do your nurses use a hallway cart to distribute nighttime medications?"

"Yes," Collingswood said. "But at all other times, medications are locked in a cabinet at the nursing station."

"Is it possible Reggie stole Haldol from the hallway cart when the night nurse delivered drugs?"

"Anything is possible. Alcoholics are devious. Denial and lying are part of the disease. But we're pretty careful with our drug documentation and nothing was reported missing."

It wasn't what Radhauser hoped for.

But at least it was a connection.

CHAPTER SIXTEEN

It was long after hours when Radhauser arrived back at the police station Wednesday night. He was exhausted and anxious to go home to be with Gracie, but instead he Xeroxed copies of the notes he took at Sunrise Drug and Alcohol Treatment Center and placed them on top of the folders Vernon had distributed around the table. They contained the information already gathered on the case.

Radhauser grabbed another cup of bad coffee, sat at the small conference table and dropped his head into his hands.

While he waited for the others, he considered Reggie as a suspect. He had opportunity—admitting to being at the Bryce home around 11 a.m. and again between 7:30 and 8 p.m. on the night Skyler died. He certainly had motivation. Radhauser had several witnesses, including Scott, who would attest to Reggie's hatred for Skyler and his belief Skyler was not his biological son. But means was a problem. Hopefully the search of his house would lead to something.

As he looked through the folder, Vernon, McBride, Corbin, and Leonard filed into the room. Murphy eventually joined them and took a seat at the opposite end of the table from Radhauser. There were dark circles under his eyes and Radhauser could smell the anxiety coming out of his pores like sweat.

Murphy didn't waste any time. "We need answers on this case and we need them now."

"We're doing the best we can," Radhauser said. "So far, we have five potential suspects. Maybe six or even seven, if we count the two unlikely ones. Skyler's four-year-old brother, and Henry

131

Evans, the son of Dana's boss." He told them about the injury Henry suffered and that he had the mental capacity of a seven-year-old.

"Reggie Sterling is my number one suspect. He believes Skyler is not his biological son. And he was given Haloperidol as part of his alcoholism treatment, but was not given a prescription upon his release."

"Dana Sterling who may have wanted to get back together with her ex by eliminating the child who stood between them."

"The next-door neighbor, Tilly Olson, who was arrested for her involvement with a drug overdose to a four-year-old in Philadelphia back in the sixties. The charges against her were dropped for lack of evidence. But we're still looking into it."

"Montgomery Taylor, an accused pedophile, who plastered his darkroom walls with photographs of Skyler. Some of them pretty disturbing."

"And finally, Caleb Bryce, the 9-1-1 caller, who has acted as father to the toddler for the past year. He admits to preparing the bottle of apple juice, but denies any knowledge of the drug Haloperidol."

Murphy shook his head and focused his gaze on Radhauser. "Potential suspects are not good enough. And you want to know why?" He didn't wait for an answer. "Because you're dragging your feet and not getting any results. Everyone and his brother wants results when a toddler is murdered. All the press this case has received is killing us. Most Ashland residents have kids or grandkids and they are horrified something like this could happen here in their safe little town. They expect us to arrest and punish someone. Most of them figure if an innocent baby can be murdered here, then their children aren't safe either. People are calling their congressmen and asking why we haven't made an arrest. They want to know what kind of police department we're running here."

"But it's only been a week since we got the autopsy results," Vernon said.

"That doesn't matter. And you know as well as I do if a murder case isn't solved in the first forty-eight hours, the likelihood it ever will be goes way down. I want a suspect in custody. And if we don't have one, I want to know why the hell not?" He paused for a moment, as if to let that sink in before he opened his folder and scanned the documents. For about ten minutes, the room was silent as each officer studied the folders in front of them.

"What about the deaf guy who called 9-1-1?" Murphy said. "He had the opportunity. Hell, he even admits to making the damn bottle. From what I understand, his girlfriend was about to leave him. One of the neighbors heard him threatening to murder the older boy." He stopped and glared at Radhauser. "You even called Child Protective Services. Maybe he was trying to punish the girlfriend by killing her baby and hurting the older boy. We've all heard that 9-1-1 tape where he keeps calling the baby *she*. Saying she was going to die. Maybe he meant his former girlfriend." He paused and held up the photo Radhauser had taken of the playhouse. "What the hell kind of a nickname is cockroach?"

"It was a pet name. A term of endearment."

"Sure, right," Murphy said. "We all know how much everyone loves a cockroach." Murphy's gaze shifted from Radhauser to Vernon. "Did the search warrant give you anything promising?"

It was the moment Radhauser dreaded.

"We found an empty bottle of Haloperidol in the bathroom trash can. It was the liquid concentrate. It's my understanding it's only available in prescription form, but it had no patient name on it. Must have come in a package of more than one."

This was incriminating evidence. But the fact there was no patient name on the bottle of Haloperidol could mean it was stolen from someplace like Sunrise Treatment Center where the drug was most likely purchased in bulk.

Vernon continued. "And the lab found traces of Haloperidol in the baby bottle we found in the crib."

"What the fuck are you waiting for?" Murphy said.

Radhauser couldn't come up with a reason why Bryce would kill a toddler he clearly loved. In Radhauser's experience with murder, the why was always inseparable from the who. "Bryce's prints were not on the bottle."

"Maybe he wore gloves," Murphy said. "He's deaf, but not stupid. Why haven't you arrested him?"

"There was a set of unidentified prints on the bottle," Radhauser argued. "They weren't in our system."

"Have you fingerprinted the other major suspects?"

"Yes. Tilly, and the accused pedophile were in the system. Reggie had a DWI, so his were on file, too. Dana wasn't a match."

"If the killer wore gloves," Murphy said. "The fingerprints could be from whoever packaged the drug."

"The truth is, I don't think Bryce did it," Radhauser said.

"Why, because he's deaf and you feel sorry for him?"

"No. The evidence against him is all circumstantial." Radhauser knew what it felt like to love a kid who died. "I think he genuinely loved that boy."

"I don't care what you think. Arrest the son of a bitch."

* * *

Thursday morning, Bryce was draped over his kitchen table gulping black coffee and rereading a collection of Raymond Carver short stories when the amplified sound of the doorbell let him know he had a visitor.

He answered and held the screen door open with his foot. A uniformed police officer, shorter than Bryce by at least six inches, and Detective Radhauser stood on his front porch.

"Are you Caleb Bryce?" the smaller officer asked.

There was a change in the weight of the air around Bryce. Something was terribly wrong. "Y...Y...Yes," Bryce stammered, his voice once again unreliable. "D...D... Detective Radhauser knows who I am." He made a feeble gesture, invited them inside.

"I'm Sergeant Leonard of the Ashland Police Department and I'm placing you under arrest for one count of child abuse against Scott Sterling and first-degree murder in the death of Skyler Sterling."

A door slammed somewhere in Bryce's head. He stared at Radhauser in disbelief. "Murder? Me? You can't be serious."

Radhauser looked stricken. "Give me a moment alone with him, Lenny," he said to the other officer.

Sergeant Leonard was built like a fire hydrant with a shaved-bald head and intense blue eyes that were difficult to read. His squared-off chin was clean-shaven, his skin tanned and taut. There was something affable in the way he nodded to Radhauser as if he completely understood his need to speak with Bryce alone.

Sergeant Leonard stepped back onto the porch.

"I'm sorry I have to do this," Radhauser said. "My captain is insisting we've got enough evidence to hold you over for trial. And, unfortunately, the DA agrees with him."

Panic rushed down to Bryce's toes and numbed him all over. "What evidence? I whacked Scott on the backside with my open hand. But I didn't do anything, at least not on purpose, to hurt Skyler."

"Listen to me. I'm going to keep digging, even if I have to do it on my own time. I'm not convinced this case is solved. Do yourself a favor. If anyone starts to question you, even if it's me and we're not alone. Say absolutely nothing. Ask for an attorney."

"I can't afford an attorney."

"The state has to appoint one for you," Radhauser said. "It's the law. And I'll do my best to see you get a good one."

"I was so sure it was an accident. A terrible accident."

"As Tilly probably told you, the autopsy revealed high doses of a drug called Haloperidol in Skyler's system. It's known to cause seizures and can result in death, especially in a young child. The officers who searched your house found the drug in your bathroom trash can and traces of it in the baby bottle in Skyler's crib."

It was a surreal moment and it took Bryce a little time to get his mind around it. "My trash can? How could it be in my trash can when I never even heard of that drug? I don't take any drugs, Detective Radhauser. Only Tylenol now and then for a headache. Was the prescription made out to Dana?"

"Not to anyone," Radhauser said. "It was in a small glass bottle, inside a Ziploc bag."

"Well, I can guarantee you I didn't put it there."

"Does Skyler take a bottle of something to drink to bed every night?"

"Yes. Sometimes water. I'm always afraid the milk will sour unless he drinks it all before he falls asleep. That night it was apple juice," Bryce said. "Dana reminded me before she left that we had to keep him hydrated."

Radhauser took out his notebook and jotted down something. "She asked you to make the bottle, specifying apple juice? Did she give you a specific baby bottle to use?"

"We only have one," Bryce said. "We were trying to wean him from the bottle to a sippy cup, but he wasn't happy about it. So we compromised, tossed most of his bottles, and gave him one only at night. We washed it out every morning and put it in the kitchen cabinet."

"The officers who searched the house collected the original apple juice container from the trash, but it showed no evidence of the drug. That means, if you had nothing to do with it, the drug was either in the baby bottle itself before you poured in the apple juice, or someone tampered with it after you made it."

Bryce told him Reggie was in the bedroom reading to Scott. And had every opportunity to tamper with Skyler's bottle.

Radhauser made more notes in this black book. "The search of Reggie's house was a bust." He kept writing while he talked, as if confirming something for himself. He called the sergeant back inside.

And Sergeant Leonard, self-confident and intelligent, looked directly at Bryce and commanded that he put his hands behind his back.

Bryce braced himself. This was no joke. He planted his feet wide apart on the living room tile, and crossed his wrists behind his back. Radhauser handcuffed Bryce, while Sergeant Leonard stood in front of him reciting his rights. The young officer sounded like a child forced to repeat a poem he memorized. His brow furrowed as he spouted off the entire paragraph as if it were one long stanza.

As he heard the click of the cuffs and felt the pressure against his wrists, Bryce stared at his boots, so far away from the rest of his body it was as if his legs stretched out. Like that green, rubber Gumby Scott liked to play with, Bryce's feet receded farther and farther away.

Near the bottom of his steps, he peered hard at the vast Oregon sky, the clear and brilliant blue that comes with autumn. And for some strange, incomprehensible reason, he thought about the enormity of space and longed to somehow reach out into the emptiness and grab onto whatever lay beyond this day.

Oddly detached from the scene now, Bryce floated somewhere outside himself, wondering about the identity of the unshaven, handcuffed man being pushed toward a police car. Sergeant Leonard nudged him gently forward, his hand pressed into the small of Bryce's back, but the forward movement only twisted the knife in his chest. Perhaps it signaled his fear, or maybe remorse, or grief. He wasn't sure. Bryce only knew that the pain belonged to him. It entered to inform him that at least his body better understood where he was headed. Leaning against the police car, he stared at the tips of his shoes.

When he looked up again, Tilly stood on her front step.

She hurried toward him, carrying the broom she used to sweep her porch. "Don't you go worrying none, Bryce. They are makin' a big mistake." She took a step toward the police car, then stopped, pushed her glasses up. "Mark my words, boy, you'll be back home before the night's over."

Bryce turned to Radhauser. "Did you give my key back to Tilly?"

He nodded.

Tilly planted her feet more securely in the gravel. Her eyes were wet and wide as she dropped the broom and wrapped her arms around herself.

"Take care of Pickles for me, would you? His food is in the kitchen cabinet next to the window." Bryce drew in a couple of deep breaths and kept his gaze away from Tilly.

"Never ya mind, boy, I'll look after everything." She tried to smile, but the tremble in her bottom lip betrayed her. "Dang fool," she hissed at Radhauser. "I thought you had better sense." She turned and walked away.

Sergeant Leonard protected Bryce's head with his hand as he climbed into the back seat. And when the cop reached down and fastened his seatbelt, Bryce believed he was being strapped into an awful mistake. The trap door opened and he tumbled into an unknown world.

Though he desperately wanted it to be, this was no joke. It was all so impossible to believe. He had never been arrested, never been handcuffed, never even been inside a police vehicle. His mind was racing out of control. Arrested for Skyler's murder. How in hell could something like this happen to him?

Outside Ashland holding, Radhauser excused himself to call his wife. Sergeant Leonard walked Bryce through two thick steel doors into the booking area that looked more like a hospital nurses' station.

He stood next to Leonard until they were waved up to the desk where he explained Bryce's hearing issues.

With exaggerated mouth movements, the guard behind the desk, a man who weighed at least three hundred pounds, requested Bryce's full name, date of birth and SSN, then asked Leonard about the charge.

"Caleb Bryce is charged with one count of child abuse of four-year-old Scott Sterling and the first-degree murder of nineteen-month-old Skyler Sterling."

The guard shot Bryce a disgusted look.

Bryce dropped his gaze to the floor.

The next thing he knew, Sergeant Leonard left and Bryce was flanked by two guards who were even bigger than the one behind the desk.

They fingerprinted him. Took his mug shot. Bryce stumbled through both procedures in a daze. He continued to be dumbfounded that he was charged with Skyler's murder.

One guard ran a chain around his waist and shackled his legs in irons, then attached a chain to his handcuffs, ran it through an O-ring on his waist chain, and then did the same thing with the leg irons.

An hour or so later, Bryce was taken into a shower room. Three more guards stood watch. Once inside the room, they removed the cuffs, unshackled him and told him to strip. They took each piece of clothing as he handed it to them, inventoried it and put it inside a cardboard box. They asked him to remove his watch and the gold band he now wore on his right hand in memory of the child who'd come from that long-ago union with Valerie.

Once completely naked, the biggest of the guards told him to open his mouth. He looked inside with a flashlight and then asked him to run his hands through his hair as if he expected tiny bags of heroin to fall out. The worst humiliation came when they demanded he bend over and spread his butt cheeks. Bryce's entire face grew hot. He and four other prisoners were led into a huge locker room. "Hit the water, boys," the guard snapped.

A short, stocky, white man with a brown crew cut and tattoos of naked women covered in snakes on his chest scooted over on the bench to make room for Bryce. "Yo, man," he shouted loud enough for even Bryce to hear him above the sound of the showers. "What ya in here for?"

Bryce kept standing. Unable to bring himself to answer the question, he clutched his soap and stepped into the communal shower, raising his face toward the water's spray.

The man, who now stood behind Bryce, jerked his shoulders and flipped him around. "You mother fuckin' deaf, man, or are ya just plain dumb?"

Water cascaded down Bryce's back. "I'm hearing impaired," he said, pointing to his ear. "You have to talk loud or face me so I can read your lips."

"I said," he shrieked the words slowly, exaggerating the movement of his lips. "What are you in for?" He leaned toward Bryce, waited for an answer.

"They claim I abused one child and killed another one."

The tattooed man stepped back. He shaped his open mouth in an O and took a step back. "Naughty, naughty. Shame. Shame." He rubbed one index finger down the other, then pointed at Bryce, wagged his finger up and down, clicking his tongue against the roof of his mouth. "That ain't good, man. Take it from me, I been in the joint enough times to know the guests don't take kindly to kiddie fuckers. That how you get your rocks off, pretty boy?" He grabbed at the air in front of Bryce's genitals. "Are you guilty?"

Bryce pulled back from the shower's spray and covered himself with a towel. "I'm not ta...ta...talking sexual stuff. I...I smacked him on the backside with my hand for biting me, then spitting in my face. If that's abuse," he looked away for a moment, "I guess I'm guilty all right."

The man faced Bryce and whistled *Rock-a-bye Baby*. He grinned, a big missing-a-tooth smile, then walked away.

When Bryce finished with the shower, the guard handed him another threadbare towel, some clothes that looked like surgical scrubs, and a pair of slippers. Bryce dried himself off, then slipped into the faded blue shirt and cotton pants, drawn with a string at the waist. The crotch hung just above his knees and fabric puddled in loose layers atop the elastic bands at his ankles. Once he was dressed, they replaced all his restraints and put a band around his wrist with a prisoner identification number.

Another prisoner, in a sweat-stained T-shirt stretched tight across his belly and chest, lingered outside the showers. He curled his top lip, hawked up a wad of spit and deposited a slimy gob on the concrete floor at Bryce's feet. Already Bryce felt the numbness and maybe it was best that way.

An hour or more passed. With his handcuffs removed, Bryce crouched on the edge of a steel bench in the holding tank with about ten other men. He and the four other prisoners who'd showered were the only ones in prison garb. The only ones who looked as if they'd bathed in the past week.

Sometime later that morning, a uniformed guard slid trays of scrambled egg sandwiches into the rank-smelling room.

A drunk, in a filthy white suit, kicked his tray across the yellow-tiled floor and screeched, "I ain't eatin' that garbage. It's poison, I tell ya. Poison. Jesus will provide the only food we need." His chalky, blood-veined eyes roamed across Bryce's face and locked. The drunk held his own, waited for Bryce to break the silence of their stare. And when he didn't, the man continued to look directly into Bryce's eyes, as if he had insights into the future that his fellow inmate did not.

The cramped room grew uncomfortably silent. Finally, a black guy wearing a faded blue tank top with so many holes it looked as if it had taken a shotgun blast, and a pair of blue jeans riding low on his bony hips, picked up the extra tray and scraped the food onto his own. "Jesus said I could have yours, too," he muttered, bits of green-tinged scrambled egg dropping from his mouth.

Bryce couldn't stop shaking his head, couldn't stop thinking this was a mistake, but with none acknowledged, he was thrust into a nightmare that stretched out in front of him like a balloon blown up way beyond its limits.

CHAPTER SEVENTEEN

Four hours later, Bryce and the four other prisoners he'd showered with were taken through the double doors to the outside and loaded into a white van. They were chained to steel rings and taken to the Jackson County Jail, where a new nightmare awaited.

Once they'd made the short trip to Medford, Bryce's shackles were detached from the ring inside the van. He was led out into the fresh air for a moment, then quickly through another set of double security doors he learned from one of the other prisoners was called a sally port. Once inside the jail, he was led to a desk where he was given a thin foam mattress, a sheet, a threadbare blanket and a paperback copy of the Bible.

After he was checked in, two more guards arrived. They each took one of Bryce's arms and escorted him down a long corridor until it ended in front of a steel door. Bryce sensed the vibrations of the guards' boots as they echoed off the ceiling and walls.

One guard pushed a button. A few seconds later, a lock buzzed, reverberating inside Bryce's damaged eardrums, and the steel door retracted.

It opened into a huge, square room with rows of gray metal cell doors along each wall. Every door had a Plexiglas window, about twelve inches square and sixty inches off the ground. In almost every cell, there was a curious face looking out the window.

Though Bryce couldn't always make out the words, the halls resounded with numerous shouts and screams—prisoners yelling to each other and jeering at the guards. Bryce wished he could put his hands over his ears to stop the vibrations.

142

They stopped in front of a cell marked *156-B*. One of the guards stepped up to the window, looked inside and shouted, "Step back, Poncho. Company's coming. You know the drill."

The guard next to Bryce turned to him and said, with exaggerated mouth movements, "You're going to love Poncho. He's a real stand-up guy." A moment later, the shackles were off and Bryce was inside a seven-by-ten-foot cell. "Turn around and face the door," the guard demanded.

When Bryce didn't hear the command, Poncho jerked him around by the shoulders. "You hard a hearing, asshole?"

There was a very loud, metal against metal sound as a tray about two feet long and four inches high appeared through the door.

"It's called a pie hole," Poncho said. "And I plan to teach you to keep yours shut."

"Put your hands through," the guard ordered.

Bryce did as he was told. A moment later, he was free of the cuffs. He pulled his hands back into the cell and the drawer slammed shut.

"You boys play nice," one of the guards said.

Poncho, a young Hispanic man, was squat, hard, and leathery and because he arrived in the cell first, he'd already claimed the bottom bunk.

Slouched over, like someone punched him in the stomach, Bryce dropped the Bible, foam pad, sheet, and blanket the guards handed him onto the top mattress. He didn't say a word, but paced the small room, then looked out into the corridor where two armed guards walked so close together their black-shirted shoulders touched.

The room held nothing except the bunks, a stainless steel toilet and a sink. Poncho had taped a few photographs on the wall above his bunk.

"So, what d'ya do?" Poncho asked, then wiped his mouth with the back of his hand.

After the scene in the shower, Bryce feared answering his question. He tried to maintain both his stare and an air of toughness while he attempted to size up his cellmate.

Poncho didn't ask his question a second time.

When Poncho stepped over to the commode and urinated, Bryce moved to the small window on the back wall of the cell. He stood on his toes to peer through a pane of filthy, shatterproof glass, inlaid with wire mesh. Nothing made sense. But one thing was certain. He was in for the fight of his life. If he was convicted of murdering Skyler, he would rot in this or some other prison.

And no one would care.

After losing his daughter, and his divorce from Valerie, he turned his back on what was left of his family and friends—convinced the only way to survive was to start over. In the years that followed, he tried to live a good life. He bought and remodeled the house in Ashland, volunteered to coach area Little League teams, and rocked babies in the hospital nursery. He had almost given up on having a family again. And then he met Dana. She and the boys were his fresh start.

Outside, a few prisoners kicked a soccer ball while others marched on the dirt track. Like refugees from something, they paced the long, oval road surrounding the prison, over and over, shoulders slumped, heads bowed, their hands stuffed into their pockets.

* * *

In downtown Ashland, wedged between a lesbian bookstore and a New Age coffee shop, The Office of Public Defense occupied the first floor of what used to be a hotel. As always when the weather was warm enough, Main Street was alive with people, most of them women.

Kendra Palmer, her heels clicking on the linoleum floor, hurried down the corridor to the small office suite she shared with Maria Fernandez, an older woman who'd worked as a public defender for more than three decades. She was a few inches shorter than Kendra and about twenty pounds heavier. Maria had a freckled nose, inquisitive black eyes and long, dark hair streaked with silver that she wore braided and piled on top of her head. She was a fixture in the department and as well-loved as anyone Kendra had ever met. Maria had two grown children, a husband who cooked, vacuumed, and came by the office once a week to take Maria to lunch, always bringing a bouquet of fresh flowers with him. She was the kind of woman Kendra hoped to someday become.

Through the window blinds, morning sunlight painted dark and light gray stripes across the metal desktops. An array of unmatched file cabinets lined the back wall. Kendra smiled at the irony and tried not to compare it to the office her father had decorated in celebration of her joining his firm. The room smelled, as it always did in the morning, of yeasty cinnamon rolls and freshly ground coffee from the shop next door.

For most of the last week, she'd shadowed Maria, following her to the courthouse for arraignments, preliminary hearings, jail visits with defendants, and a felony assault trial that only lasted one afternoon. Kendra was learning the ropes. And for the most part, she was loving every minute.

Maria dropped a manila folder on Kendra's desk. "You ready to fly solo?"

Kendra opened the file. A thirty-five-year-old hearing-impaired man accused of one count of child abuse of a four-year-old boy, and the first-degree murder of a nineteen-month-old toddler. *Holy crap*. Her first case. A child abuser? A kid murderer? A deaf man? Maria must be kidding.

Swallowing back the lump of anxiety that seemed to have taken up residency at the base of her throat, Kendra glanced over at Maria. Sooner or later she was going to have to get a grip on herself and perform. She was a Harvard-trained lawyer, prepared to handle this or any other case the judge appointed to her. "I don't know sign language," her mouth said, though her mind had meant to assure Maria she could handle herself in court.

"No one here does. But you're in luck. He suffered an injury as a child so he had already developed speech. It's muddled, but understandable. And if you look at him when you talk, he will read your lips."

"This is my first case."

"No shit, Sherlock." Maria shrugged. "The investigating officer is Winston Radhauser—one of the good ones." She paused and smiled. "Easy to look at, if you like cowboys. He's happily married and a little old for you. Almost everyone finds him instantly likeable. You can trust what he says."

"Do you think I'm ready?"

Maria gave Kendra a big smile. "I do. But I probably wouldn't have assigned you a murder." She shrugged. "I guess the boss figures you must have learned a few things from your old man."

Her father was almost as well known throughout the world as F. Lee Bailey. Nearly everyone had heard of him and his reputation for winning. Kendra had hoped Ashland was a place where she could escape being her father's daughter. It looked like she was wrong.

"Mr. Bryce refused to talk to the arresting officers and has asked for a state-appointed attorney," Maria said. "I suggest you get over there as quickly as you can. They've already transferred him from Ashland holding to the Jackson County Jail in Medford."

Kendra was packing her briefcase when a man ducked his head to get through the old, six-foot doorway into their office. In his jeans, cowboy boots, and western cut jacket, he looked like a handsome cattle rancher. With his gray Stetson dangling from the index finger of his left hand, he stopped in front of Maria's desk and dropped a manila folder of his own.

Maria looked up at him and smiled. "We were just talking about you. If it isn't my favorite cowboy detective."

He ran the fingers of his right hand around the edge of the cowboy hat. "Has the Bryce murder case been assigned yet?"

Maria nodded toward Kendra. "You're looking at her. Detective Radhauser, meet Kendrick Huntington Palmer IV. She's a Harvard graduate, passed her bar on the first go around. And clerked for Judge Wallace Turnbough up in Portland."

The cowboy raised his eyebrows.

"And yes," Maria said. "She's *his* daughter."

A red-faced Kendra offered her right hand. "Please call me Kendra." His dark blue eyes were striking in their sapphire color and reminded her of Crater Lake in the sunlight. But he couldn't hide the disappointment in them. He wanted Maria, or someone more experienced, to handle this case.

He turned back to Maria and confirmed Kendra's suspicions. "No offense to your no doubt brilliant young colleague, but I was hoping you'd handle his defense."

"What's so special about this one?" Maria asked.

"He's innocent."

She shrugged. "Aren't they all?"

"This one is different. I'd bet my badge on it."

Maria shook her head. "It's your case. If you're so sure he's innocent, how come he's in the pen?"

"I wasn't ready to make the arrest. Murphy ordered it. I told him he was pulling the trigger too soon, that the case was thin. But you know how he can be when the press is on his tail. Despite the circumstantial evidence against Bryce, I'm certain he didn't do it." He paused and smiled. "Come on, darlin'. I need someone with experience to work with me on proving it."

"Don't try that country boy charm routine on me. I know you have the instincts of a bloodhound and are probably right, but it wasn't my decision," Maria repeated. "Give the kid a chance. She may be new, but she's brighter than most."

Kendra suppressed a smile. For a moment, she stared at Radhauser's hands. They were the calloused hands of a working man with nails that were clean, but slightly uneven. A nice person's hands. Even though the detective was very good looking, he was somehow regular and approachable.

Radhauser picked up the manila folder and handed it to Kendra. "This is everything I have so far connected to Bryce's case. Be sure to read all of these reports before you see him. I made extensive notes on everyone I've interviewed so far."

"I was headed over to County when you got here," Kendra said.

"Where are you parked?"

"In the lot behind the theater."

After he ducked through the doorway, he put his hat back on. "I'll walk you to your car. I can fill you in on the way."

As they walked down Main Street, with its green and gold

147

Shakespeare banners flapping in the wind, Radhauser told her everything he knew about Bryce, Dana and Reggie Sterling, and their four-year-old son, Scott. The summer tourist season was over and the streets finally belonged to the residents of Ashland again. "You've come here at a good time," he said. "It's always a relief not to have to dodge window-shopping tourists and hundreds of high school students bused in for the theater."

While they walked, Radhauser suggested she take depositions from Bryce's neighbor, Tilly, and from his supervisors at both Gilbert's Grocery Market and the hospital where he volunteered in the newborn nursery.

"You know I'll be called as a witness for the prosecution, but I'm not going to stop investigating this case," he said. "Even if I have to do it in my spare time. So, feel free to contact me." He pulled a business card from his wallet and jotted his home phone number on the back. "Anytime. And I mean it."

She took the card and tucked it into her jacket pocket.

"Oh, and one more thing. Here's a list of things Bryce needs to know about prison." He handed her a sheet of paper. "He's a lamb ripe for the slaughter. His neighbor told me he's a poet. Anyone who commits a crime against a child, or is even accused of one, becomes a punching bag. If someone doesn't give him a crash course in prison life, they'll eat him alive in there."

* * *

After spending fifty minutes in her car, digging through the copies of Radhauser's reports, looking for any detail that might have been overlooked, Kendra took a deep breath, straightened her back, and strode up to the Jackson County Jail.

Exude an air of confidence. Pretend this isn't your first murder case. Who was she kidding? This was her first solo case, period. What would her father think if he knew? She toyed with the idea of calling him later. It was a huge case as far as publicity, the kind he loved, and that was pretty exciting, but it was also a first-degree murder charge, and that meant the stakes were high for her client. She decided to wait on telling him until she had a better handle on her defense.

Once inside the jail, she stopped at the reception area where a pudgy, middle-aged man, with a mostly gray crew cut sat behind a wall of what she assumed was bulletproof glass. Though she visited the prison twice last week with Maria, she'd never seen him before. He wore a black pullover shirt with a stitched badge on the right arm. Beneath the badge were the words *Jackson County Jail* in gold letters. As Kendra approached, he spat a wad of tobacco into a Styrofoam cup. Nothing like making a good first impression.

She picked up the sign-in sheet. "I'm here to see Caleb Bryce."

"We go by inmate numbers here, pretty lady," he said, with a twinkle in his brown eyes.

She opened the folder Radhauser had given her. "Number 4795." As she recited the number, she felt the wrongness of inmates not being called by their names. The place was dehumanizing enough without being issued a number.

"Do you have ID?"

She reached into her purse, pulled out her driver's license and Oregon Bar Association card, and slid them into the metal tray at the bottom of the window. "My name is Kendra Palmer," she said. "I'm Mr. Bryce's attorney."

"Lucky him," he said. "You'll most likely raise the morale in this joint. Do you know the way to the visitors' area?"

In San Francisco, the guard would be slapped with a sexual harassment charge. She fought the temptation to threaten him, and simply nodded. She'd been to the visitor area as part of her training and knew it didn't offer much privacy. Next time she'd call ahead for an attorney's room.

"I'll buzz you on through."

Kendra made her way through the maze of gates and steel doors and took a seat at a scarred wooden stool inside a compartment not much larger than a telephone booth. While she waited, she leafed through Radhauser's reports one more time. The evidence against Bryce seemed sketchy and circumstantial. He had opportunity— no doubt about that. And he did admit to preparing the baby's bottle of apple juice. There were two eyewitnesses who'd swear Bryce had threatened to murder Scott—but the witnesses were a four-year-old boy, and Harold Grundy, a cranky old neighbor man bordering on senility.

Half the neighborhood had overhead Bryce call Dana a selfish bitch on the morning before Skyler's death. The prosecution would claim he had motive—that he wanted to get even with the girlfriend who'd threatened to leave him.

The means was another issue. Bryce had no history of alcohol abuse or mental health issues. Why would he have a drug like Haloperidol in his possession and where would he have gotten it?

It was a high-profile case. Radhauser had been pressured by his captain to make an arrest. She was new at defending alleged criminals, but she'd learned from her father that it would be a rare detective or prosecutor who'd question the gift of a murder weapon found in a suspect's house—no matter what the circumstances.

CHAPTER EIGHTEEN

B ryce sat on an aluminum picnic table in the yard, watching other prisoners shoot hoops. The warm autumn morning expanded with shouts, threats, and rowdy exchanges of profanities. A thud of multicolored flesh collided on the court, and a long-haired white boy caught a swift elbow in the stomach as he jumped after a rebound. When the wind came up, a lone big-leaf maple tree in the yard shed its leaves in a flurry of huge, golden snowflakes.

"Yo, 4795," one of the guards shouted, then strolled up to him. "You got yourself a visitor."

"Me?" Bryce said. Who could possibly be visiting him here? He followed the guard inside where he was shackled again. They meandered down the winding corridors, past the other pods where the clamor of prisoners arguing, playing cards, and shouting at a television talk show host sent their vibrations booming and echoing through the hallways.

The visiting room was divided into small cubicles with a Plexiglas wall separating the prisoner from his visitor. Bryce was still wearing his shackles and waist chain, but his hands had been left free. He thought for the hundredth time just how surreal his life had become.

Smeared with handprints and lipstick smudges, the glass also held small fingerprints and palm marks, from children who must have pushed against the unyielding pane, hoping to dissolve into the arms and laps on the other side. The sight of those tiny fingerprints filled him with sadness.

When the guard pointed to the second booth, Bryce shuffled

inside, sat on the metal stool and picked up the telephone receiver. He flipped on the amplifying device and stared into the face of a young woman who looked like an Ivy League college student dressed up for Parents' Day.

She was slender and wore a tailored, gray-striped suit, with a pale pink satin blouse. Her face was beautiful and flawless, her blonde hair clipped with a barrette at the nape of her neck to hold it in place.

"Who are you?" he asked.

"I'm your attorney."

"You look like a kid."

She slipped her business card through the narrow slot in the Plexiglas.

Bryce studied it for a moment. *Kendrick Huntington Palmer IV, Office of Public Defense.*

"I understand you requested a court-appointed attorney." She dove right in. "You can call me Kendra." She spoke slowly, articulated each word. "I'll be your representative in the state's case against you." She placed her notes on the small ledge that served as a table and held his gaze. Her fingers long and slender, nails unpolished. Her blue eyes were specked with green, and very beautiful.

"You don't look old enough to represent yourself," Bryce said.

She smiled, a rich girl's smile, her teeth white and perfectly even. "I'm old enough to have graduated from law school, passed the bar and clerked for a judge. I'm old enough to get a job in the public defender's office. So, I suggest you stop worrying about my credentials and start worrying about your case."

He wasn't sure how to respond—hadn't meant to offend her.

She didn't wait. "I also understand you're hearing impaired. Are you able to hear me all right?"

"You don't need to speak so slowly," he said, tired of all the exaggerated mouth movements he'd encountered since his incarceration that morning. "I read lips and can make out what you're saying just fine as long as you articulate. And face me when you talk."

"I assume you've been charged by now and know what we're up against." She looked straight into Bryce's face, her clear blue eyes serious and doused with something that looked like sympathy.

But Bryce watched her mouth, because for him, the mouth revealed more than any other facial characteristic. He could spot a lie through a twitch in the corner, read tenderness in a certain droop that could later darken into indifference. An eye, altered by a shadow or a beam of soft light, could mislead him, but the mouth remained reliable and certain.

"Tell me why you think you are here," she said.

He told her about hitting Scott on the backside with his open hand and what had led up to it. "I lost my temper, and if that's child abuse, then I guess I'm guilty. As for Skyler, I can't begin to imagine how anyone could charge me with his murder. I loved that little boy like my own son." Heat pulsed behind his eyes. He looked away and swallowed. In prison for less than eight hours, Bryce had learned one thing. Don't show weakness.

"The state's going for first-degree murder. Do you understand what that means?"

"Not exactly."

"They intend to prove you killed Skyler Sterling with malice and forethought."

"That's ridiculous. I n…never laid a h…h…hand on that baby. And I certainly didn't give him some drug I've never even h…h… heard of. It makes no sense. If I wanted him dead, I mean…why would I ca…ca…call for help? I gave him CPR." Bryce shuddered. "I was frantic."

She told him what Radhauser already had, about the medical examiner's findings and the drug residue in the baby bottle. "The state will claim you felt remorse and that's why you tried to save him."

Bryce closed his eyes. He moved his hand away from his ear and slammed it against his right thigh. He was the one who'd made the bottle for Skyler that night. But he sure as hell hadn't laced the apple juice with some drug.

When he loosened his grip, the receiver dropped and dangled

just inches above the floor. Bryce held his head in his hands. As he slumped on the stool, a steady, throbbing rhythm in the back of his neck echoed the hard, slapping beat of his own heart. And the noise pounded in Bryce's head, drowning out all other sound.

"Bryce," Kendra shouted. Then, getting no response, she beat her fist on the Plexiglas until he finally lifted his head, picked up the receiver and pushed it against his ear again.

He opened his eyes.

"Look, you have to listen to me," she pleaded. "I've read your statements and those of Detective Radhauser. I plan to talk with some of your neighbors and with your boss at Gilbert's. Detective Radhauser believes you are innocent. And, so do I. I'm here to help you, but you have to cooperate. You have to listen. And you have to be involved in your own defense."

The imploring tone of the young attorney's voice and the sure movement of her mouth comforted Bryce. "I'm listening," he whispered, then licked his dry lips.

"Detective Radhauser wanted me to tell you a couple things about prison. For your own safety."

Bryce was grateful. "God knows I need all the help I can get."

"Rule number one. You'll be in lockdown twenty-three hours a day. Use the hour in the yard wisely. Get some exercise. Rule number two. Keep your mouth shut and your eyes open. Stand up for yourself. Fight only if you have to, but don't let anyone walk all over you. Once you do that, you're lost. Rule number three. Don't trust anyone. That means other inmates, the guards, your cellmate. Trust only me and Detective Radhauser. Rule number four. Don't stare at anyone, ever."

"Is that all? Four basic rules for survival in the slammer?"

"You're going to need some things like underwear, socks, soap, shampoo, and a toothbrush. You'll have to buy them from the commissary. I'll deposit some money in your account."

"I can't let you do that."

"You can't stop me. You can pay me back when you get out of here. And don't tell any prisoner or guard how much you have in your account."

"I'm scared, Ms. Palmer," he said. "I know I shouldn't say that out loud. And I hate to admit it to you or anyone else, but I'm afraid."

She moved slightly toward the Plexiglas. "Call me Kendra."

He closed his eyes for a moment, ashamed of his confession.

"I know," she said. "And I'm scared, too, but I want you to remember something. No matter what happens at your arraignment and trial, I won't quit my attempts to prove your innocence. And neither will Detective Radhauser."

"I'll be back tomorrow," Kendra said. "And I'll reserve a conference room. I'll ask the warden to provide you with pencils and paper in your cell. In the meantime, I want you to review the events of the day Skyler died." She told him to go over the details again and again, and make notes.

"I don't care how insignificant you think something is, Bryce, I want to know about it, okay? A lot of lawyers don't ask their client to do this because they'd rather not know if he's guilty. But I want the absolute truth from you. I already believe you're innocent. So, tell me everything that happened. Every word you can remember that anyone said to you. Everyone you talked to or who came by your house. I want it all. Think of it as a minute by minute accounting—paying special attention to the time after you put Skyler to bed."

Bryce swallowed hard, then nodded. He was a poet who liked to write. He could do what she asked. It was up to him now and he intended to fight.

"One more thing," Kendra said. "Because of your hearing impairment and the nature of the charges against you, I'm worried about your safety. I've requested protective custody—a private cell for you. But with crowded conditions…" She paused, shook her head. "It may take a little while for it to happen. So be very careful."

Something about her filled Bryce with hope that he might someday regain the freedom he'd so recently taken for granted. Kendra became, during that first brief encounter, a symbol of everything lost.

She stood, then packed and closed her briefcase. Within another minute, the only thing left was the faint scent of her perfume, something powdery and sweet—like lilac—seeping through the small opening at the bottom of the Plexiglas.

Oddly calm now, Bryce followed the guard back to his cell, still wondering how something like this could happen in his world.

As a little boy, he longed to go hunting with his big brother, Jason, and Isaiah Bryce—the man he'd believed was his father. But when it finally happened, the deer spotted and in his rifle's sites, six-year-old Bryce couldn't pull the trigger. His father had been livid and backhanded Bryce across the face. How could anyone think him capable of murdering a baby?

* * *

Bryce passed the remainder of the afternoon drifting between the scenes in the prison yard and staring out into the corridor until a bell rang and he was herded into a dining hall for dinner.

And it was there, seated at a long, metal table with an assortment of other prisoners, that Poncho dropped a torn page from the evening newspaper, *The Medford Tribune*, onto Bryce's dinner tray.

TOT DEAD, SIBLING CLAIMS ABUSE
By Lauren Armstrong
Nineteen-month-old Skyler Sterling was buried on Saturday, but no one can say why he died...

As he stared at the article about Skyler's death and his own arrest, a circle of grease from his gravy-topped mashed potatoes seeped through the headline and slowly spread across the page.

After dinner, Poncho shoved Bryce into the table, then thrust another newspaper in front of him. "Hey Cryin' Shame," he bellowed, loud enough for everyone to hear. "Is that you, man, the faggot poet, turned baby-killer? Why don't you pick on someone your own size, asshole?" Poncho glared into Bryce's face, then pranced off, swaying his hips and swishing his hand up and down to the frenzied laughter of his cronies waiting at another table.

Without looking at it, Bryce folded the paper with trembling hands. He wondered how Poncho could possibly know he wrote poetry. When the bell rang, Bryce kept his gaze planted on the floor and hurried back to his cell.

His bunk was stacked with legal size tablets and a half dozen fat pencils like the ones first graders used. Did they think he was going to stab himself with a pencil?

Poncho must have gone to the recreation room to watch television or play pinochle before lockdown. Relieved to be alone, Bryce unfolded the newspaper and stared at the headline:

POET CHARGED WITH MURDER IN DEATH OF TOT
By Wally Hartmueller
My precious, precious, child
Dying was one thing,
Being left behind you quite another.
Oh, if we could only change our places.

Those words are from a poem by Caleb R. Bryce, a poem that appears to have risen out of a gentle man who cherishes children. But the Caleb Bryce who wrote that poem is in the Jackson County Jail in Medford charged with murder in the October twelfth death of 19-month-old Skyler Sterling.

An autopsy revealed extensive internal bleeding and more than twenty bruises on the child's battered body...

An ocean of nausea washed over Bryce. Where had that reporter gotten his poem? He'd filed it away with the journal entries, photographs, and memories of that other dark time in his life he'd tried so hard to forget. How dare they rummage through his personal life like that? It was one thing for Dana to pack up boxes, probably her own things, before she moved out. But complete strangers, newspaper reporters, that was a different issue.

When he shifted his gaze to the right of the article, he recognized himself staring up from the front page. In the photo he appeared haunted, his dark eyes wide and dead-looking. His matted hair clung to his forehead in sweaty strands. And even though it was his face, the mug shot taken at his booking, even though he remembered every second of what happened, it still seemed unreal to Bryce. It was as if someone awakened him from a deep sleep by throwing a bucket of ice water in his face.

He read the entire article, the sluggish way someone half asleep incessantly rereads the same paragraph, attempting to discover a correlation between sentences, something that connected the words to his life, to the person Bryce thought himself to be. He yearned for something that made sense to him, something he could believe was the truth.

With his back to the door, he didn't hear Poncho's return, didn't anticipate the fist that seemed to explode the right side of his head and knocked him to the concrete floor.

Poncho pinned Bryce's arms to his sides, then plastered them against his crumpled body with knees as powerful as a vice. "It's plum pitiful, ain't it, Shame? Grown man like you killin' a little bitty baby. A cryin' shame, I tell ya."

Bryce felt his lower lip split against his front teeth and one of the blows to his chest sent out a pain so sharp he believed Poncho had stabbed him in the heart. Despite the rules Radhauser delivered through Kendra, Bryce didn't fight back. He closed his eyes, half unconscious, the taste of blood rising in the back of his throat while Poncho hurled his rage into Bryce's face until his battered head tottered on his neck like a punching bag.

Somewhere inside his confusion, Bryce acknowledged that, guilty or not, he had begun to pay his debt for the death of Skyler Sterling.

When he awakened, many hours later, he lay on clean, white sheets in the prison infirmary, limp and lifeless as a rag.

A nurse, tucked into the corner of the room, stuffed salad into her mouth with a plastic fork.

Bryce moaned, but she continued eating as though he wasn't there. He struggled to raise himself up on an elbow, but the throbbing in his head blinded him and he was violently ill, vomiting onto the floor.

"Jesus, Mary and Joseph." The nurse leaped to her feet, lettuce and carrot slices scattering across the white, tile floor. "Couldn't you have felt that coming?"

CHAPTER NINETEEN

When Bryce opened his eyes again, he stared down the length of the prison infirmary bed and into the concerned face of his attorney.

"Good God," Kendra said, moving alongside the bed. She touched his cheek. "That thug Poncho really did a job on your face." She paused and smiled at him. "You used to be handsome."

For a moment, Bryce, baffled and confused over his whereabouts, rode the dizzy ship of whatever painkillers they'd administered intravenously. He glided along, his sense of time and locality hazy.

When he stared into the mirror Kendra held up for him, Bryce scarcely recognized the man staring back. Encircled in black that faded into blue and yellow at the edges, his dark eyes sank into his skull, barely more than slits. His nose was splinted and packed with gauze and three inches of stitches crisscrossed the space above his right eyebrow. "I'm sure no beauty queen now," he said.

"Look, I'm furious about what happened to you. I screamed at a couple guards. And if I could, I'd kick Poncho where it would hurt the most."

He tried to smile through his busted lip. "You're braver than I am."

"I think you should file charges."

"What's the point? It's over now."

Kendra tucked the mirror back into her purse. "I know it's a little late, but my screaming got you a private cell. It's not exactly isolation, but you'll take your meals in there from now on and leave only when a guard accompanies you. Got that? And we'll have our meetings in there from now on, too."

Bryce nodded, and with the movement the ache in his head arched in an enormous V from the base of his neck, over his skull, and into each eye.

"When you feel up to it, I still need you to write out the things we talked about before Poncho beat the crap out of you." The set of her jaw told him she was madder than the proverbial hornet. "You sure you don't want him punished? Thrown in some dark hole with no food or water?"

"As you've mentioned before," he said, attempting another smile, "I have more important things to think about right now. And a writing assignment to complete for my attorney."

Kendra started to leave, then turned back. "One more thing. The press is all over this. Even the local tabloids have picked it up. Tomorrow, I'm going to ask for a temporary restraining order and see if we can block further coverage."

"I want to know what they're saying." Bryce heard the deadness in his own voice.

"No, you don't." Kendra moved to the edge of the bed and dropped her right hand onto his shoulder. "The truth is I need you to concentrate all your energy on your defense—on remembering that night. I don't want a bunch of newspaper hype distracting you."

"Don't I have a right to know what's being said about me?" Bryce tried to sit, but the pain in his head thrust him back against the pillow.

"Of course you do, but please...trust me now. I'll save everything and you can read it all you want once we get you through this. Now we need to concentrate on your preliminary."

"You might not believe this," he said. "But I don't even know what a preliminary is."

"A preliminary hearing. They listen to the prosecution's evidence and decide whether or not to indict and hold you over for trial. You don't have to be present for the preliminary."

He asked the next two questions with his aching eyes closed. "What will happen? What are they going to do to me?" He opened his eyes.

Kendra sat on the edge of the bed and positioned herself so he could read her lips. "First, there's the arraignment," she explained. "You'll go before a judge or a magistrate, or maybe a justice of the peace. The charges against you will be read, and then they'll ask how you plead to both charges. Your plea will be officially entered."

"After that?"

"The DA's office will turn the prosecution's evidence, a list of witnesses, and any depositions they've taken over to me after the hearing. Radhauser already gave me copies of his reports, but they may have other things I don't know about yet."

"I want to be there. I'd really like to know what evidence they have against me." Bryce lifted his hand to his head, then grimaced as he accidentally brushed the line of stitches above his eye. "When do I show up in court?"

"They postponed the arraignment because of your beating, but it's rescheduled for tomorrow morning at nine. There's not much to it, really. The charges against you will be read, and when asked how you plead to both charges," Kendra paused, tapped Bryce on the forearm as if to make certain he was paying attention, "I want you to look straight into the eyes of the judge or magistrate and say, 'not guilty,' with as much confidence as you can muster."

Later that afternoon, Bryce was accompanied by a prison guard to his private cell. In the corridor, as he passed the cubicle they'd shared, Poncho hissed, "If it ain't the Cryin' Shame. Feelin' better, Shame? Where they takin' ya, tough guy? To the nursery so you can suck on yo mama's titty?"

"Shut your fat mouth, Poncho." The guard jerked his baton from his waistband and waved it in front of Poncho's face, then shifted Bryce to his other side and continued until they stopped in front of a dim, gray room. After unlocking the door, the guard prodded Bryce inside and released him from his shackles and handcuffs.

A toilet stood exposed in the right corner. Moss-colored stains encrusted the bowl. To the left, a concrete table and stool-like chair—the words *Jackson County Jail* stenciled on the backrest.

The table was piled with a stack of legal pads and a new paper cup full of fat pencils with dull points.

Next to the table, in the room's left corner, a gray-striped mattress, dusty and stained, hung partially off the bed's concrete frame. Tucked in the sagging center was a makeshift tinfoil ashtray stuffed with crushed-out cigarette butts. No maid or cleaning service in this place.

The smell from the old ashes turned his stomach.

"Sheets will be passed out after supper." The guard slammed and locked the door behind him, then disappeared.

Bryce flushed the cigarette butts down the toilet, then sat on the concrete chair in front of a blank yellow pad. He wondered what information about that night he could provide Kendra that she didn't already have access to through Detective Radhauser. He stared around the cell again, trying to find something to hold his attention, something to postpone the inevitable.

Through a small, wire-meshed window near the ceiling, the final rays of the sun fell in a patchwork pattern across his forearms. It was amazing how few details infiltrated a jail cell, a place pared down to the barest of necessities, a place with virtually no color, just concrete, steel, a dull, striped mattress, and a thin blue blanket. A place where a single beam of sunlight or the vibrant color of the yellow-lined pads stacked on the table in front of him suddenly loomed up as extraordinary.

Bryce stood, shook his head, determined to settle his thoughts, to clear the way for Kendra's assignment. He paced the five steps from one end of his cell to the other, again and again, until he finally sat, slumped with his eyes clamped shut and focused his thoughts on the day Skyler died.

He needed to stop beating himself up over the things he hadn't done. No precaution he might have taken would have saved Skyler. Not if the medical examiner was right and he died because of a drug overdose. The only thing he might have done differently was to keep a closer watch on Skyler's bottle. Who had access to that bottle? He tried to remember if there was any fluid in the bottle when he took it down from the overhead cabinet and poured in the apple juice.

When Bryce picked up a pencil and began to write out events, he hoped the words would gush out in a trance-like unconscious torrent, but it didn't happen that way. They came slowly, and again and again, his thoughts trailed off from the assignment in front of him.

If there was anything in the bottle, Bryce hadn't noticed. But there must have been. Somehow that drug got into Skyler's bottle, and there was one thing Bryce was certain of—he didn't put it there.

Henry had delivered the bottle to Skyler. Could he have tampered with it before giving it to Skyler? Henry was nothing but a big kid himself. But maybe someone else instructed him. Reggie was in the bedroom reading to Scott. Could he stoop so low as to poison a toddler—a child he claimed was a bastard? Bryce made a note on his pad. And how about Scott? When Dana called and talked to him, she asked that he take care of Skyler and make sure he drank his apple juice. But Scott wouldn't have access to drugs. Again, Bryce wrote it down.

Could Dana have tampered with the bottle, knowing he wouldn't notice? Was she so enamored with Reggie that she would kill her own child to be with him again? And leave Bryce to take the blame? Dana was an immature kid, but he couldn't imagine her doing something that horrific. But Reggie? That man was a totally different story and capable of anything. Bryce jotted down his suspicions.

One memory arrived and before he could write it all out, another followed, until there was a dense accumulation of details inside his head.

When a guard shoved a set of dingy sheets and a dinner tray through the pie hole in the door, Bryce didn't bother to pick either of them up. He wasn't hungry. And he wasn't in the mood to make his bed.

For the remainder of the evening, one false start after another plagued Bryce. When he finally gave up and stumbled across the room to pick up the sheets and make his bunk, the concrete floor was strewn with mounds of crumpled yellow paper.

163

After breakfast the following morning, Bryce gathered up his efforts, tossed them into the garbage can next to the toilet, and started over again. But in spite of his attempts to accommodate his attorney's request, when, an hour before the arraignment, one of the guards escorted Kendra to his cell, Bryce handed her a single sheet of paper with the words: *Forget it. I'm guilty. I was the responsible adult and if I'd kept better watch over him, Skyler Sterling would still be living. And that's the only truth, the only words, the only details that really matter.*

He gave her the sheet of paper.

She read it, wadded it up, threw it back at him, then took him by the shoulders. "Listen to me, Bryce. I know what's happening here. My father always said guilt hangs on to no one the way it does the innocent. I know how shocked you must be. If you'd committed a crime and were caught, you wouldn't be surprised. But when you know you didn't poison Skyler, when you would never have thought of doing something so terrible, it starts to eat you alive. You think no one believes anything you say. It erodes away at you until you begin to wonder if you should stop believing in yourself."

Bryce remained silent. She'd nailed it. That was exactly how he felt.

After a few seconds, Kendra squatted beside his bunk, her face pushed so close to his that the tips of their noses nearly touched. "I believe with all my heart you are innocent. I'm fighting for justice for you, Bryce. Not for myself. I've been up half the night, spending every spare minute I can extract from my life for you. I need to know you're going to fight as hard as I am on this case. Or I'm going to walk away. Do you hear me?" She waited for his answer.

"I hear you," he finally said. "But do you really think I have any hope of beating this?"

"Not if you give up. It's way too early to make any prediction as to how this will go. I have no idea what kind of evidence the state has against you. But from my education, what I've learned from my father, and my own experience with the DA's office, they don't arrest someone unless they have a pretty good case—or at least believe they do."

"No matter what anyone thinks. I didn't put drugs in Skyler's baby bottle."

She seized his hand and squeezed. "I know. First-degree murder is unlawfully taking the life of another with malice aforethought. Think about that for a minute. Your actions, trying to reach the phone for help, to get Skyler to breathe again, in no way contributed to his death. If you deliberately gave him that drug, if you wanted him to die, why would you have tried so hard to save him?" The attorney's voice softened a little. "The prosecution will make it sound like you felt remorse after the fact."

"If that were the case," Bryce said. "And I knew I'd poisoned him, I would have tried to induce vomiting."

"Exactly. That would have been the logical and intelligent thing to do. But here's the truth as I see it. You've got no time to wallow in your passive self-pity. We need to find out who put that Haloperidol in Skyler's bottle. This is the rest of your life we're talking about here, Bryce. Possibly your death."

He stood.

Kendra took his shoulders and held firm as they faced each other, her breath raking across Bryce's neck. "And if you're not willing to fight for your life, why should I?"

"I'll fight. I'll give it everything I have."

She grinned, a smile that lit her blue eyes. "Now you're talking."

CHAPTER TWENTY

As the sun rose, golden, pink, and a little hazy over the Siskiyou Mountains, Radhauser headed up the gravel drive toward their barn. There was a bounce in his steps. Gracie had come home from the hospital yesterday. And, so far, the prognosis looked good.

It was a brisk autumn morning, the kind that made him want to leap into the air and celebrate his life. He reached down, picked up a small rock, and heaved it high into the sky over one of the big-leaf maple trees that lined their driveway. A few seconds passed before he heard it rustle through the tree top and come back to earth.

Fallen leaves covered the ground in shades of rust, yellow and orange. A brown oak leaf clung to the top of one of his black rubber boots as he slid open the double barn doors and greeted their horses. Though he often helped Gracie in the barn on his days off, the morning feedings had always been her job and he wondered if the horses missed her. He reached into the first stall and stroked Mercedes' neck. She nipped at his hand. "I know. You expected someone prettier, but you're going to have to put up with me a while longer."

Radhauser would probably never think of himself as a genuine rancher. He was a detective first and foremost. But he loved starting the day in the barn with its smells of sawdust, alfalfa, leather, and sweaty horse blankets. Just as Gracie had taught him, he poured two cups of grain topped off with a little sweet feed and molasses into their feeders, ran fresh water in their troughs and forked a two-inch flake of alfalfa into each stall.

After Bryce's arraignment, he planned to return and release the horses into the back pasture so he could muck out the stalls. Gracie was fussy about her barn. And taking good care of it for her was his job while she recovered from the mastectomy. Maybe that was the secret to love. Sometimes it carries you and other times it's your turn to carry it.

Gracie's mother, Cynthia, felt guilty about not being with her daughter during surgery. But Gracie said she needed childcare for Lizzie more than her mom's presence at the hospital. Yesterday morning, Nana Cynthia moved into the guest room to help take care of Gracie and Lizzie. Radhauser was grateful. Lizzie adored her nana and he didn't know how they'd manage right now without her.

After Bryce's arrest, Murphy had eased up and Radhauser was able to take some time off to be with Gracie, but he also wanted to help Kendra Palmer free Bryce. Having Cynthia here would enable him to offer more support.

When he returned to the house, Lizzie was dressed in her favorite cowgirl outfit—a denim skirt with fringe, and a red and white checked blouse with tiny white buttons. She had on her red cowgirl boots and her nana had pulled her hair into two ponytails, each one tied with a red ribbon.

He patted her on the head. "You look very pretty this morning, Lizzie. Your nana is an excellent hairdresser."

She grinned up at him, her baby teeth stained slightly blue from the berries in her oatmeal.

Cynthia was making a breakfast tray for Gracie. "Are you hungry? I've made enough for both of you." She nodded toward a plate heaped with scrambled eggs and thick slices of bacon. A smaller plate held a stack of toast. And if that wasn't enough, she included a salad bowl of fresh fruit. Enough food for a family of five. "I thought you might like to have breakfast together."

He glanced at his watch, then kissed her on the cheek. It was only seven. Bryce's arraignment wasn't until nine. "You're amazing. If I wasn't already married to your daughter, I'd be on my knees proposing."

Lizzie threw her head back and laughed. "You can't marry Nana, Daddy. Besides, I'm gonna marry you when I grow up."

Feeling another rush of happiness, he yanked on one of her ponytails. "That's right, Lizzie, girl, but a man can't have too many wives."

She batted his hand away from her hair. "Mommy would be mad if you had another wife." Her brow furrowed as she thought for a moment, then added, "Unless it was me."

Cynthia slapped him on the shoulder. "And I'd be mad, too. It's taken me years to get used to having a detective for a son-in-law." She handed him the breakfast tray.

When he carried it into the bedroom, Gracie was propped up in their king-sized bed, her dark hair fanned out against the stack of pillows behind her back. Her pajama top was unbuttoned, exposing the bandages around her chest and a drainage tube that stuck out from the gauze just under her right armpit. It had a bulb on the end to help suction out excess fluid.

"How's my beautiful wife this morning?"

Her eyes got glassy and she gave him a closed-mouth smile that didn't reach them. "I hurt. Feels like an elephant is sitting on my chest."

"Do you want me to drain off the fluid?"

She nodded toward a small glass measuring cup on her bedside table half filled with a murky liquid. "I already did."

He set her breakfast tray on her lap while he carried the cup into the bathroom, recorded the quantity of fluid on a chart the surgeon provided, and poured the opaque and strong-smelling fluid into the toilet and flushed. After rinsing out the cup, he hurried back to his wife.

"I can get that prescription filled McCarthy gave you for pain pills."

She shook her head, fiddled with the hem of her pajama top. A single tear rolled down her cheek. "No. They're bad for the baby."

The doctor had warned him she might be depressed after the surgery, might think losing her breast had made her less of a woman—and would make her less of a mother to their new baby.

Radhauser set the tray on the bed and carefully put his arms around her. "The horses miss you. Mercedes was so unhappy she nipped at me when I tried to rub her neck."

Gracie swallowed and took a deep breath, as if trying to get herself through the pain and back to composure. Her breath smelled like toothpaste. "That's just her way of saying 'hurry up, I'm hungry'."

He reached down and gently rubbed her swollen belly. "How's Jonathan Lucas Radhauser this morning?"

She smiled for real this time. "Happy to be home. And hungry."

He tucked a napkin around her neck. "Looks like your mother is intent on fattening up all three of us."

They ate for a few minutes in silence.

Gracie's brush with cancer had given him a new awareness of what she meant to him. It seemed as if everything in his life was so different now. And so much more than he expected it to be again after the loss of Laura and Lucas. Sometimes, like now, he didn't recognize his own life—like he awakened to find himself seven feet tall and wealthy beyond all measure. Now, he was the one who swallowed.

"How's your case going?" Gracie asked. It was her attempt to take the focus off herself and he went along with it.

"I'm worried. I've never investigated a murder when I was so sure the man I arrested was innocent."

"Do you have any other suspects?"

"No one new. I'm still looking at the mother, Dana Sterling, and her ex-husband, Reggie Sterling. And Henry Evans, he's the son of the man who owns the Lasso." Kendra had called earlier to report that Henry had taken the bottle of apple juice into the bedroom for Skyler, while Reggie read to Scott. Bryce claimed Henry liked to play with the boys and visited them often. He enjoyed pretending he was their daddy—and loved to deliver the nighttime bottle to Skyler.

"Have you talked to him?" Gracie asked.

"Once. But he wasn't much help. Henry suffered a traumatic brain injury and has the mind of a seven-year-old. The chances are pretty slim he'd have access to a drug like Haloperidol. And he really liked Skyler. I can't imagine a motive. But I now know Reggie was in the bedroom with him. Maybe Henry saw something."

"Lizzie's only four," Gracie said. "But she can sure tell you what she saw."

Time to re-interview Henry Evans.

When she squeezed his hand, her fingers were icy. "I know you feel terrible. I wish Murphy hadn't pushed you so hard to make an arrest."

"As far as he's concerned, our job is over, except for helping the prosecution convict." He shrugged. "Boss doesn't know it, but I'm working with Bryce's attorney." He told her about Kendra Palmer, how young and relatively inexperienced she was. How much he hoped she inherited some of her father's legal instincts. "I'm nervous about it. But I keep telling myself I have to trust that somehow if I keep gathering and examining it, the evidence will eventually lead me to the truth."

* * *

A confusion of flashbulbs and reporters with tape recorders and video television cameras greeted Radhauser as he walked up the Jackson County Courthouse steps for Bryce's arraignment. He hurried past them, opened the door into the courthouse and passed through security, then up the stairs to courtroom 3-B. When he opened the door, the room was packed with reporters and cameras. A huge mirror, with a gold-leaf frame, hung on the west wall of the courthouse. Radhauser looked into his own eyes and made a promise. *You will get Bryce out of prison.* And while it was in violation of his sacred rule: don't get personally involved with a suspect, he never meant any statement more.

Court wasn't due to start for another fifteen minutes, but Kendra was already seated at the defense table. He wanted a moment to talk with her before the DA arrived and became suspicious. He touched her shoulder. She turned to face him, wearing a pair of dark-rimmed glasses he suspected she didn't need. They gave her a studious, slightly older and more professorial look.

"Judge Shapiro is going to deal with the Bryce case first thing because he fears we're going to have a media circus," she said. "They brought him over from the jail about a half hour ago. He's in a holding cell. There are already two television cameras in here and a half dozen newspaper reporters. Not to mention the ones on the courthouse steps."

Radhauser took a seat behind her and leaned forward. "How is he doing?"

"Not good. Spectators and reporters were waiting in the parking lot by the prisoner entrance. When he got out of the county van, they shouted things like 'baby killer' and threw plastic rattles and stuffed toys at him. The police finally broke them up. Sometimes I think Bryce has given up. He believes Skyler's death is his fault since he was the adult in charge. And to make matters worse, we got Marshall's statutory notice informing us the state is seeking the death penalty."

"Give him an attitude adjustment. We need him pissed off at the injustice and ready to fight for himself."

"Believe me, I've tried. Something isn't right. I want him to see a forensic psychiatrist. I suspect there's more to his hearing loss than he's telling us. He strikes me as a man who suffered a lot of abuse and neglect in his childhood."

"Fine," Radhauser said. "Poor Bryce. We might be able to make the jury feel sorry for him, but not sorry enough to forgive a kid murder."

"Maybe it's got nothing to do with the case," she said. "But there is that 9-1-1 call. The prosecution is going to have a field day with the way he kept referring to Skyler as 'she'. They'll claim he meant Dana—that she's the one he wanted dead, and killing Skyler was his way to get even with her for leaving. But all my instincts tell me there's another reason for his confusion. And I plan to find it."

Radhauser was impressed by her conviction, but suspected the underfunded Public Defender's Office wouldn't spring for the fee. "Women's intuition, huh? Is your office prepared to pay for the psychiatrist?"

"If they aren't, I will."

He had no doubt the daughter of Kendrick Huntington Palmer, III could afford to pay the psychiatrist, but why would she want to? He thought about that for a few seconds. This was her first case. And she was determined to get justice for Bryce. Was it to impress her famous father? Or was it something else? Something like her sharing his belief that her client was, indeed, innocent.

While he examined her motives, he took a look at his own. In general, once the DA charged someone, the police stopped looking for another suspect and worked with the prosecution as a conviction machine. And they wouldn't stop until they got either a guilty verdict or a plea.

Why was he helping the defense? As the investigating officer, he would be called as a witness for the prosecution. Radhauser might even lose his job if Murphy knew his detective thought Bryce was innocent. But Radhauser believed in justice more than he believed in keeping his job. And that little voice inside his head said justice would not be served by convicting Caleb Bryce of a murder he didn't commit.

But why was he so certain Bryce didn't kill Skyler? It was a rare suspect who didn't claim he was innocent regardless of the evidence against him. There was something gentle and decent about Bryce. What was the old saying? *Still waters run deep.* Either he was the best con man in the business, or innocent. Radhauser would put his money on the latter.

A reporter stuck a microphone in Kendra's face. "Is this your first case, Ms. Palmer? Does your father plan to help you win?"

At first Kendra looked away and said nothing, but then she raised her shoulders, took off her glasses and faced the reporter head on. "I'm a Harvard-educated attorney. I passed the bar and clerked for a year. I don't need my father or anyone else to hold my hand. I will represent my client to the best of my ability," she said, her cheeks reddening. "I'm convinced he's innocent and my responsibility is to prove to the jury that I'm right. Now get out of my face. I've got a job to do."

The reporter backed away.

Radhauser couldn't restrain his smile. She looked young

enough to be carded in bars, but Kendra Palmer was tougher than she appeared. Still, he wished for a way to keep the reporters and cameramen away from the arraignment.

Judge Steven Shapiro, a devout Christian, was usually at his most intractable when there were cameras in his courtroom. He believed in the Ten Commandments and thought the public wanted judges who were tough on criminals, especially murderers. Add the fact that the victim was a toddler, and there were people ready to lynch Bryce on the plaza—you had a formula for chaos. When the media was present in the courtroom, Shapiro made it a point to live up to his hard-earned reputation.

Four uniformed Jackson County sheriff's deputies flanked the corners of the courtroom. The gallery was nearly full. Many of the occupants were other criminal defendants, charged with lesser crimes, whose arraignments would follow Bryce's.

The door to Judge Shapiro's chambers opened, and he seemed to float through it. His salt-and-pepper hair was freshly cut, not one strand out of place—as if he used hairspray. He was about fifty, with strong, chiseled features, and looked almost otherworldly, his black robes flowing behind him. Radhauser supposed Judge Shapiro was handsome. Based on all the mirrors in his chambers, the judge certainly thought he was.

The bailiff stood and faced the crowd. "All rise," he commanded. "The criminal court for Jackson County is now in session, the Honorable Steven J. Shapiro presiding. Please come to order."

Judge Shapiro climbed the steps to his bench and took his place in the high-backed leather throne. He was a slender man and the robe hung loosely over his shoulders.

Everyone sat.

"Good morning," Judge Shapiro said.

Nearly the entire courtroom responded. Many of them nodded their heads like a row of bobble-head cats in the back of a 1955 Chevy Bel Air.

"The first case we are going to address this morning is the state of Oregon versus Caleb R. Bryce." Judge Shapiro turned to the prosecution. "And I see that Assistant DA, Andrew Marshall, will be prosecuting the case."

Marshall's face flushed a little and he looked down at his shoes.

Judge Shapiro turned to Kendra. "And who might you be, Ms. Kendrick Huntington Palmer IV?" Judge Shapiro raised his eyebrows, as if recognizing the famous name. But to his credit, he didn't comment.

"Please call me Kendra," she said. "I've recently joined the Public Defender's office. I'll be representing Mr. Bryce."

Shapiro turned toward the deputy closest to the door. "Bring in the defendant."

The deputy disappeared for a moment, then returned with Bryce beside him.

The shackles on Bryce's ankles forced him to shuffle with each step. Every camera was pointed toward him. It was so silent in the courtroom the clanking sound of the chains on Bryce's waist and wrists as he moved toward the defense table were audible.

Radhauser thought it was overkill, forcing Bryce, beaten almost beyond recognition, to wear shackles and a waist chain. So much for the presumption of innocence. Bryce had never been arrested before, never had a speeding or parking ticket. But defendants accused of murdering children were shown no mercy.

He looked scared, battered and bruised, as if beaten half to death. The gash above his eyebrow was still covered in gauze.

Kendra stood.

Bryce took his place beside her.

The judge studied the charges, then handed them to the bailiff. "Give this to Ms. Palmer. And let the record show the defendant's counsel has been provided a copy."

"Caleb Bryce, you've been charged with one count of child abuse of the four-year-old child, Scott Sterling. And murder in the first degree for the October twelfth death of nineteen-month-old Skyler Sterling in Jackson County, city of Ashland. How do you plead?"

Bryce lifted his battered face, glanced at Kendra Palmer, then stared straight into Shapiro's eyes and declared, in a loud and muddled voice, but as if he really believed it, "Not guilty to both charges, Your Honor."

The judge looked at Kendra. "What about scheduling?"

An advantage of a small town like Ashland was there weren't many murder trials. That meant an inmate's right to an expedient trial was more likely to be accommodated.

"My defendant would like a speedy trial," she said. "And we request bail be set at $25,000."

Shapiro gave her a look that could have melted wax. "In a capital murder case involving a nineteen-month-old? You must be dreaming, Ms. Palmer."

"My client does not have the financial means to post any larger bond. He maintains his innocence and wants a trial as soon as possible. I believe I can be ready in four weeks."

Marshall stood up. "There's no way the state could be ready in less than three months."

"If our good Lord, as is stated in Genesis, created the heavens and the earth in less than one week, I think you should be able to get ready for a pretty standard trial in four times that amount, Mr. Marshall."

Shapiro turned back to Kendra. "How long do you anticipate the trial will last?"

"A week. Maybe a little more."

The judge turned the pages of his calendar. "I have an opening November fifteenth. That's just a little less than four weeks from now, Mr. Marshall, and I expect you to be ready."

"Mr. Bryce," the judge said. "When you're brought into my courtroom on November fifteenth, I personally guarantee you a fair trial. It will be your responsibility to wear civilian clothing. The jury will not see you restrained in any fashion as long as you behave yourself. Do you understand?"

"Yes," Bryce said. "Thank you, sir."

The bailiff took him by the arm and led him toward the door. Bryce's face was a deep red, as if hearing his name and the word murder in the same sentence had set him on fire.

CHAPTER TWENTY-ONE

It was around noon when Radhauser arrived at the Lazy Lasso. The restaurant was crowded. He waited on the lobby side of the swinging oak bar doors until the crowd thinned out, then passed through them and stood in front of the hostess podium until the couple ahead of him was seated. As usual the place smelled fabulous. Nothing like the sizzle sound of prime meat over an open grill to make a man's mouth water. How long had it been since he and Gracie sat down to a normal dinner? Once she felt up to it, he planned to bring her here for a steak.

Angela smiled. "Detective Radhauser. Dana's not here yet. She's got the three to eleven shift today."

"I'm here to see Henry Evans."

A look of concern swept over her face. Her smile faded. "Wait a minute, I'll call Bear."

"I don't want to talk to him. It's Henry I need to see."

Across the restaurant, Henry was sitting alone at a table by the window, drinking a soda and eating a hamburger and fries.

"Bear said I should call. He doesn't want you to talk to Henry again unless he is there, too." Angela picked up the phone.

Radhauser darted over to Henry's booth and slid onto the bench across from him. "Hi, Henry, do you remember me?"

"Sure," he said, his mouth filled with French fries. He wore a lightweight gray hoodie with elastic at the wrists. "You're the policeman that talked to me at the place where Skyler was in the pretty white box. My dad says it's a coffin. I never saw a coffin before."

"Yes," Radhauser said. "You're right. I was there. But let's talk about the time you went over to Mr. Bryce's house with Reggie."

"I do that a lot. We go there before Reggie takes me to the car lot to wash the cars."

"I want to know about the last time. You gave Skyler his bottle of apple juice that night. Am I right?"

Henry bobbed his head up and down three times. "I like to pretend I'm the daddy and Skyler and Scotty are my boys."

"That sounds like a fun game. Did you give him his apple juice on other nights?"

"Sure. Mr. Bryce always lets me."

"Did you watch Mr. Bryce make the bottle for Skyler?"

Again, he nodded three times. "In the kitchen."

Bear and Henry lived in a modular home in a wooded area about one hundred yards behind the restaurant. Radhauser didn't have much time. "What did he put inside the bottle?"

"He poured in a little jar of baby apple juice, and then he put water from the spigot, and then he put the top on and shook it up real good." Henry raised his right hand and made a shaking motion. A small dab of ketchup flew off his finger and landed on the table in front of Radhauser. He wiped it up with his napkin.

"Did he put anything else in the bottle?"

"Nope."

"Where did Mr. Bryce go after he made the bottle?"

"He went back in the living room to watch TV."

"And you took the bottle into Skyler's room?"

Another three nods. "It's Scotty's room, too. They share."

"Was Reggie there?"

"Yep."

At that instant, Bear Evans stormed through the swinging doors and crossed the restaurant in record time, his long, thick arms sawing the air like some irate windup doll. "What's going on here?"

"I'm asking Henry a few questions about the night Skyler Sterling died."

"Not without me, you aren't."

"He's eighteen. It's not against the law for me to talk with him without a parent present. And I can also take him down to the police station for questioning."

Bear slapped his hand on the table, causing Henry's soda to spill over and puddle under his glass. "My son had nothing to do with that Sterling mess."

Henry cleaned the soda up with his napkin, then tucked his hands into his lap.

Radhauser could tell by the movement of Henry's arms and the slight snapping sound that he nervously stretched and released the elastic on one of his sleeves.

Bear's voice was raw with anger. "You're exploiting my son, Detective Radhauser. You know as well as I do, it's advisable for someone with Henry's issues to have a parent, guardian or legal counsel with him when being questioned by a fucking police officer."

Henry shuddered.

Bear slid into the booth next to him and put his arm around the boy's shoulders. "I'm sorry, Henry. That wasn't a nice word."

"It's okay, Dad. He's a nice policeman."

"He's a stranger, son. Remember what I told you about talking to strangers."

Henry looked down at his lap. "Stranger danger."

Outside the window, a bird began to sing. Henry scooted over and pushed his hands and nose against the glass. "Listen. It's a sparrow." He searched for the bird, but unable to find it, turned back to his dad.

A moment later, he leaned across the table as if he were about to tell Radhauser a secret. "Bird songs speak to our souls. Because words are too little."

Radhauser couldn't help but smile. Even with his limitations, or maybe because of them, Henry was a charming boy. As gentle as they come. Bryce told him Bear raised Henry by himself. The man did a great job.

"Very good, Henry," Radhauser said. "You sound like a bird expert and a philosopher all rolled into one."

Henry gave Radhauser a ketchup-mouth grin. "What's a philosopher?"

"A wise person."

Bear's face softened. No doubt this man loved his son. "What do you say when someone gives you a compliment, Henry?"

"Thank you, Mr. Policeman."

Bear beamed. "He likes birds, so I taught him to identify the more common ones by their songs."

"I only have a couple more questions, Mr. Evans. And you're more than welcome to be present. Henry was one of the last people to see Skyler alive, and he was the one who gave Skyler his bottle of apple juice." Radhauser was careful not to mention the drug, for fear Bear would silence Henry.

"You can't think Henry—"

"I don't," Radhauser said. "But Henry wasn't the only one in Skyler's room that night."

A look of understanding passed over Bear's face. "Go ahead. But don't expect me to stay quiet if I don't like what you're asking my boy."

Radhauser waited until Henry looked at him. "You already told me Reggie was in the room. Did he say or do anything to Skyler?"

Bear looked skeptical, but kept quiet.

"Skyler screamed. He screams a lot, but then he laughs. Reggie hates it. Me and Mr. Bryce think it's cute. Reggie put his hand over Skyler's mouth like this." Henry slapped his right hand over his mouth and held it there. "He said 'shut up you little...' And then he said a not very nice word."

Bastard. The unspoken word echoed in Radhauser's mind. He waited to see if Henry had anything else to add.

"He always says mean things to Skyler." Henry's face crumpled up, and for a moment Radhauser thought he was going to cry. "It makes me sad."

Bear tightened his grip on Henry's shoulders.

Radhauser waited a few seconds for Henry to collect himself before asking his next question. "Did you see Reggie put anything in Skyler's bottle?"

"Mr. Bryce already put apple juice and water in it."

"Yes, I know, but did you see Reggie open the bottle and put anything else inside?"

He shrugged. "After I gave Skyler the bottle and he stopped screaming, Scotty and me played on the floor with his Matchbox cars."

"What was Reggie doing?"

Again, Henry shrugged. "I don't know. I didn't look."

"Thank you for your time," Radhauser said to both of them, then turned to Bear. "My wife is pregnant with a boy. I hope my son grows up to be as good-hearted as your Henry, Mr. Evans."

A smile blew wide across Bear's face. "Call me Bear. Everyone else does."

Radhauser had no doubt that Henry had told the truth as best he could. The boy didn't have an ounce of duplicity in him. He'd confirmed Bryce's story about the apple juice and his returning to the living room. And he shed some more light on Reggie's character and feelings for Skyler. At least Radhauser knew Reggie had every opportunity to taint that baby bottle.

Now, all he had to do was prove it.

* * *

"Lookie here, Shame. You done made me a famous man." Poncho slipped the two-day-old tabloid under the door to Bryce's cell on his way to the dining hall.
PRISONER TAKES JUSTICE INTO HIS OWN HANDS
by: Wally Hartmueller

Echoing public opinion, a prisoner identified only as Poncho, convicted a fellow inmate and administered his own sentence yesterday when he severely beat Caleb R. Bryce, thirty-five, charged with one count of child abuse of four-year- old Scott Sterling and with first-degree murder in the death of nineteen-month-old Skyler Sterling. Jail authorities discovered Bryce, unconscious and bleeding, on the floor of the cell he shared with Poncho.
When asked to comment on what he did, Poncho said, "Even us convicts got some standards. And baby killers don't measure up."
Prison authorities are still looking into the matter.

* * *

Just as Kendra warned, publicity became a major issue in Bryce's case. The South Carolina incident where a mother rolled a car into the lake, her two small children strapped into the back seat, had horrified and enraged the entire country. Ashland was no exception.

Local newspaper reporters and television broadcasters detailed elaborate conjectures as to how and why Skyler Sterling died. One news anchor announced, "Police Chief Murphy says motive is jealousy over girlfriend's relationships with other men, particularly her ex-husband, Reggie Sterling."

Associated Press picked up the story. Bryce had no idea where that trumped-up motive came from, but the press, determined to convict, did everything in their power to guarantee nothing short of death by lethal injection.

Public interest was further fed by child abuse stories of other children. On an order by Judge Shapiro, who would preside over the trial, the public and the press were not admitted to the pretrial hearing.

Before the preliminary, picketers, mostly women, paced the sidewalks outside the courthouse, thrusting handmade signs into the air—*STOP JEALOUS BOYFRIENDS FROM ABUSING AND KILLING OUR CHILDREN.*

When they spotted Bryce, a group gathered around him and hissed, "Baby killer... slime... I hope you rot in hell," as he stumbled, shackled and handcuffed, through the prisoner's entrance and up the stairwell to the courthouse.

On Thursday, October twenty-eighth, black paper, taped from the inside, covered the small glass windows on the courtroom doors. Another window, left open for ventilation, was guarded by a deputy who shook his head at the few reporters below, then closed the blinds.

Everything considered, Kendra indicated she was pleased with the assignment of Judge Shapiro and told Bryce the judge had a reputation for fairness, keen legal insights, and a great sense of humor.

Bryce stood before the bench, his face faintly discolored, his eyes puffy and the line of stitches still visible above his right eye. He was cleanly shaved and dressed in baggy blue prison pants and shirt. As he confronted the judge, a part of him still believed this was all a huge mistake, a bad dream from which he would eventually awaken.

Judge Shapiro leaned forward in his chair and let his gaze settle on Bryce's face. "How are you feeling, Mr. Bryce?"

"Much better, Your Honor."

"I want you to know I spoke with the warden at county jail. Poncho will be punished for what he did to you. I also apologize for the hecklers outside the courthouse. Unfortunately, there isn't much we can do about them. I've requested more police protection for you as you enter and leave the court."

"I appreciate the concern, Your Honor." Bryce wasn't sure if punishing Poncho would make his life better or worse.

His preliminary hearing lasted less than three hours. At the close, Judge Shapiro commented. "All the state has to do at a preliminary hearing is produce probable cause to believe a crime was committed. And the person in custody had the opportunity and means by which to commit that crime."

To no one's surprise, except Bryce, the judge believed this had been done. "But the defendant, Caleb Bryce," Judge Shapiro added, "is innocent until such time as the state of Oregon can prove, without a reasonable doubt, that he indeed abused Scott Sterling and murdered Skyler Sterling."

Kendra's motion for a temporary restraining order against the Medford, Talent, and Ashland newspapers to block out further coverage until after the trial was denied. However, Judge Shapiro did approve an injunction that prohibited police and sheriff's officers, the District Attorney and his deputies, from any further discussion of the Bryce case with the news media.

"One more thing." Judge Shapiro turned to Bryce and smiled, the lines on either side of his mouth deepening. "Try to stay out of the ring. From the looks of that face, Joe Frazier wasn't one of your childhood role models."

"Yes, sir," Bryce said, grateful for a likeable and seemingly fair judge.

Later that same evening, Bryce slumped over the table in his cell, a tray of barely-touched fried chicken, soggy string beans, and instant mashed potatoes, beside him. Having heard Assistant District Attorney Andrew Marshall's spiel about the medical examiner's report, he thought about what it would be like to be poisoned.

He imagined Skyler's life trickling out of him like air leaking from a balloon. Caleb had studied enough anatomy to know a severed hepatic vein would cause a lot of blood to pool inside his tiny body. A red wave that heaved up and toppled the sleeping baby toward death, even without the added drug.

For an instant, he felt it again, that need to disappear the way he had so many years ago after he and Valerie divorced. And with that need came a realization of how he'd started his lifelong pattern of isolation and silence. Once he opened the door to them, they barged in and almost took over his life. He couldn't—no, he wouldn't, let that happen again.

A slow and certain understanding dawned for Bryce.

He paced his cell for another hour.

Bryce didn't know where the anger came from, but when it rippled inside his chest and rose into his throat, he stifled the urge to scream, kicked the concrete wall instead, then grimaced in pain.

It wasn't so much the isolation of prison that ate away at him. He had always lived inside his mind or the cover of a book. It was the kind of child, and later the kind of man he became—a river of silence.

But much more than loneliness, it was the terrible sameness of prison, the dull steel world of concrete and fluorescent lights that devoured him. He mourned for the small things—sunlight releasing the night from its shadows, walking under a black sky heavy with stars, the pungent smell of roses after rain, iridescent drops beaded on spider webs crisscrossing the delicate branches of the Japanese maples in Lithia Park.

Pausing in front of the trash can, Bryce stared at the discarded, crinkled newspaper. In the photo, he walked through the doors into the courthouse for his preliminary hearing. His first inclination was to laugh at the haggard and battered face staring up at him.

The humiliation of the newspaper article critical of his hospital volunteer work ripped at him. Joselyn Kennedy, the program director, befriended Bryce at a time when he desperately needed it. And the implication that she be held accountable, reproached somehow, for allowing a person like him, an accused child abuser and killer, to touch the newborn babies made him angrier than hell.

Something had to change, and he couldn't depend on anyone except himself to make that change happen.

CHAPTER TWENTY-TWO

The guard thrust open Bryce's door and Kendra stepped inside. He blinked, startled and confused for a second. With the sleeves of his shirt pushed up over his elbows, he was buried in yellow sheets of paper, his hairy forearms resting over them like giant paperweights.

He'd met with Sandra Shortbridge, the forensic psychiatrist Kendra sent, three times, and each time painful memories were unleashed. Memories he hadn't thought about in years. And despite the psychiatrist's assurance it was a good thing, Bryce wasn't so sure.

The lawyer dropped her briefcase on the table and stood beside Bryce, her hands woven together in front of her. "At least we know what we're up against. We've got our work cut out for us, Bryce, there's no doubt about that, but I still believe we can beat this thing."

When Bryce stood, stepped over to his bunk, and retrieved the most recent newspaper article he found in his cell, Kendra unlaced her thin fingers and separated pale hands that always appeared to be so clean.

"I want you to throw this where it belongs."

She grabbed the paper from Bryce, glanced at the headline, *ACCUSED CHILD MURDERER WORKED AS VOLUNTEER IN HOSPITAL NURSERY*, crumpled the page, and tossed it into the small rubber trash can next to the toilet.

"The prosecution wants the jury to hear what Scott has to say in person. I argued for videotaping the testimony, but Judge Shapiro interviewed Scott in his chambers. He thinks the boy knows truth from lie and is more than capable of telling the jury what he saw. And his mother has no objections."

"What about me? I have an objection. He's just a little kid."

"Your objection doesn't count," she said. "They'll be calling Scott to the stand. We know that for sure now."

"Won't that be risky? Scott tends to lie when he knows he's done something wrong."

"Cross-examining a small child can be dangerous, and the truth is we'll have to be very careful not to antagonize the jury." Kendra wiped her forehead with the back of her hand, then sat at the table. "We can make this work for us, Bryce, everything inside tells me that. But you have to help me know that little boy inside and out, what pushes his buttons, where he's insecure, how he really felt about his little brother. His mother. His father. And most of all, you."

"Why?"

"Lawyers should never ask a question when they don't know what the answer will be. I have to plan my questions by predicting his responses." She fumbled with the latch on her briefcase, then added, "That boy's testimony can make or break our case."

"I'll do the best I can," Bryce said, and meant it. He was tired of being a victim. And it was going to stop. Now.

He took the concrete chair, and Kendra sat on the bunk across from him. "But I still don't get how anyone could think I had malice toward Skyler and planned his murder."

"The legal concept of malice doesn't incorporate ill-will, hatred, or even carrying a grudge against the victim," Kendra said. "For example, a mother who kills her illegitimate child to hide her shame may have no ill feelings against the child. She may, in fact, love him or her. Or a wife who kills her husband to avoid his suffering from a hopeless disease."

"That's considered murder with malice? If you ask me, the law sucks."

Kendra laughed. "I know, but even cases as extreme as those fill every legal requirement of malice aforethought. There were murder convictions when defendants were shown to possess a man-endangering state of mind, even if that state of mind was unrelated to the victim."

"You think Marshall will try to show I was so angry with Dana that the thought of killing Skyler to get even with her entered my mind. And I translated that thought into action. Took advantage of the situation and deliberately killed Skyler."

Kendra nodded. "It's not an easy concept to grasp, but that's precisely what he'll attempt to prove."

"God." Bryce swallowed the lump that crept up his throat. "That's ridiculous, but how will we show he's wrong?"

"That's my job," Kendra assured him. "Yours, for the moment anyway, is to tell me about Scott Sterling."

Occasionally consulting his yellow pad of notes, Bryce talked nonstop for more than an hour. He answered every question Kendra asked, always careful to tell nothing but the truth. But as he listened to himself, heard one truth follow another, the body of evidence against him seemed to accumulate. Until, truth by truth, it assumed the shape of an incriminating and monstrous lie.

* * *

"Keep going over this, Bryce. I think we're on to something." Kendra needed to talk with her client about the 9-1-1 tape, but wasn't sure how to approach it. She decided to plunge forward. "Before I go, I need to know about Valerie and your daughter."

"I ca…ca…can't," he said. "I already talked with Sandra about them. Please don't make me go through it again."

"You have to. I know it's a cliché, but the rest of your life could depend on it."

As the memories of his infant daughter crowded inside his head, Bryce attempted to push them away. But they remained, more persistent than usual, fluttering around inside him like tiny, pure white birds.

And he wondered how many people in the world lived whole and happy lives because the one chain of events that could press them over the edge never occurred.

"I met Valerie Simmons at the University of Utah. During our junior year, she got pregnant."

"All by herself?" Kendra asked.

Bryce laughed. "No, I had something to do with it. Her family was Mormon."

"So, you dropped out of college and got married."

"Yes. It was hard to leave my roommate to fend for himself, but it was the right thing to do." He explained that Noah Morgan was a blind boy he'd been paired up with after Child Services took him away from his mother and put him into foster care. After a couple stints in various foster homes, they placed Bryce in the Lake Institute for the Deaf and Blind. "I became Noah's eyes. And he was my ears. We were inseparable. It was like *together we were a whole boy.*"

Together we were a whole boy. Funny how a single phrase could bring back a memory Bryce thought long buried.

He'd been ten years old and written a letter to his mother in the care of the Robertson Inn where she worked for years. The Institute put on a spring carnival and Bryce invited her. When she failed to appear, he wandered around in a daze, looking for Noah. He found him, lying on the ground under one of the big fir trees on the east side of the Institute.

Noah lifted his head. "Your mother didn't show, did she?"

"How'd you know?"

"I recognize your footsteps and they're sad today." Noah sat, brushed the needles from the back of his blonde hair, then lifted his face toward the sun. "I used to dream my mother would come for me—the wish I made with every birthday cake. But now, if I had only one wish, it would be to see the sky and know what blue is."

The first surge of understanding swelled in Bryce that there were ways of being in this world for which no grown up could offer an explanation. Things he would never be able to comprehend and must, somehow, come to accept. This peculiar wisdom was too huge and risky to articulate and so he turned his thoughts to something he could do for Noah. "Wait right here," Bryce said. "I got a great idea."

When he returned, he dropped to the ground beside Noah.

"Tell me what you imagine the sky looks like."

"Sometimes, when I lift my face toward it, my skin gets hot. So, I imagine the sky looks real hot, even though I know blue is a cool color."

"No. The sky looks crisp and frosty cool, even when it's hot." Bryce wrapped Noah's hand around a cold bottle of sparkling water. "Take a big gulp and hold it in your mouth for a few seconds."

Noah filled his mouth. His cheeks puffed out in rosy globes on both sides of his freckled face.

"Spit out the water and think about chapel, the time that choirboy sang *Amazing Grace* without any music and his voice sent goose bumps down our arms."

Bryce placed a polished stone in Noah's hand and told him to rub it. "The sky is dazzling today. It's everywhere, all around us—so blue that it changes everything else. The grass is greener, the water in the pond is a brighter shade, even your yellow hair is lighter under a blue sky as dazzling as today. In a way, it looks like this rock feels, like that boy in the choir sounded." Bryce leaped up, raised his arms. "And it makes your eyes tingle the way your mouth felt, just after you spit out the sparkling water."

Taking the stone and putting it down, Bryce then wrapped Noah's hand around a paper cone of cotton candy. "The sky has a few high, puffy white clouds today, and when one of them floats across the sun, the air gets cool. Stick out your tongue."

He put his open hand behind Noah's head and pulled his face to the mound of cotton candy. "Feel how it dissolves, disappears almost as fast as it hits your tongue. Clouds look the way that feels. All wispy and soft."

Bryce grabbed a wad of cotton candy and smeared it across Noah's face.

Within seconds the two boys fought a candy battle that left them pink and sticky. The bright sound of their laughter had risen like a bunch of colored balloons, their pastel ribbons streaming beneath them in the wind.

Kendra's voice brought him back. "Why were you removed

from your mother's custody?"

For a moment, Bryce was taken aback by the question. It was a subject he hadn't visited in years, and yet there it was, his childhood all around him like broken glass. "My father, or the man I thought was my father, committed suicide. Jason, my older brother by twelve years, joined the army. My mother was a drunk who left me in a motel room to fend for myself when I was six."

"Did you ever learn the identity of your birth father?"

"Not really. I think I met him once—the night they left me."

"Did you stay in touch with Noah?"

He shook his head. "I lost touch with everyone after…after…" Memory could be a floodgate—once opened, it was hard to close.

Kendra gave him a moment to collect himself. "So, Noah wasn't happy about your getting married and leaving school."

"We both won scholarships to the University of Utah. Noah begged me to stay and graduate, but I had to be a father to my baby. I watched her being born, February ninth, 1984, and I cut the cord. It was the most amazing moment of my life, Kendra. I spent the night in the hospital with Valerie and our daughter, drifting in and out of sleep. And when the new day awakened, it was like a bright blue miracle, right outside our hospital window."

"God," Kendra said. "I can't imagine what it feels like to watch a baby come into the world, especially your own."

"I hope you get the chance, Kendra. Because it's…" Bryce stopped, shivered slightly, then focused his gaze on the wall, as if searching for the precise word. Unable to decide on just one, he said, "Amazing. Awesome. Wonderful. I don't know, maybe it was just me. There was so much missing from my childhood. I wanted, just once, to feel endlessly connected to another human being." His eyes locked with Kendra's. "That's what happened with my daughter. With Courtney. And she made me believe, at least for a little while, in God, in some electric improbable being all charged up with love and goodness."

Kendra scribbled her notes, periodically interrupting the flow of his thoughts with a specific question. "Wow, Bryce. You could make a woman change her mind about having kids."

He had something else he needed to say and again, he struggled to find the words. "It's funny how time usually fades memories. I never talked about her, but she changed me into someone better than I am. I remember every detail about that year."

"Tell me about it," Kendra said.

"Christ, I don't know where to begin."

"Just start at the beginning. I've got time."

"Noah flew out for the christening. We named her Courtney Morgan Bryce. Noah was thrilled that we named her after him. But before we even took her home from the hospital, we found out she had a ventricular septal defect. The doctor told us it was the kind of defect that often corrects itself without surgery. So, we were optimistic and brought her home."

"And she was fine?" Kendra said.

"She was perfect. And I was crazy about her. To the rest of the world, Courtney Morgan Bryce was an ordinary miracle, but she was the wonder of my life. I couldn't get enough of her. Night after night, I dug her out of her bed, just to hold her, stare at her, and make sure she was still breathing."

"As the months passed, Courtney revealed her many faces and I felt nothing short of simple awe at this little daughter, whose life was already separate from mine. During those early months, her dark blue eyes paled into the light blue eyes of my mother, Rachael Bryce. They sparkled whenever Courtney spotted me. It was like getting to see how my mother's eyes would have shone, had happiness ever filled them."

He became more assured with each day Courtney lived that she would be okay. It was as if the longer she stayed in the world, the more firmly she'd be anchored to it. By continuing to breathe, she staked her claim on life. He was wrong. So, so wrong.

Less than a month before her first birthday, the nightmare he'd experienced since her birth didn't stop when he opened his eyes in the morning. Tests revealed an enlarged and overactive heart. The aortic leaflets inadequately supported in the region above the ventricular defect prolapsed and there was nothing left for them to do except a repair, which meant open-heart surgery.

"Two days before the surgery, she looked up at me and uttered her first word, 'Da'. In that moment, I saw her in every conceivable stage of her life—swinging in the park, playing inside the tiny wooden playhouse I already planned to make for her. I was going to teach her to swim the following summer."

A bone-chilling panic silenced him now. He couldn't go through that night again.

Kendra reached across the table to touch his arm. "Courtney died before her surgery, didn't she?"

"Yes," Bryce choked out. "She died."

"And you were thinking about her when you found Skyler, when you saw his blue fingernails and when you placed that call to 9-1-1?"

"Yes. I couldn't help it. It all came racing back."

The whole terrible time in his life spilled out. Courtney had been the reason for the marriage. She forced them into the confines of a family. She was the moon that controlled their tides. The baby had forged Bryce and Valerie into a life, and once the baby was gone, that life disappeared, too.

CHAPTER TWENTY-THREE

As soon as Kendra returned to her office, she phoned Radhauser. "I'm going to take you up on that offer to help me with the Bryce case."

"What do you need?"

"Any possibility you can spare me a few minutes?" She wanted to talk with him face to face about what she learned from Bryce and how she planned to use it for his defense.

"I'll be there in ten."

Maria, Kendra's office mate, was visiting a client booked at the Ashland holding and Kendra had the office to herself. She sat at her desk and cradled her head in her hands. Though sure it was the right thing to do, she was uncertain how Bryce would feel if she brought his family to see him before the trial? Would it give him the support he so desperately needed? Or would he be angry with her for meddling in a past he wanted to forget?

She had stopped at the District Attorney's office on her way home from the prison and picked up police reports, hospital records, a tape of the 9-1-1 call, photographs of the crime scene Radhauser had taken, fingerprint results, a preliminary list of witnesses for the prosecution, and the autopsy and other forensic examinations—everything the defense was entitled to for her preparation. She spread the documents out on her desk, then studied them for a few minutes and began writing cross-examinations of the prosecution's witnesses and direct examinations of her own.

A nineteen-month-old toddler had been murdered and the details summarized in less than three pages of a handwritten report. That was the way the system worked. The criminal courts were full of cases like this one, and the jails were filled with people like Bryce—some of them innocent.

Scott Sterling reported that Bryce hit him and when CPS investigated, they found a neighbor who witnessed the event and heard Bryce threaten Scott. From the account Bryce had given Kendra, it would have taken a saint to remain patient and not slap that boy's behind. Years ago, this was considered discipline. *Spare the rod, spoil the child.* But times changed. And Kendra needed to get to work.

This is what she knew from law school and from living with her father. The prosecution was sworn to do justice. The defense attorney was sworn to protect the interests of his or her defendant. It didn't matter if she thought, or even knew, her client was guilty. What mattered was whether or not the prosecution could prove their case beyond a reasonable doubt.

Was it better to let a guilty client go free than for an innocent man to be convicted?

For Kendra, the answer was an unequivocal yes.

The front door opened.

A moment later, Radhauser appeared in her office doorway. He removed his Stetson and ducked to avoid hitting his head on the doorframe. Plopping into the chair beside her desk, he then stretched his long legs into the aisle between Kendra and Maria's desks.

"You look tired," she said.

"It's been a rough week."

"How's your wife?"

"A little depressed about the mastectomy. And pretty sore. But things look good so far. We're waiting for the biopsy results from the lymph nodes. If they are clean, we have every reason to be optimistic."

"I'm happy for you both. And the baby?"

"Apparently he came through his mother's surgery like a trooper. But you didn't call me over here to talk about Gracie and our baby. What's up?"

"Despite all the circumstantial evidence pointing to him, I'm convinced Bryce is innocent of both charges."

"You're preaching to the choir. And I'm depending on you to prove it."

"My father always told me you are better off defending the guilty. I didn't understand what he meant until now. He claimed the cases that eat you alive are the ones where you're absolutely certain you are defending someone who didn't commit the crime."

"Seems like it would be easier to defend someone you know is innocent. Who'd want to argue a case when they knew their client was guilty?"

"I've had some time to think and this is what I believe. If you know your client is guilty, the trial is only a game you're playing— like those practice cases we tried in law school. There's nothing to lose. If the jury finds your client guilty, so what? Justice is done."

"And if they find them not guilty often enough," Radhauser added. "You can become as famous as your father."

She tensed and sat straight up. "That's not fair. I don't want to be compared to my father and I don't care about being famous. I want my instincts to be right. I want to serve my clients to the best of my abilities. And I want to find a way to keep Bryce alive and out of prison."

"Lighten up, Kendra. I was only joking. I know you didn't join the public defender's office to become your old man. Or to make money."

Kendra relaxed. He was right, and unless she changed her name, she might as well get used to sarcastic references to her father. "Do you know any good private investigators?"

"Sure. Is your boyfriend cheating on you?"

"I don't have time for a boyfriend. It's about the Bryce case."

"I use Tommy Henderson pretty frequently."

"Is he good at finding missing people?"

"As good as any. Why?"

"Bryce finally talked," she said. "Seems his meeting with the forensic psychiatrist loosened his tongue. I was right about the 9-1-1 call. There was a very good reason for his confusion." She told him what she learned about his childhood, his wife, and their infant daughter.

"Do you plan to call his ex-wife as a witness?"

"I will if you or Tommy can find her. She'll be a perfect rebuttal once Marshall introduces the 9-1-1 tape. I'm building my defense. And I want to find his mother, his brother, and his best friend, Noah Morgan, fast. Before the trial begins if possible."

"That's not a good idea," he said. "Have you asked Bryce about this?"

"I don't want to take the chance he'll say no."

"What if he's pissed off and goes even further into his shell?"

"My intuition tells me he needs family support. It's a chance I'm willing to take," she said. "You know what the prosecution is going to do with that 9-1-1 tape."

"Okay. The ex-wife will be a great surprise and negate their efforts, but I'm not so sure about his birth family. Given his mother's drunken history, what makes you think her visit would be helpful?"

He might be right. Maybe she should reconsider the mother, especially if she was still drinking. What could she offer her son except painful memories of a past he wanted to forget?

"If she's sobered up and is sorry for the way she neglected Bryce, her presence might be a comfort and shed some light on his seeming willingness to take the blame for something he didn't do. And my bet is she'll have some Alcoholics Anonymous 9th step work to do—some amends to make to her son."

"And if she hasn't quit?"

"Then we leave her in Utah, the box under the freeway, or wherever the hell she is."

He stood to leave.

"Oh, and Radhauser. One more thing."

"Yeah?"

"About Tommy Henderson's fee. I've got it covered."

"This case is going to drive you into bankruptcy," he said, placing his Stetson back on his head.

She laughed.

* * *

When Bryce wasn't lying on his narrow bunk drifting down the stream of his life, positioning himself somewhere along the rocky shores of his early days in Wheatley, Utah, he was bent over the small table in his cell, determined to overcome his sense of failure and do what Kendra asked of him. For now, he was writing down everything he knew about Scott Sterling.

At the very least he would record the facts of his relationship with the boy, offer them as candidly as possible, and allow them to divulge whatever they could. But he didn't allow himself a lot of hope they'd change anything. Bryce had recently discovered facts don't always tell the truth.

In spite of the pain of remembering, Bryce scrawled long into the night, recognizing that no matter how worthless the words might appear, they stood between him and the old silence that now terrorized him.

When, in the early hours, he finally collapsed on his bunk again, Bryce lay awake, his eyes open in the semi-darkness. With the impossibility of sleep, hour after hour, he tried to imagine the remainder of his life. To see himself free and back in his little house next door to Tilly.

He was glad they'd taken his wristwatch away. It would make him all too aware of the passage of time.

The sound of a guard pushing a breakfast tray through the slot in the door signaled the timeless onslaught of another day. When Bryce lifted himself from his bunk, the routine was always the same. Standing in front of the stained sink, he splashed cold water on his face, neck and arms. After brushing his teeth, he ran the Bic razor over his beard, then handed it to the waiting guard.

Finally, seated at the concrete table, Bryce jostled his food around the plastic tray and spooned up a bite or two of soggy pancakes and scrambled eggs made from powder.

He burned few calories and was seldom hungry. Since placed in isolation, he rarely visited the yard or exercise rooms. Once in a while he worked out on the cell floor, a few sit ups and pushups, but for the most part he spent his day hunched over the concrete table writing a psychological profile of a little boy he knew for just over a year.

When the guard announced his visitor, Bryce was surprised. It was too early for Kendra. And she wouldn't have him called to the visitor room. They held their meetings in the cell Kendra jokingly referred to as the board room. "I'm bored all right," Bryce had laughed.

As he spotted Tilly seated on the other side of the Plexiglas, he couldn't help his grin. But realizing the front guard had searched the old woman, asked her to remove her watch, turn over her pens and keys, leave her purse and other belongings with the guards in the reception area, his smile faded. He hated to imagine his proud friend shoved with all the others through a series of doors and corridors that finally opened into this awful room.

His imprisonment didn't make sense to him and there was no way to interpret it for Tilly. He had tried to break through the confusion and shame of his lost childhood, find respect and control as an adult. But it was hard to make it happen in this place, with his best friend and neighbor sitting across the wall from him. It was as if his imprisonment stained not only his life, but hers as well.

Bryce slipped into the cubicle, then picked up the phone, turned on the amplification, and, in spite of himself, smiled again. "Tilly, it's so damn good to see you. You look downright beautiful." He nodded admiringly.

She was dressed up for her visit, in a flowing, bright, flowered skirt and a purple blouse, with a matching hat perched on her gray curls. From her ears hung a pair of purple beaded earrings with feathers on the end.

"How's Mister Pickles?"

"I swear that cat is an eatin' machine. He's done finished off a whole bag of Purina Cat Chow. Pickles would eat till his belly exploded."

"Thanks for taking care of him." Bryce, unable to meet her gaze, stared at the graffiti scribbled on the booth wall. *Why the fuck am I here? I used to be human.*

He finally looked into her eyes. "I don't know what I'd do without you. Do you need any money for cat food or anything?"

"No. That lawyer lady of yours, that Kendra Palmer, dropped by a couple times now. She said you told her it was okay if I let her into your place. When she finished pokin' around, she slipped a little roll of cash with the key. Said for me to put it in my pickle jar for takin' care of that cat and anything else I notice needs doing around your place."

"Kendra did that?"

"Yeah, and she asked me millions of questions about you. I came here because I wanted to tell you myself about answering them. I even told her things you'd told me about your family back in Utah. She's a good person and she wants to help you, I'm sure of it. So, I want to help her, too." Her dark eyes were big and round behind her glasses.

"I don't know what to think, Tilly. The world isn't making a lot of sense to me these days. You're right, Kendra seems to care, but I sure as hell don't know what's in it for her."

"Maybe she just believes you're innocent. Give that idea a try."

"Maybe so."

"I also wanted to give you this." She slipped a photograph through the small drawer in the Plexiglas. "The guard said it was okay."

Bryce stared at the photograph of a man with a camera around his neck, entering Bryce's front door. At first, he thought it might be Monty Taylor, the man who wanted to photograph Skyler at Lithia Park, but the size and hair color were all wrong. "Who is this?"

"I don't know for sure. But I think it was one of those newspaper reporters who been writing that trash about you."

"Are you saying he broke into my house?"

She gave him a half smile, a sheepish look on her face. "I'm sure I locked the front door after I fed Pickles. I mean, I'm almost sure."

Tilly was getting old and didn't always remember everything. "Don't worry about it. When someone wants to get in, they usually find a way."

"Maybe he picked the lock like you see on television. But I

figured he was the one found that poem you wrote about your baby girl. I want you to give this photograph to Kendra. Maybe that cowboy detective can find him and arrest his good-for-nothing ass. Isn't breaking and entering a crime?"

He smiled at her to protect her feelings, but inside he was furious. And he would ask Radhauser to look into it. With any luck, the man who did this would be held accountable.

They made small talk about what was going on in the neighborhood.

"Been all kinds of activity around your place since you been in here. Dana and Reggie packed up all the kids' stuff. That Andrew Marshall DA guy was poking around. I told him I didn't have a key. But when the cops came by with another search warrant, I let them in. Kendra said I was right to do that."

Bryce stared at his fingernails. "There's no such thing as privacy once they get you into this place."

"I'm sorry for you," Tilly said loud enough to raise his eyes again. "You be needing anything, boy?"

"I could use a sunset." He shook his head and smiled. "But you wouldn't be able to get it past the guards."

"What's it like here in this jailhouse? Is it awful?"

Bryce struggled for a response, but couldn't find one.

"You be out soon, Bryce. That Kendra is one smart cookie and she won't let you stay in this place for something you didn't do no how."

"It feels good to know you believe in me, Tilly. You've been a great neighbor and friend, much better than I deserve." He bowed his head.

"What you mean by that? You been downright wonderful to me and my grandbabies. You patched my roof during that bad rainy spell. And hauled in three wheelbarrows of top soil for my vegetable garden. What kind of man does something like that for a fat ole colored woman like me?"

She paused and waited, expected an answer, but his gaze remained averted, his head down. "Look at me, boy. I want you to answer."

Her demand raised Bryce's head and he stared directly into her eyes.

"You are very good," she said again, dropping her hands into her lap and jutting her chin toward the ceiling. "You are one fine man and I oughta know. Now tell me what it's like here."

He still had no answer, so he chatted with Tilly about her family and Mr. Grumpalump's latest fiasco. When the buzzer sounded and she stood to leave, Bryce hated to see her go. She reminded him of the other life, the world he used to live in, where people struggled to survive and helped each other cope with day-to-day problems.

As the guard escorted him back, he sealed himself off from the jeers of the other prisoners and didn't allow their words into his consciousness. Once inside his own cell, the place he came in some strange way to welcome, Bryce crouched at his little table and pondered Tilly's question. "What's it like in this jailhouse?"

Staring at the blank yellow tablet in front of him, he thought about an answer, wished he'd been able to form the words for her, then flipped to a clean page and drafted a poem.

A Prison Letter to Tilly

When you asked what it's like here
No words rose to describe it.
Without answer,
I hung my shameful head.

Now, I can tell you that prison
Is a cubicle where a man lingers
With his guts stretched like barbed wire.
Early mornings that roll
Out into months that rise
Like a tide around your throat,

Until you are demented
And believe the morning is an ocean,

Green water, white crests, an island
Where you lie under bright sunlight,
And orange bird of paradise
Blossoming from your palm.

But there are no flowers in these cells,
No sea, and you hold nothing
In your hands except fear
That survives the absence of sunlight,
Something that vacates
The mind to expand the darkness
Rising like an ocean against your thighs.

It rises and there are no words for it,
Though you search for them,
Flip on the dim imprisoned light and watch it
Float down your yellow blanket
Over black water, the light arresting
The dark for just an instant
Opposing what coils inside your throat.
It is a type of dread,
A foreboding for which
Your world, Tilly, has no words.

CHAPTER TWENTY-FOUR

When, less than twenty-four hours after Tilly left, Bryce was called out for another visit, it mystified him.

"Number three, Bryce." The guard nodded toward the third booth where a tall man, casually dressed in pressed blue jeans and a gray, chambray short-sleeved shirt, stood on the other side of the Plexiglas wall. His graying, teak-colored hair was combed back from his high forehead and hung just over the collar of his shirt. A trimmed reddish beard, laced with gray, gave him the look of a country western singer.

For an instant, Bryce panicked, feared Kendra Palmer had been removed from his case and someone else assigned. But this man didn't look like an attorney—his tanned skin was weathered like a man who worked in the sun. Their eyes met and held as Bryce took his seat, picked up the receiver, and turned on the amplifier. The man, following Bryce's lead, pressed the phone against his ear, his pale blue eyes never leaving Bryce's face.

"You don't know who I am, do you, Cale?" The man swallowed as if he were nervous. The muscles in his throat tightened above his shirt collar.

No one had called him Cale since he left Wheatley, Utah. He started calling himself Bryce at the Institute—an attempt to forget the life that seemed to have forgotten him. Was this someone who knew him in Wheatley? As he stared into the face on the other side of the glass, Bryce rummaged through his memory for a name, but came up with none. Still, there was something vaguely familiar about the way his blue eyes caught the light and twinkled. "Should I know you?"

The man smiled, a sad closed-mouth grin. "Yes. Indeed you should. But if you suddenly appeared in front of me after all these years, I wouldn't have the faintest notion who you were, either."

"So, are you going to tell me?"

"I'm Jason," he said. "Your big brother."

For a moment, Bryce was too shocked to speak and kept shaking his head. "Holy shit," he finally choked out. "Jason. I was six years old and you weren't more than eighteen the last time I saw you. I don't believe it. I just don't believe it."

Flooded with emotions and old memories, Bryce struggled to find the words to talk to this brother he hadn't seen since childhood. With such an expanse of time between them, a kind of mourning rose inside him. It was something as tender and terrible as grief over the lost years and broken dreams. Jason had always been so kind to his little brother. But then, like everything else, Jason disappeared.

Bryce trembled, blinked away tears. "What in the hell are you doing here? How long has it been? How did you find me?" All the questions he'd saved up for years ran together in that first blush of fever at seeing Jason again.

"Whoa, Cale, one question at a time. I'm here to see you. Best I can remember, the last time I saw you was the day before you and Mom disappeared with her boyfriend. Dad shot himself the next morning—less than a week before I left for basic training. "

"I begged the social worker to let me come home, but she told me Dad was dead and you'd joined the army." Again, Bryce locked eyes with Jason. "Of course, he wasn't really my father, was he?"

It was strange, but ever since he started talking to that psychiatrist and writing out things for Kendra, his entire life seemed like one enormous boil. And the pressure had finally reached the point where the only relief was to lance it, to drain away his own spiritual abscess through facing the truth.

"No, I don't think he was..." Jason hesitated, stared at his brother as if seeking permission to go on, and to Bryce's relief, he found it. "He told me the last time we went hunting together that Mom had an affair with some big shot from Kennecott Copper she met waitressing at Robertson's Inn. She was a real looker then. Every man she met was a little bit in love with her. But especially Dad. Her leaving ate him alive. I figure that's why he did it."

"I was so young," Bryce said. "I didn't know what was going on half the time."

Jason leaned forward. "I still miss him. Can you believe that? He's been dead more than half my life. For years, I thought I was going crazy. When I was stationed in Germany, I'd see him walking down a street in Munich, kind of bent over like he was. Then when I believed I'd gotten over it, there he was again on a shopping mall escalator in Salt Lake." Jason shook his head. "My wife, Katja, says it's because I never saw him dead. It all happened so fast, there's nothing for me to remember except that closed box sitting over a big hole in the ground."

Bryce wanted to put his arm around Jason's shoulder, tell him what a good son he'd been and how much Isaiah Bryce had cared about him. "He sure as hell hated my guts." The hardness of his own words jolted Bryce, but shock didn't silence him. "I couldn't figure it out and I tried and tried to get him to love me."

Jason was quiet for a few seconds, and then, his voice low, said, "Yeah, I know it must have seemed that way. You were a constant reminder, I guess, but I think it had more to do with his loving her than his really hating you. God knows why, but he did. Love's a strange bird, little brother. No telling where it's gonna fly."

Bryce laughed. "I finally figured it out."

"Figured love out?"

"No. I figured out the man who took Mom and me to that fancy hotel in Salt Lake was my birth father. I think I caught on that night, he was so nice to me. It's just that I didn't know what to do about it."

Jason nodded. "Yeah, that's what I think, too, and I'm pretty sure he's the one who flew off with Mom's heart, but she never admitted it, at least not to me. After Dad died, I didn't hear from her for years. Of course, I didn't try to get in touch with her either. I blamed her for Dad's suicide. Actually, I thought I hated her. Then one day I got a letter."

Jason gestured with his right hand, turned the palm toward the ceiling. "The army's pretty good about keeping track of its soldiers. Her letter found me. She wrote that she went to Alcoholics Anonymous because she wanted to make amends. I guess she stopped drinking, cold turkey, then got herself a job in a hospice."

"Is she...I...I...mean...do you know if she's still alive?"

"Yes, very much so," Jason said. "She lives in Salt Lake."

Bryce closed his eyes for a second, trying to imagine their mother now, then opened them again. "Do you ever see her?"

"Yeah, pretty often. She's not more than five miles away from Katja and me. We have her over for dinner almost every week. Always on holidays. What she lacked in being a mother to us, she's found with her grandkids. They adore her."

Unlike Bryce, Jason had managed to move forward and forgive their mother. And that forgiveness somehow weaved itself around his brother and held the past in its place behind him.

"She got married again," Jason said. "To a nice guy whose wife died of cancer. She met him in the hospice. Regrets have nearly eaten her up, especially about you. When I told her what happened, that I was flying to Oregon, she hid her face in her hands and sobbed."

"How did you know where to find me?"

"I didn't." Jason's eyes widened. "Not really. I read about the case in the paper, saw a few news clips on television, but I thought it was just a coincidence, a man with the same name. I couldn't imagine you in Oregon, and the mug shot, well, it didn't exactly look like the six-year-old I remembered. And then a private investigator found me. He said he was working with Detective Radhauser and was hired by your attorney."

"You're kidding." How could he repay Kendra Palmer for everything she'd done for him?

Jason continued. "The PI said you were in trouble and needed all the support you could get from family and friends. He's a hell of a nice guy, even offered to send me the ticket. So here I am. It's about time, don't you think?"

Again, Bryce swallowed in a futile attempt to keep the tears from flowing. "Thanks for coming," he whispered. "I've thought about you a million times."

"I'm sorry, Cale. I should have tried harder to find you when you were a kid. I was told you were placed with a foster family. I guess I wanted to believe you were better off."

"Maybe I was eventually," Bryce said. "The school they put me in was a good one."

Your attorney is convinced of your innocence, and if you want to talk, I'll be happy to listen. If you don't, that's all right, too. I just want to be here for you."

"I spend every waking moment exhuming the past for my lawyer. And you're right, she believes in my innocence, maybe even more than I do. But if it's all the same to you, I'd like to hear about your life."

Jason refused to talk about his tours in Vietnam, but told Bryce he married Katja while stationed in Germany. They had two children—a daughter, Brianna, and a son they'd named Caleb. For years, they'd moved from one post to another, but once the kids were in high school, Jason retired and opened a small landscape business in Salt Lake. Now, Brianna would graduate from high school next spring and Caleb was a freshman at the Southern Oregon University, right there in Ashland.

"When I left Utah, I didn't think I'd ever go back," Jason said. "But as I got older, it pulled me and I wanted to see Wheatley again."

"Has it changed much?" Bryce asked.

Jason laughed. "Changed? Has it ever. I figured you heard—it's under a hundred and fifty feet of water now. They dammed up the Provo River, call it the Jordanelle Reservoir."

"Maybe it's just as well. It's not as if we have a lot of happy memories of the place. But..." Bryce shook his head. "I still can't believe you named your son after me. Does that mean you actually liked your pesky little brother?"

"Yes," Jason said, swallowing hard and dropping his gaze to his lap. "And I never stopped thinking about you, Cale." He raised his watery eyes. "I always told people I had a little brother even when

I wasn't sure you were still alive." Jason fiddled with the button on his shirt pocket, then removed a stack of snapshots of his family. He pressed them, one by one, against the Plexiglas wall.

A little blond girl with sparkling blue eyes stood on tiptoes and smiled up at Bryce from a ballet recital.

Then, slightly older, decked out in a bunny Halloween costume, long, pink ears flopping against her rosy cheeks.

Standing at home plate, a serious, thin-faced boy, maybe seven or eight, in a miniature Dodger's uniform, a wooden bat slung casually across his thin shoulders. His namesake, Caleb.

A beautiful teenage girl in a prom dress.

A boy who looked to be about sixteen, heavier, with a wide grin and a line of pimples across his forehead.

Picture after picture.

One of a tall, slender woman sitting in front of a Christmas tree, a young boy and girl on the floor next to her, ripping off wrapping paper.

"Is this your wife?"

"No," Jason said. "It's Mom with my two kids, quite a few years ago. She looks a lot older now."

Bryce stared at Jason, but said nothing. He tried, but couldn't state why the photograph of his mother disturbed him so much. His breathing grew shallow, and he wiped at his eyes. His throat and nose seemed blocked. He'd had panic attacks before and tried to slow down his breathing so he wouldn't hyperventilate.

After a few seconds, Jason flattened another photograph against the glass—one of the last photos of their father. Dressed in the dusty clothes and helmet he wore into the mines, Isaiah Bryce stood between eighteen-year-old Jason and six-year-old Bryce. One pale arm dangled at his side, the other draped over his elder son's shoulders.

When the buzzer sounded to signify visiting hours had ended, Bryce was not ready to say goodbye to his brother or to his niece and nephew whose whole lives had spread out on the wall in front of him, like a picture book. A nephew, named for him, right under his nose in Ashland and he didn't even know it. Perhaps they'd passed each other in the halls of the Modern Languages building where Bryce took a class, or on the tree-lined mall in front of the student union, or seated at a small desk by the windows in the library.

"I'll be back," Jason said.

"How long are you staying?"

"I leave tomorrow. But I'm coming back for the trial and will stay until it's over. I'm gonna stop by my son's dorm on my way back to the hotel." Jason stood, the phone receiver still pressed against his ear. "He doesn't know I'm here. Won't he be surprised to see his old man? Hope I don't catch him with his pants down." He grinned, dropped the phone back into its cradle, and hustled from the room behind the other visitors.

* * *

Within an hour of returning to his cell, Bryce lay on his bunk, wondering if he imagined or dreamed his brother's visit. They grew up in the same family, the same town. And, though he didn't know it until recently, when he was taken away, he carried enormous hunks of Wheatley, Utah, Isaiah, Rachael, and Jason Bryce with him.

Jason had been the only person in his early childhood that Bryce could consistently depend upon. But as the years passed, all tangible traces of that family had disappeared except for the vivid memories Skyler's death and Bryce's incarceration had ironically released.

For days and nights on end, Bryce recalled things in the obsessive detail of someone who was finally disentangling himself from the past. And he came to the late conclusion that the details of his childhood, in some harrowing and illogical way, still mattered.

Nearly overwhelmed by it all, Bryce closed his eyes, and, without any desire to go, drifted into that place between sleep and waking where memory lived. Once there, outside of real time, the invisible clock in his body ran backwards once more, toward the early childhood he spent with Jason.

He began to think memory was a reward we received for each day's death. It was the place we went to revise and reshape our lives. A way of giving ourselves another chance. And today, in the Jackson County Jail, of all places, Bryce got one with his brother.

* * *

The creak of the cell door opened Bryce's eyes to the present as Kendra slipped inside. His attorney stood beside the bunk. One hand held her briefcase, the other rested on her hip. "It's awful early to hit the sack, Bryce. Are you sick or something?"

"I'm recovering from a shock." Bryce sat. "But then I guess you know my older brother was here today. I haven't seen him for almost thirty years. I guess you know that, too."

"Yes, to both guesses." Kendra dropped her briefcase on the table. "He wanted me to give you these." She handed Bryce the stack of photographs Jason had pressed against the visiting room glass.

Bryce stacked them on the shelf above his bed, wiped his eyes with his fists, then stood and stretched. "Did you and Radhauser hire someone to find him?"

"We did," she said.

"Your budget allows for private investigators? No wonder us poor taxpayers are pissed off." Bryce suspected Kendra paid the PI out of her own pocket, but didn't want to risk another scene over money.

She smiled, opened her briefcase and laid out the evening's work.

"I've had nothing to do but think since I was put in here," he said. "And sometimes I think about you and the way you were brought up. Affluent, with highly educated parents. I'm assuming you must have had everything you needed or wanted. So, what makes a rich person like you happy?"

Kendra rubbed her jaw, and thought before answering. "First of all, I didn't have a mother. She died when I was seven. And you'll probably think this is strange, or worse yet, corny, but people like your neighbor, Tilly, make me happy. She hasn't got an extra dime, a pot to piss in as you'd say, but that woman would gather soda cans and take in laundry to feed your cat and keep you from losing your house. You may not believe it, but to me that's real wealth,

Bryce, the kind that makes people happy. My father, with all his millions, doesn't have a single friend like her."

"That reminds me. Tilly gave me a photo of a reporter entering my house. I suspect that's how they got the poem I wrote about my daughter. I think the reporter's name is Wally Hartmueller. He's at that tabloid called *The Talent Tattler*."

"I'll ask Radhauser to investigate," she said. "If nothing else, we can scare the crap out of him with an arrest warrant."

"Good," Bryce said. "I'm sick to death of people walking all over me."

Kendra smiled. "That's what I want to hear. The guard told me Poncho is in solitary for a month. Hopefully he'll learn how to keep his fists to himself."

Tilly was right, Bryce thought, as they settled into the night's work. No matter what Kendra's real motivation for helping him, or what the future held, he'd lucked out when the state of Oregon assigned Kendra to his case.

It was after ten when she left.

Alone in his cell again, Bryce stretched out on the bunk. About a week ago, he had discovered pencil drawings and words written on the cinder block walls, hidden by the mattress. He lifted the thin foam, stared at the scribblings and sensed the spirits of nameless prisoners in this cell before him. Men who had lives, as aching and real to them as Bryce's was now.

Today is Abby's third birthday. She won't remember me.
My father died yesterday, August second, 1997.
My wife got married to my brother. I hate them both.

Bryce felt the other men close by, thinking their thoughts, fearing their fates, and jotting private messages into circles with scalloped mythical wings surrounding them.

A moment later, Bryce stood, rummaged through the cardboard box of tablets and pencils for the tape Kendra had used to piece back together one of the lists he tore in half.

When he found it, he stuck Jason's photographs on the wall and laid down again, staring up at his family until sleep finally pulled him away.

CHAPTER TWENTY-FIVE

Each morning, Radhauser helped Gracie change her bandages and empty the drain tube above the place where her right breast had once been. Darker skin, slightly crinkled like parchment, spread across her thin chest like a flower. Its petals blossomed over the area where her nipple had once been. But the stitches had dissolved and the skin begun to smooth over her wounds, making them easier to look at now. He reached for the gauze wrap.

"Don't look at me," Gracie said, taking the roll of gauze away from him and struggling with her left hand to wrap herself.

"Please let me help you," he replied.

She threw the gauze on the bed and some of it came unrolled.

Radhauser rerolled the gauze and gently wrapped it around her chest, careful not to disturb the tube under her right armpit.

She kept her gaze on her lap.

Outside the window, an autumn rain fell, cold and heavy, the kind that sunk into your bones and made them feel weighted and soggy. The only time Gracie seemed happy now was when Lizzie was lying on the bed beside her, pretending to read her mother a story. The doctor said it would take time. That what for many women started out as shame and repulsion turned into a kind of survivor pride.

Still, he was puzzled by her demand not to look at her. They'd been together for nearly a decade. He held her head when she puked, and cleaned the bathroom floor when she was too sick to make it to the toilet. They'd shared so many intimacies. He watched their daughter emerge from her body. How many times had they made love, he wondered? A thousand? Fifteen hundred?

And yet sometimes, like now, she felt unknowable to him. He understood she might be ashamed or embarrassed by her wound. But what he didn't understand was why she was so self-conscious around him.

A blur of red leaves swept back and forth across the panes as the wind picked up, tossing a Japanese maple branch against the window.

Stepping back over to her bedside table, he picked up the small measuring cup of fluid they'd drained, then pressed a kiss to her forehead. "I love you," he said softly. "You're the most beautiful woman in the world to me."

Tears welled in her eyes. She leaned into him, keeping her head down to pretend she wasn't crying. And he pretended he didn't know she was. "It wasn't bad news, Gracie. It was inconclusive. So, we have to wait a little longer. Your nodes are going to be clean. And once the baby is born and you complete your radiation and chemo, we'll find a good plastic surgeon and start reconstruction."

"It feels like such a long way off. She glanced down at the flat side of her chest. "Such a long time to look like this. And what if the nodes are positive? I won't abort our baby. I don't care what anyone says."

"As soon as you heal, we'll get you a prosthesis."

It was hard to watch someone he loved close the door of every optimistic solution he offered. He stepped into the bathroom and recorded the quantity of fluid.

When he returned to the bedroom, she cocked her head slightly, her gaze holding steady with his own. "I'm not a very good patient, am I?"

"I'll say it again. You're the most beautiful woman in the world to me."

When she smiled, he wanted to tell her that nothing was ever as bad as it seemed. But then he thought about Skyler Sterling's death and the fact that an innocent man was about to go on trial for murder. Some things were every bit as bad as they seemed. And some were even worse. To make things more difficult, the media were crawling up their butts like cheap underwear.

Murphy ran a tight ship and he made it clear to all of them that the person they worked for was not him or the people of Ashland. They worked for the victim, and had to become the voice of the voiceless—the righter of wrongs for those who couldn't right them. But the way Radhauser saw it, Bryce was just as much a victim as Skyler Sterling. And he couldn't live with himself if he didn't find a way to right that wrong.

The phone rang.

Gracie's mom answered in the kitchen. A moment later, she carried the phone into the bedroom and held it out to him. "It's for you. An attorney named Kendra Palmer."

"Tell her to hold on a second."

He tucked the tube back into place under Gracie's arm, kissed her on the forehead, then took the phone. "Kendra?"

"I need a favor," Kendra said. "I'm up to my eyebrows in depositions and I need you to make an airport run."

"Sure. I can do that. Who am I picking up?"

"Bryce's mother. I want you to take her directly to the jail, stay with her throughout her visit, then drop her off at her motel in Medford."

He hated visiting anyone in prison. It was crazy and made no sense, but whenever he did, he felt like he was being punished for some unknown deed. Steel doors slammed behind him. And there was a locker-room smell, male sweat and fear, that seemed to swallow him. Even as a detective, he was searched, counted, required to sign in, and record his visit on an official roster. Every time he entered the county jail, he had a terrible feeling that he wouldn't be allowed out. Maybe everyone should have the experience, he thought. A specific kind of education. A realization that it was a privilege to be able to exit the steel doors and enter the world again.

"Come on," Kendra said. "You told me you'd help. This is what I need from you."

For a moment, a silence fell over him. Disgust began its slow crawl up his spine as he imagined Bryce's mother—the alcoholic who'd abandoned her six-year-old son. Without warning, his thoughts jumped to Flannigan, the man in jail for killing his first wife and son. "I'm not the best person to do that," he said. "I have a thing about drunks. I practically break out in hives whenever I'm around one."

"She's been clean and sober for more than a decade. I think it might help Bryce to have her and his brother here for the trial."

Outside the bedroom window, rain fell in gray veils across the gravel drive and pastures and dripped from the monkey bars on Lizzie's jungle gym. It clattered against the rooftop and boiled and snapped in the dark pools that had gathered beneath the swings.

A few minutes before Kendra's call, Radhauser had the thought he couldn't live with himself if he didn't do something to help Bryce. Maybe Kendra was right. Maybe having some family support would make him fight harder for himself. "Okay," he said. "What time does her flight get in?"

* * *

Bryce studied the Thanksgiving decorations provided by a local third grade class that graced the visiting area of the Jackson County Jail. Linked circles of autumn-colored construction paper and glittery glue-streaked margarine lids with photos of turkeys on them dangled on pipe cleaners from the popcorn strings.

He smiled, thinking about the small hands, their sticky fingers gripping dull scissors, intent on cutting out their turkeys. The guard led him to one of the larger booths—with a visitor bench that could seat three. Had Jason changed his mind, stayed longer and returned with his son?

Radhauser led an older woman into the booth and waited until she was seated before sitting beside her. He picked up the receiver.

Bryce grabbed his own and turned on the amplifier.

"There's someone here who's anxious to see you." Radhauser handed a second receiver to the woman.

"I wouldn't blame you if you never wanted to set eyes on me again."

And then Bryce knew. It was his mother.

She lowered her gaze as if embarrassed to look at him. Tendrils of gray hair had loosened from their pins and were suspended in front of her ears. Her face, though lined, was still thin, with prominent cheekbones and beautiful blue eyes framed by thick, black lashes. For a woman of sixty-five, she was hauntingly beautiful.

Unable to respond to his mother's words, Bryce stared at her wrinkled hand as it clutched the phone receiver. Her veins rose in pale blue cords beneath her translucent skin and that obvious evidence of aging caught him off guard, although Jason had warned him. The last time Bryce saw her, she was young.

The image of his mother and the man he now understood was his birth father rose. Though he had no desire to go back to that night of joy and horror, before he could stop it, the memory rushed by him.

* * *

Bryce had been six years old. His mother shook him awake. "What's wrong, Mama?"

She sat on the edge of the mattress and turned on the light so he could read her lips. "Put these clothes on, Cale." She handed him the plaid shirt and pressed blue pants he usually wore for church or special occasions. "We're taking a little trip." She bustled around his bedroom, packing a small suitcase.

"What about Jason and Dad?"

She lifted her index finger to her lips. Through the flowered fragrance of her perfume, he detected the funny smell on his mother's breath that meant she was drinking. "They'll be okay. Jason will be leaving for the army in less than a week. Now get your clothes on and be quick about it."

When he finished dressing, she led him into the kitchen, ran water over a comb and parted his dark hair, carefully arranging it as if he were going to Sunday school.

"You look pretty, Mama." His gaze traveled over the dress, stockings and high heels she usually saved for weddings and holidays. His mother was tall and slender, with long hair that fell in shiny copper waves over her shoulders. Cale could tell men thought she was beautiful by the way they stopped to talk with her on the street, her laughter rising like a bright yellow ribbon in front of her.

She took his hand and they stepped outside into the crisp, November air, then hurried past all the other houses on their street. They passed Clemson's barn and the old brick schoolhouse nobody used anymore and headed toward the Robertson Inn. Like most everything else around Wheatley, Utah, the Robertsons owned the house his family lived in as well as the mineral rights to the mine where Isaiah Bryce and the other local men dug.

At the edge of the Inn's wooded drive, Cale and his mother waited, hands stuffed in their pockets, until the lights of an oncoming car washed over them.

"Here he comes." She brushed Bryce's hair off his forehead with her fingertips and straightened the collar of his jacket.

A car jerked to a stop and the passenger door opened. His mother pulled the seat forward and he climbed in back. The car still had that new leather smell and the seats were as soft as the fur on his pet lamb. He watched as she slid all the way across the front seat until her shoulder brushed against the arm of a tweed jacket. Then she flung herself into the man's arms and kissed him on the lips.

The man had black hair, and when he broke away from her embrace, he pivoted in the seat and stared at Cale over his shoulder for what seemed like a long time. Then he leaned forward, started the car and pulled out of Wheatley toward Route 40 and the big city of Salt Lake.

A few minutes later, the man picked up a bottle from the floor at his feet, unscrewed the top and swallowed several times, shaking his head as he finished. When he passed it to Cale's mother, she took a long pull, trying to make it look like a sip. They chattered in low, comforting voices that sounded like humming as they passed the bottle back and forth between them. Eventually, Cale curled into the corner of the back seat and drifted into sleep.

When he awakened, the man was carrying him toward a big bed with a puffy flowered cover and a pastel mural of a country landscape painted on the wall above it. A television set on brackets hung just under the ceiling.

"You have your own room, big guy." He untied Cale's shoes,

217

then slipped them off, along with his socks. He bounced him on the bed, tickled him under his arms for a moment, then pointed to a door in the wall next to the television. "Your mother and I are right over there. So, you don't have to be afraid."

He paused and looked at Cale's mother. "Does the big guy talk?"

"Sure. And he can read, too. He's not even in first grade yet. He's a little shy, but real smart, and he has eyes just like his daddy." She giggled, tilted her head and looked up at the man from beneath her eyelashes. "He knows his numbers all the way to a hundred."

The man picked up a tablet from the table next to the bed. "I'll write these numbers down for you. Tomorrow morning when you wake up hungry, dial zero for the front desk. Tell them you want room service and that you are in room 840. Then order whatever you want—eggs and bacon, a hamburger, fries, even a milkshake. They'll bring it right up to you." He smiled and patted Cale on the top of his head.

He tried to concentrate on the man's lips, but he kept thinking about the bright blue color of Isaiah's eyes. They were nothing like Cale's dark brown eyes. He tried to figure out what his mother had meant.

"It's like magic," the man said. "*Presto*—all the food you can eat appears on a cart in front of you." He snapped his fingers and his happy dark eyes sparkled.

His mother showed Cale the bathroom, then helped him out of his shirt and pants. When she tucked him into the fancy hotel bed, she called him precious and sweetheart, her love child. She hugged and kissed him on both cheeks the way she used to before all the fighting with his father began. "Now, be a good boy and don't leave the room," she said, squeezing his nose with her thumb and forefinger.

He breathed in the sunshine smell of the starched white sheets as she disappeared through the door, the man's right arm wrapped around her waist, holding her up.

Pulling the covers around his neck, he turned on his side, floated into sleep, and the night passed.

When sunlight streaming through the east window awakened him, he padded across the room wearing only his underwear. His bare toes sank into the thick blue fibers of the carpet as he tapped on the door connecting the two rooms.

No one answered.

He gradually increased the intensity of his knocking until he finally pounded with both fists.

Still, no one answered.

He tried to turn the knob. The door was locked.

The world dropped away. The walls, even the floor itself, tumbled and he was drowning in an infinite ocean of empty space, the size and shape of his fear. He slipped into his clothes, and sat on the edge of the bed. His gaze darted around the room and landed on the numbers the man wrote out for him.

He dialed zero, ordered scrambled eggs, toast, and bacon, a large Coke and a bowl of Frosted Flakes. And just as the man promised, about a half hour later someone tapped on his door and wheeled in the magic cart with more breakfast food than Cale ever saw before.

The waiter spread a blue linen cloth over the small round table in front of the window, then positioned a single rosebud in a polished silver vase at the table's center. He pulled out the chair for Cale and once the boy squirmed into place, he lifted a silver dome from the steaming plate of eggs and bacon. "Is there anything else I can get you, sir?"

Cale grinned back. "No, thank you, sir. This is just great."

He spent the day watching television game shows, soap operas, and *The Andy Griffith Show*. He turned the volume real high so he could hear it because he liked the whistling music as Opie and his pa walked down the road together at the beginning and end of the show.

When darkness fell again, he adjusted the volume of the television even louder and waited. He thought about his pet lamb, Oscar, and hoped Jason would remember to feed him. Bored and hungry again, he picked up the telephone, ordered another Coke, French fries, and a hamburger. He ate, waited some more, then fell asleep.

The next day, the front desk called. Cale whimpered into the phone. "I don't know where Mama is. I keep knocking on the door to their room, but no one answers."

They said something, but he couldn't hear. A few minutes later, one of the hotel clerks joined Cale in the room, asked the boy his name and some questions about his mother. "Why don't you come downstairs with me?" he finally said. "You can be my helper behind the front desk."

"No," Cale cried. "I can't. Mama said for me to wait here, she said not to leave the room."

"Okay, calm down," the hotel clerk said. "It's all right. You lock the door behind me and wait here. I'm going to get help. Will you be okay?"

Cale nodded.

An hour or more later, another knock rattled the door. Thinking his mother and the man had returned, he smiled, leaped from his perch on the bed, pulled the desk chair over and stood on it so he could slide the dead bolt to the left. He thrust open the door.

A tall lady in a blue suit with a small hat balanced on top of her wavy, brown hair stood before him.

Cale moved aside and she stepped into the room, her eyes surveying every corner from behind her round, wire-rimmed glasses.

She bent down so close to his face that he could smell coffee, and see the golden flecks in her brown eyes. "I'm Corinne from the Child Welfare Department. You don't have to be afraid, Caleb, we're going to help you."

He later learned his father shot himself in the head after discovering his wife was gone. Less than a week after their father's funeral, his big brother Jason left for the army.

After two stays in foster homes where he refused to utter a single word, the state of Utah did some testing and discovered the extent of Bryce's hearing deficit and the many ways in which he was gifted. Two months later he was placed in the Lake Institute for the Deaf and Blind.

He never heard from his mother again.

CHAPTER TWENTY-SIX

After almost thirty years, Rachael Bryce sat in front of him. "I'm so sorry, Cale," she said. "I know I hurt you. And I'm ashamed of the mother I was. I hope you can find it in your heart to forgive me."

For a moment, Bryce said nothing. "I go by Bryce now," he said, attempting to keep the hurt and anger out of his voice. "I don't like to remember what it was like to be Cale."

"Is there anything I can do to help you? Do you need money? I got married again to a really a fine man. His name is Theodore Clark. He said to tell you he'll hire a good lawyer, do anything he can to help." Rachael spoke rapidly, as if she feared this might be her only chance.

"I have a very good lawyer." He nodded toward Radhauser. "And a detective who is on my side, too."

Radhauser cleared his throat. "I feel like I should leave and give you two time alone. I can wait in the car."

"No," Bryce said. "Please. I need you to stay."

Rachael wiped her face with her free hand. "I wish things were different. I wish I gave you the family you deserved."

Bryce stared at her thin lips, watched the movement of her tongue behind her teeth, trying to connect the words with his life, with what he remembered of this mother and his childhood. He swallowed hard against the anger and hurt that kept rising. He had been a little boy, barely older than Scott, and it had all been so unfair. But fairness was for happy people who've been fortunate enough to live a life defined by love and certainty. Not the abuse, hate, and ambiguities he'd suffered.

"You were such a sweet boy," his mother said. "After I joined AA, I wanted to find you and make amends, I swear to God I did." Her gaze shifted to the back wall, but she kept talking as if she had practiced her speech and now recited the words by heart. "I eventually found out you'd been placed in that school, but when I called they told me you'd gone to college. When I tried the University of Utah they said you'd withdrawn. I kept telling myself you were better off without me and I wanted to believe people loved you...took care of you." She paused, studied her son. "I used to imagine a woman with soft hands and a kind voice tucking you into bed at night."

Rage flared hot in his chest. No woman with soft hands tucked him into bed at night or offered him any kindness or comfort. The one woman who was supposed to love him, loved her vodka more. Words were lost to him and he stared at her in disbelief.

As if privy to his thoughts, she shook her head and raised her trembling hand again to touch her cheek. "Alcoholism is a disease."

He shut his eyes. Under his closed lids, Bryce was at the mercy of the throbbing sound of his own pulse. He felt it in the sides of his neck and the tips of his fingers.

Then, disgusted with himself, Bryce opened his eyes and tried to clear his thoughts, tried to stop the clock from racing backward toward the boundless possibilities of another childhood. The air around him filled with blame. Without any help from this woman who was supposed to love and guide him, he had made some kind of life for himself.

Or had he made even more a mess of his life than she had hers?

His mother, as far as he knew, had never been arrested for child abuse and murder. How unfair was that? She was more responsible for Isaiah Bryce's suicide than he was for Skyler's death. Did he really want this woman back in his life?

"...it's a 12-step program." His mother hadn't stopped talking, but her voice entered his consciousness again. "The 9th step says the alcoholic needs to make direct amends to the people we've hurt except when to do so would injure them or others. I contacted Jason to apologize and ask his forgiveness. And even though he'd been dead for years, I wrote a letter to Isaiah. But you...I just..."

She turned her head, tears streaming, then turned back, as if remembering he couldn't hear her if she weren't looking at him. "I couldn't find you, but even if I could, I didn't know how to begin. None of it was your fault," she sobbed. "You were just a little boy and well...forgiving me...it's so much to ask."

Something inside Bryce softened. He'd fought so hard to forget his past, forget who he once was and where he came from that his childhood felt more like fiction than truth. He could have won an Olympic gold medal in the sport of being silent. But what good had it done him? He hadn't really run away from his past. Hiding from a monster in the living room doesn't make it go away.

When he glanced up, his mother had flattened her hand, fingers spread, against the window between them. And, instantly understanding what she wanted, part of him yearned to accommodate her, to raise his own hand and press it against the glass, matching finger for finger the hand of his mother. The depth of sadness in her eyes startled Bryce, but his arm hung limp, too heavy to lift. He stared at the lines in Rachael's palm until she pulled it away, tucked it into her lap. But the moist print on the glass lingered for a long moment before it slowly lightened and disappeared.

"Would you rather I left?" Again, she lowered her gaze, avoiding his eyes. "I don't want to intrude and make anything worse right now. I know what a hard time this has to be for you."

Bryce found his voice. "I thought about seeing you again so many times. I thought about what it would feel like to face you. My mother. The woman who abandoned me at six years old."

Her mouth remained open for a moment, as if the full implication of that was hitting her for the first time.

"And believe me," he said. "No woman with soft hands ever tucked me into bed at night." His eyes started to well up. Her reappearance was an array of contradictions. Of light and air infused with something darker, like thunder. "It's just that I didn't know seeing you again would be so confusing."

She looked into his eyes. "It's not easy for me either. I can't begin to tell you how sorry I am..."

The word forgiveness grazed his mind like a bullet. It sped by him, slowed, then speeded up as if it had no idea of its target. Over the years, he thought about forgiveness many times. Thought about forgiving the man he believed was his father. The man who hated Bryce because he was betrayed by his wife. Could he forgive this mother who took so much from him? *Forgiveness.* The word meandered down long and convoluted paths, but never found its mark.

"I would do anything if I could go back in time and change what happened," his mother said.

"Why did you leave me in that hotel room?"

"I was a selfish drunk who put myself above the welfare of my own child. I'm so sorry, Cale."

With the sincerity in her voice, pity rose inside Bryce. After all, his life had hardly been perfect—he made his own set of mistakes and in spite of good intentions ended up divorced from Valerie and now in jail.

Radhauser hung up his receiver and Bryce understood this was too personal for him, and that he wanted to give them some privacy.

"Please stop apologizing," Bryce said.

"I'll try," she said.

"We can't change the past. I mean, I'm glad you stopped drinking and put your life back together. I'm glad you found someone to love. Do you still see my father?"

She looked at him as if seeing a ghost, someone once significant, but now gone. Unable to meet his gaze, she finally answered, talking into her lap. "He's dead. You know that."

"Don't you think it's time we stopped pretending that Isaiah Bryce was my father? We both know he wasn't."

Bryce hadn't meant to sound cruel and was startled by the heartlessness of his words. He merely wanted to face the truth about his life. A relationship with his mother was impossible so long as that huge lie lay between them.

She sucked in a breath. "Your birth father had a wife and three children in Salt Lake. They moved to the east coast just before I joined AA and I never saw or heard from him again."

"What's his name?"

"Elliott Cummings. He was an administrator at Kennecott Copper in Salt Lake and used to visit the Wheatley mine when I worked at the Robertson Inn."

"Did Isaiah know about him?"

"Not at first. But later, after you were born, he suspected. No Bryce ever had brown eyes."

Bryce shook his head. Shades of Reggie Sterling and little Skyler. "So that's why he hated me so much?"

"He didn't hate you. He was hurt and angry with me. It was entirely my fault, not yours. We didn't have much money and he did the best he could. No matter how many times I got drunk, made a fool out of myself, and ran off, he took me back. It's not easy to live with an alcoholic and most men would have kicked me out the door without a cent."

"Did you love him?"

"I was young and stupid and I used him as a ticket to get away from my own messed-up family, but I wasn't in love with him."

Bryce laughed. "I meant the other guy. Did you love Elliott Cummings?"

"I was crazy about him and would have done anything he said, or at least I thought so then. But now I don't know what was me and what was the alcohol. I sure like to believe I couldn't leave you alone in that hotel if I wasn't a drunk." She shifted her gaze to the wall behind his head. "But things happen in our lives, Cale—I mean Bryce, and we try to make sense of them."

All the pieces of his life broke apart. There was a jab of pain behind his eyes, so quick and sharp he had no time to prepare for it. He dropped the receiver onto the small shelf in front of him for a moment and cradled his head in his hands. When he finally looked up, his mother began to speak.

He read her lips.

"I'm sorry. None of it was your fault."

It was her resilience and acceptance of the blame for what

she did that inspired him to be a person who at least considered allowing her this righting of a wrong. She made no excuses for her behavior. She held herself accountable. He picked up the receiver and smiled at her. "We agreed to stop apologizing, remember?"

"I agreed to try," she said.

They spent the remainder of the hour talking about their lives, her new husband, how much she loved Jason's kids, and how she thought about her younger son every time she uttered her grandson's name. As if to prove it, she pulled a worn, black and white photograph from the pocket of her skirt. In it, a boy Bryce recognized as himself sat on the concrete steps in front of their Wheatley clapboard house. In his lap, he held the pet lamb he'd named Oscar.

Bryce felt an ache so profound he nearly gasped for air. It sneaked up on him, paralyzing him with sadness for all the years he'd lost with Jason, his family, and their mother. If he were honest, he wanted many things for the remainder of his life and continued estrangement from his family was not one of them.

When the buzzer sounded, Rachael didn't rise with the other visitors. Her knuckles whitened as she clenched the phone as if it were some kind of lifeline. "Now that I've found you, I don't want to ever lose touch again. I want to be part of your life, if you'll have me."

"The way things are headed, I don't know what kind of a life I'll have. I may well spend the rest of it in jail. Or end it quickly with a lethal injection."

"I can't believe that will happen. From everything Detective Radhauser and Kendra Palmer told me, I know you'll be found innocent. We all make mistakes. You didn't hurt that little boy on purpose. God forgives us. I'm living proof."

When the guard nodded to Radhauser, he touched Rachael's shoulder.

She stood and once again pressed her open palm flat as a moth against the clear plastic wall.

This time Bryce matched it with his own, the smooth Plexiglas between them. Their eyes met and held as his fingers stretched over hers. Bryce took a deep breath. The invisible bands that bound him for so long loosened.

"Visiting hour is over," the guard said.

Radhauser tapped her shoulder again.

She crumpled into sobs.

Bryce watched as the hard-nosed detective, who told him how much he hated drunks, slipped a white handkerchief from his pocket and handed it to her. He put his arm around her shoulders, then guided her gently from the cubicle.

For hours after he returned to his cell, Bryce sat on the floor. He pulled the soles of his prison slippers together and gripped his ankles like a little boy. He rocked back and forth, continuing to feel that long, invisible thread that connected him to his mother.

CHAPTER TWENTY-SEVEN

Kendra measured Bryce's waist, sleeve, and pant length, and the distance across his shoulders and around his neck. "I know you don't like this, but the truth is a jury makes judgments based on the way a defendant appears. Besides that, your picture will be plastered in every newspaper from New York to Los Angeles, and I want you to look like a million dollars."

"Oh, I see. You're sprucing me up, afraid the old man's gonna pick up a newspaper and see his daughter standing next to a loser." He twisted away from the tape measure to get a better view of Kendra's face. "Who's going to pay for my new duds?"

"Hold still and let the rich girl with the good teeth worry about that. You have far more important things to ponder."

Kendra confided that her prime concern was to find a pool of potential jurors from which twelve impartial ones could be selected. Beyond the basic problem of locating jurors able to accept presumption of innocence, the prosecution and defense attorneys both had their own particular interests to protect.

"Something I learned from my father was that, whatever preconceived ideas a jury may have about a defendant, it is essential they see his lawyer as a person who believes in his innocence and is acting in good faith. When that happens, the lawyer wins a lot of support from the jury. In a close case, it can make all the difference."

"Do you think that's even possible, given all the crap they've read about me in the papers?"

She tried to protect Bryce from the press, but Poncho and his cohorts consistently undermined her efforts. "I won't have any problem convincing them I believe in your innocence because I do. But the most we can hope for is a jury who will listen to what we have to say before they judge. I've made copies of the police reports and other documents the DA provided." She slid the folder from her briefcase. "Read everything. Take a pencil and make a check mark next to anything you think is wrong or anything that reminds you of something you think I should know. We'll talk about it when I come back."

* * *

On her next visit, Kendra arrived toting a black garment bag from Macy's. "I bought this off the rack," she said. "Forty-two long. I sure hope it fits." She slipped the suit out of the garment bag.

Bryce tried on the jacket. It fit perfectly.

"Tilly polished your black shoes and ironed some shirts. The tie belongs to an old boyfriend of mine, so it's on loan. Don't spill any caviar or red wine on it, okay?"

He raised his eyebrows. For some unexplainable reason, the fact that she called the tie man an old boyfriend made him happy. "What's up with that? You break up and you get custody of his ties?"

"Just a couple he left in one of my dresser drawers."

"You're too much, Kendra. And you're not giving me any choice about my outfit, are you?"

"No way, Bryce. I'm calling the shots on this show now and the next stop is the barber."

"Great," Bryce said. "I've seen the way the prison barber cuts hair. Just what I need to sway the jury's vote. The skinhead look. Did you arrange for a tattoo as well?"

"I'm bringing someone in this afternoon from the outside to cut and style your hair. You need to look clean-cut and respectable, like a man who doesn't belong in a prison cell. Someone the jury sees in a positive light and can identify with." She paused and looked at him. "Like the man you really are."

Bryce fidgeted in his chair, clearly uncomfortable with the plan, but said nothing.

For nearly three hours they reviewed the prosecution's case.

Kendra asked and Bryce answered questions. And at the end he told her nothing she hadn't learned from their very first talk. He told the truth.

"Try to make eye contact with each one of the jurors. Show them you have nothing to hide, that you are there to tell the whole truth."

She pressed the button so a guard would come and let them out of the cell.

The same guard accompanied them down the corridor to the room used as a barber shop. "This is Wendy," Kendra said. "She cuts my hair, too."

A pretty, dark-haired woman shook Bryce's hand, then got to work. She washed his hair, opened her bag of tools, and started to cut. When she finished blowing his hair dry, she held a mirror up for Bryce.

"Once I put on that suit, I'm going to look like a hotshot lawyer." He nodded toward Kendra. "You need a new partner, Palmer?"

"I'll see you tomorrow, Bryce. Get some sleep. I'll have your clothes waiting for you in the holding cell. Wear the gray-striped tie. Trust me, it'll make a good first impression."

* * *

On a clear November fifteenth in Medford, the sky the bright color of a blue-throated hummingbird, Caleb Bryce's murder trial began. As Bryce stepped through the door from the stairwell where they'd kept him in a basement holding cell, television and newspaper reporters lined the second-floor corridors. There was an armed guard on either side of him.

He kept his head down, but, recognizing the cowboy boots, paused briefly in front of Detective Radhauser. The detective had been nothing but kind and helpful to him since called to the scene before Skyler's death.

Radhauser reached out and touched Bryce's shoulder in a gesture of support. "Good luck with the trial."

Bryce blinked, hoping to avoid tears of gratitude from rising.

Because of the media hype, they were using the largest available courtroom. It had bronze reliefs of past presidents framing the judge's bench. Bryce took his seat beside Kendra at the wide oak defense table and rested his right hand on one of the volumes of a blue bound set of books with gold lettering—*Oregon Revised Statutes Annotated.*

"You ready to fight?" she asked, flashing that rich girl smile.

"Yes," Bryce responded, trying to sound as confident as Andrew Marshall, the county prosecutor, looked as he stepped through the door into the courtroom. Marshall carried two huge manila folders which Bryce assumed contained the state's case against him.

With his newly-cut and styled hair, the starched white shirt, conservative tie, and the dark-colored suit, Bryce looked pretty damn good. He would have guessed himself to be an investment broker.

Kendra's motion to exclude the press had been denied, and reporters filled seats on both sides of the courtroom. One burly newsman's leg was propped up on the wooden railing that separated the gallery and behind which spectators and witnesses sat, their eyes glued on Bryce.

In addition to the new clothes, Bryce had been fitted with a hearing aid to amplify proceedings. And he heard things that he wished he hadn't—like the disappointment in one woman's voice as she muttered to her neighbor, "I expected him to be bigger. He doesn't look like a baby killer."

"Look at his hands," a man said, leaning toward a thin woman in a paisley dress. "They're huge and powerful looking."

Bryce removed his hands from the table top and folded them on his lap. Kendra advised him to sit quietly, look directly at the witness stand, and listen to everything he could hear.

The attorney had also arranged for a young woman from the Oregon School for the Deaf, a board-certified interpreter, to sit in front of Bryce and sign so he would always know what questions were asked, even when the attorneys had their backs to him. Bryce had learned to sign at the Institute, but rarely used it because his speech was understandable to most hearing people.

Finally, the wood panels behind the bench opened and the

presiding judge, the Honorable Stephen Shapiro, entered and took his seat on the bench. On either side of him, on the back wall, American and Oregon State flags drooped in the still air.

While the clerk read the roll of prospective jurors, Bryce glanced around the courtroom. Extra chairs had been brought in to accommodate the overflow of reporters.

In the selection of jurors, it soon became obvious to Bryce that the prosecution wanted individuals unopposed to a death sentence. Only a few seemed to object, and some of those expressed a willingness to reconsider when dealing with this type of case. Jurors with any reservations were asked a question by Marshall, "Even when it deals with the murder of a child—a nineteen-month-old toddler?"

Each time Marshall asked, slightly rephrasing the question after Kendra's objection, Bryce cringed. He twisted his sweaty hands under the oak table as jurors with substantial reservations about a death penalty were, one by one, disqualified by the prosecution.

The jury selection was slow and tedious. Kendra asked the same question of each juror. "Do you think Mr. Bryce has done anything wrong?" And often enough to frighten the wits out of him, the answer she received was positive.

Kendra stood in front of one prospective juror, a well-dressed woman in her forties, the wife of a local pediatrician. "And why, Mrs. McIntyre, do you think so?"

"Because he's here," she replied, her voice clear and assertive. "Why would he have been arrested and brought to trial if he did nothing wrong?"

"That's a very good question," Kendra said before she dismissed that potential juror.

Another prospective juror, a man in a three-piece suit, tried to get himself exempted. "I can't be impartial in this case. I have a son, just about the same age as Skyler Sterling, and it makes me so mad to think of that son of a bitch hurting someone that innocent and small." He turned to face Bryce and spat out the remainder of his words. "I want to kill him myself."

Kendra made a motion for a change of venue stating this

answer showed the hostile attitude of the entire community and demonstrated that a fair trial for Caleb Bryce in Jackson County, Oregon, was impossible.

Judge Shapiro denied the motion.

To nearly all the jurors, Kendra asked one final question. "Can you assure me that you will base your verdict on the evidence deemed admissible in this courtroom and not on anything you've seen on television, heard on the radio, or read in the newspapers?"

A twelve-member jury was finally selected. It included a school janitor, a car mechanic, a hospital marketing director, a nursing home kitchen worker, a clothing saleswoman at Macy's, a Medford school bus driver, the manager of Appleby's Restaurant, three homemakers, the owner of an apartment complex, a local high school math teacher, and two alternates.

The jury was a good mix of races, ages, occupations, educational backgrounds, and sexes. "All in all," Kendra mouthed to Bryce, "I'm pretty pleased."

With the jury dismissed from the courtroom, Kendra rose from her chair and submitted a motion to bring Dr. Martin Gerhardt, a clinical psychologist, to testify that the jurors selected were subconsciously affected by the pretrial media coverage concerning the case.

"All twelve jurors and the two alternates read about this case in the newspaper," Kendra said. "Ten have admitted to seeing it on television and six admit to having discussed it with other people." She paced in front of the judge's bench. "Now don't get me wrong, Your Honor, I'm not trying to say these people lied about their ability to remain impartial. I know they told the truth to the best of their ability. But I propose to show that subconsciously they absorbed much of the media information."

Judge Shapiro agreed to hear Gerhardt's testimony the following morning in the absence of the jury.

At eight-thirty the next morning, Kendra carted a box filled with newspaper clippings, and television and radio tapes into the courtroom. "Your Honor. These exhibits are intended to support my contention that the jurors, even though they are honest and forthright, may be mistaken in stating they have not already made up their minds about my client's guilt or innocence."

When Dr. Gerhardt took the witness stand, he looked over the exhibits, thought about each question carefully and finally concluded, "In my opinion, it would be impossible for a juror who has read and seen these accounts to completely disregard the information when it comes time to reach a verdict."

Despite Gerhardt's testimony, Judge Shapiro denied the motion for moving the trial to another location. He concluded the court must take the jurors at their word and all of them stated they would be fair and just in their deliberations.

When the bailiff left the room to summon the jury, Bryce glanced around the courtroom. His mother and brother were seated behind him in the second row. As his eyes connected with hers, Rachael held on for a moment, then smiled, blew him a kiss and bowed her head. When Jason winked, Bryce nodded and swallowed. He wasn't alone anymore.

Turning his attention back to the defense table, he jotted a note on a yellow sheet of paper and passed it to Kendra. *And now it begins...*

She nodded, then covered Bryce's hand for an instant with her own.

CHAPTER TWENTY-EIGHT

Bryce sat quietly behind the defense table and watched the jury assemble and settle into their seats. If one of them made eye contact with him, he met their gaze, looking directly into their eyes as Kendra had instructed.

Judge Shapiro called the court to order. He spent a half hour instructing the jury, reviewing his courtroom schedule. They would start promptly at 9 a.m. Lunch from noon to 1 p.m. A fifteen-minute morning and afternoon break. And Maria already told Kendra he meant what he said. Shapiro was the kind of judge who tried a full day, every day.

When the judge finished, Andrew Marshall stood, buttoned his jacket, then consulted a sheet of paper on his table, laid his pencil aside and turned to the jury. He wore a navy-blue suit, gray shirt, and a blue, red and gray tie. An American flag was pinned on his lapel. His wingtips were spit polished. He was armed and ready.

"Ladies and gentlemen of the jury," he began. A portable lectern was available, but Marshall elected not to use it. He had no notes. A man who spoke from the heart. "I'm Andrew Marshall and I'll be presenting the state of Oregon's case against the defendant, Caleb Bryce. This trial will not be a pretty one. It involves the death of a nineteen-month-old boy." He paused and held up a photo of Skyler Sterling on his first birthday for the jury to see.

It was one of Bryce's favorites. There was cake smeared on the toddler's cheeks.

Marshall waited the appropriate amount of time to have the enormity of what was lost sink in. "It will be told by about ten witnesses, the 9-1-1 tape, doctors at Ashland Hospital, the police detective who investigated the case, the medical examiner, the ex-husband of the victim's mother, and the victim's four-year-old brother."

"And when you hear their stories, when you piece it all together, you will see that the state of Oregon has proven to you, without a reasonable doubt, that Mr. Bryce poisoned Skyler Sterling and then tried to cover it up by calling 9-1-1 and claiming the child seized and stopped breathing." Marshall paused and sighed, as if to let the jury know he took no joy in doing his job on behalf of the people.

"If it pleases the court," Kendra Palmer interrupted the prosecutor. "If counsel may approach the bench."

"You may," Judge Shapiro replied.

Bryce strained to listen to what was said in front of the judge, but he was unable to make out a single word. His interpreter's hands were still.

When they finished, Kendra pivoted and returned to the defense table, her face revealing nothing. She wrote Bryce a note. *I asked the judge if Marshall could cut the theatrics—the long sighs and hangdog looks.*

Marshall appeared slightly flustered, but resumed his address.

"The beginning of this story goes back to Caleb Bryce's meeting Dana Sterling, the mother of Skyler and Scott Sterling. You will hear testimony regarding the volatile and abusive nature of that relationship." Marshall removed his horn-rimmed glasses, rubbed the bridge of his nose, then replaced them.

"On the morning before Skyler Sterling's death, neighbors overheard Mr. Bryce fighting with his girlfriend. Later, he admitted to Detective Radhauser that he had a rough day with Scott, and hit him harder than he intended. He put both boys to bed early." Marshall paused, stepped a little closer to the jury box.

"And you'll see that Mr. Bryce finally reached his limit—had all he could stand. Dana was about to leave him. She was young, beautiful, and had many friends. Bryce was a loner, on medical leave from his job, and alienated from his family and society. He was a man angry enough to hurt someone. He was jealous and desperate, mad enough to strike out at a four-year-old. He was resentful of his own situation and impotent to change anything. His rage built and built until somebody did die, a nineteen-month-old child. A substitute for Dana."

"The state intends to show that Caleb Bryce was so enraged and out of control in the 9-1-1 tape that he says, not once, but five times, "She's gonna die." Marshall frowned, and laced his hands together in front of him.

"She, Dana Sterling, didn't die. But her baby, Skyler Sterling, did, ladies and gentlemen. And his testimony can only be heard through the medical examiner's report. When you see the slides of that little boy's body, hear the extent of his internal injuries—injuries the doctors repaired, but they couldn't repair the damage caused by the drug overdose—poison given to him in his bottle of apple juice. A bottle the defendant admits to preparing. There is only one conclusion to be drawn in this case and that is this defendant," he paused, unlaced his hands and turned toward Bryce, "murdered Skyler Sterling in order to get even with his girlfriend, Dana, for threatening to leave him."

Marshall took a deep breath. "As for the child abuse accusation, you'll read the deposition of an elderly neighbor who witnessed the defendant's attack on a helpless four-year-old boy and heard his threat to murder Scott Sterling. You'll also hear from Scott himself, who claims the defendant hated him. The evidence presented in the murder case will make it very clear Mr. Bryce was capable of anything."

Completing his opening statement, Marshall stood perfectly still for a moment, bowed his head as if he were about to pray for guidance, then walked briskly over to his table and sat down.

When Judge Shapiro shifted his gaze to Kendra, it was their turn to face the jury. Bryce's shoulders slumped and again he doubted himself. A little boy was dead, and maybe he wouldn't be if only Bryce hadn't entered his life. He straightened his shoulders. What was he thinking? He didn't lace Skyler's bottle with Haloperidol. Whatever he might be guilty of, he did not kill Skyler.

Kendra, poised and self-confident, stood at the end of the defense table, her right hand slipped casually into the pocket of her gray blazer, her left rested on a statute book. She didn't pace during her statement, but spoke directly to the body of jurors, making eye contact at least once with every one of them.

After introducing herself, Kendra began. "There is no dispute that a terrible tragedy unfolded in the late evening of October eleventh and the early morning of the twelfth. The defense is not, in any way, trying to diminish that tragedy. A baby is dead. And all the possibilities for Skyler Sterling and what he might have brought into the world are no more."

"But think about it. There could be nothing worse for anyone who loved that little boy than to be falsely accused of having killed him. The state is trying to compound the tragedy of Skyler's death by sending an innocent man, a man who loved that child, to death by lethal injection." Kendra lifted her left hand to touch Bryce's shoulder, just as she'd told him she would—showing the jury she believed in him and had no fear.

"From the beginning, I'll make it clear that anything you hear in these opening statements from either the prosecution or myself is not evidence." She paused and moved closer to the jury box. "The evidence comes after the witnesses are sworn in by the clerk, seated in that chair next to the judge, and talking to you, the jurors, who will ultimately decide the fate of Caleb Bryce." She pointed toward the wooden witness box to the right of Judge Shapiro.

"Our opening comments are designed to orient you, in a kind of outline form, about the case you will hear. A whole lot of small pieces will come out in this case and it is your responsibility to assemble them, once you have them all, and come to your own conclusion about what happened on the night of October eleventh and the early morning of October twelfth."

"The defense intends to show you that Mr. Bryce loved Skyler Sterling. He loved him so much that he offered him a place in his home, and actually took care of him and his older brother during the day while Skyler's mother slept and again at night when she worked. He made toys and a playhouse for him."

Bryce tried hard not to crumple at the memory of the playhouse. The way Scott and Skyler played so peacefully together. He sucked in a craggy breath and forced himself to return his concentration to Kendra's opening statement.

"We will review the events leading up to that night. And, while perhaps Mr. Bryce could have acted in a different manner and left Skyler in his crib while he phoned for help, that isn't what he did, ladies and gentlemen. He picked up the toddler, and, not thinking about anything except the fact the child wasn't breathing, raced across the room, tripped over a toy, and stumbled into the coffee table in his desperate effort to telephone for help."

Kendra was smooth in her presentation, didn't miss a beat, and the jury listened as if mesmerized.

"Ladies and gentlemen, when Mr. Bryce walked into that bedroom to check on the boys and discovered Skyler in his crib, blue and not breathing, he simply reacted as any parent would."

At this point, Kendra stepped even closer to the jury box, centered herself in front of it and spoke directly into their faces.

Because he could no longer see her lips, Bryce watched the hands of the young woman who signed for him. "And if that's a crime, then my client is indeed guilty. But it is our contention that he behaved, not like a murderer, but like a man terrified for the life of a child he considered his own. He behaved, I venture to say, exactly the same way you or I might have behaved in the same petrifying situation."

"The prosecution will be hard pressed to find a motive. Because there is none. Mr. Bryce had no reason to kill a child he loved. We subpoenaed his medical records and he is not taking, nor has he ever taken, Haloperidol—the prescription drug that killed Skyler Sterling."

"You'll clearly hear the terror in his voice on the 9-1-1 tape, you'll hear testimony from the investigating officer and the paramedics who found Mr. Bryce with his index finger clamped between Skyler's jaws, the toddler's teeth actually exposing the bone. They found him, despite the pain he must have felt from the injury to his hand, frantically trying to administer CPR. And it succeeded. When paramedics arrived, Skyler Sterling was breathing again."

"As to the child abuse charge, you'll hear testimony from the victim's mother that her older son, Scott, was a handful and that she told Mr. Bryce he was too easy on Scott. Indeed, you'll hear testimony he never laid a hand on Scott before that day when the boy kicked, bit and finally spat in Bryce's face. At his wits' end, he struck Scott on the butt with his open palm. If that's child abuse, I suspect most every parent in the world is equally guilty."

As Kendra completed her opening statement, turned away from the jury and started back toward the defense table, her face turned to stone.

Bryce followed his attorney's stare to a well-dressed, dark-haired man with strands of silver at his temples. He stood at the back of the courtroom. As Bryce watched, the man slipped up the center aisle and squeezed into the third row.

He was over six feet tall, tan and fit, and looked like he should be on the cover of some American Bar Association journal. His gray, pinstriped suit was obviously expensive and an alligator briefcase lay across his lap. The man didn't look at Kendra, but rather kept his gaze straight ahead, focused on Judge Shapiro as he dismissed the jury for lunch.

"Oh, shit," Kendra whispered as she sat down next to Bryce. "What's he doing here?"

* * *

"I can't believe my father had the balls to just show up. He didn't even call and tell me he was coming." Kendra paced the basement holding room, ignoring her lunch tray on the conference table across from Bryce. "Listen to me," she raged on. "Whining about him not telling me he was coming. He didn't even ask if I wanted him here. He just assumes…"

"It's a public place. He didn't need your permission. Maybe he wanted to surprise you. Maybe he wanted to see his daughter in action," Bryce said. "I think you put on a pretty good performance. And who do you think you're kidding? I thought part of the reason you took on my case was because you wanted him to notice you."

Kendra stood in the corner of the windowless room, staring at an ugly painting as if it had something important to tell her. "I took your case because it was assigned to me."

"Come on, Kendra. What's the worst thing that can happen?"

"How would you feel if your father showed up without warning?"

Bryce locked eyes with Kendra and he tried hard not to smile as he said, "I don't know, Kendra. The man I thought was my father is dead, but I'd like to think I'd give him another chance, the same way I did my mother."

"Give me a break, Bryce, it's not the same and you know it. Your mother was sick, suffering from alcoholism. The truth is, she had no real idea what she did to you until after she got sober and thought back on it. My father thinks I'm a child and can't handle a high-profile case. That I need my daddy's help."

"No breaks, Kendra. I can be as ruthless as you when I know I'm right."

"You don't know shit," Kendra grumbled, unable to stop the smile from spreading across her face.

"The way I see it, this is your opportunity. Rise to the occasion and show the old man what you're really made of. Show him the apple didn't fall far from the tree."

* * *

Her father waited for her on a bench outside the holding cell. He stood and wrapped his arms around her.

For a moment, she was comforted, taken back to childhood by his clean smell of soap and the evergreen aftershave he wore her entire life.

"I hope you don't mind my coming," he said. "I finished my case early and wanted to see where my daughter lived and what she was doing."

Kendra wasn't fooled by his contrived concern for her well-being. He heard about the case and wasn't sure she could handle it without him. "Where are you staying?"

"I booked a room at the Mark Anthony on Main Street. You're

right. Ashland is a charming little town. I got in early last night and walked around for a while. I can understand why you like it here."

"It's very different from San Francisco."

"I sat in on your opening statement. Looks like you've got yourself a tough case right out of the starting gate."

She waited for him to compliment her on the opening statement.

He didn't.

"It is going to be hard, but I'm pretty sure I can win it."

He looked at her for a minute as if trying to decide whether or not to ask. "Would you like some help?"

There it was. The truth. "I don't know, Dad. I'm confident I can poke some serious holes in the prosecution's case. But probably not enough to guarantee reasonable doubt. My client doesn't have a motive. I'm one hundred percent certain he's not guilty. And I keep remembering what you told me about how hard it is to represent someone you know is innocent."

"Is the prosecution trying to fabricate motive?"

"Yes. They'll say he killed the toddler to get even with Dana, his mother, because she threatened to leave him."

"Marshall can speculate your client sought revenge against his girlfriend. But that's all it would be. Speculation. He'll need evidence to prove it beyond a reasonable doubt."

"He's got some witnesses who heard him call her a selfish bitch the morning before Skyler died, but not much more than that."

"I'm happy to go over the prosecution's case and see if I can find any weaknesses that might help you. Do you have other suspects?"

"The investigating officer, Winston Radhauser, believes my client is innocent, too. He suspects Reggie Sterling, the father—who claims Skyler was not his biological son and has repeatedly told others he couldn't stand the kid. The mother, Dana Sterling, is another possible suspect. She was hardly mother of the year material. Let's face it, anyone could have tampered with that bottle. From what I understand, Haloperidol, the murder weapon, is a clear liquid and it would have gone unnoticed in the bottom of that baby bottle."

"You told me Detective Radhauser believes Bryce is innocent. If that's the case, why did he arrest him only eleven days after the murder?"

"Radhauser went so far as to tell me he was pressured by his boss. Ashland is a small town and the press went crazy. Murders are rare here. And the murder of a toddler is unheard of. There were demonstrations in the streets demanding someone be held accountable."

"Look, sweetheart. I know how you feel about wanting to prove yourself and make your own reputation, so I won't do anything you don't want me to. But it sounds to me like you need a plausible alternative to Bryce as the murderer."

Wow. That was a change. Usually her father just moved in and took over. An innocent man's life was at stake. Her father was one of the best criminal defense attorneys in the country, maybe even in the world. She couldn't let her pride get in the way of doing the right thing for Bryce. And the truth was, she needed help.

"Okay, Dad. Sure, I'd love it if you'd take a look at the case. Maybe I can bring Detective Radhauser in to talk to you as well. I know what a stickler you are for detail, and he's a good detective who knows more about what happened that night than anyone. There's a little conference room in our offices you can use. I'll call Radhauser and set it up."

"You want to grab some dinner? I saw some charming little restaurants overlooking the creek."

"That sounds great. I'll meet you in the lobby of your hotel at six."

"Let's celebrate that opening statement you gave today. You made the old man proud."

CHAPTER TWENTY-NINE

When Winston Radhauser was called as the first witness, he hurried up to the stand. He was in a precarious situation—a witness for the prosecution who believed the defendant he had arrested was not guilty of the crime. He needed to find a way to tell the truth without damaging the reputation of either himself, Captain Murphy, or the Ashland Police Department.

After Radhauser was sworn in, Marshall asked him the usual identifying questions. Name. Job. Duration of employment.

"Were you the investigating officer sent to the scene on Pine Street in Ashland after the defendant called 9-1-1?"

"Yes, I received notification from dispatch about 12:15 a.m. that a small child had been injured. She said the 9-1-1 caller sounded drunk. Felix Murphy, my boss, decided a detective should investigate."

"What did you find when you arrived?"

"I knocked several times, but no one answered. The front door was unlocked. I went inside and yelled out, but still no one answered." He described the overturned coffee table, the tarot cards scattered about the floor, the broken glass from the oil lamp globe, and the spilled vase of daffodils.

"Where was the defendant?"

"At first I didn't know. I kept calling out, but got no answer. I noticed a trail of blood drops on the tile floor that led into what I believed must be the kitchen. I placed my hand on the Glock in my holster and followed them. I found the defendant in the kitchen administering CPR to a small child. I called out again, but there was no answer. He had his back to me. I soon realized he was hearing impaired."

244

"Was the defendant intoxicated?"

"Objection," Kendra said. "Since there were no blood alcohol levels taken, this calls for an opinion."

"I'll allow," Judge Shapiro said.

"No, he was not. The 9-1-1 tape sounded garbled because of his speech impediment."

"I understand you photographed the scene."

"I did."

Marshall handed him a stack of photographs. "Are these the photos you took that morning?"

Radhauser looked at them for a moment. "Yes." He gave the photos back to Marshall, who handed them to a clerk for delivery to Kendra and then the jury.

"Did you determine the source of the blood?"

"It came from the defendant's finger. The victim clamped his teeth down on it during a seizure when the defendant was attempting to clear the child's airway."

"Did you interview the older child, Scott Sterling?"

"Yes. After the ambulance left with Skyler, Scott wandered into the living room. At first, I didn't realize there was a second child."

"What was the nature of your conversation?"

"Scott accused Bryce of hitting him on the backside and making him go to bed too early."

"Was this a concern for you?"

The question stopped Radhauser and he thought about it for a few seconds. "At first, I was shocked and angered by what the child said, but after hearing the whole story and witnessing the way Bryce interacted with the boy, I felt differently."

"I later learned the boy was upset because he wasn't allowed to eat ice cream before dinner. And that he pushed Skyler, resulting in a fall down some concrete stairs. I have a four-year-old and I know how they love to exaggerate and claim things aren't fair."

"If you weren't concerned, why did you file a report with Child Protective Services?"

"Because I'm required by law to do so with even the slightest suspicion of abuse."

"So, you had a slight suspicion."

"I had the boy's testimony."

"Did officers with a search warrant look for evidence at the Bryce home?"

"Yes."

"What did they find?"

Radhauser knew where Marshall was going with this and he dreaded giving his answer. "They found an empty bottle of Haloperidol in the bathroom trash can, and the baby bottle in the victim's bed."

"What did forensics on the baby bottle show?"

"There was residue of both Haloperidol and apple juice in the bottle."

"No further questions."

On cross-examination Kendra asked, "What was the state of mind of the defendant when you arrived at his house?"

"Objection," Marshall said. "Calls for an opinion."

"I'll rephrase, Your Honor. What did you observe in the kitchen?"

"I saw a man frantically administering CPR to a young child. I saw that the child had clamped down on the defendant's finger and it was dripping blood. But the defendant continued to do everything in his power to get the toddler to breathe. When paramedics were able to release the finger, the defendant's bone was exposed."

"Did the defendant tell you it was his fault the child stopped breathing?"

"No. Not directly. He blamed himself because he fell asleep and hadn't checked on Skyler as often as he planned to after his fall down the steps. He was afraid the toddler might have sustained a concussion and that was the reason for the seizure."

"How would you characterize his behavior?"

"Objection," Marshall said. "Again, she is calling for an opinion."

Judge Shapiro overruled the objection.

"He behaved like a man who'd do anything to save a child he

obviously loved." There, he said it. The truth. And he sure hoped it wouldn't come back to bite him in the ass.

"Did forensics check for fingerprints on the Haloperidol bottle?"

"Yes. They did, but the prints were not in the system."

"Were they compared with the defendant's?"

"Yes. They were not a match."

"From the evidence collected so far in this case, do you believe, beyond any reasonable doubt, that Caleb Bryce deliberately poisoned Skyler Sterling?"

Despite his understanding of why Kendra asked it, this was the one question he'd hoped he wouldn't have to answer. He waited a second, hoping Marshall would object.

Although he knew there'd be consequences from ADA Marshall and Captain Murphy, his innate sense of integrity wouldn't allow him to answer any other way. "No," he said. "I can't truthfully say that I do."

"Objection, Your Honor," Marshall said. "Yet another opinion."

Now, Radhauser understood. Marshall had expected a much different answer from a member of the prosecution's team.

"Sustained," Judge Shapiro said. "Jury is instructed to ignore that question and response."

"No further questions," Kendra said, a slight smile on her face.

* * *

The prosecution's next witness was the medical examiner, Dr. Steven Heron.

Bryce had never met him before and there was something about Dr. Heron that reminded him of Isaiah Bryce. Probably the leanness of his body and length of his neck. The way he seemed to lope, rather than walk, up to the stand. After the court clerk swore him in, Marshall introduced his credentials, his numerous board certifications, and established him as an expert in the field of forensic pathology.

Marshall blocked Bryce's view of Dr. Heron so he watched the woman sign in front of him, even though he could hear much of the testimony thanks to the device in his ear.

"Did you perform the autopsy on Skyler Sterling?"

"Yes, I did."

"Would you please review your findings as to cause of death?"

Dr. Heron referred to his report, spread out on the stand in front of him. "Skyler Sterling died from an overdose of Haloperidol, a drug used for certain psychiatric disorders. Skyler Sterling was poisoned."

"Were there other injuries?"

"Yes, some pretty severe ones. He suffered a lacerated spleen and hepatic portal vein. The spleen was removed and the vein repaired by a pediatric surgeon at Ashland Hospital."

"Would you please educate us, in layman's terms if possible, as to the function and importance of this vein?" Marshall stepped back from the stand, and Bryce, his eyes now planted on Heron's face, could lip read what he couldn't hear.

"It's part of a major network that returns blood to the heart. The hepatic portal system includes veins that drain blood from the pancreas, spleen, stomach, intestines, and gall bladder and transport it to the portal vein of the liver. Ultimately, blood leaves the liver through the hepatic veins, enters the inferior vena cava, and is carried into the heart."

"So, is it accurate to say Skyler Sterling would have bled to death from his injury on October eleventh had the surgeon not repaired the vein?"

"Yes," Dr. Heron replied. "He likely would have."

Marshall asked that the lights be dimmed so the medical examiner could review slides of the dead toddler's body before autopsy. "Ladies and gentlemen of the jury," Marshall announced, "these may be difficult to view. If you feel queasy, take a deep breath. Sometimes it helps to oxygenate."

Dr. Heron presented five slides. One of Skyler's head. There was a blue knot the size of a large egg above his right eyebrow. He showed two views of his chest area, revealing numerous black and blue marks, and one of his lower extremities. The toddler had scrapes and bruises on both legs. The last slide was a close up of the child's penis which showed a bruise and human teeth marks.

Two jurors gasped.

"All in all," Heron testified. "There were twenty bruises on Skyler Sterling's body."

"Did you see evidence of sexual abuse?"

"I'm not sure," Heron said. "There was no anal tearing or bruising. But he didn't bite himself on the penis."

"So, you're saying sexual abuse is a possibility."

"I wouldn't rule it out without further investigation."

"In your expert opinion, Dr. Heron, what would cause the severing of a hepatic vein?"

"A severe trauma. Sometimes a bullet. But most often we see this kind of blunt force injury when a child is struck by a car or a baseball bat, or a heavy object falls on their abdominal region."

"Could an adult foot cause such an injury, Dr. Heron?"

Knowing Marshall had carefully plotted his questions, Bryce wondered where he was headed with that one.

"Objection, Your Honor. Leading the witness." Kendra stood, and took a step toward the bench.

"Overruled," Judge Shapiro said. "You may answer the question, Dr. Heron."

"Yes," he said. "I believe an adult who kicked or stepped on a child of Skyler Sterling's size and weight could inflict this type of injury."

"Thank you, Dr. Heron." Marshall stepped away from the witness stand to take his place at the prosecution table. "I have no further questions."

On cross-examination, Kendra had only a few questions. "Could the type of injury sustained by Skyler Sterling have occurred as a result of a fall down three concrete stairs?"

"It's possible, but not very likely unless he hit the edge of the concrete with great force," Dr. Heron said, shaking his head. "Kids fall all the time. Ordinarily they're pretty resilient."

"How about a fall sustained when a frantic adult raced across the room to call 9-1-1, a child blue and not breathing cradled in the crook of his arm? If that one-hundred-and-eighty pound adult tripped over a coffee table and fell on top of that twenty-five pound child, is it possible, Dr. Heron, that such an injury could be sustained?"

"Objection, Your Honor." Marshall was on his feet. "Connection," he demanded.

"I move that Your Honor receive the evidence to which my opponent has just objected subject to later connection." Kendra approached the bench. "I present to the court it is my intention to connect this fall by testimony from the paramedics who first appeared on the scene. They will testify they observed evidence, as well as my client's statement, to such a fall. The jury has already seen the photographs Detective Radhauser took of the overturned coffee table and broken oil lamp globe."

"I'll allow," Judge Shapiro said. "You may answer the question, Dr. Heron."

"Yes. Given the probable force of a running one-hundred-and-eighty pound adult falling on top of a twenty-five pound child, I would say injuries of the type Skyler Sterling sustained would be quite possible."

Kendra continued with her questioning. "The drug found in Skyler Sterling's blood, Haloperidol—isn't it also used to treat symptoms of severe alcohol withdrawal?"

"Yes," Heron replied. "It's been shown to be very effective in treating delirium tremens."

"Was there something in particular in the autopsy that made you suspect Skyler had been poisoned?"

Heron told the jury what he told Radhauser about the EKG and how unusual it was for a young child with a healthy heart to have QT interval prolongation. That it was a measurement of the time between the start of a Q wave and the end of a T wave in the heart's electrical cycle. "Often prolongation is a risk factor for sudden death."

He told the jury after more laboratory work, they found high concentrations of Haloperidol and its metabolites in Skyler's blood and urine, and upon microscopic examination of his tissues. "This drug can cause seizures and heart rhythm abnormalities and would explain the QT interval prolongation."

"I'd like to revisit the bite marks on Skyler Sterling's penis," she said, handing him a copy of the photograph Radhauser had taken of the bite mark on Bryce's arm. Please compare this to your photograph of the victim's bite marks."

The medical examiner studied the photos for a moment. "Both bites show small teeth indentations, likely those of a child."

"Thank you, Dr. Heron. I have no further questions." Kendra laid her hand reassuringly on Bryce's shoulder as she settled back into the seat beside him. Another gesture to show the jury she saw him as a decent human being and not a penis-biting child killer.

Andrew Marshall called Dr. Carter Barrows to the stand and after he was sworn in questioned him with regard to his credentials, the medical school he attended and his board certifications.

"Where do you currently work, Dr. Barrows?"

"I'm an emergency room physician at the Ashland Hospital."

"Were you on duty the night of October eleventh and early morning of October twelfth?"

"Yes, sir, I was."

"Did you treat Skyler Sterling?"

"Yes, sir, I did."

"Would you please describe the condition of the child, Skyler Sterling, when you examined him?"

"His respirations were shallow and he was cyanotic. Paramedics reported the toddler had been found in his crib, stiff and apparently not breathing. CPR was administered at home and breathing resumed. At first, it appeared to be a seizure."

"Were you suspicious of any other injuries?"

"Objection." Kendra stood. "Leading the witness."

The judge overruled and directed Barrows to answer.

"There was a large contusion on the child's forehead, just over his right eye, several other bruises on the chest, but no obvious external injury to suggest something like a ruptured hepatic vein." He paused, shuddered visibly, then continued. "We did have difficulty getting a vein to start IV fluids, but that sometimes happens with small children. They get dehydrated easily."

"Were the number of external bruises unusual in a child of that

251

age?" Marshall stood with his hands planted on his narrow hips.

"Yes and no," Dr. Barrows answered. "We see all sorts of things in the ER. Kids that age are eye level to many surfaces that can cause injury to them. But we're required to report any suspicion of child abuse to the authorities, and I did the following morning."

"Were you informed by Mr. Bryce or the paramedics of any trauma to the child preceding the incident, any fall?"

"No. But the circumstances were unusual. The paramedics got another call for an automobile accident. They left in a hurry. Mr. Bryce was not with the child. Skyler was brought in by ambulance, without either of his parents. When the parents arrived, maybe fifteen minutes or so later, neither had been with the child at the time of the alleged seizure. And Skyler was already in surgery."

"Would you have taken a different course of treatment had you suspected other trauma?" Marshall asked, then turned toward the jury.

"I doubt it would have changed the outcome very much," Barrows said. "We got him to surgery pretty quickly. If we'd known he ingested Haloperidol, we might have pumped his stomach before surgery. It's possible that could have made a difference."

"No more questions, Your Honor." Kendra sat beside Bryce. She scribbled a note on her yellow pad to reassure him.

Once Marshall was finished with his cross-examination, Kendra stood again. "Were the bruises on the child's chest consistent with attempts to perform CPR by an untrained adult?"

"Possibly," Barrows replied. "Pediatric CPR is different from adult CPR. Few lay people, even when trained, administer it to a child in a life-threatening situation without some evidence of injury."

Kendra stepped closer to the stand for her next question. "Dr. Barrows, were you aware my client, Caleb Bryce, did come to the hospital that night after he arranged care for Skyler's older brother? Mr. Bryce checked in at the emergency room and was sent up to the third-floor surgical waiting room. He would have been more than willing to talk with the physicians treating Skyler."

"No, ma'am. We were not informed of Mr. Bryce's presence, or that he had any pertinent information about the child."

"So, no one at the hospital asked Mr. Bryce what happened that night?"

"Not to my knowledge."

"Thank you," Kendra said. "No further questions."

CHAPTER THIRTY

When Andrew Marshall called Reggie Sterling to the stand, dread wrapped its hands around Bryce's throat. Reggie hated him and Bryce had no idea what he might say. After Reggie was sworn in, Marshall surprised Bryce with his line of questioning.

"Are you the biological father of Skyler Sterling?"

Reggie paused, stared at his lap. "I don't think so," he said in a voice Bryce couldn't hear even with the aid. He read the interpreter's signs. "Dana had a one-night stand when we were still married, but having some problems."

"His birth certificate has your name on it, doesn't it, Mr. Sterling?"

"No, well, not exactly. You see Dana kept the Sterling name. So, you could say Skyler's birth certificate has her name on it. I didn't acknowledge him as my biological son."

"Do you know who Skyler's father is?"

He glared at Bryce. "I have a pretty good idea, but I can't be sure."

"How about Scott? Is Scott your son?"

"Yes, he's my boy, all right. Our baby pictures are identical. You can't tell us apart," he said, his chest swelling.

A giggle escaped from one of the younger female jurors who quickly covered her mouth and lowered her head.

"Did you continue to have a relationship with Dana after she moved in with Mr. Bryce?"

"I saw her once in a while after she got off work. And sometimes during the day when I came to visit Scott. Before Bryce hurt his leg and hung around all the time. Me and Dana were talking about getting back together."

"And was Dana agreeable to that?" Marshall stepped back and Bryce could read Reggie's response on his lips.

"She said she wanted to, but was afraid of what Bryce would do if she left him."

"She was afraid of Mr. Bryce? Do you know why?"

"Objection, Your Honor." Kendra leapt to her feet. "Calls for an opinion on the part of the witness."

"I'll rephrase the question, Your Honor." Marshall glanced at Kendra and smiled. It wasn't a nice smile. "Did Dana Sterling indicate to you why she feared Mr. Bryce?"

"He stabbed her with an ice pick."

The whole court sucked in a breath, followed by what seemed like an eternity of utter stillness.

Bryce couldn't believe he really heard Reggie's testimony and asked the interpreter to repeat her signs. When she did, his stomach curled into a knot as if to shield a kick. He never laid a hand on Dana, not once. And she told him the small scars on her abdomen were made by Reggie.

"Objection, Your Honor." Kendra broke the silence and again rose to her feet. "That's hearsay. Mr. Sterling was witness to no such act."

"Please bear with me, Your Honor," Marshall asked. "This is important to the defendant's state of mind and may help establish a probable motive."

"Objection overruled. State of mind and evidence of motive is admissible." Judge Shapiro readjusted his weight on the bench.

Reggie concluded his testimony for the prosecution by stating that Dana showed him two tiny scars on her abdomen.

"Your witness," Marshall said. As he turned his body toward Kendra, the corners of his mouth lifted in another faint smile.

Kendra did not cross-examine. "I'd like to reserve the right to call Mr. Sterling to the stand at a later time."

Judge Shapiro granted her request and due to the lateness of the hour, dismissed the court for the day, instructing the jury not to talk about the trial, not watch TV, and not read the newspapers.

Bryce was led downstairs to the holding room, Kendra at his heels.

When the door closed, she turned to him, her face contorted and red. "Why in the hell didn't you tell me about that? We had an agreement, Bryce, that you'd tell me everything, that there wouldn't be any surprises in court. The truth is this little bombshell could kill our case."

He slammed his fist on the table. "It was a surprise to me, too." The shock of Reggie's false testimony under oath had torn the entire framework of Bryce's belief system away. He collapsed in a heap on the chair. "I...I...never laid a hand on Dana. I swear it. He's lying." With those words, Bryce dropped his head into his hands. "Jesus Christ, Kendra," he muttered. "I don't know how to fight this thing anymore. Maybe I should just give up and let them do whatever they want to me. Sometimes I think I'd rather be dead anyway. But I can tell you one thing about the truth..." He lifted his head. "It isn't being told here."

"So, what is the truth? It's about time you told me all of it."

"You've got to believe me." Bryce's mind was racing. "I've turned myself inside out to tell you the truth. I feel as if I'm going crazy. Dana told me the exact same story about Reggie. She pointed to those little scars and said, 'Reggie Sterling put them there with an ice pick.' She claimed it was why she really left him. I swear to God, Kendra, that's what she told me, but I can't imagine anyone, even you, believing that. Not now."

Kendra stepped behind Bryce and dropped both hands on his shoulders.

He turned to face her.

"Look, I'm sorry I flew into you like that. I do believe you, and this is no time for you to give up. I need you to be madder than hell about this. Either Dana or Reggie is lying and that pisses me off, Bryce, and it sure as hell should piss you off, too. Do you understand?"

"Yeah," Bryce said. "I understand. But my being pissed off isn't going to change what that jury heard. No matter what happens, they'll believe I stabbed Dana with an ice pick. You saw the shock on their faces. And it won't be too far of a stretch for them to think I murdered a baby, too. Not to mention taking a bite out of his penis."

"If we can prove she or Reggie is lying on the stand, the jury's faces will change in a hurry. As far as the bite is concerned, we'll clear that up on cross-examination of Scott. Think about those scars on Dana's abdomen and see if you can come up with an explanation, anything."

"But I already told you she said Reggie put them there."

"I suspect she's lying to both of you. I'll be by later tonight after I have dinner with my father." Kendra patted Bryce's shoulder. "Before I go, is there anything else you haven't told me?"

He lowered his head. "I didn't tell you the ice pick story because I didn't do it. Why should I think it had anything to do with the case?"

"It does now," she said, then shook her head, turned and left the room.

When the guard handcuffed and escorted Bryce out of a side door into the parking lot where a police car waited to take him back to the county jail, he stared into space. A dust devil picked up a piece of scrap paper and it danced madly in circles all by itself on the asphalt.

Ignoring the taunting insults of the small crowd that gathered, Bryce watched the swirling scrap of paper. The old Bryce would have yearned to disappear, to drag his suit coat over his head and hide. But the new Bryce breathed in the clean scent in the air and decided, once and for all, his life was worth the fight. People were lying about him. And that made him mad as hell.

Even Reggie Sterling had better sense than to testify under oath to something that didn't happen. Dana must have shown Reggie the scars after she started living with Bryce. He didn't dare pursue the other implications of that, but it probably meant she didn't have those scars when she was married to Reggie.

Alone in his cell, Bryce jotted down the information available to him, writing out dates and possible scenarios. By the time Kendra arrived back, the seed of an idea popped its tiny head through the darkness.

"You may think this is farfetched, Kendra, but you should check the hospital records. If someone really stabbed her, she would have sought medical care. Believe me, Dana runs to the doctor every time she sneezes."

Bryce handed Kendra his notepad, with the time frame between when Dana left Reggie and when she and the boys moved in with him. "I'd start with Providence Hospital. It's where she delivered Skyler, and her gynecologist is there, in those offices right next to the hospital. Oh my God—"

"What is it, Bryce?"

"I just remembered something. Before all this happened, I suggested we have a baby together and Dana claimed she couldn't. I didn't think much about it then, thought she meant psychologically she couldn't handle another one. But maybe, just maybe…"

"Great idea, Bryce. Brilliant. You sure you didn't go to law school?"

"It's all those *Matlock* and *Law and Order* reruns I watched after my Achilles surgery." He attempted a laugh.

"Do you know the name of her gynecologist?"

He thought for a moment. "Dr. Herrington."

"Sometimes it's hard to get a warrant for medical records, but we can try. Can you draw me a diagram of those scars, size, shape and location?"

"I'm no artist, but I'll do the best I can." Bryce sketched a rough outline of a woman's body, then made two small circles with his pencil, one just below the waist and another just above the pubic hairline.

"Don't worry," Kendra said, as she packed her notes and the sketch into her briefcase. "We'll get to the bottom of this. I promise."

* * *

Kendra returned to her office. Both her father and Detective Radhauser sat at the table inside the small interior conference room the public defenders called 'the war zone'. She left them reviewing her plan for cross-examining Reggie and Scott Sterling. The conference table was cluttered with files, legal pads, medical examiner and police reports. And the trash can was overflowing with the remains of the dinner Radhauser ordered from Greenleaf on the plaza.

Kendra had no more than sat down at the table when the telephone rang. She picked it up.

"Bryce didn't kill that baby," a man's voice said.

"Who is this?"

Both her father and Radhauser stopped working and looked up at her.

The caller continued. "It doesn't matter what my name is, because I won't implicate someone I love. But I don't want to see an innocent man punished either."

"Tell me who this is," Kendra demanded.

"All I'm willing to tell you is that Bryce is innocent." The man hung up.

Kendra did the same.

The curious expression on her father's face ratcheted up a notch. "What was that all about?"

She relayed what transpired on the call.

"I'll see if I can trace it," Radhauser said. "It won't help our case if he isn't willing to come forward. Sounds like someone the caller is close to is the actual killer, if it isn't a prank. Do you think it could be Reggie's father?"

"Not a bad thought," Kendra said. "Any possibility you could check him out for me before Monday?"

Radhauser agreed.

"From what I gleaned so far," her father said, already refocused on the case. "If you go by the old adage of motive, means and opportunity, the prosecution doesn't have much."

Kendra hoped she hadn't made a mistake in giving her father access to the case. She wanted to handle her first case—wanted to prove she was a competent attorney in her own right. She'd spent a lifetime riding on her famous father's shoulders. It was time to stand on her own.

But she didn't want to risk Bryce's freedom because of her pride. Maybe the mark of a competent attorney was the acceptance of help when needed. "The prints on the Haloperidol bottle were not in the system. And Bryce wasn't a match."

"Great," her father said. "Did the jury hear that?"

"They did." She told him the prosecution would claim his motive was revenge against Dana and the fact that the drug bottle was found in his house provided the means.

"I tried to get a warrant for pharmacies and psychiatrists to see if anyone who'd been prescribed the drug had a connection to Skyler Sterling, but the judge wouldn't grant me one," Radhauser said. "He claimed too many innocent people with psychiatric issues would have their rights violated. I do know that Reggie Sterling took the drug when he was in a treatment center for alcoholism last summer."

"Could you get a warrant for Dana's medical records from Dr. Herrington? He's a gynecologist in the medical building next to Providence Hospital," Kendra asked.

"I can handle that," her father said. "And make sure the jury hears that Reggie Sterling took Haloperidol in the treatment center. It might be enough for reasonable doubt."

"I'm going to talk to Henry Evans again. I want to ask him about the rubber band," Radhauser said. "It's troubled me since I learned it wasn't a medical alert bracelet—the one little detail of who put it on Skyler's wrist and why. And when I interviewed Henry, I noticed that when he was nervous, he snapped the elastic on the sleeve of his hoodie."

"Did you ask Scott about the rubber band?"

"The kid claimed he didn't see it. And Bryce said it wasn't there when he gave the boys their baths and put them to bed."

"That leaves Reggie Sterling and Henry Evans," her father said. "My bet is on the Evans boy."

"Why?" Kendra asked.

"Call it a hunch. It sounds more like something a kid would do. I'd check it out. Who knows, it may have relevance to the case."

That was her dad. He never made assumptions. Never let anything slip by uninvestigated.

Radhauser stood. "Oh, by the way, Kendra. I've got some irony for you." He handed her an envelope.

Both Kendra and her father studied its contents.

"I recommend you reveal this fact in Reggie's cross-examination," her father said. "He may break down on the stand and admit he poisoned Skyler. I've seen it happen before. We need to take the shot while we have it."

Kendra swallowed her reaction to his use of the pronoun *we*. Once again, she reminded herself Bryce's life was at stake and her vain need to prove herself shouldn't play a part in this battle.

"One thing is certain," her father continued. "We need to win. Because if the jury convicts in a death-penalty case, the odds of ever overturning that verdict are minuscule."

Radhauser shook her father's hand. "Thanks for your advice on the case." He put on his Stetson. "I'll talk to Reginald Sterling, senior, then see what I can find out from Henry Evans. Hopefully without his father around."

* * *

Radhauser walked the short distance from Kendra's office to where he left his car parked outside the police station. When he saw the envelope beneath his windshield wiper, he was certain it was a ticket. And he laughed. Some gutsy meter maid giving a cop a ticket.

He opened the envelope.

I WANT TO SEE YOU IN MY OFFICE NOW. It was Murphy's handwriting, his printing in reality, and he wrote his command in red ink with all capital letters.

The boss no doubt got a call from Andrew Marshall about Radhauser's testimony. *Oh well*, he thought. *It's time to pay the fiddler.*

The lights were on in the police station and the door unlocked. Determined to tackle Murphy's anger head-on, Radhauser strode directly to his office. He tapped on the glass.

"Get the hell in here, Radhauser." It was Murphy's most pissed-off voice.

Radhauser took off his cowboy hat and entered.

Murphy sat behind his desk, his face red and sweaty like it always got when he was furious. "What the hell do you think you're doing?" His unblinking eyes never wavered off Radhauser.

"Andrew Marshall—you know, the ADA you're supposed to be helping convict our murder suspect—called me right after court adjourned for the day. Five hours ago, by the way. Where the hell have you been?"

"You know I took time off. My wife is recovering from cancer surgery."

"I know all about Gracie's surgery, damn you. But I called and your very nice mother-in-law informed me you weren't home. She thought you were out working on a case. What case? A suspect has been arrested and is on trial. Our police work is done on the Skyler Sterling murder, Radhauser. Unless you've already undone it with your testimony."

The air in Murphy's office was electric and the hairs on the back of Radhauser's neck lifted as if an invisible finger had zipped up his spine.

"What the fuck are you trying to do by telling the jury you don't believe Bryce is guilty? Your job is to back Marshall up, help him prove guilt."

"Are you finished?" Radhauser asked.

"No. I want some answers."

"I've always been a good detective, right?"

"I thought you were one of my best." Murphy spat out the words as if it hurt him to say them.

"I've never done anything like this before, right?"

"You wouldn't be here if you had."

"I'm sorry, Captain Murphy, but I don't believe Bryce killed that baby. And I tried to tell you that before we arrested him. I have a reputation, too. I won't risk my integrity and go against my own belief system."

"It doesn't matter what you believe. You have a job to do."

"If it gets to the point where my job is to send someone to his death for a crime he didn't commit..." Radhauser paused, shook his head. "Then I no longer want this job." He turned on his heels and left the police station.

Murphy chased after him. "You're suspended," he yelled. "Until further notice."

CHAPTER THIRTY-ONE

Bryce watched the jury as they filed into their places. Some of them looked tired and he wondered if the trial was getting to them, the way it was getting to him—a roller coaster ride that never ended. Down one day. Up the next. Kendra told him about the anonymous caller who claimed to know Bryce was innocent. A little good news. But that caller wouldn't leave his name so he couldn't be called to the stand to testify. More bad news. It seemed every day the idea he might be convicted and put to death hovered over the courtroom like a giant hammer, ready to drop on his head.

Andrew Marshall called Dana's friend, Angela, to the stand. She testified to Bryce's anger, the way he screamed "selfish bitch" at Dana and threw a rock at her car on the day Skyler died.

The prosecutor was setting the stage for the 9-1-1 tape. But when Marshall actually played it, Bryce sat, horrified, by the amplified sound of his own voice.

The tape was disjointed, slurred, and difficult to understand, with periods of silence and dull thudding sounds in the background, mumbling and occasional profanities. The words he spoke and his pauses, indicated by three consecutive dots, flashed on a large, white screen for the jury to read.

Bryce referred to Skyler as "she" on numerous occasions.

The 9-1-1 operator interrupted him repeatedly with words of assurance. "Calm down, Mr. Bryce," she said. "I've called for help. It won't be long. Just hold on, help is coming."

And then, at the very end of the tape, Bryce shouted, "...die dammit...she's gonna die." Those final words echoed through the silent courtroom.

For Bryce, the indisputable word *don't* lay hidden inside those three dots in front of the word *die*, but he didn't have any idea how Kendra could convince the jury to hear or see that word.

While workmen carted the screen and sound equipment from the room, Kendra approached the judge. "May it please Your Honor, I move for permission to call Mrs. Valerie Thompson, Bryce's ex-wife, as a witness for the defendant at this time. I know it's an unusual request, but her testimony will shed important light on the exhibit just presented to the court. And she is flying to Europe tonight."

After conferring with Marshall, the judge granted his permission and Valerie stepped up to the witness stand.

It had been more than twelve years since Bryce saw his former wife. She was thinner than he remembered and appeared mature, grown up, no longer the young girl he married. Dressed in a long-sleeved flowered dress, her hair was darker and cut shorter than she wore it when they were together—just brushing her dress collar. Her face was serious and composed while the court clerk swore her in and Kendra asked the usual opening questions.

Valerie stated her full name, the fact that she lived in Mesa, Arizona, with her husband, Charles Thompson, and their two sons.

Somehow, Valerie had managed to move on from Courtney's death and carve out a new life for herself. A swell of happiness washed over him.

"Do you know the defendant, Caleb Bryce?" Kendra nodded toward the defense table.

"Yes," she replied in a strong, clear voice Bryce could hear easily. "We were once married."

Kendra led Valerie expertly through the birth, the ventricular septal defect, the short life, and finally the death of their daughter, Courtney Morgan Bryce. She told the jury how deeply Bryce had loved Courtney and how hard he took her death. "It was a nightmare from which Bryce couldn't seem to awaken. Without the daughter who'd brought us together in the first place, our marriage didn't survive and we divorced."

When she finished, Kendra asked one final question. "Do you have any idea why your former husband repeatedly referred to Skyler Sterling on the 9-1-1 tape you just heard as 'she'?"

"Objection, Your Honor." Clearly disturbed by the testimony that could go a long way in invalidating the defendant's motivation, Marshall leaped to his feet, his chair scraping the floor behind him. "This calls for an opinion."

"Sustained," Judge Shapiro ruled.

"I'll withdraw the question," Kendra said. The dimple on the side of her cheek deepened slightly, but she didn't actually smile.

Bryce understood Kendra asked that question, knowing Marshall would object. But it didn't matter. Thanks to Valerie, everyone in the courtroom understood what happened inside his head during that awful phone call to 9-1-1.

Andrew Marshall stood perfectly still for a moment, then took a breath deep enough to raise his shoulders. "I have no questions for this witness."

Valerie returned to her seat near the back of the courtroom.

Marshall called Scott Sterling to the stand.

When Scott climbed up the steps leading to the witness stand, Bryce's heart ached for the little boy. He looked so scared. Scott was dressed in a pair of new jeans and a western shirt. His cowboy boots were clean and polished, and his red hair recently cut and slicked back. Bryce wondered where Scotty spent the last month and how he coped with the death of his little brother.

As the boy settled into the chair, Reggie nodded to him from his seat in the front row. Scott was barely visible behind the wooden stand and the clerk smiled as he toted in a booster chair to raise the little boy high enough for the jury to see him. The clerk then asked him to hold up his right hand and promise to tell the truth and nothing else. Scott promised.

Marshall's expression was sympathetic and he smiled. "You remember me, don't you, Scott?"

"Yes." Scott nodded, but he kept his gaze on his mother who sat in the third row back with a grief-stricken expression on her face.

"Just try to relax," Marshall said. "You have nothing to be afraid of. I'm going to ask you a few questions and all you have to do is tell me the answer. And if you don't know, that's okay, too. Just say, 'I don't know'."

"Okay," Scott said, leaning back a little bit.

"Could you tell me your whole name?"

"Scott Allen Sterling," he said emphatically, tilting his head a little bit to the right.

A warm chuckle arose from the jury.

Bryce saw what Kendra meant—they already loved the little boy.

"Do you know what the truth is, Scott?"

"Sure, I do." He looked at his mother again and she nodded for him to go on. "That's when you tell something the way it really, really happened."

"Very good," Marshall said. "And how about a lie? What's a lie, Scott?"

"It's when you play pretend. When you make something up that didn't really happen."

"Excellent," Marshall said, again smiling at Scott. "You're a smart little boy."

Scott grinned back at him.

"And how old are you, Scott?"

"I'm four and a half."

"Do you know that man sitting over there?" Marshall pointed at Bryce.

"Sure," Scott said, taking a quick sideways glance toward the defense table. "That's Bryce. Caleb Bryce."

"And you and your mom and Skyler used to live in the same house with him. Is that right?"

"Yeah." Scott lowered his head and added, "But Skyler died already."

Marshall bowed his head, shaking it slightly from side to side, a gesture of pity. "Yes, I know. And I'll bet you miss him a lot, don't you?"

"My mom cries sometimes when she talks about him. But me

and Dad don't. We're braver."

Several members of the jury smiled.

"When you lived with Bryce." Marshall nodded again toward the defense table. "What did he call you?"

"You mean my name?" Scott wrinkled his nose and glanced at his father who signaled his approval with a somber nod.

"Yes," Marshall confirmed, his arms folded over his chest.

"Scott. He always called me just plain Scott. Or sometimes Scotty." The boy shrugged, as if to say what a stupid question, but Bryce knew where Marshall was headed.

"What did he call Skyler?"

"Cockroach."

There was a loud sucking sound from the jury, as if all of them had inhaled in unison.

"He always called him that," Scott added.

"Do you know what a cockroach is, Scott?"

Understanding Kendra's fear about Scott's testimony now, Bryce swallowed hard, but kept his eyes on the little boy just as Kendra instructed him to do.

"Sure." Scott nodded, as if pleased he could answer his question. "It's a bug. A yucky, poopy, brown one. It's kind of long and skinny."

A few giggles erupted from the jury.

Marshall took a step toward the witness box, his left hand slipped into this pants pocket. "Have you ever seen a cockroach in real life?"

"Sure." Scott grinned, as if he were happy with his knowledge. "One time we had millions of them in the house. Under the sink and stuff. Sometimes in the bathtub. They're really, really, really gross."

"What did you do with them?"

"I didn't do nothing with them. But Bryce, he smashed them with his foot, then he flushed them down the toilet. Finally, a stermanator man came. And we had to go live in a motel so he could put poison in the house to kill them."

Again, the jury sucked in a combined breath, and despite

Kendra's orders, Bryce couldn't help himself and he lowered his gaze, stared at the shiny top of the defense table.

"Scott, did Bryce ever hit you?"

"Yeah. Really hard, and it hurt, too. He hated me." Although Scott's gaze was already focused on his lap, he lowered it ever further, pushing his head down, too, as if trying to escape into himself. "He was bad to me and said he was going to murder me." The boy shot a quick glance at his father.

Oh my God, Bryce thought. *I did say that. How could I have said something so awful to that poor little boy?*

"Thank you, Scott. You've been a big help."

It was late in the afternoon when the prosecution finished its examination of Scott Sterling and Judge Shapiro recessed for the day before Kendra had a chance to cross-examine.

The boy's testimony was damaging. But the child didn't lie, and as he stepped down from the witness box, Bryce's impulse was to reach out and hug him, to assure Scott Allen Sterling that he didn't mean what he said that night. He didn't hate him and he could never, not ever, do anything to hurt him.

CHAPTER THIRTY-TWO

As Bryce entered the courtroom the following morning, his gaze darted around the room for Scott. He found him on Dana's lap, her arms wrapped around the boy's narrow shoulders.

When Kendra called Scott to the stand for his cross-examination, the boy strutted across the courtroom. Again, he was dressed in blue jeans, with a different western shirt. Knowing what to anticipate this time, he climbed into the witness box a bit more confidently, the booster chair already placed by the bailiff.

Kendra introduced herself to Scott and chatted a few minutes, reminding him that he was still sworn in and that meant he had to keep on telling the truth, just like he did the day before.

"I will," Scott announced.

"Skyler Sterling was your baby brother, right?"

"Sure," the boy said, his forehead furrowing. "Everybody already knows that. Except my dad said Skyler was only my half-brother. I don't know how you get half a brother."

Several jurors smiled. Someone behind Bryce laughed out loud.

"Dad and me, we didn't like Skyler very much. He screamed a lot."

"But you played with him sometimes, right?" Kendra stood slightly to the left of the witness stand, close enough to appear friendly, but not so close as to intimidate the little boy. "You played together in the special playhouse, right?"

"Yeah. It was really fun. We put our stuffed animals inside and pretended like they were our kids."

"And sometimes Bryce played, too, didn't he?"

"He always played with Skyler. He liked him better than me." Scott's lower lip trembled.

270

Kendra stood quietly for a moment, her arms bent, hands woven together in front of her. "Why do you think Bryce liked Skyler more than you?"

"Because he had a special name for him. And he made him a playhouse and only put that special name on it. He didn't make me nothin'."

"Tell me about the playhouse." Kendra's voice raised a little, as if very interested in what Scott had to say. "What did it look like?"

"It was so big I could stand up inside it…and really, really cool. It had windows and a door and everything. I helped Bryce paint blue shutters on it." He stared directly at Kendra, then added, "And I stayed inside the lines he drew really good."

Kendra addressed the bailiff and retrieved one of her defense exhibits, an eleven-by-fourteen photo of the cardboard playhouse. After identifying it to the court, she presented it to Scott who said it was the playhouse he and Bryce made for Skyler. The words *Cockroach's House* were clearly legible over the doorway. Kendra handed it to the bailiff who passed it around the jury.

"Scott," Kendra said. "I want you to think real hard now. Do you remember the night Skyler got hurt?"

"I was sleeping," he said, raising his chin. "I didn't even know he died. Bryce lied. He said Skyler would be okay."

"Did that make you angry, Scott?"

"Yeah, I hate him." He pointed his index finger toward Bryce, but didn't look up.

"Do you remember what happened in the daytime before you were sleeping?"

"Bryce hit me." His gaze darted to the defense table and then quickly away.

"Why do you think he hit you, Scott?"

"Objection," Marshall said. "Calls for an opinion."

"Acknowledged," Shapiro replied. "But I'll overrule in this instance." The judge directed his next words at Scott. "Tell Ms. Palmer why you think Bryce hit you."

"Because I wanted ice cream."

Aware that wasn't the answer Kendra anticipated, Bryce held his breath.

She backed up a step, then treaded forward again, smiling at Scott. "Did Skyler fall down the steps that day?"

"Yeah, but it wasn't my fault." His gaze dropped to his lap, then raised again. He searched the courtroom, then connected with his mother. "The door—it just falled open."

"Where was Bryce when the door opened?"

"He was on the sofa with his hurt leg up on the chair."

"Sometimes baby brothers make us mad, don't they, Scott?"

The boy shrugged. "I guess so."

"Did you ever bite Skyler?"

"Objection." Marshall raised his voice slightly. "She's leading the witness."

"Overruled." Judge Shapiro wiped his forehead with a handkerchief. "Answer the question, Scott."

"Yeah," Scott said. "But that time in the bathtub was an accident. I only wanted to blubber his tummy, but his penis got in the way."

The courtroom grew silent.

"Were you angry with Skyler?"

"He always knocked over my forts and stuff. And then he laughed about it, like it was really funny or something."

"What did you do when Skyler knocked down your forts?"

"Mostly I just pushed him away. Mom got real mad when I bit him or hit him. She said he was littler. It wasn't fair."

"Did you push him the day he fell down the steps?"

"Not very hard." Scott frowned and stared at the ceiling. "The dumb door was broke."

"Yeah," Kendra said, sympathy in her voice. "And that wasn't your fault, was it?"

"No."

"What did Bryce do when Skyler fell down the steps?"

"He jumped off the sofa real fast and ran outside and picked him up and hugged him and stuff."

"What did you do?"

"I was scared he'd be mad like Mom gets when I hurt Skyler. So, I ran behind a house and climbed up a tree. Really, really high."

"Did Bryce find you?"

"Yeah." The boy wiped his nose on the back of his hand. "He said I had to go to bed."

"And you didn't want to do that, did you?"

"It wasn't even dark yet. Besides, he's not my real dad." Scott paused and pointed to Reggie Sterling. "That's my real dad over there. He says Bryce is a jerk and he can't boss me around."

Kendra nodded. "It's hard when big people who aren't our real parents tell us what to do, isn't it?"

"Yeah. But I showed him. I bit his arm really hard. He bleeded and everything." Scott paused for a moment, swiped his top lip with his tongue. "I kicked him, too. It wasn't my fault. Dumb door."

"Yeah," Kendra agreed. "I get real mad too when I think things aren't fair. Is that when Bryce hit you? After you bit him?"

"No, he didn't hit me then."

"When did he hit you, Scott?"

"After I spit on him." Again, the boy's head lowered and Kendra waited patiently until Scott lifted his eyes and said, "I don't wanna talk anymore."

"Okay. I just have two more little bitty questions and all you have to say is yes or no."

"All right," Scott muttered.

"Did Bryce ever hit you before the night Skyler fell out the front door?"

Scott appeared to be thinking and he didn't move or blink for a second.

Bryce held his breath. Said a silent prayer that Scott would continue to tell the truth.

"Nope. That's the only time."

"Did you ever see him hit Skyler?"

"No. No. No." Scott punctuated each no with a shake of his head, then added, "He wouldn't never hit Skyler."

Bryce breathed.

Relief flooded over Kendra's face.

Bryce lowered his head in an attempt to hide the tears puddling in his eyes.

"All right, Scott," Kendra said. "You did a very good job. Thanks for telling the truth. You're a brave little boy."

* * *

After a fifteen-minute break, Kendra called Reggie Sterling to the stand for her cross-examination and reminded him he was still under oath to tell the truth. Reggie was dressed in an expensive grey suit, with a black silk shirt and black and red striped tie. His black loafers were polished to a bright shine.

"Is it true you were hospitalized at the Sunrise Drug and Alcohol Rehabilitation Center for alcohol addiction?"

"I thought medical records were confidential," he said. "Protected under some government regulation or something?"

"That's true," Kendra said. "Most of the time. But not in a murder case."

"Since you already know, I might as well tell you. I was going through a hard time after Dana and Scott left. And I drank too much. I wouldn't call it an addiction. But my father was worried, so he did an intervention and I completed the program at Sunrise."

"Were you given the drug Haloperidol for the treatment of your delirium tremens?"

"Yes. But I didn't leave the center with a prescription in my pocket if that's what you're driving at."

"Did you take it from the nurses' cart?"

"No way. I'm not a thief. Why would I?"

Kendra changed her line of questioning. Hopefully, the fact that Reggie had a connection to the drug would help create reasonable doubt in the jurors' minds. "Is it true you divorced Dana because you believed Skyler was not your biological son?"

"Yes. And can you blame me? Dana didn't even have the good sense to lie. She admitted to screwing around on me. What was I supposed to do? A man has to have a little pride."

"Did you have Skyler's DNA tested?"

"No."

"So, you had no real proof of paternity at the time of the divorce."

"That's right. I didn't need proof. I could tell by looking at the kid."

"As a matter of fact, with your permission, Detective Radhauser had your DNA compared to DNA the medical examiner had taken from Skyler. We got the results back yesterday, Mr. Sterling. The match was ninety-nine point nine percent conclusive. It proves you are indeed Skyler's birth father."

Reggie's head spun around as if it had been struck by a fist. For a second, he seemed almost speechless. "I don't believe you. He looks nothing like me."

Kendra read his face. It was filled with righteous conviction.

She handed him the DNA results.

He studied them. Something passed over him, like a shadow crossing in front of the sun. His face drained of color and his whole body trembled. He closed his eyes. "I'm sorry, Skyler," he whispered. "I'm so sorry." Reggie dropped his head into his hands and howled. It was one of the worst sounds Kendra had ever heard. A mournful, animal-like sound that came up from his chest and reverberated across the courtroom.

* * *

The prosecution completed its case against Caleb Bryce on Thursday afternoon and Judge Shapiro opted to recess rather than start the defense so late in the day.

"Marshall's running scared," Kendra announced to Bryce as they reviewed the day's findings in the courthouse basement. "He wants to make a deal. They drop the murder one charge and you plead guilty to manslaughter."

Bryce pushed his chair away from the table and stretched out his bad leg. "What exactly does that mean?"

Kendra leaned forward, her elbows on the table as if settling in for a long explanation. "Manslaughter is the unlawful killing of another without malice, either expressed or implied. It may be in a fit of rage when two people are fighting and one kills the other, or while in the commission of some unlawful act."

Bryce frowned. "I'm not sure I understand."

"Let's say you were driving your car and a child ran out in front of you. You hit him. He died. He came out of nowhere, you didn't see him until it was too late."

"That would be an accident, wouldn't it?"

"Yes," Kendra looked at her hands, then back at Bryce. "Unless you were driving over the speed limit, or under the influence of alcohol, or breaking the law in some way when the accident occurred."

"Okay, but I still don't grasp what unlawful act Marshall thinks I committed in trying to get Skyler to breathe."

Kendra laughed, a sweet bubbling sound Bryce wanted to hold on to for hours. "Me either."

"Would I serve time?" Bryce picked up a paper clip, then nervously unwound the silver coil.

"Seven and a half to fifteen years. You might get out in four with good behavior."

"I'd be out by the time I'm forty?" Bryce raised his eyebrows. "A sure thing?"

Kendra nodded. "Pretty much."

"And if I don't agree?" Bryce paced across his holding room, his hands still fingering the now straight wire of the paper clip.

Kendra grabbed his arm to stop the pacing. "We fight. Take our chances, present our case, and let the jury decide."

"I say we go finish the trial and let the jury decide." Bryce dropped back into the folding chair and tossed the useless paper clip into the garbage. "I'm tired of this victim shit. And I don't like the idea of admitting to something I didn't do."

"Good for you." Kendra reached across the table to shake Bryce's hand, that rich girl grin spreading across her face. "One more thing," she added. "I want you to know I'm calling Dana as our first witness tomorrow."

An uneasiness fluttered in Bryce's chest. "I'm not sure that's a good idea, Kendra. I haven't spoken a word to her since she and Scott moved out. For all I know she hates me and believes I'm responsible for Skyler's death. I mean, maybe she'll corroborate Reggie's lie about the ice pick."

"Look," Kendra said. "Trust me on this. She'll be a great witness. No one will have more influence with that jury than the child's mother. She refused to testify for the prosecution and I think that tells us something. Besides, my old man is working on a lead."

"I hope your hunch is right, Kendra."

CHAPTER THIRTY-THREE

On Friday morning, Bryce took a deep breath and waited as Dana was sworn in and asked the usual questions.

"How long have you known the defendant, Caleb Bryce?"

"About a year." Dana was dressed conservatively in a pale pink knit suit, her dark hair pulled back with a matching ribbon. Looking somehow innocent and childlike, she cupped her chin in her fingertips, the nails short and painted a soft rose color.

"What was the nature of your relationship?"

"At first we were just friends. He offered to give the boys and me a place to stay until I could afford an apartment. So, we moved into Bryce's house in Ashland."

"Was he good to your boys, Ms. Sterling?"

She hesitated for an instant. "Yes."

It was difficult for Bryce to look at her because he could see Skyler in her face, something soft and glowing he never noticed before. He focused his gaze on the rapidly moving hands of the young interpreter signing in front of him.

"Did you ever see him mistreat either of your sons or suspect that he might have?"

"No, I never saw him hit either of them. Bryce was generally too easy on them, especially Scott. My Scotty can be a handful."

"Did you ask Bryce to stay home with Scott and not come to the hospital the night of his seizure?"

"Yes, but I didn't think Skyler was hurt so bad. I didn't think he would die."

Bryce glanced up as she hung her head and closed her eyes. When she opened them again, tears dropped from the corners.

He glanced toward the jury box where two women dabbed at their own eyes.

"But," she said through her sniffles. "He should have fixed the door." She looked at Reggie Sterling, then quickly averted her gaze.

"Did you know Mr. Bryce at the time he ruptured his Achilles tendon?"

"Yes, ma'am, we were living together. The boys and I were in the stands at the baseball field when it happened."

"How did the accident affect him physically?"

"Objection, Your Honor," Marshall called out from the prosecution table. "Calls for a medical opinion. This witness is not a physician."

"Overruled." Shapiro jotted something on a legal pad in front of him. "You may answer the question, Ms. Sterling."

"He was in a cast for about six weeks. When they removed it, he had treatments—physical therapy. He was getting better, but still unsteady on his feet. He tripped and fell pretty often, especially if he tried to run."

"Did you ever know Bryce to have in his possession or to use the drug Haloperidol?"

"No, ma'am. I never even heard of that drug. Bryce didn't take any drugs stronger than an aspirin. He didn't even get the prescription filled for his pain pills after his Achilles surgery."

"Before I ask the next question, I want to remind you that you are under oath to tell the truth. Perjury is a punishable crime." Kendra stepped back. "Do you understand that?"

Bryce lifted his gaze and locked on Dana.

"Yes, ma'am." Her face tightened.

"Did Mr. Bryce ever hurt you in any way?"

She made a low sound in her throat, then focused her gaze on the far wall of the courtroom. A distant look came over her face, as if she had somehow disappeared into the mahogany paneled wall.

"Please answer the question, Ms. Sterling." Judge Shapiro was patient, but stern.

Dana swallowed, her eyes hooded. "No."

"Specifically," Kendra continued. "Did he ever threaten you or stab you with an ice pick or anything else?"

Dana glanced at Reggie as if seeking permission, but he didn't meet her gaze.

Anxiety grew, like an air bubble, in the center of Bryce's chest. He held his breath. *Please, Dana. Tell the truth.*

"No," she said quietly. "Bryce never hurt me."

Bryce breathed. *Thank you.*

"Isn't it true, Ms. Sterling, the small scars on your abdomen are from a surgical procedure? A tubal ligation?"

"Yes," she whispered. "It's true." With those words, Dana Sterling lowered her head and burst into tears.

The court recessed for ten minutes so Ms. Sterling could gain control of herself.

On cross-examination, Marshall asked only three questions. "Did Mr. Bryce mention Skyler's fall down the front steps or his own alleged fall into the coffee table to you either on the phone or when you saw him in the surgical waiting room?"

"He told me about the fall down the steps in the surgical waiting room."

"When did you learn of Bryce's tripping over the coffee table?"

"The coffee table...let's see..." Dana paused, clamped her eyes shut for a moment. "I think I heard about it for the first time when Ms. Palmer gave her opening statement."

"Didn't you think it strange his not mentioning something that important?" Marshall stepped from behind his table and stood only a few feet in front of the witness box.

"Not really," Dana said, shaking her head. "It all happened so fast. Skyler was in surgery. We had more important things to worry about."

Kendra made a note on her pad and passed it to Bryce. *See, I told you, she made a great witness. And besides, my father found the doctor who performed her tubal ligation. She wasn't about to lie with him sitting right next to my old man in the third row back.*

* * *

It was nearly 2 p.m. on Sunday when Radhauser parked in the

Lazy Lasso parking lot, near the back dumpster and waited. He knew if he went inside the Lasso, Bear Evans would be on him, like a bee on honey.

With some help from Kendra and her father, they were granted a subpoena for Henry to appear as a witness for the defense, but Radhauser wanted to talk with him again first, without his father lurking over him. Henry bused tables and did odd jobs in the kitchen. With any luck, he would step outside to empty the trash.

When Radhauser met with the senior Reginald Sterling earlier that morning, he gleaned nothing new except that he was an even bigger pompous ass than his son. Mr. Sterling claimed Dana was nothing but a slut, his grandson a brat who needed discipline, and that Reggie was an idiot, but had his sobriety to worry about now and was much better off without either of them. He hadn't come across as a man who'd risk anything to protect his son.

And that got Radhauser thinking about Bear, the way he put his arm around Henry's shoulder—the way it appeared he wanted nothing more than to keep Henry safe. Radhauser also knew that Bear was fond of Bryce. It made much more sense that he was the one who placed the anonymous call to Kendra.

After an hour, Radhauser's intuition paid off and Henry appeared carrying two large, black trash bags toward the dumpster. He wore a pair of high-top red Converse sneakers, pressed jeans, and a butcher-type white apron over his light blue T-shirt. His hair was cropped shorter than when Radhauser had last seen him.

He opened the car door and got out, then walked over and held the heavy dumpster lid open for Henry. "How's it going, Mr. Philosopher?"

Henry looked up at him without a trace of guile. "I'm not really a philosopher. I'm just plain Henry."

"Okay, just plain Henry. How's it going for you?"

"My dad said I'm not supposed to talk to you unless he's with me." Henry pulled up the sleeve of his shirt, exposing a wide rubber band on his wrist. He snapped it several times, hard enough to sting. "I'm afraid my dad's gonna be mad."

Looking back on his earlier interview with Henry, Radhauser

realized Henry hadn't been snapping the elastic in the sleeve of his hoodie—he was snapping a rubber band on his wrist.

Radhauser smiled. For the first time since he arrested Bryce, he had a glimmer of hope that things might just work out for Bryce.

"No, he won't be mad," Radhauser said. "He likes me. I'm not stranger danger anymore. We're just two people who bumped into each other in the parking lot. We're talking. Like friends."

"Sure. Reggie and Dana are my friends, too." Henry snapped the rubber band again.

"Doesn't that hurt?" Radhauser said.

"A little."

"Why do you do it?"

"Dr. Durham showed me a trick for when I get nervous or feel like I'm going to shout out bad words. If I sting myself with the rubber band, I forget to say the cuss words. And that makes my dad happy."

Radhauser gave him a big smile and tipped his Stetson. "That, Sir Henry, is a really great trick."

Henry bowed.

"Did you know Skyler had a rubber band on his wrist?"

"Sure," Henry said. "I gave it to him. Skyler screams a lot and Reggie hates it. I showed Skyler the trick Dr. Durham taught me. If he stopped screaming, Reggie and Dana would make up and Scott and Skyler could live with both their mommy and their daddy. My mom left when I was little. I miss her."

"That's a very nice thought, Henry. Did you do anything else to help Skyler?"

"Yeah, I—"

The door from the kitchen opened.

Henry stopped talking and backed up against the dumpster, snapping the rubber band on his wrist again and again.

Bear stormed out. "Go back inside, Henry. You've got tables to bus."

He waited until Henry closed the door into the kitchen, then grabbed Radhauser by the shoulders. "What the hell do you think you're doing?"

"I was preparing Henry for his testimony on Tuesday."

"What are you talking about? Henry's not testifying. I already told you, he didn't have anything to do with this mess."

Radhauser handed Bear the subpoena. "Have him in court at 9 a.m. sharp, or you'll be arrested for impeding a murder investigation."

"He doesn't know anything. He follows Reggie around like a puppy. Henry's got the mind of a seven-year-old. He's not responsible..." Bear stopped himself. His face went dark for an instant before he turned and hurried into the restaurant without saying another word.

Radhauser drove to the police station, hoping Detective Vernon, a well-known workaholic who often came in on a Sunday afternoon, might be available to help him. And sure enough, Vernon's car was parked in the lot and Murphy's wasn't.

The sun streamed through Vernon's first-floor window, the low blinding sun of a late November afternoon. "I know I'm suspended," Radhauser said. "But I'm close to solving the Sterling murder case and I need your help."

"No problem," Vernon said. "Murphy screwed up. He should have given us more time."

He asked Vernon to find every Dr. Durham in a twenty-mile radius of Ashland. "Start with psychiatrists. Bryce said Henry had some psychiatric issues."

"I'll get right on it," Vernon said, then turned to go, but Radhauser stopped him.

"One more thing. What's the name of that condition people have where they shout out cuss words? You know what I mean? It starts with a t and it's on the tip of my tongue, but I can't seem to spit it out. The one where people are sitting in church or at their doctor's office and say things like 'fuck you' to no one in particular."

"Tourette's Syndrome," Vernon said. "I had an aunt with it."

"That's the one." Radhauser flipped on his computer. Once it booted, he read everything he could find on Tourette's until he stumbled on something he couldn't wait to tell Kendra and her father. Now, all he needed was confirmation that Henry Evans was treated for Tourette's.

A half hour later, Radhauser stopped in front of Vernon's desk. "How you coming with that list?"

"I only found one Dr. Durham who is a psychiatrist. His office is here in Ashland. Maple Street, near the hospital."

There was no way Dr. Durham would release Henry Evans' medical records without a court order or subpoena.

Radhauser called and left a message for Kendra. Perhaps she, or the great Kendrick Huntington Palmer, III could get Judge Shapiro to grant another subpoena.

* * *

When court resumed on Monday, Kendra called various witnesses to the stand. An emergency room physician in another Medford-area hospital testified that, in his professional opinion, at least fourteen of the twenty bruises on Skyler's body could be accounted for by attempts at resuscitation.

A forensic pathologist from another state interpreted the autopsy report, stating his contention that Skyler Sterling's fall down the concrete steps could be responsible for the other bruises as well as the ruptured hepatic vein. Kendra called him in to testify in an attempt to establish doubt in the jury's mind.

One of the paramedics at the scene attested to the broken globe of the oil lamp, the overturned coffee table, and Bryce's valiant efforts to administer CPR with his index finger clamped between Skyler's teeth.

Kendra called the director of the preschool Scott and Skyler attended and she testified that the boys' attendance, behavior, hygiene, and attitude actually improved after Dana moved in with Bryce.

The Director of Volunteers at Ashland Hospital where Bryce spent a few hours every week rocking infants testified to his reliability and his gentle nature with the babies.

When Marshall finished his final cross-examination, Judge Shapiro addressed the jury. "Ladies and gentlemen. Due to the lateness of the hour, we'll adjourn for the day. We'll begin closing arguments tomorrow. I think we'll have this wrapped up by noon and then you can start your deliberations."

CHAPTER THIRTY-FOUR

After the jury filed out, the guard escorted Bryce back to the holding room. As had become their daily custom, Kendra followed and they spent a half-hour sitting across from each other at the small conference table, reviewing what had happened in the courtroom that day. "Don't look so worried," she said. "Everything is going to be okay. I've got a very good feeling about tomorrow."

Despite his nervousness, Bryce pulled an envelope from his breast pocket and handed it to Kendra before he lost his nerve. "I wanted you to have this before the jury reaches its verdict."

She reached out and took the envelope. "What is this, anyway?"

"It's your payment. Not much, but the best I could do." Bryce shifted his gaze to the wall as she opened and read the poem he wrote.

This Brightness
For Kendra

All night I stood waiting
for sun to fill the cell's small window,
the glass still black where I pause
looking out as if for a signal
and remembering how dawn
releases the trees, mountains and each
fence from its shadow.
Still holding the nightfall between my hands
I whisper, "it will come."

The dark yields slowly and this day

might have traveled here from the other side
of the earth, might have first lit the sky
over Europe, an avenue in Warsaw and a house
where a man has paced since midnight
the musty stillness of his attic, thinking
each time a board creaked that soldiers
moved on the stairs and imagining
that these would be his last moments.

Words like moths kicked up
from the tall grass could
trace his story back to its ink.
He knows the meaning of all time is words—
those small unstoppable sounds
that fold, finger by finger,
across our bodies.

He would understand morning
is a kind of reprieve, its slow coming
the affirmation of everything night
called into question, and he might believe
that light passes from country to country,
one man to another, a sharing
that becomes personal like the space
between the living and the dead—
that otherness inside us we never touch
no matter how far down our hands might reach.

Morning allows us to survive
our separate lives, step before windows
two continents apart, opening our hands
to the light of another country, this brightness
that comes to us from across the world.

For a moment, Kendra didn't say anything. "God, Bryce. You're really something." Her voice was pillow soft. "I've never written a poem in my life. Where does it come from?"

Again, Bryce dodged Kendra's gaze and stared at the wall. "It starts with something inside me, like a hunger to say or to understand someone or something. It is so fierce that it hurts, and then that ache, well…sometimes it finds a way out in a poem."

She gave him a hug.

Something shifted. It was as if an internal mountain range had moved. He felt it in his toes. Kendra smelled like peaches. He held on a second too long.

She pulled away, her cheeks flushed. "I don't know what to say. The truth is this is the nicest thing anyone has ever done for me."

"It was a lot cheaper than a retainer." Her compliments embarrassed him, along with the way her hug felt. There was no doubt about it, he had a slight crush on his attorney. Who wouldn't? She was beautiful and smart. And, with any luck, she was about to save his life.

But who was he kidding? She was twenty-six years old and graduated from Harvard. He was thirty-five years old and on trial for murdering a child. He hadn't completed his BA in night school. There would always be a sliver of uncrossable distance between him and Kendra.

"I'm going to frame it and hang it on my office wall." Kendra carefully placed the poem in a manila folder in her briefcase. "You know, the way some people frame the first dollar they ever made."

As the overhead light caught in her blue eyes, he imagined he could see into her, a clarity and openness that drew him. No one had ever done as much for him as she had. Kendra pulled him out of the darkness and showed him how to flip on a light bulb and save his own life.

"I want you to know something," he said. "Whatever happens in the courtroom tomorrow, I'm grateful for everything you did for me. Even tracking down my family. You taught me something. Your family is never really in the past—you carry them around with you no matter where you are. Like those Russian dolls, their lives just sit inside you waiting to be acknowledged."

"Radhauser did most of the work finding your family," she said. "But you did a few things for me, too, Bryce. My father just handed me two season tickets to the Oregon Ducks home basketball games in the Matthew Knight Arena in Eugene. Center court, no less. And if it weren't for you and your little lecture on forgiveness, I'd have told him where he could put them." Kendra shook her head. "I still can't believe it. Kendrick Huntington Palmer III snaps his fingers and season tickets magically appear. Do you like basketball, Bryce?"

It took all the strength he had to keep his hands from sweeping the wisps of blonde hair off her face. They kept brushing across her cheeks and he longed to touch them. "I love basketball," he said. "But I've never seen a live Ducks game."

Kendra smiled. "I'll tell you what, when we beat this thing, one of those tickets is yours."

"You don't have to do that, Kendra."

"And you didn't have to write me a poem, either." Kendra patted her briefcase. "Keeping a professional distance notwithstanding, I think we've adopted each other. Two social orphans become friends."

Bryce smiled back.

It was their beginning.

* * *

On Tuesday morning, November twenty-third, 1999, just two days before Thanksgiving, Bryce struggled to keep his hands from shaking as Judge Shapiro called the courtroom to order. Both the prosecution and defense were scheduled to make their final arguments.

Kendra asked if she could approach the bench.

The judge nodded.

Kendra stepped up, Marshall at her heels. "Your Honor, I'd like to call one final witness to the stand. Henry Evans."

"I object," Marshall said. "This witness is not on the defense list."

"Some new evidence has come to light. Henry was the one who delivered the bottle of apple juice to Skyler Sterling and one of the last people to see him that evening. His testimony is imperative to our case, Your Honor. I promise you, it will change everything."

"I'm going to grant it, Ms. Palmer," he said. "But it better be good."

Marshall stomped away.

Kendra explained the witness's special circumstances to the judge, then called Henry Evans to the stand.

Henry appeared terrified as he walked up to the aisle. He was dressed in a dark suit with pale blue shirt, and a gray and blue striped tie. Two times he turned around and his gaze found his father in the back of the courtroom. Henry kept snapping the rubber band against his left wrist.

Bear nodded to the boy, as if to encourage him.

When he was seated and sworn in, Kendra approached the stand. "Hello, Henry," she said. "How are you today?"

"I'm scared. I don't want to say the wrong thing." Again, he snapped the rubber band.

"There is no wrong thing you can say, Henry. Only the truth. Do you know what the truth is?"

"Yes, ma'am," he said. "It is when you say what really happened and don't make anything up, pretend, or lie."

"Very good, Henry."

He smiled.

"I want you to go back and remember when you went to Caleb Bryce's house with Reggie Sterling and you asked Bryce if you could deliver the bottle of apple juice to Skyler. Do you remember that night?"

He nodded. "Yes."

"Did you like Skyler Sterling?"

"Objection," Marshall said. "Calls for an opinion."

Judge Shapiro sighed. "You are right, Mr. Marshall, but these are special circumstances and I'll allow. Answer the question, Henry."

"I don't remember the question."

"Did you like Skyler Sterling?" Kendra repeated.

"Yes," he said.

She needed to ask him something that couldn't be answered with a yes or no. "Why did you like him?"

"He screamed a lot. And Reggie said he couldn't live with him. But I liked him. He was a cute baby. And I liked to pretend he was the baby and I was the daddy."

"You wear a rubber band on your wrist, don't you, Henry?"

"Yes."

"Why?"

"Because it helps me not to scream out cuss words and make my dad and customers at the Lasso upset."

"Do you have a condition known as Tourette's Syndrome?"

He nodded. "I can't always remember the name."

"Did you go to see Dr. Durham?"

"Yes, he's my doctor."

"Did he tell you to wear the rubber band?"

"He said if I flick my wrist and it hurts a little, it might help me forget about screaming out bad words."

"Did you put a red rubber band on Skyler Sterling's wrist that night when you gave him the apple juice?"

"Yes. So he could stop screaming, too."

"Why did you want him to stop screaming?"

"Because of Reggie and Dana. They're my friends. I wanted them to be married again and Scott and Skyler could live with their mom and their dad."

"Did you give Skyler anything else that night you thought might help him stop screaming so much?"

"Objection," Marshall said. "Leading the witness."

"Under the circumstances," Judge Shapiro said. "I'm going to allow."

Henry nodded.

"You need to say yes or no, Henry, so our court reporter can hear you."

"Yes," he said.

"Tell us about it, Henry."

Bear stood up at the back of the courtroom. "Don't say another word, son. I plead the fifth amendment on behalf of my son. He's nineteen, but I'm his legal guardian."

The judge slammed his hammer against the bench and ordered

the bailiff to remove Bear from the courtroom.

Everything stopped while Bear was led out, screaming, "Stop talking, Henry. I mean it."

"What else did you do to help Skyler?" Kendra continued.

"My dad said I shouldn't talk."

"You are in a court of law, Henry. And you have promised us and God that you'll tell the truth, the whole truth. That is what you must do."

"What about my dad?"

"He was wrong to tell you to be quiet. We need to hear what really happened that night and how you tried to help Skyler."

"Will you explain to my dad?"

"Yes," Kendra said. "I will. Now, what else did you do to help Skyler?"

"I gave him some of my medicine."

"Do you know the name of your medicine?"

"No. It's a hard word to say. But I take it every day. And it made me better." He snapped the rubber band again. "I hardly ever scream now."

"Is your medicine called Haloperidol?"

"Something like that, but shorter."

"How about Haldol?"

"Yes. That's my medicine."

"How did you give Skyler your medicine, Henry?"

"I poured it into his bottle of apple juice, 'cause I wanted him to stop screaming and get better like I did."

"Thank you, Henry. I have no further questions." Kendra took her seat next to Bryce.

When Radhauser leaned forward and squeezed Bryce's shoulder, a streak of joy, as real as a lightning bolt, shot down Bryce's back.

The courtroom grew so quiet, even Bryce could hear the silence. He had nearly given up, resigned himself to a conviction and death row in a Salem prison. His feelings about his future had been a muddle, like dirty water sloshing around in the bottom of a boat.

But now it was so clear. He wanted freedom with an almost

fierce desire. He wanted to know Jason's wife and kids. He wanted to get to know his mother again. Maybe even find Noah, his old friend from The Lake Institute.

But what about Henry? He leaned over and whispered to Kendra. "They can't put Henry in jail. He won't make it."

"Don't worry," she said. "It won't happen. No way will he serve any time. I'll represent him myself if it comes to that."

Marshall stood. "I have no questions of this witness, Your Honor."

"The defense rests." Kendra stood and moved closer to the judge.

Bryce stared at Kendra's back for a moment, then turned to his sign reader.

"I move the murder charges against Caleb Bryce be dismissed," Kendra said.

Judge Shapiro granted the motion, offering the state of Oregon's sincere apology, but reminded the jury they still had to decide on the count of child abuse of Scott Sterling. And then he called for the closing arguments.

Marshall asked if he could approach the bench.

Both he and Kendra did.

"I prepared a closing for a murder charge," he said. "I barely mention the child abuse."

Judge Shapiro shook his head. "Well, you'll just have to ad-lib, Mr. Marshall. I think our jury is ready to go home. Not to mention our defendant. We'll hear your closing arguments after a fifteen-minute break."

CHAPTER THIRTY-FIVE

In the holding cell during the break, Bryce, Kendra, and her father couldn't stop smiling. They slapped Bryce on the back, then embraced him. The celebratory mood in the room was so tangible you could reach out and touch it. Outside, the late morning sun filtered through the bare limbs of the trees and left a subtle yellow glow over the room.

"I knew it was in the bag," her father said, looking trim as an athlete and fashionable with his gray streaks in his dark hair an exact match for his obviously expensive three-piece suit. There was a splash of sapphire-colored silk in his breast pocket.

Kendra laughed. "Oh yeah, Dad, when did you know that?"

Her father winked, then gave her a huge grin. "The minute you were assigned to the case."

Kendra shook her head. That would be her dad—so self-confident it would never occur to him that he might lose, only how big his win would be.

The truth was, she couldn't have done this without Radhauser and her father. It took all three of them to solve the case. Radhauser got a subpoena for Henry's medical records. And her father convinced Dr. Durham to testify, should Henry fail to tell the truth.

Her father stopped grinning and turned serious. "Let's take a look at your closing."

"Oh no, you don't," she said, "You gave me my wings and I'm flying solo on this one."

* * *

Andrew Marshall didn't say anything new in his closing statements, he merely reemphasized the state's contention that Bryce abused Scott Sterling, and possibly even Skyler, based on the bruising reported by both the ER physician and the medical examiner.

Marshall claimed Bryce had a man-endangering state of mind when he chased after Scott for pushing Skyler. And that he was enraged with Dana and wanted to get even by hurting her children. He again showed the jury photos of Skyler's battered body and reminded them of Scott's testimony that Bryce threatened to kill him.

All in all, Bryce could see Marshall's arguments lost their steam, didn't convey the weight they'd carried before Valerie untangled the 9-1-1 tape, Dana admitted the scars were from a tubal ligation, not an ice pick, and Henry confessed to putting the drug in Skyler's bottle.

When Kendra stood, Bryce sucked in a deep breath and sat, straight backed and still, nearly afraid to breathe.

"Ladies and gentlemen of the jury, when this trial began, my client was charged with murder in the first degree and one count of child abuse. You've heard the prosecution's case against Caleb Bryce and our defense. You heard Henry Evans come forward and admit he was the one who put the Haloperidol in Skyler's bottle."

"When you entered this courtroom," she said, pausing to look directly into the eyes of each juror. "You were charged to administer justice. Your job is to weigh the facts honestly and sincerely, not influenced by emotions. The scales of justice must always be balanced by an honest gauge. You will provide the gauge, I'm sure, and weigh the facts that determine the truth of this case." She addressed them the way she'd talk if she stood in front of the twelve most intelligent people on the planet.

"And perhaps the most compelling testimony on the child abuse count came from Scott Sterling, the alleged victim. He told you, in the honest voice of a child, that Bryce never struck him before that night. After a day when Scott pushed his baby brother down the stairs and ran behind a neighbor's house because Bryce refused to give him ice cream before dinner. A day when Bryce learned Dana planned to take the kids and move back in with her ex-husband, Reggie."

She moved closer to Bryce.

He knew her hand was on his shoulder, he could feel the gentle weight of it. But, intent on her closing, he was aware of it only fleetingly, like a thought that passed through his mind and disappeared.

"Caleb Bryce is not a violent man. You heard Dana Sterling testify she lied to Reggie about Bryce stabbing her with an ice pick. That the scars on her abdomen were from a tubal ligation surgery. You also heard her say that Bryce would never deliberately hurt her children."

"Yes, it's true that after being kicked, bitten and spit on by Scott, Bryce slapped him on the behind with his open hand. And yes, he threatened him. It was not a death threat, ladies and gentlemen, it was the frustrated voice of a man pushed to the limits of patience by a four-year-old boy. What parent among you has never been pushed to a similar limit?" Kendra sighed and shook her head.

Calling for logic and fairness from the jurors, Kendra stood by her client's side and kept her hand on his shoulder. "My client is a good man who has been put through hell by the state of Oregon. He was charged with a murder he didn't commit and was so severely beaten in jail for being a child murderer that he could have died from his injuries. The newspapers and television reporters have slandered him."

"The responsibility for trying this case has been a heavy one," she said. "And, throughout it, I have felt my duty to Caleb Bryce. It is a duty I now hand over to you, to render justice fairly and impartially. Let your verdict be based on the law and the evidence you heard here and I am confident you will free him from the one-count of child abuse and allow him to go home and piece his shattered life back together."

After delivering his instructions, Judge Shapiro charged the jury to deliberate.

The twelve jurors walked, solemn-faced and single file from the courtroom, down the hallway and into the jury room. The alternates were dismissed with the thanks of the court.

Kendra gathered her papers, then shook Bryce's hand before he was led back down the stairs to the basement holding room.

When, about five minutes later, Kendra joined him, Bryce looked up from his untouched lunch tray. "What do you think will happen?"

She settled into the chair across from him and gave him a big smile. "I'm going to adopt my father's strategy and believe there is no way we can lose."

* * *

When Judge Shapiro granted the brief recess, Radhauser slipped out of the courthouse and drove home to pick up Gracie. After he'd discovered Henry's involvement, Tilly and Bryce's mother were so certain of release, they planned a celebration of his homecoming, just in time for the Thanksgiving holiday. It was Gracie's first time out after the mastectomy. Lizzie was spending the night at her nana's house to give Nana a chance to catch up on bill paying and other chores around her house.

He pulled into his driveway. As he neared their house, he spotted a bronze SUV with Arizona plates parked in the circular drive just outside their front door. He studied the car for a moment, uncertain what to think.

Once inside his house, he found his wife in the living room, dressed in a red gingham blouse, a long denim skirt and red leather boots. She looked beautiful, all made up and ready for the party.

A young woman who appeared to be in her early twenties was sitting across from Gracie at a small table in front of the bay window. Gracie had made tea. The room smelled like cinnamon and orange peels.

As soon as she saw him, the young woman leaped up and held out her right hand.

Radhauser took it.

She was pretty, tall and slender with long dark hair, smooth skin and dark eyes that seemed to search inside him. She wore a pair of jeans and a navy-blue sweatshirt with the University of Arizona Wildcat's logo. "I'm Lisa Flannigan," she said. "I drove from Tucson to see you."

He let go of her hand. His body reacted before his brain did—accelerating his heart rate. A vein pounded in his temple and a sudden, bone-chilling panic washed over him. This was the daughter of the man who killed his first family. Lisa had been thirteen, the same age as Lucas, and was home with her mother the night of the collision.

He tried to fight the images inside his head, but they kept coming. The smell of the morgue in the basement of Tucson Medical Center. Two little boys in body bags. Laura and Lucas so silent and still on those stainless steel gurneys, white sheets covering them.

Lisa must have spotted the horror on his face, because her look became one of despair.

Gracie stood and began to clear the dishes from the table. She looked at Lisa, her face as tender and kind as he ever saw it. "I'll give you two some privacy." Before Gracie left the room, she stood on her tiptoes, kissed him on the cheek, and whispered three words. "Listen. Consider. Forgive."

A wave of something like fear hit Radhauser and nearly knocked him over. He could listen. But forgiveness? Considering how much this girl's father took away, how could forgiveness be possible?

Neither of them moved or spoke until it seemed like the roof might fall in on them under the unbearable weight of their silence. Dust motes spun in the pewter shafts of light that slanted through the west windows.

Lisa was first to speak. "Is it okay if we sit and talk for a few minutes?"

Radhauser nodded, then took one of the brown, leather wingback chairs in front of the fireplace.

Lisa sat on the sofa directly across from him. Her hopeful, homecoming queen smile had returned. "I'm getting married on Christmas Eve."

"Congratulations," Radhauser said. "December is so beautiful in Tucson."

"I'd like to tell you about my father."

"I don't want to hear anything about him." He closed his eyes for a moment in which he could feel the anger, the familiar heat churning inside, try to rise to the surface.

When he opened his eyes, Lisa gazed at him, the hope on her face morphed into doubt. "I know my father stole something precious from you. He took my little brothers from my mother and me, too. Along with his presence in my life. But please, won't you just listen?"

"Didn't you ever visit him at the prison in Florence?" Radhauser said. "It's not like he's dead."

"My father didn't want me to visit. I lived eleven years without seeing my dad. But he wrote me letters every week. They arrived on Tuesdays, like clockwork. But I was living a nightmare of my own—you have no idea what's it like to be the daughter of a man in jail for murder. Four murders. And as I'm sure you already know, my father is up for parole."

"I won't change my mind," he said. "What you're about to ask of me is too much."

"Please listen, Mr. Radhauser. I spent my teenage years hurt and livid with him." She took a photograph from her sweatshirt pocket and handed it across the coffee table. "Because of them." A tear rolled down her cheek. She quickly wiped it away.

Radhauser stared at the photo. Twin boys, around five years old, sat on a tree limb, one in front of the other. They were dark-haired like their sister, grinning, and as cute as they come.

"For ten of those eleven years, I never answered a single letter. But to his credit, he didn't give up. He kept writing them."

Radhauser returned the photo.

She tucked it back into her pocket. "Believe me. I know what it's like to think you hate, to be so full of rage you can barely stand to keep living. But I also know what rage can do to your soul." Her voice was soft now, sweet in a way that tore at him.

"It's different for you," he said. "You're his daughter."

She bowed her head, as if in prayer. "I didn't always want to admit that. But yes, I am his daughter. And I finally visited him last week. He's changed. My father has been sober for eleven years."

"That's not much of an accomplishment in his current location." Aware of the cruelty in his voice, he tried to swallow against it. Prisoners had ways of getting drugs and alcohol.

"My dad joined AA. And now he runs the in-house program. He sponsors some of the younger inmates and they tell him things they can't tell their family. He counsels them toward sobriety, love and forgiveness. And at the same time, he's trying to find forgiveness for himself."

"Am I supposed to give him a trophy?"

"I understand your bitterness," she said. "When I finally went to see him, he cried and apologized through most of our visit. He was so ashamed. And I realized he also lost two sons. Yes, he behaved irresponsibly. He should never have allowed my little brothers to ride in the back of the truck, or driven so drunk he drove the wrong way on the freeway. It was his fault, and, don't you see, that only makes it worse for him. In my opinion, everyone deserves a second chance."

Radhauser thought about Caleb Bryce and the scene he witnessed between him and the mother who left him to fend for himself in a big-city hotel room at six-years-old. The way he listened to her apologies, fought his hurt and rage, and finally pressed his hand against hers on the Plexiglas wall. Bryce found a way to forgive his mother and had gazed at her with such longing Radhauser looked away—felt small, ashamed, and a little unworthy.

Rachael Bryce would have done anything for a second chance with her son. Maybe Lawrence Flannigan felt the same way about his daughter. Maybe he wanted nothing more in the world than to be with her and his wife again.

"Detective Radhauser," Lisa said, tears welling in her eyes again. "I want my father—no, I *need* him, to walk me down the aisle at my wedding."

Radhauser had a sinking feeling in his stomach.

Their eyes met.

In hers, he saw the pain of losing her little brothers and growing up without a father. It pierced him inside, knowing he had the power to make some of that hurt go away. He understood something new about life. You live it forward, but understand it in retrospect.

A comradeship hung in the air between them, like they were two veterans of the same awful war. He wanted to say he understood how she must feel about her lost father. Wanted this beautiful young woman to have her dream wedding. Didn't Lisa deserve happiness?

Someday, if he was lucky, he would walk Lizzie down the aisle on her wedding day.

What did he have to gain by giving a victim statement that might prevent Lisa's father from his parole? Keeping Lawrence Flannigan in jail for another ten years would not bring Laura or Lucas back. He had a new life—Gracie, Lizzie, and the little boy they were all so eagerly awaiting. Maybe the anger he'd harbored all these years added to Gracie's stress. Maybe it even contributed to her breast cancer.

This was Radhauser's chance to be a better man. A man who listened, considered and let go. The man Gracie wanted him to be.

As the words formed inside his mind, he felt a cool tunnel of air loosening in his chest—releasing everything clenched and bitter that had lived inside him for over a decade.

"I'll walk you to your car," he said.

Outside, the sun had gone down, and the sky turned silver and darkened to a light purple near the horizon. The trees had been stripped almost bare by November.

He opened her car door, then turned to face her. "Tell you what, Lisa Flannigan. I'll tear up the victim impact statement I wrote." He thought about Rachael Bryce again. "Everyone who has worked as hard as your dad to be a better person and make amends to the people he hurt deserves a second chance. I wish you every happiness in your married life. And I hope I'm around to walk my daughter down the aisle someday."

Her smile was as big as Texas. She hurled herself toward him and wrapped her arms around his neck. "Your wife told me you're a good man, Detective Radhauser. I didn't believe her at first. But, she was right."

When Radhauser turned and headed back to his house, Gracie stood on the porch, a mixture of tears and laughter in her eyes.

"The doctor called. My lymph nodes are negative." She wrapped her arms around his waist and hugged him hard, then put her arm inside his. "I'm so proud of you," she said. "Come on Mister I-won't-ever-change-my-mind. I want to meet Bryce, Miss Tilly and Kendra. Not to mention the great Kendrick Huntington Palmer III. We've all got some major celebrating to do."

She paused and gave him a big grin. "And by the way, Murphy called. He sounded a bit sheepish, but he's lifted your suspension."

CHAPTER THIRTY-SIX

Exactly twenty minutes passed before a buzzer sounded and the bailiff stuck his head into the holding room door. "We've got a verdict," he said.

Kendra and Bryce locked gazes.

"We've called Judge Shapiro," the bailiff continued. "He slipped home—guess he didn't expect anything so soon."

The courtroom filled rapidly and there were more spectators than earlier in the day, more reporters and cameramen than the courtroom could contain. They pushed together in front of the door as Bryce was led to the defense table, his arms folded in front of him, his breath coming hard. He lowered his head and tried to regulate his air intake and prevent a panic attack.

Kendra's father walked up to the defense table and stood in front of them. "You did a fine job with your closing," he said, holding out his hand. "I never thought I'd say this to a public defender, but I'm proud, and your grandfather will be, too. You're one of the best damn lawyers this family ever produced."

Kendra gripped her father's outstretched hand. "Thanks. Coming from you, that means something. And thanks for your help finding Dana's surgeon and Henry Evans' psychiatrist."

He flashed another rendition of his daughter's rich girl smile, then turned to Bryce. "Good luck to you, son." He firmly shook Bryce's hand, then took his seat behind them in the first row.

A few minutes later, Judge Shapiro entered. "Ladies and gentlemen of the jury," his booming voice echoed in the suddenly quiet courtroom. "I understand you have reached a verdict."

"We have, Your Honor," the foreman answered.

"Pass it to the bailiff, please."

The bailiff crossed the courtroom to the jury box, took the folded piece of paper from the foreman, and delivered it to Judge Shapiro.

Judge Shapiro unfolded the paper, raised his eyebrows as he read the verdict, then handed it back to the bailiff who returned it to the jury foreman.

"Will the defendant please rise?" the judge said.

Bryce and Kendra rose, the rustle of papers on the defense table the only sound in the courtroom.

"Mr. Foreman," Judge Shapiro said. "On the second count of the indictment, the child abuse of Scott Sterling, how does the jury find?"

"In the case of the state of Oregon versus Caleb R. Bryce, on one count of child abuse of four-year-old Scott Sterling, we find the defendant, not guilty."

* * *

As cheers echoed through the courtroom, the words repeated themselves inside Bryce's head. *Not guilty. Not guilty.* The room whirled around him.

His mother let out a cry and began to sob.

Bryce stopped breathing and didn't move.

The courtroom broke into applause.

When the noise level decreased, Judge Shapiro turned his attention to the jury, thanked them for their swift administration of justice, then dismissed the jurors.

Before they could leave the courtroom, spectators nodded and smiled as Bryce, dumbfounded, drew in a breath.

It was finally over.

He stared in disbelief at the jury, some of whom wiped their faces with handkerchiefs as they filed out of the room. When he turned to Kendra to shake hands, she threw her arms around him. "We did it, Bryce."

Stunned, he couldn't quite follow the thread of what went on around him anymore. All Bryce knew was that he and Kendra Huntington Palmer, IV, were standing at the front of a courtroom where people he didn't even know applauded his innocence.

Judge Shapiro stood and, without precedent, came down from his throne. He shook Bryce's hand. "You're free to go, Mr. Bryce. I'm sorry, truly sorry, for what you went through here. But the system worked. And justice has been done. May the rest of your life be filled with happiness." He turned and left the room.

A free man. God, what did it mean to be a free man? He looked at Kendra. "What do I do now?"

"Well, you could check back into the prison hotel for the night, have a few drinks and a quiet dinner with Poncho and your other intimate friends, or go home. Take your pick."

"I think I'll go home."

She smiled. "You can pick up your things tomorrow or next week. Or never."

"I don't have anything in that jail I want, except my watch and ring. And the photos of Jason and his family."

Kendra took his arm. "I'll make sure you get them," she said as they left the courtroom.

Reporters flocked around them, and camera flashes exploded in their faces. A young reporter thrust a video camera in front of Bryce. "How does it feel to be exonerated of all charges?"

"I don't know," Bryce said. "I haven't had time to feel anything yet."

When they finally emerged from the wall of reporters, Bryce and Kendra stepped onto Oakdale Avenue. "I have a surprise for you, Bryce."

"I don't know how much more I can handle today."

A sandy-haired man rose from his perch on a wooden bench just outside the courthouse. He stood in front of Bryce, his old white cane discarded in favor of a beautiful German Shepherd seeing-eye dog in a harness with a handle attached. "I got one question for you, Caleb Bryce." Noah Morgan smiled. "How's the sky look?"

"Dazzling," Bryce said, staring into a blue-spun universe that suddenly swelled with hope. "Noah. Noah. Noah. I can't believe it's really you."

Noah reached down and petted the dog. "This is the guy who took your place. He's my eyes now. And besides that, he's a chick magnet, and far more handsome than you ever were. His name is Vision. Go ahead. Shake his paw."

Bryce squatted and held out his hand. Sure enough, Vision gave him his paw.

"I'm pleased to meet my replacement," he said. "Looks like you've taken good care of him."

"Let's get moving," Kendra said. "There's a party waiting at your place. Tilly and your mother have been cooking for days."

Bryce climbed into the front seat of Kendra's car. Noah removed Vision's handle before they both climbed into the back. Through the rearview mirror Bryce watched Noah pet the dog's sleek coat.

On the short drive to Bryce's house, Noah leaned forward and turned his face so Bryce could read his lips, then filled him in on the details of his life, told him he was married, lived in Salt Lake City, and had two young daughters. That he taught creative writing at the Lake Institute where they'd spent their boyhoods.

"I'm sorry I didn't do a better job of staying in touch, but after Courtney died…" Bryce shook his head. "And now you're a father."

Noah grinned. "You were right. It's the best thing that ever happened to me."

"Tell me about your job."

"The Institute has over two hundred students and you wouldn't believe what a difference technology makes. Our blind kids have talking computers. They actually tell the students what they've written. It's fabulous."

"Is Dr. Russ still headmaster?"

"He retires later this year. He sends his regards, says he wants to see you again. I was so sure you weren't guilty I told him I'd bring you to his retirement party."

Kendra pulled up in front of Bryce's house. The driveway and all the parking places on the street were taken.

"I'll drop you three off, find a parking place and be back."

Bryce, Noah, and Vision got out of the car. Noah reattached

the handle to Vision's harness.

The front door flew open and Tilly hobbled out to greet them, making a gallant and hilarious effort to run. "I knew it would be all right, Bryce. I just knew it." Her heavy feet crunched the gravel driveway as she enveloped Bryce in a bear hug and didn't let go until he finally untangled her arms.

"Tilly, I'd like you to meet my other best friend in the world, Noah Morgan."

"You're the one from the school for the deaf and blind. The one Bryce named his baby daughter after."

"That would be me."

"I've heard many a tall tale about all the mischief you boys got into at that school. I feel like I've known you forever." Tilly hugged him, too.

But when she spotted Kendra, she let go of Noah and stumbled down the driveway, then threw her arms around her. "I swear to God. You are smarter and more beautiful than that Perry Mason fella ever dreamed of bein'." When she planted a big kiss on Kendra's astonished face, Bryce burst out laughing.

Noah took Tilly's arm and they walked up the steps. "I'm very happy to know that Bryce has you for a best friend now."

Bryce took Vision's handle and stepped into his house. The living room was decorated with crepe paper streamers and balloons and a long table filled with food. Above it, a hand-painted sign read *Welcome Home, Bryce.*

Neighbors, Kendra's father, Radhauser and his wife, co-workers from Gilbert's, his family, Jason and Katja, his niece Brianna, his mother, and his nephew, Caleb, cheered and applauded from the kitchen doorway.

Bryce hugged each one of them. And in that split second when he reached for his mother, he caught a glimpse of all the beauty and symmetry in the world, like the first glare of sunlight on newly-fallen leaves.

Tilly's grandson, Lonnie, headed for the food table. "Can we eat now, Grandma? I'm starved." He pointed at Bryce and grinned. "Or do we have to wait for him to stop huggin' people?"

Tilly patted her grandson on the belly. "You don't much look like you're starvin', boy. And if you know what's good for you, you'll wait till our guest of honor fills up his plate."

She gently nudged Bryce toward a table of the best looking and smelling food he'd seen in months.

* * *

After the party, as Noah and Vision snored peacefully in the room Scott and Skyler had once shared, Bryce stood in front of his bedroom window, staring out into the moonlit garden behind his house.

Like most everyone else, Bryce carried a whole community around inside his head—people like Isaiah Bryce, Valerie, Courtney, and Skyler, places like Wheatley, Utah, The Institute, and a way of life that had long ago disappeared. And he hoped no amount of time or pain would ever blot out his memories of Courtney and Skyler. Somehow, the shame and guilt for their deaths had been replaced with ordinary love and grief.

For the first time, he realized there were many other worlds that breathed side by side. The criminal world was only one. There were the soft, padded worlds of the insane; the hazy, hopeless, drug-filled worlds of the terminally ill; the waist-high, wheelchair worlds of the crippled. Perhaps even the dead inhabited a tufted, satin, haloed world of their own, somewhere just outside organic confines.

He slipped into his own bed and realized Tilly had washed his sheets and hung them outside to dry. That night, he slept in a bed that smelled like lemons and sunshine.

In the morning, he made a pot of coffee, fed Pickles and waited for Noah to shower.

After breakfast, they lingered over coffee and the warm sticky buns Tilly provided. On the way to the airport, they stopped by the cemetery. It was a magnificent Ashland day, the sky bright and clear, the sun warming the early December air to a balmy sixty degrees.

"No wonder you like it here so much," Noah said. "I can smell the snow on the mountain tops."

They sat on the ground in front of Skyler's grave. The ragged edges of turf had knitted together into a thick blanket of soft green grass. Bryce traced Skyler's name with his fingertip. "It's so hard to let go, especially with little kids."

"On the plane coming here," Noah said. "I tried to imagine what it would be like if one of my girls died. I got choked up just thinking about it. When Courtney died, you nearly drowned in your own pain. You've got to let it out, Bryce. Let it break loose. Maybe you're afraid there won't be anything left if you do, but you're wrong." Noah said softly. "The heart is a silent river. But it keeps flowing and there is always more. We all die, my friend, and those who are left go on loving and remembering. You can't hide the dead away or you'll never heal."

Bryce leaned forward, put both hands on Noah's shoulders, and retold the story of his love for Courtney, of how, for a year, Skyler had filled the empty place. The words rose from some bottomless and essential place inside him and declared themselves as if they'd been there waiting all along.

Noah was right—they were both part of the same stream, as surely as they'd been as boys together in the Institute. It was sorrow and shared grief that ripped down the walls that divided people. In some strange way, Bryce's imprisonment had been a gift, a way of finding his way back to his family and Noah.

He no longer believed himself responsible for Skyler's death. It was a terrible tragedy. And Henry was as innocent as a seven-year-old who'd believed he could help Skyler stop screaming and reunite Dana and Reggie.

Sitting with his oldest friend on the cemetery grass, Bryce knew he had come there to weep, then rejoin the living. His entire life was the sum of all the other lives he touched, of the people, living and dead, he had loved. It was the accumulation of remembering that mattered.

"Well," Bryce said, rising to his feet. "I better get you to the airport or you're going to miss your flight."

Bryce dropped his arm over Noah's shoulders as they walked, Vision trotting alongside. A shower of happiness fell over him.

And the sudden, unexpected extent of his joy at being reunited with his family and his childhood friend was as mysterious as love itself.

On the way to the airport, Noah made Bryce promise to come back to Utah for Dr. Russ' retirement party and meet Noah's wife and daughters. That he'd consider applying for a teaching position at The Lake Institute once he completed his degree.

As his friend's plane lifted up and disappeared into the dazzling blue sky, Bryce glanced at his wristwatch. He needed to hurry. The Oregon Ducks were playing a home basketball game tonight and Kendra was picking him up in an hour for their drive to Eugene.

AUTHOR NOTE

Thank you for taking the time to read *A River of Silence*—the third book in my mystery series featuring Detective Winston Radhauser. If you enjoyed it, please consider telling your friends and posting a short review on Amazon. Word of mouth is an author's best friend and very much appreciated. I wish you all the best, Susan Clayton-Goldner

ABOUT SUSAN CLAYTON-GOLDNER

Susan Clayton-Goldner was born in New Castle, Delaware and grew up with four brothers along the banks of the Delaware River. She is a graduate of the University of Arizona's Creative Writing Program and has been writing most of her life. Her novels have been finalists for The Hemingway Award, the Heeken Foundation Fellowship, the Writers Foundation and the Publishing On-line Contest. Susan won the National Writers' Association Novel Award twice for unpublished novels and her poetry was nominated for a Pushcart Prize.

Her work has appeared in numerous literary journals and anthologies, including Animals as Teachers and Healers, published by Ballantine Books, Our Mothers/Ourselves, by the Greenwood Publishing Group, The Hawaii Pacific Review-Best of a Decade, and New Millennium Writings. A collection of her poems, A Question of Mortality was released in 2014 by Wellstone Press. Prior to writing full time, Susan worked as the Director of Corporate Relations for University Medical Center in Tucson, Arizona.

Susan shares a life in Grants Pass, Oregon with her husband, Andreas, her fictional characters, and more books than one person could count.

FIND SUSAN ONLINE

Website
susanclaytongoldner.com

Facebook
www.facebook.com/susan.claytongoldner

Twitter
twitter.com/SusanCGoldner

Blog
susanclaytongoldner.com/my-blog---writing-the-life.html

Tirgearr Publishing
www.tirgearrpublishing.com/authors/ClaytonGoldner_Susan

BOOKS BY SUSAN CLAYTON-GOLDNER

WINSTON RADHAUSER SERIES

REDEMPTION LAKE, #1
Released: May 2017
ISBN: 9781370712939
Tucson, Arizona–Detective Winston Radhauser knows eighteen-year-old Matt Garrison is hiding something. When his best friend's mother, Crystal, is murdered, the investigation focuses on Matt's father, but Matt knows he's innocent. Devastated and bent on self-destruction, Matt heads for the lake where his cousin died—the only place he believes can truly free him. Are some secrets better left buried?

WHEN TIME IS A RIVER, #2
Released: September 2017
ISBN: 9781370576975
Someone is stalking 2 year old Emily Michaelson in Lithia Park playground as she plays with her 18 year old half sister, Brandy. Not long after Emily's disappearance, Detective Radhauser finds her rainbow-colored sneakers in Ashland Creek, their laces tied together in double knots. He insists Brandy stay out of the investigation, but she's obsessed with finding her little sister.

A BEND IN THE WILLOW
Released: January 2017
ISBN: 9781370816842
In 1965, Robin Lee Carter sets a fire that kills her rapist, then disappears, reinventing herself as Catherine Henry. In 1985, when her 5-year-old son, Michael, is diagnosed with a chemotherapy-resistant leukemia, she must return to Willowood and seek out the now 19-year-old son she gave up for adoption. Is she willing to risk everything, including her life, to save her dying son?